www.united-pc.eu

EVER A CROSS WORD

J.J.FALLON

For Paul - for everything

A good name is rather to be chosen than great riches, and loving favour rather than silver and gold.

(Proverbs Ch XXII, v.1)

SKELETON

The black squares have to be filled in as well as the words.

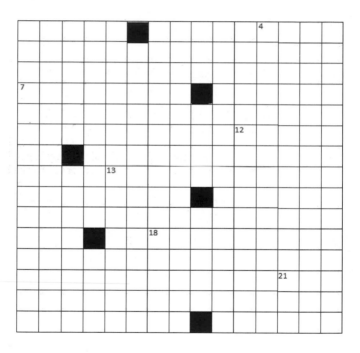

9 ACROSS, 22 ACROSS, 23 ACROSS

Overdone hag, nay (3,3,8 anag.)

When Chief Superintendent Sean Pollock awoke on Sunday morning he couldn't quite remember how he'd got home. The thumping headache playing the drums very loudly at the front of his head explained why.

They'd been celebrating Inspector Liam Kinsella's retirement. After thirty years in the force Kinsella had decided that he'd had enough and it had been abundantly clear last night that, although he felt a certain regret at leaving his colleagues, the Inspector was only too happy to be ending his working life. He'd already started making plans, beginning with a lengthy visit to Montreal to visit his daughter and grandchildren.

A lot of drink went into a retirement party – especially one as excellent as the one which Geoff Hughes had organised for his friend and colleague. No effort had been spared in making Liam Kinsella's farewell celebration a very special occasion. The upstairs room at the Seanachai pub – the local for many of the city's gardai – had been transformed. Colourful streamers snaking across the ceiling had met at intervals under a swathe of huge paper bows and vivid balloons while a large banner had proclaimed the force's good wishes to Kinsella. Immediately underneath this banner the bar had done great trade all evening as the guests competed with each other to reinforce the banner's sentiments with alcoholic sustenance. No wonder Pollock's head felt like a ton weight.

He hadn't been helped by the fact that, prior to the night's entertainment, Sean Pollock had accepted an invitation from his Inspector, Chris Murphy, to share his family's evening meal.

"Fiona thought it might be a good idea to have a decent meal inside us before we head out for the evening," Murphy had explained. "Nothing fancy but enough to balance the beer intake."

"Nothing fancy" had been a somewhat misleading description. As usual Fiona Murphy had produced a wonderful meal – a delicious beef casserole followed by a mouth-watering lemon meringue pie, baked to utter perfection, the whole lot accompanied by a full-bodied red wine. Small wonder his head was now punishing him.

He wasn't sure how many pints he'd downed during the course of the evening but as he stared at the bloodshot eyes gazing back at

7

him from the mirror of the bathroom cabinet he assumed that it had been far too many. It must have been a really good evening for him to have let himself go so much although, if he were honest, the last thing he could remember with any measure of clarity was making a small presentation to Liam Kinsella on behalf of the whole squad.

What was it Kinsella had said about being part of a team? Pollock struggled through the fog in his brain, trying to remember the exact words.

"It's a lot like family, working with our kind of team." Those had been the sentiments expressed. "I'll miss it, that's for sure."

****

Sean Pollock had understood exactly what he meant. Looking at them as they'd raised their glasses to toast their colleague's future health and happiness Pollock had experienced a similar emotion.

They were all there – the five of them. Chris Murphy, mid-forties now, his dull blond hair showing more than a few signs of grey, his glasses perched dangerously on the tip of his nose as he became increasingly caught up in an apparently intense discussion with the barman. He was, Pollock knew, far more than just a colleague. Over the years he and his family had provided much-needed support for the Chief Superintendent.

Geoff Hughes, the driving force behind this particular event, was clearly basking in the praise his efforts had earned him. Once described by a friend of his sister as 'cuddly' he was well aware that his rounded figure topped with a neat brown beard and a head of somewhat unruly, curly brown hair could perhaps give that impression. "Like a big teddy bear," the girl had said. Such a description didn't trouble him too much; in fact, on more than one occasion it had proved an asset since, during his career, several criminals had misjudged the nature of the man, assuming, wrongly, that his appearance was a true reflection of his character. True, he could be soft in the right circumstances but when the need arose he was hard, conscientious and anything but the 'easy touch' some misguided felons considered him..

Not surprisingly, Pollock thought, as his gaze wandered further round the room the two younger men, Phil Coady and Noel Lawson, were definitely enjoying their fair share of female attention. Not that this was any surprise in Phil Coady's case. At just over six feet tall with slightly longer than regulation jet black hair and deep blue eyes it was easy to see how such film star looks could

8

attract many a young woman. By the look of things, Pollock mused, as he watched his young colleague, tonight was definitely proving this to be the case.

Rather more surprising, the Chief Superintendent realised, was the attention young Noel Lawson was receiving. An unassuming young man - tall, thin, with dark hair and glasses - in many ways he resembled the typical comic-book boffin. 'Nerd' was the current term as far as Pollock knew. Clearly, if the reaction of the young women clustered around the two detectives was anything to go by, appearances could, indeed, be very deceptive.

Two very different young men Pollock realised. Yet each - Coady with his occasionally cavalier attitude, his dry sense of humour and his often challenging manner and Lawson, the new boy but an expert in the modern technology which was becoming so much more important in detective work - had already shown that they were very much a part of the Chief Superintendent's close-knit team.

And then there was Mags. The lovely and very efficient Margaret Power whose small, slim figure, pale features and mousy brown hair had, on more than one occasion, fooled criminals into believing she was a push-over. They soon discovered that her apparently meek exterior hid a quick mind and, more surprisingly, nerves of steel. Watching her now, secluded in a corner with her newly promoted fiance Sean Pollock could not avoid a pang of disappointment at the fact that, within a few short weeks, Mags would soon be leaving the group to join her fiance in New Zealand .

"Yes," he'd thought, giving way to an unexpected wave of sentiment, "they are like family. And maybe that's why I don't want to make any decision about my own future."

****

That, he now realised staring again at the face in the mirror, explained why he'd drunk more than he usually would – even on special occasions. Since the unexpected death of his wife, Claire, at the early age of thirty-nine he'd devoted his whole life to the force. At first it had been therapy, then habit. But now? Lately he'd suffered from a growing sense that he might be losing his grip, no longer showing the keen instinct which had led him to the top job in the city's serious crimes unit. And, as a result Chief Superintendent Sean Pollock felt uncertain of his future. Several times since Inspector Kinsella had announced his decision to go Pollock had asked himself whether it was time for him, too, to consider retirement. Unfortunately it was not a pleasant prospect.

It wasn't as if he'd be financially stuck. He'd have a good pension despite the upheavals of the recent recession and it would surely be beneficial to his health to put an end to the inevitable stress which came with the job. And, of course, it could be really good to have time to do all those things he'd had to leave to one side because of the demands of the job. But therein lay his problem.

He'd never been much of a one for hobbies or sports, even as a young lad. All the usual retirement pursuits – golf, gardening, bridge – held no appeal. And then, of course, there was the loneliness. That, if he were honest, was what really lay at the root of his indecision. With Claire still alive it would have been so different. They could have shared so many things together. As so often in the past he cursed the cancer which had so swiftly and suddenly robbed him of his beloved wife. They'd not been blessed with children but their devotion to each other had been such that they'd never felt the lack. As friends, as lovers, as partners they had truly felt that they had no need of anyone else. How wrong they had been. And how wrong he had been, throwing himself into the job so completely, leaving himself no time for any other life. Work had become his life. Without it – nothing.

That, he realised grimly as he fumbled through the medicine cabinet in search of the pain killers that he was sure must be there somewhere, was why he'd envied Liam Kinsella last night. And why he'd agreed with the sentiment that the team had become like family to him. And, most damning of all, why he'd drunk so heavily. He'd wanted to escape the inevitable – for a little while longer, at least.

He wandered dismally back into the bedroom, dressed slowly and made his way downstairs to the kitchen. By the time the kettle had boiled the painkillers had begun to take effect. The crescendo of drums in his head had subsided, giving way to a small but persistent trio of woodpeckers hammering away inside his skull. At least this condition was slightly more manageable.

As he drank his mug of tea and set about making some toast for his breakfast his thoughts returned once again to the previous evening.

Dinner with Chris Murphy and his family had, as always, been a happy, relaxed occasion. Not only had he enjoyed a good meal but he'd also found pleasure in the company of the Murphy's three children for whom he had become, in effect, almost a surrogate uncle. And, as the boy's godfather, he felt a very special bond with eight year-old Joe, the Murphy's second son; a bond which he felt was getting stronger every time he was with the lad. All three children had provided great entertainment during the meal as they'd vied with one another to provide the most outrageous stories and the most ridiculous jokes. Following the meal Pollock had been subjected to a familiar ritual: a brief – and, for him, unsuccessful – attempt at a Play Station game with both of Chris's sons, Joe and ten year-old Matthew and then a story for four year-old Maeve. A typical family behaving in a typical family way. This was an extra bonus which his friendship with Inspector Chris Murphy had created. It was one for which he was extremely grateful.

Inevitably his thoughts were then drawn back to the rest of the evening. As his headache finally receded and memory returned he realised that it had been, as everyone had agreed, a very successful evening. Geoff Hughes had outdone himself in making sure his colleague had a good send-off and all had passed without a hitch.

Liam Kinsella, as guest of honour, had clearly been overwhelmed by it all, especially by the number and variety of people who had taken the time to come and wish him well. To his amazement, and amidst the greatest emotion in what had been quite an emotional evening, Hughes had even managed to track down a couple of the men who had trained with Kinsella at Templemore over thirty years earlier. There had been champagne and speeches, food and presentations and, Pollock was sure, more than a few sore heads as a result.

'It's a good job I'm off duty this weekend,' he thought, as he began buttering the toast and settled down to read the morning paper. 'What I need now is a very quiet couple of days to recover.'

****

As things turned out it was a quiet weekend for most of the guests who'd attended Inspector Liam Kinsella's retirement party. The uniformed gardai had their usual quota of drunks and petty crimes to deal with but for Chief Superintendent Sean Pollock's serious crimes unit there were no major incidents. It was just as well. It was to be the last quiet few days for quite a while.

****

THE MOTHER

I suppose I must have been about three when I first became aware of the absence of a father and by then my child's mind already knew better than to ask questions. I'd somehow learned never to question anything.

My mother tolerated me and that with obvious ill grace. Love never entered the equation. It took me some years before I fully realised this truth: years in which, no matter how hard I tried, I could find no way of pleasing her. If I spoke I was wrong but being silent left me equally at fault. When I behaved and was really good – as much as a determined child could be – I was ignored. Misbehaving, if only in order to get at least some reaction, was always a big mistake leading, inevitably, to one of a variety of drastic punishments ranging from a beating (which I soon learned to endure) to no food for twenty-four hours (a much harder torment to bear.)

It was only when I became fully aware of my sister's role in our family situation that I began to understand a little of my own predicament – and even then not fully. Just as I could do no right my sister –eight years older and far more ill-disciplined – could do no wrong. When I was cheeky I suffered: when she behaved in a similar fashion she was praised as having a mind of her own. Late arrival at meals meant, for me, an empty plate; for her, a mild reminder of the importance of eating the food while it was still hot.

It was an unfairness which, naturally, led to a series of revolts as a consequence of which I spent several years in a constant state of hunger and painful bruises. Eventually I surrendered, withdrawing into my own quiet, shadowy world and trying, as much as I could, to come to terms with my mother's unexplained hostility.

It might have been different if my brother had lived. At least then there would have been two of us to share the pain. But that was not to be and his early death became just another reason to treat me like dirt.

****

I was already in my early teens before I learned the truth behind my mother's harsh attitude and even then, though I could feel a certain sympathy towards her, I still couldn't reconcile what I heard with how I felt.

It was my cousin, my mother's only sister's child, who told me the story; whispering conspiratorially in the seclusion of the garden shed where we'd sought shelter after a sudden summer downpour had interrupted a somewhat desultory game of tennis. Neither of us had wanted to play – indeed, we didn't even want to be in each other's company – but my sister had already escaped into the town and, as my cousin and I were of a similar age, our mothers insisted that we find something to keep us 'out of the way'. Since neither of us was willing to face the consequences of ignoring such an order the tennis game had seemed the best solution. Until the rain came, of course.

"What do you know about Grandad?" my cousin asked abruptly, as soon as we'd pushed our way through the cluttered contents of the shed and managed to find two faded but useable garden chairs on which to rest until the rain abated.

"I don't know anything about any of my family," I confessed, a little shamefaced that I had to make such an admission.

"Oh, don't worry," my cousin reassured me. "I only found this out by accident. I don't think my mother would be too pleased if she knew."

So saying she looked around nervously as if she half-expected our mothers to pounce on us at any moment.

To be honest, I wasn't particularly interested in indulging in any family gossip but, since I could see that she was determined to share her discovery with someone, I chose to encourage her. At least it would pass the time until the shower had ended .

"O.K. So what's this big secret then?" I tried hard to sound enthusiastic but her reply showed how miserably I'd failed.

"Well, if that's going to be your attitude," she shrugged, "I just won't bother saying anything. Not that I should be surprised. Given your background I don't blame you for not wanting to know."

Now she had me hooked, as she probably knew she would. This was clearly going to be something relevant to my own life. Maybe it would even explain why I suffered the way I did.

"Don't be like that," I cajoled. "I didn't mean to sound off-hand. Honestly." I leaned forward, hoping that my expression now showed the genuine interest I'd begun to feel. It worked.

"Well," she began, looking round once more before continuing in hushed tones, "it seems our grandfather was ...." She paused for dramatic effect before pronouncing the damning accusation. "A bigamist!"

I'm not sure what I'd expected to hear but my reaction was almost one of disappointment. I have no idea what misdeeds I'd thought she might reveal – murder? bank robbery? espionage? – but somehow bigamy didn't seem, to me at least, such an outrageous crime.

Fortunately, my lack of any dramatic reaction was misunderstood. My cousin clearly believed I'd been rendered speechless with shock as she continued hurriedly.

*"Yes. It's true. I heard my mother talking to Don, her fellow, about it. She didn't know I was listening, of course. Anyway, it seems Grandad not only married twice. He actually had **three** wives – all at the same time."*

"What happened to him?" I felt obliged to show some interest.

"He got found out eventually and put in prison – though I don't think he was there for long before he was let out on the grounds of ill health. Anyway, he died not long after but by then, of course, the whole city knew all about him. Imagine how it must have been for our mothers. Having to live here, going to school and all of that, knowing that everyone knew the story."

"Was their mother the legal one?"

My curiosity was beginning to revive. Maybe this explained why my mother found it hard to show any emotion – to me, at least.

"That's the point, stupid. He was already married when he met our Nan. And since his first wife wouldn't give him a divorce he just moved here and married Nan as if he was a free man. Then, when he got fed up with her, he moved on, leaving Nan and her two daughters with nothing."

She fell silent for a while and I assumed that, now the big family secret had been revealed, there was nothing more to be said on the subject. One look at the sly expression on her face warned me that I was wrong.

"What?" I asked innocently. "What else is there?"

"Oh nothing," she said casually. "I was just thinking, that's all."

"Thinking what?"

Like all girls in my experience – limited though that was I must admit – she liked to spin out a story, almost making her audience beg for information.

"Well. It just strikes me as funny – not in a laughing way, mind you – that history almost repeated itself with your mother."

"What do you mean?"

I was alert now, certain I was about to learn a vital fact about my parentage; uncertain whether I really wanted to know.

"Well, your dad did pretty much the same thing, didn't he."

I'd never really considered my non-existent father. He'd never featured in my life and, since it was clearly a forbidden topic, I'd never heard him mentioned before, by anyone. This really was getting interesting.

"I've no idea."

I tried hard to sound nonchalant: for some reason I was embarrassed by my own ignorance. It seemed wrong that this cousin, just a couple of months younger than me, should be so much more aware of my background than I was.

"No." She looked at me shrewdly, the expression on her twelve year-old face already displaying a female wisdom that I would never understand. "I don't suppose you would have. I don't suppose your mother would want to talk about it."

"So how do you know then?" I asked scornfully, trying to conceal my own unease with a bravado I definitely didn't feel. "I bet you're just winding me up. You don't know anything."

"Oh yea, I do," she snapped back. "It's part of what my mum was telling Don. Your dad did a runner the same as Grandad. He found someone else and upped and left your mother a couple of weeks before your brother was born. No wonder," she concluded, with an understanding way beyond her years, "she doesn't like you very much. It must seem that all the men in her life are just no good."

So that was it. My father had betrayed my mother as had her father before him. Men were bad and if she had to put up with a male in the house she was going to do all she could to make him suffer as she had suffered. At last I understood. I was to be punished for the sins of my forefathers. And, for the time being at least, there was nothing I could do about it.

****

Knowing the cause of my misery in no way changed things. Naturally I said nothing to either my mother or my sister about what I'd learned. To have done so would, I knew, have unleashed a far greater wrath than any I had previously experienced. Far better to stay silent and endure.

Through my teens I retreated into a world of my own. I watched my sister blossom under the loving care of an indulgent mother – and I held my peace. I became, to all intents and purposes, a non-person, a scapegoat for all the household ills, a slave for all the household tasks. And I said nothing. Life, I decided, was easier that way.

For the first twenty years of my life I don't think my mother ever addressed me by my name. I was 'you' or 'fool' or 'idiot'. I think that the habit became so deeply ingrained that she didn't even realise what she was doing. Maybe she'd even forgotten my real name. Even in public it was the same, which was, naturally, a source of acute shame for me. But though I cringed inwardly every time she spoke to me in that way in front of people I said nothing. There was, I knew, nothing I could say.

****

Why did I stay? I don't know. Perhaps I was afraid to face the uproar that any suggestion that I was leaving might cause. Or maybe, and this might be nearer the mark, I simply didn't want to make it three in a row. Her father had deserted her, so had her husband. Even her infant son had left her, although that, tragically, had not been by choice. Perhaps I simply couldn't let her remaining son do the same ....

And, to be honest, once I'd created my own private world within the confines of my room and my head, I felt I could put up with her for as long as was necessary. After all, sooner or later she was going to die. That much was certain. And then I'd laugh.

Oh, how I'd laugh.

****

RICHARD

I

"Get your lazy arse down here now!"

Richard Corcoran flinched at the sound of his mother's voice. It surprised him that he should react so, since this had been the familiar wake up call for as long as he could remember, certainly since his first day at school. Nothing gentle, nothing kind. Just the shriek from the bottom of the stairs, cutting its harsh, demanding way through the layers of his mind and dragging him back from the protective security of sleep into the harsh reality of his daily existence.

He rolled over and rubbed his eyes. He knew better than to try and go back to sleep. To have delayed in a vain attempt at grabbing another few minutes of what he considered well-earned rest would have meant risking a further torrent of verbal abuse. It wasn't worth it. He knew that from bitter experience. Instead, he crawled out of bed and stumbled to the bathroom.

It was six forty-five. He didn't need to look at the clock to know that. He always got woken at six forty-five: summer or winter, it made no difference. His mother's routine was steadfast. She got home from her shift in the hospital laundry by six-thirty at the latest, made herself a cup of tea and then, at six forty-five on the dot, let out the clarion cry which marked the end of her day and the beginning of his. Occasionally she would wait until he was in the kitchen before retiring to her room for some much-needed sleep: more often she was already half-way to dreamland before he'd reached the bottom of the stairs.

'Still,' he thought as he locked the bathroom door behind him, 'at least my mornings are quieter when she does that.'

It was a thought which had reassured him many times over the years.

Six forty-five. Usual time, usual routine. The voice echoed up the stairs once more.

"For goodness sake, you lazy lump, get up."

"Coming, Mum," he called, as he looked at his reflection in the bathroom mirror, pondering once again the image before him and the niggling problem that image had recently created. His was a thin, pale face, dotted here and there with the occasional hint of

17

teenage acne. That, however, wasn't the problem. No, his difficulty was simpler in many ways but, for lads his age he suspected, no less important. He rubbed his chin. There was no doubt about it. The faint, dark stubble which had been there for a couple of weeks now was definitely becoming more apparent. He wondered whether it was time he started shaving but he didn't know quite what to do.

Exactly when should a boy have to start shaving? And what was the best method – electric razor or not? And how did a person manage to use an ordinary razor without cutting his face to ribbons? And, come to think of it, what about the many other mysteries which adolescence brought with it – questions about relationships, for example, and how to behave with girls? Not that he could ever imagine that sort of dilemma arising in his case. He had very little opportunity to mix socially with anyone, let alone start thinking about girlfriends.

This, he realised, having decided to leave the matter of the stubble for another twenty-four hours, was one of the many unexpected ways in which he missed having a father. Of course, there were plenty of other ways although, for the most part, he'd got used to them. But this was one of the questions that a father would understand, a father could tell him what to do. He laughed, without mirth. A father was one thing, one of many, that Richard Corcoran had never known.

Perhaps these seemingly minor dilemmas might have been less pressing if he'd had any close friends but, thanks to his mother, that particular solution was not available. She discouraged any visitors in such an alarming manner that few youngsters would be prepared to risk her wrath. As far as she was concerned Richard's only social outlet – if it could be described as such – was school. And that was only available for the strictly-observed hours of nine in the morning until four in the afternoon. Any other absences from home were either strictly monitored or totally forbidden.

"Are you deaf or what?" Another screech accompanied this time by a loud knocking on the door.

Richard jumped with a mixture of guilt and alarm. His musings had distracted him and the resulting delay had been sufficient to arouse his mother's unpredictable temper. This, he knew, was not a good way to start the day. He sighed.

'So what else is new' he thought.

II

Only when he was safely in the classroom during another tedious day could he allow himself a return to his earlier thoughts. The school day had begun with a double science lesson – not one of his favourite subjects but one for which the teacher demanded total concentration, with serious consequences for any student caught day-dreaming. The third lesson, however, was an unexpected study period caused by the absence of the English teacher. Work had been provided but not enough to interfere with the occasional quiet reverie – as long as it was not too obvious, of course.

Richard, safely situated in the centre of the room – far less likely to attract the supervisor's attention there than in any of the more popular seats at the back or in the corners – was taking time writing his answers to the questions before him when the title of the poem on the opposite page caught his eye. *'In Memory of My Father.'*

My father. The completely unknown character in his life and yet, he had only recently begun to understand, the one who might possibly be most responsible for his miserable existence. After all, if his father were dead he would surely have been told by someone even if his mother found the subject too painful to discuss. The only other explanation, it appeared, was that, for some unknown reason, his father had chosen to leave his family. That might explain his mother's harsh attitude. Either way it struck him, more and more, how amazing it was that such a total stranger could exert so strong an influence on his life. And, more to the point, how different things might have been.

He'd never asked about his father, not directly at least although there had been many times when he'd wondered. He'd learned from a very early age that his position in the family was, to say the least, precarious. Some children sometimes feel unwanted: he hadn't been many years old when he knew that he definitely was unwanted. So much so that of late he'd begun to wonder more and more why his mother had even bothered to keep him.

He couldn't actually remember when he had first become aware that he lacked a father. His early years had vanished from his mind and, as far as he knew, it was only when he began nursery school and had his first experience of mixing with other children that he became conscious of a major personality absent from his life. The discovery was not an easy one, brought about as it was by the heedless cruelty of other children.

"You're odd," they'd taunted. "You don't have a daddy."

19

Thanks to his mother's apparently unusual ideas about child-rearing he was already becoming aware of the differences between himself and other children. At an age when being the same as everyone else was of vital importance he couldn't bear the thought of yet another possible peculiarity separating him from others. To avoid this he'd created his own escape mechanism. Being, as he was, unable to ask his mother for the true explanation – to do so, he'd discovered very quickly, would inevitably draw an angry, bitter response from her – he'd sought refuge in his own imagination.

Using the example of a story he'd once seen on television he created a father - a man of mystery whose high-powered government job took him away from home for months at a time and whose work was so secret that the family were never allowed to talk about him. The story was so good that, for a while, he'd almost believed it himself. Certainly it impressed the other children and their jeering ceased. But not for long.

As he grew older and others saw through his make-believe he drew more scorn. Humiliation had led, initially, to invention: that, in turn, led to isolation. He withdrew even further into the protective shell he'd been forced to build around himself. He was seen as being odd and odd children don't win friends.

Strangely, though, a part of him still clung to the myth he'd created. Even after he'd discovered other 'fatherless' children, even after he'd realised, as he progressed through school, that there was no real shame in not knowing his father, there were still times when he thought of that imaginary figure who would one day walk back into his life and transform it. As oppression at home worsened this make-believe father became a vital emotional shield.

'Life,' he thought, 'might be tough now but one day my dad will come back for me. I know he will.'

Such thoughts lifted his spirits when he most needed. In calmer times he was forced to accept the truth. He didn't know why – he might never know – but his father had chosen to abandon him a long time ago. He was never coming back.

One fact he did come to understand more and more as he grew older. His father's absence was at the root of most of his troubles. What was for some children a tragedy and for others a relief was, for him, a disaster since it left him open to constant attack from his one remaining parent. Until he was fourteen he didn't know why this should be. Unfortunately the explanation, when it finally came, although it clarified things a little did nothing to improve his situation. For him knowledge did not bring power.

III

"Who's the fellow in the corner?"

"Him? Oh, that's Richard Corcoran. You don't want to bother with him. He's an odd-ball."

"How come?"

"Makes up stories like a kid. Says his dad's some sort of special government official. Some kind of secret agent or something equally daft."

"And is he?"

"'Course not. Corcoran made the whole thing up years ago. Still goes on believing it – or at least telling people - even though everyone knows it's not true."

"So what does his dad do? Cleans sewers or something."

The laughter which followed this comment tore through Richard's usual protective shell. The other boys made fun of him whenever they could: he was used to that. The fact that this newcomer – a boy who'd only joined the class that morning – could be so easily turned against him came as no surprise. It was the cruel humour the newcomer had so quickly shown which really hurt. Who was he to judge Richard or his father? What did he know that gave him the right to comment? He wasn't even from the city. What did he know about Richard's life?

Of course, the obvious thing to do would be to get up and walk away. There was another ten minutes or so before the bell rang to mark the end of the lunch break. Time enough for a brisk walk around the school grounds even though it was still pouring with rain.

Damn rain! It was that which had forced him to break his usual routine and remain in the classroom instead of escaping to the sheltered corner he'd found behind the caretaker's shed. Surprisingly, none of the other boys had found it – even the most determined smokers hadn't made the effort to push through the tangle of shrubs to reach the small open space beyond. Richard had: and most days this was where he spent the lonely hour allowed for lunch. On one occasion he'd even managed to drag an old chair into the space without being spotted. Its broken leg had made it useless

21

in a classroom but he'd found a way of propping it up enough to provide him with a seat while he drifted into his own solitary world.

Not today, though. Today the rain had been coming down in such torrents that even he could see the folly of sitting outside for an hour. Instead he'd retreated to the back of the classroom where, he'd hoped, his silent presence would be ignored by the others. It was not to be. The new student, anxious to become part of the class as quickly as possible, had spotted him and started asking questions. It was like manna from Heaven for the others, giving them the opportunity to pour out their scorn without any restrictions. And for Richard there was no escape. To move now would not only draw attention to himself it would also show them that he'd heard what they'd said. And that, he knew from previous experience, would only add to their spiteful pleasure and provide more fuel for their mockery. He kept his head down, trying to focus on the work in front of him, struggling in vain to blot out the cruel chorus nearby.

"Why does he do that? He must have a screw loose or something."

The newcomer was clearly intrigued by the notion of one of his classmates inventing such fairy stories. That, in his limited experience, was something only little children did.

"Like I told you." The speaker was John Nicholson, class bully and the one person everyone knew could make school life intolerable. Richard avoided him as much as was humanly possible. "He's an odd-ball."

Actually, John Nicholson had, for the most part, given up tormenting Richard. After the first ghastly term in secondary school he'd realised that his victim was, on the surface at least, quite immune to his verbal attacks. And since that took away all of the fun – and since he was far too smart to indulge in any form of physical abuse – he'd given up and turned his attention to some other poor soul. That didn't stop him returning to the challenge whenever the occasion arose. The newcomer had presented him with an opportunity that was far too good to miss and he was determined to use it to the full.

"Of course, with a mother like his I'm not surprised." He launched his attack. "She treats him like dirt and the silly sod lets her. Hell! If my old woman spoke to me the way she talks to him I'd tell her where to get off straightaway."

"He does nothing I take it."

"Not a thing. Just lets her rant and rave at him as much as she likes."

"His sister's just as bad." A new voice spoke. "She copies her mother in everything."

"Everything?" Nicholson's voice had a touch of sarcastic humour in it. "I'll have to get to know her in that case, if you get my drift."

He gave a suggestive laugh which made Richard stiffen. What exactly was he hinting at? It was a question the new boy voiced for him.

"Well," came the answer, "according to my old man, Corcoran's ma liked to put it about a bit when she was younger. Quite a goer by all accounts. Didn't even learn her lesson when she got knocked up the first time. As soon as the fellow knew there was a kid on the way he did a runner. Didn't stop her though. Within months she had a new guy in tow. 'Course, same thing happened."

"Are you saying that he's got no dad at all?"

"Not one he knows anyway. His dad took off just like his sister's."

"So that means...." A different voice this time.

"That means that when we call Corcoran a thick bastard that's exactly what he is," Nicholson declared grandly, delighted to produce the barb which, he was sure, must have pierced Richard's defences.

"I suppose," the newcomer reasoned once the laughter following Nicholson's comment had died down, "his mother learned her lesson after the second chap ditched her."

Nicholson gave another cruel laugh.

"You'd think so but she must be as dumb as he is. According to my ma she still likes to entertain fellows – if you know what I mean. But none of them has stayed very long."

"I bet she hates men by now."

It was such a casual comment and from the loud laughter which followed Richard was certain they were all looking at him. He had no intention of finding out. Not that he wanted to. His mind was in turmoil.

What was it they'd said? He'd never had a father – apart from in the biological sense, of course. And, if John Nicholson was to be believed, his mother, although she called herself Mrs Corcoran, had never actually married. Not only that, Angela, it appeared, was only his half-sister. He thought again about the newcomer's final remark. Twice his mother had, he presumed, had been rejected by a man as soon as complications – in the form of a pregnancy – had arisen in the relationship. Instead of standing by her, marrying her, doing the 'right' thing not one but two men had deserted her. No wonder she considered men worthless. And no wonder she treated him the way she did. He was living proof of the worthlessness of men. Angela, he reasoned, would have to be nurtured and protected, at least in his mother's mind, in order to prevent the same thing happening to her. He, on the other hand, was to be punished. He was to be living proof that never again would any male get the better of Bridget Corcoran.

'It explains so much,' he thought, as the bell rang and his tormentors finally moved away. 'And there's not a thing I can do about it.'

He was right. Knowing the truth – and he saw no reason to doubt that John Nicholson's story was basically true – changed nothing. There was no point in saying anything about what he'd heard either to his mother or to Angela. After all, what could he say? It was all in the past so there was no point in trying to revive what must surely be painful memories. All that would do would be to make his mother even more bitter. And he'd suffer more as a consequence. No; better to just accept the truth and say nothing. Life could just go on as before.

IV

John Nicholson had been right about one thing. From time to time Bridget Corcoran would introduce a new man into the house. Each one only stayed for a short time and since they were all quite similar in character – loud, rough, coarse – Richard often wondered if this was what his father had been like. Had his mother always been attracted to that type of person? At first he'd also wondered why his mother continued to welcome these men into her home, given the way she treated him. The noises he heard at night on the odd occasion when he couldn't sleep gave him the answer to that particular mystery. He soon came to understand that sex was probably the only reason these men were allowed into her life and her home. Certainly, there were few other signs of affection although her abusive treatment of them was far milder than that shown to Richard. Nevertheless it had the predictable effect: none of them stayed longer than a couple of months.

It therefore came as a great surprise when he arrived home from school one day to find his mother up, the house tidy and delicious smells coming from the kitchen. This was most unusual. Normally his mother was still in bed when he got home, catching up on her sleep before her night's work. It always fell to him to do the clearing up and get whatever food he wanted. His mother rarely cooked and by the time he'd reached the age of eight she'd already made it very clear that he was old enough to fend for himself. Since, for the past six years, both she and Angela were able to get a cooked meal at work he'd made do with tinned or packet food, anything which required minimum fuss and even less cleaning up.

'So what makes today different?' he asked himself.

The answer came as soon as he entered the kitchen.

"Oh, it's you." His mother's tone was, as always, far from welcoming. "You can get upstairs straightaway. Angela's bringing her young man to dinner and she won't want you hanging around."

He knew better than to protest so, grabbing the couple of slices of bread and an apple grudgingly allowed by his mother, he hurried to the seclusion of his room. Here he was left in peace to ponder this new and surprising development.

Richard had never been close to his sister, eight years and a lifetime of hostility separated them. The knowledge, recently gained, that their relationship was even less than he'd believed only added to the huge gulf separating them. Apart from the fact that she'd left school at eighteen and, after a year at the technical college, had got a job in a local beautician's, he knew nothing at all about her life. The fact that she now had a boyfriend – and one about whom she was serious enough to invite home – was complete news to him. What was even more astonishing was the fact that his mother not only accepted this but actually appeared to be encouraging the romance. Given all the animosity he'd witnessed over the years this new development seemed, to him, very strange.

Then it dawned on him or, at least, he thought he'd found a fairly credible explanation. His mother had been betrayed by two boyfriends and, as a result, had been left to raise two children on her own. She would, therefore, be determined not to let her daughter fall into the same male trap. Far better to encourage a suitable young man in the hope that he would settle down and stay. A welcome home, a good meal, a pleasant evening – and no younger brother around to cause any awkwardness – would go a long way to achieving that aim.

This logic proved correct and within six months Angela and Colin had become engaged. They were married three months later.

Richard didn't attend the wedding. He wasn't asked nor did he expect to be. On the contrary, he was told, in no uncertain terms, by both his mother and his sister that he was to remain in the house, preferably in his room. He didn't mind. At fifteen he'd become so used to his own company that he actually found it difficult being among people, especially people he didn't know.

So, while the bride and groom and their guests celebrated the big event with a four-course dinner and endless glasses of champagne, followed by dancing till late to the music of a well-known local band, Richard sat in his room enjoying a microwave curry and a mug of tea with 2FM radio for company. It suited him better.

For Richard the one truly astounding thing about Angela's marriage had been finalised only a few days before the event. At least, that was when Richard was told about it.

"Angela and Colin are going to live here after they're married," his mother had announced. "He's away a lot with his work so it makes sense. You'll have to keep out of their way, of course."

That was all. His opinion – if he had one – was neither asked for nor given. It was assumed that he'd accept the situation.

In fact he didn't mind. He'd only met Colin twice, each time very briefly, but thought he seemed a nice enough sort of person. His close-cropped hair, sturdy figure and the large tattoo on his left arm all suggested a fairly tough character although, in fact, he was quite mild. Certainly he acknowledged Angela as the dominant partner in their relationship, placidly accepting her ideas – and occasional tantrums – with little or no protest. He'd got a comfortable home, a steady job, an attractive wife and he was happy. Richard figured that he probably didn't even realise that it was only this complete subservience which made him acceptable to Bridget. Here was a man who knew his place and did exactly what was expected of him. Unconsciously, perhaps, he was allowing the two women to dominate him just as Richard did. He was both useful and obliging to them: for that reason the arrangement worked.

V

At eighteen Richard left school. His final exams had not produced any outstanding results in spite of the huge amount of time he'd spent over the years shut away with his books. Consequently jobs were hard to come by.

He wasn't helped by his mother's attitude. Despite the fact that he was now a grown man she continued to undermine him with no thought whatsoever to the effect this continued abuse was having on him. When no job was immediately forthcoming she even insisted on accompanying him to the Social Welfare Office, monitoring his every move and then ensuring, when his unemployment benefit was eventually agreed, that every last cent was handed over to her. Every time he went to sign on she was at his side. Every time he went to the local post office to collect his money she went with him. He had no life of his own, no funds in his pocket, no freedom.

It was a situation which couldn't last. It didn't. And it was his lack of employment which proved the final catalyst.

The economic recession and the resulting rise in the number of people unemployed had led to certain necessary changes in the operating of the city's Social Welfare Office. In the past, when the Celtic Tiger was roaring loudest, it was possible to saunter into the large room, sign on and stroll back out all in the space of about five minutes. However, as the boom collapsed taking thousands of jobs with it, the queues of people waiting to sign their names in order to receive financial assistance grew to such dramatic proportions that, in spite of there being several clerks available, they stretched out of the building and into the adjacent car park. To try and ease this pressure the authorities decided to introduce an appointments system. Signees were instructed to attend only at specified times. Failure to do so, they were warned, could affect their benefit payments.

Richard knew all this. He'd received notification of his official sign-on day and time several months previously and, accompanied as always by his mother, had dutifully presented himself at the unemployment office according to these instructions.

He had no idea how or why he'd got confused. Certainly his life had undergone no dramatic change, nothing that could cause a sudden upheaval to his routine. He still spent most of his time closeted in his room, when he wasn't busily trying to do the multitude of chores his mother automatically demanded of him.

Even more astonishing was the fact that his mother – always complaining about his faults, always monitoring his life – also managed to make the same mistake.

They both got the wrong day.

Unfortunately, it was only when he reached the desk that Richard became aware of this.

"Name?"

The soft-spoken man on the other side of the glass-fronted counter didn't bother looking up, choosing instead to keep his attention focussed on the box of cards in front of him.

"Corcoran. Richard Corcoran."

The man began flicking through the cards, resignation turning to irritation when he discovered that the relevant card was not in this particular box.

"Are you sure you're supposed to be here at this time?" he demanded, looking up. Only then did he discover what a can of worms he might just have opened.

"You idiot," Bridget Corcoran snapped at her son, not bothering to lower her voice. "You stupid great idiot. Can't you ever do anything right?"

Her fury was fanned by the realisation that she had also been at fault, although this was a fact she would never admit to anyone. Grabbing him roughly by the arm she dragged him across the room, loudly berating him the entire time in tones of such scorn that the other occupants began to turn away in embarrassment.

He was, according to her loud accusations, a hopeless waste of space and the world – certainly her little corner of it – would be a far better, much easier place if he were no longer in it.

For the first time in his life Richard felt a flicker of hatred stirring inside him. He said nothing, bearing his humiliation and the taunts which were causing it in silence. But the damage had been done: the flicker became a flame. On the bus journey home – a journey accompanied by an almost ceaseless tirade from his mother, much to the obvious discomfort of the other passengers – that flame became a fire. And, by the time they entered the house, the fire was an inferno, completely out of control.

"How dare you!"

Richard didn't shout. To do so would have put him on the same level as his mother. Instead his tone was one of cold calm, far more dangerous had Bridget taken proper notice.

28

"How dare you humiliate me like that in front of everyone."

His mother, after one brief moment of surprise, opened her mouth to speak. His rage would not let her.

"I'm nearly twenty-one. I'm a grown man. And all my life you've treated me as if I was a piece of dog shit you'd picked up on the sole of your shoe."

She winced at his choice of language, little realising how much he was controlling his words. There were, he knew, far worse words he could have used against her but even in his rage he sensed that to resort to a torrent of effing and blinding would somehow make him no different from her. And never in his life had he felt more strongly how little he wanted to be in any way connected to her. Instead he chose to maintain the cold voice and the restrained language.

"Well," he continued, "I'm not. What's further more I'm not taking any more. I've had my fill. You're a bloody disgrace as a mother and I'll not put up with it any longer."

"What did you say?" screamed Bridget, seizing a pause in his words to vent her growing outrage. "Don't you dare speak to me like that. You're a complete waste of space and you know it. I know it. Everyone knows it. I should have got rid of you long ago. Before you were born even. You're just as big a disaster as your father was. He was a useless nobody and so are you."

The venom in her voice and the rising volume which accompanied it brought Angela and Colin hurrying in from the small back yard where they had been sitting out enjoying the warm, late August sun. They were just in time to hear Richard's next words.

"I don't know who my father was and I no longer care. But I don't blame him in the least for leaving you. You're a bitter and twisted old woman. You have been for as long as I can remember so I doubt if you've changed much throughout your life. Bitter and twisted you were; bitter and twisted you are; and bitter and twisted you'll always be."

Angela immediately joined in the attack.

"Don't you dare speak to Mum like that," she shouted, her tone alarmingly similar to her mother's. "You ungrateful little sod!"

Even the normally mild-mannered Colin was roused to enough concern to join in the row in support of his mother-in-law.

"Come now, Richard, there's no need to speak to your mother like that."

Richard, however, would not be silenced. Almost twenty years of pent-up suffering finally erupted in a torrent of abuse. All his suppressed resentment met all her well-nurtured bitterness in a storm of emotion that moved from room to room as the war of words grew ever more heated. It finally came to a head as he stormed into his room, slamming the door in Bridget's furious face. By the time she'd opened it he had already ripped open drawers, flung a few things into a hastily opened rucksack and was ready to march back down the stairs.

His mother stood before him, her hands on her hips, her face a blaze of pure hatred.

"Where do you think you're going with that?" she screeched.

"It's obvious isn't it," he replied, calmly. "Or are you blind as well as spiteful. I'm leaving. I should have gone years ago. I should have woken up to the fact that you're never going to let me have a life. Well," he pushed past her, "I know now. And I'm bloody well going to get out and make one."

"You go, you stupid cretin, and you'll never be allowed back," she threatened, slightly subdued now as if she realised she was perhaps fighting a losing battle.

She tried one final onslaught.

"Don't think I'll ever let you darken my door again. You think you should have gone long ago. I should have thrown you out, more like. And more's the pity I didn't. Get a life?" she sneered. "You don't know how. You'll be back within days looking for help. Well you won't find it here."

He stared at her for one long moment in silence. Then he continued down the stairs.

"Come back here to this prison?" he laughed as he opened the front door. "I'll see you dead first."

The door slammed shut behind him.

****

ONE ACROSS, SIX DOWN

I

It was Geoff Hughes who took the call. Chief Superintendent Sean Pollock had just eased his six foot frame into a more comfortable position in the big leather chair in his office where he'd been studying the crime figures for the previous six months. He let out a sigh of satisfaction. His calculations had been correct. The figures were definitely down compared with the same period last year. Well, for serious crime anyway and that was what concerned him most. He was smiling broadly when the younger officer knocked on the door and, without waiting to be asked, hurriedly entered the small room. The smile soon vanished.

"A call just came through from uniform, Sir," Hughes announced. "A body's been discovered on some waste ground out by the Ballyglass Industrial Estate. Female. Strangled by the look of things."

Pollock was on his feet immediately, almost toppling the heavy chair in his haste. He was as aware as any other officer how important it was in cases of violent crime to seal off the crime scene as soon as possible – before the inevitable ghouls came to gawp and stare, destroying valuable evidence as they vied with one another for a better look at some poor unfortunate fellow-human's untimely end. As far as Sean Pollock was concerned people were no more civilised in such matters than they had been during the days of public hangings and the burning of witches.

"I take it someone's already notified the medical officer," he asked, as he pulled on his heavy black overcoat. It was a cold, dull October morning with rain threatening and he had no desire to risk a soaking.

"Mags is onto it now, Sir," Hughes replied. "And Noel's organising the forensic team."

"Inspector Murphy not here?" he asked

"He's out on a robbery case, Sir," Hughes replied. "Seems he has a contact who might be able to assist the uniform guys with their enquiries."

"You'd better come with me, then," Pollock said.

He hurried ahead of the younger man, pausing just long enough to put his head round the door of the main office to leave a message for Chris Murphy.

"Let him know what's going on when he gets back." Pollock was already moving again. "And tell him I've taken Hughes with me. The quicker we see this murder victim the better."

With that he hastened along the corridor, down the stairs and out into the car park, closely followed by Hughes. In a matter of minutes they were manoeuvring their way through the city's mid-morning traffic as they headed towards a large and partially abandoned industrial estate which stood on the western fringes of the city.

****

The Ballyglass Industrial Estate had certainly seen better days. Established in the mid-nineteen nineties at a time when the birth of the Celtic Tiger had promised endless growth and prosperity to the hitherto frail Irish economy it was a mute witness to the folly of such uncontrolled optimism. It had gone from being the ultimate symbol of the city's new-found wealth to being the miserable haunt of many of the city's hopeless outcasts. Despite the recent upturn in the national economy most of the thirty-six units which made up this particular estate remained empty; their boarded windows, covered with a huge variety of graffiti, and the rain-splattered 'To Let' signs providing clear evidence of the major financial damage the recession had caused to so many small businesses.

"It doesn't matter what the politicians say," Pollock remarked, grimly, "it'll be a long time before places like this are fully up and running again."

"And meanwhile," added Hughes, as they rounded a corner where a pile of empty bottles, beer cans and cigarette packets provided ample proof of the most recent use which had been made of the place, "it becomes the haunt of drunks, druggies and Lord knows who else. Small wonder there's now been a murder here. I'm surprised it hasn't happened sooner, given some of the types that congregate here of an evening."

"It doesn't make our job any easier, that's for sure," Sean Pollock agreed. "Especially for these young uniform fellows."

They had pulled up beside a young guard apparently deep in conversation with a short, thick-set man who looked to be in his

32

early forties. They stopped talking as the car halted, the guard moving away from his companion ready to report to the senior officer as soon as Chief Superintendent Pollock climbed out of the car.

"Garda Martin Maguire, Sir," he introduced himself. "They radioed me from the station. The serge knew I was on duty in this area so asked me to follow up on the call. This," he indicated the man beside him, "is Mr O'Malley. He found the body."

"Gave me a hell of a shock," the man said in response to the reference to his name. "I usually take a short cut this way on my way to the shops but I've never seen the like of this and that's the truth. I had quite a turn I can tell you. To begin with I thought it was some drunk sleeping it off but see for yourself ...."

His voice trailed off as he began to look decidedly uncomfortable, the realisation of what he'd unwittingly become involved in hitting him with full force.

'The discovery of a murder victim,' Pollock mused 'is never any good to a person's constitution, no matter how strong they think they are.'

This wasn't, however, the worst case he'd seen. As he turned his attention to the victim, leaving Garda Maguire to finish getting the basic information from Mr O'Malley, the first thing that struck him was the apparent neatness of the body. Lying there, clothes tidily, respectfully arranged, it would, the Chief Superintendent realised, be easy to mistake this for someone sleeping. Apart, that was, from the brightly coloured scarf pulled tightly round the woman's throat, the unnatural pallor of the skin and the bloodshot, sightless eyes.

The victim, quite a large woman, was probably in her middle years. Her clothes – brown trousers, thick green sweater, tan-coloured anorak – gave no immediate clue as to what she might have been doing in this particular part of the city although their neat, orderly appearance suggested that there had been no sexual motive behind the attack. Appearances, however, could be deceptive and, as Sean Pollock well knew, in a case like this nothing could be taken for granted. Only the probing and testing of the pathologist could produce anything like the definite answers he was going to need to assist him in this investigation.

As if the thought had summoned up the reality a small black Renault pulled up alongside his own car and out stepped an

33

immaculately dressed, middle-aged woman. Dr Elizabeth Mason, the pathologist.

Pollock joined her as she moved to the boot of her car and began organising herself, shedding her dark blue coat and replacing it with a familiar white protective suit of the kind always used in investigations such as this.

"Elizabeth." Sean Pollock greeted her as a familiar friend. "Long time, no see."

"Getting on for a year by my reckoning," she answered. "Not since that awful cocktail party at the court-house."

They both laughed at the memory. The city's Victorian courthouse had been transferred to a completely different premises about ten months earlier and nothing would suit the newly-appointed mayor but to hold a gathering of the city's elite to celebrate the move. It had been a disaster. The caterers had underestimated the amount of refreshments needed, the speeches had been even more tedious than usual in such events and, in the end, Pollock and Dr. Mason had slipped away like truanting schoolchildren and enjoyed an excellent dinner at Les Oliviers, the city's increasingly popular French restaurant instead.

Recalling it now Sean Pollock realised what an extremely pleasant evening that had been. Embarrassingly, he also remembered his parting remark to Elizabeth Mason at the end of that evening.

"I've thoroughly enjoyed myself," he'd said. "We must do this again – and soon."

"I'd like that very much," she'd agreed.

That had been ten months ago. To his immense chagrin he'd done nothing more about it, with the result that he'd not met the doctor again until now.

He reddened at the blunder his words had just made.

"I'm so sorry," he struggled to apologise. "I've been so caught up in work I ...."

She laughed, a pleasantly confident sound cutting off any further apology from him.

"Don't worry, Sean," she said. "I understand."

He wondered if she did. Come to think of it, he wasn't even sure whether he did. Still, this was neither the time nor the place to be pursuing personal interests. Time enough for that later.

"Our victim's over here," he said instead.

Business superseded pleasure once more.

****

They found the victim's handbag just a few feet from the body. Although it was open it looked as if its contents had been left untouched by the killer.

"By the looks of things we can rule out a mugging gone wrong then," said Hughes, as he pointed to the small brown and white bag.

Pulling on a pair of thin gloves Sean Pollock carefully opened the bag fully and began sifting through the contents. There was the usual female clutter – a bit of makeup, a comb, a couple of tissues, a mobile phone - and a purse, still containing forty euro in notes and a handful of loose change. There were no credit cards but a crumpled invoice, hastily stuffed behind the banknotes, and a membership card for the city's central library both suggested that their victim's name was Mrs Bridget Corcoran. The address on the invoice was in the West Thorn Estate, not far from where they now stood.

Sighing Pollock carefully replaced the purse's contents and returned it to the bag.

"Someone is about to have their whole life turned upside down," he said, sadly. "And they have, as yet, no idea what's about to hit them."

He sighed again and, leaving Geoff Hughes to work with the forensic team and report back later, turned back towards the car.

The forensic team, hastily summoned and already wraithlike in their white overalls, had begun their intricate inch by inch search of the ground surrounding the body. Meanwhile, Garda Maguire, the Chief Superintendent noticed, having finished taking down details from Mr O'Malley, was busy keeping ghoulish onlookers away from the scene, the bright yellow tape, which he and Geoff Hughes had strung up around the crime scene area, providing a very flimsy barrier.

"What is it about violent death that attracts so many on-lookers?" Pollock asked no-one in particular.

He didn't expect a reply knowing, as he did, that there probably wasn't one. Or perhaps there was sound psychological reasoning to explain why violence in death had such an attraction. A case of 'At least it isn't me' perhaps. Whatever the reason it didn't stop him feeling a surge of anger, especially when an eager young man with untidy dark hair and an even untidier overcoat pushed his way across to Pollock's car. Simon Moran. Pollock recognised him at once – and was not pleased.

"Excuse me, Chief Superintendent." The young man already had his notebook at the ready and was anxiously looking around, trying to catch the attention of a similar-looking young man armed with a camera. "Can you tell us who the victim is and how she came to be here? Anything at all you can give the local paper."

For some reason Chief Superintendent Sean Pollock – usually quite patient with members of the press, knowing, as he did, how often the gardai had need of assistance from the 'fourth estate' – saw red. Angrily he rounded on the unfortunate young reporter.

"Listen, Moran," he snapped. "I've now got to go and give some poor family shocking and heart-breaking news the like of which you and I can probably never imagine. The last thing they want is people like you pestering them. You'll get your story when we're good and ready and not before. And," he added, darkly, "if you or your photographer friend try to get anywhere near the crime scene or cause any trouble for any of my officers I'll personally see to it that you get locked up for obstruction."

So saying he climbed into the car, started the engine and drove swiftly away, heading in the direction of the West Thorn estate. He hadn't gone very far, however, when a change of mind took him in a different direction. There were, after all, certain advantages to being in charge and, in any case, he knew someone far better suited than himself to talk to Bridget Corcoran's family. Slower now and thoughtfully, he made his way back to the garda station.

II

It fell to Margaret Power –soon to depart from the serious crimes unit for an entirely new life in New Zealand – to visit the family and notify them of Bridget Corcoran's untimely death. In previous cases Chief Superintendent Pollock had been very impressed with the sympathetic way in which the young woman had dealt with some of the families who had come face to face with sudden, dramatic bereavement. Only later had he learned, from Geoff Hughes, that her tactful skills were based on her own personal experience. Her own father had been the tragic victim of a fatal accident at work, caused, it was later discovered, by sheer negligence on the part of his employers. No wonder she could show so much sympathy to victims' families: she knew better than most exactly how they might be feeling.

She felt it now as she sat on the edge of the red leather settee in the front room of Bridget Corcoran's home. She'd been met at the door by an anxious-looking young woman in –Power guessed – her late thirties.

"It's about my mother, isn't it," the young woman cried as soon as she'd opened the door and Mags had introduced herself. "Have you any news? I've been almost out of my mind with worry. She's never this late getting home from work."

"Shall we go inside," said Mags, gently, not wishing to draw too much attention from the neighbours. The news she was about to impart did not need an audience.

She'd been led into this small sitting room, a room made even smaller by the amount of furniture crammed into it. There was not one but two leather settees plus an easy chair as well as a sideboard, a bookcase and three small tables. It seemed as if every inch of the blue-carpeted floor had to be covered. Not only that but every available surface was cluttered with a variety of ornaments while the pale pink roses on the wallpaper were all but lost behind an array of pictures ranging from family photographs to familiar framed prints. It was a room guaranteed to create a sense of claustrophobia and Mags couldn't help wondering how anyone could feel comfortable in such chaos.

She broke the news gently. Mrs Corcoran's daughter might have already been anticipating bad news; it didn't make the giving of it any easier. The gasp of horror was swiftly followed by a flood of tears and Margaret Power found herself yet again offering words of comfort to what she always thought of as one of the other victims of violence. Her offer of tea – the traditional cup of consolation – was rejected and the two women sat in that over-crowded room, each lost in her own thoughts, the silence only broken by the sobs and sniffs of Bridget Corcoran's grieving daughter.

****

"The victim is Bridget Corcoran. Aged fifty-two. Lives, or rather lived, with her daughter and son-in-law at 17, Holly Avenue on the West Thorn estate."

Chief Superintendent Sean Pollock was back at the station where, thanks to Inspector Murphy's foresight, a special incident room had already been set up in one of the lesser-used rooms at the rear of the building. Extra phone connections had been installed, computers brought in and a large white-board had been erected at the front of the room. On this, Pollock was pleased to note, someone had already marked out the basic details acquired so far along with a photograph of the dead woman. All these preparations might, he realised, prove totally unnecessary if, as they all hoped, the case proved straightforward. On the other hand, past experience had taught him that it was far better to have a designated incident room ready at the start of a murder case rather than face the necessity of trying to create one later if a case proved less simple.

"As far as Dr. Mason could tell from her preliminary examination there appears to have been no sexual assault. Certainly her underwear was still neatly in place, an unlikely situation if she'd been the victim of rape. In fact none of her clothes had been disturbed. And, according to her daughter, since she didn't own a scarf like the one the killer used, he must have brought that with him which might suggest some sort of premeditation. I suppose we could be dealing with a random attack or, more likely, it could mean that Mrs Corcoran might well have been the intended target. Either way let's start by looking very closely at everyone connected with our victim, no matter how remotely."

"You said him," Noel Lawson remarked. "But could it not just as easily be that the killer's a woman? That would explain the scarf, which doesn't look much like one a man would have."

"Possibly," agreed Pollock "but unlikely, I think. Mrs Corcoran was quite a big woman both in height and build. It would have taken an extremely strong female to overpower her and pull the scarf tight enough – and for long enough – to strangle her."

Margaret Power looked at the solitary photograph on the incident board. The vivid shades of the murder weapon stood out sharply against the awful colour of the dead woman's face.

"It's such a pretty item," she murmured. "Seems so wrong that it could have been used for such a gruesome purpose."

Pollock nodded briefly, then continued: "We found her handbag close to the body. Since the contents seemed untouched - forty euro might not seem a large amount for a thief but I'm reliably informed that the mobile phone is quite an expensive model and certainly would fetch a bit. Anyway, since these were still in the bag I think we can also rule out a mugging gone wrong."

"Do we assume therefore that this was a straightforward and possibly premeditated murder?" It was Geoff Hughes who voiced the question that was in everyone's mind.

"It would seem so," Sean Pollock replied.

"Does that mean that she might have known her killer?" asked Phil Coady.

"Or at least that he knew her," added Noel Lawson.

"Let's hope so," Pollock replied.

He was well aware that the alternative was that this was a purely random killing. And if that were the case it could mark the start of some lunatic's private killing spree.

"Anyway," he went on, "we'll start with the obvious candidates. As I say, I want to know all there is to know about Mrs Corcoran's family, friends, work-mates. If she knew her killer it's got to be one of them." He turned to Margaret Power. "So, Mags, what do we know about the family?"

"Well, Sir, she lives with her daughter and son-in-law. Apparently she has done so ever since the daughter married, about eight years ago. I think that it was actually a case of daughter and son-in-law moving in with her rather than the other way round."

"Any other family?" Hughes asked. "Husband? Other children?"

"There was no mention of any husband. Angela, that's the daughter, was very vague about that when I asked about him although given her distressed state that's no surprise. However, there was a load of what I took to be family photos in the room where I was and, as far as I could see, apart from one small wedding photo tucked away in a corner, none of them had any men at all in them."

"Not even this Angela woman's husband?" Pollock asked.

"Only the one, Sir. And, as I say, the way it was half-hidden suggests it wasn't really welcome. Otherwise, no men at all."

"That's a bit odd," the Chief Superintendent remarked. "Still, Inspector Murphy's with her at the moment. He's taken her to make a formal identification of the body. Maybe he'll be able to get a bit more information from her after she's done the identification.

That's if she's in any state to talk. Meanwhile, Phil, I want you and Mags to go back to Holly Avenue and start talking to the neighbours. See what they can tell you about our victim.

"Mags," he turned to the team's solitary female representative, "where did the daughter say her mother worked?"

"She works in the laundry at the hospital, Sir. On the night shift. Her daughter was already getting a bit anxious because her mother was late coming home; although she did admit that sometimes her mother went home with a couple of the other laundry women and had a bit of breakfast with them first."

"Right, Noel, I want the names of these women and I want any information they can give you about her."

"Sir, if they've been working all night they might not appreciate a visit from the gardai just yet. They're probably catching up on their sleep at the moment."

Sean Pollock was about to insist but then hesitated. Noel Lawson was right. If they were trying to sleep they certainly wouldn't welcome any of his people arriving on the doorstep with a load of questions. And they might therefore decide to be awkward. If that were the case they might not give as much help.

"I take your point," he now said. "We'd better leave them until later this afternoon. But in the meantime you can at least get over to the hospital and get details of any of the people she might have come into contact with. Talk to anyone there who knew her. Get any information you can. By the way," it seemed a sudden afterthought but they all knew the Chief Superintendent well enough to know he'd already considered many of the different strands that would make up this investigation, "where's the son-in-law at present? What do we know about him?"

Mags Power consulted her notes.

"His name's Colin, Colin Molloy. He's a long-distance lorry driver. Apparently on his way home from delivering a load to somewhere in France. He should be arriving on this afternoon's ferry."

"Which will certainly rule him out of our list of suspects," Hughes commented.

"Only if he told his wife the truth," retorted Pollock. "Although that should be easy enough to prove."

He couldn't help a slight feeling of disappointment. If, as might be possible, Bridget Corcoran had known her killer then the son-in-law might have been an obvious candidate. He shrugged. They couldn't be that lucky.

"I'll get you to check that out, Geoff," he said as the others left the room. "And while you're at it you might see if we've got him on record at all. Who knows? If he had any kind of strong grievance against his mother-in-law he might be the type with associates who could have got rid of her for him while he was out of the country." He laughed as he saw the sceptical look on Geoff Hughes' face. "O.K. I know you think I'm clutching at straws but I'm determined to leave no stone unturned.

"And when you've done that I think it might be a good idea to grab a couple of uniform fellows and head back out to the industrial estate where the body was found. I know it's partly disused but I want you to question people in the units which are still occupied. They're all small-scale businesses so it should be quite straightforward. We need to know if anyone saw anything unusual out there over the past few days. People loitering about there for no clear reason, unfamiliar faces, anything like that. It's a long shot, I know, but it's worth a try. It could be that the killer chose that spot deliberately and if that's the case he may well have been hanging around there earlier, sizing up the place. You never know: we could get lucky.

"And," he added, almost as an afterthought, "see if there's any CCTV coverage. I know a lot of cameras - if there were any in the first place - will have been taken away or turned off but still. Maybe luck will be on our side in this one.

'But somehow,' he muttered to himself, 'I've a feeling that won't be the case.'

III

Alone in his office once more Chief Superintendent Sean Pollock began to mull over what they had so far. Until they received the final post-mortem report information on the victim's death was, of course, incomplete – a lot of things just guesswork for the time being. They had no official time of death, for instance, although she certainly couldn't have been dead for more than twenty-four hours since someone would surely have noticed the body sooner. Added to which her daughter would, presumably, have reported her as a missing person. He was fairly confident that rape or mugging could be ruled out but, again, only the post-mortem could prove this for definite. And Elizabeth Mason might find evidence of other injuries although, to his untrained eye, it certainly looked as if strangulation was the cause of death.

'Which,' he said to himself 'makes it murder. So what we now need to find out is what was so bad about Bridget Corcoran that made someone want to kill her. And that,' he concluded, 'might not be easy.'

****

Sean Pollock was right. The information they gathered over the next twenty-four hours gave no clue about why Mrs Bridget Corcoran had met such a violent end.

The post-mortem report confirmed that death had been caused by strangulation, the pretty scarf being the killer's chosen weapon. Time of death was estimated as being approximately two to three hours before the body was discovered. Three at the most. The body had been discovered at about eight o'clock, making it round about five-thirty, six o'clock in the morning when the killer had struck. The impression left on the victim's neck was horizontal at the same level of the neck, indicating that the murderer had attacked Mrs Corcoran from the rear. It also suggested that her attacker was at least as tall as her, if not a little taller. Although scratches on the victim's neck suggested that she had attempted to loosen the fatal cloth there were no signs of any major struggle. Nor were there any other injuries. As Pollock had suspected, this had been no sexual attack. As well as being similar in height the attacker, the report concluded, was almost certainly stronger than the victim – all of which suggested, to the Chief Superintendent at least, that they were looking for a man and a fairly tough one at that. Unfortunately, however, most of the team's investigations had provided very few clues.

As was half -expected, Geoff Hughes' return to the murder site had yielded nothing in the way of witness accounts.

"As you know," he reported back to Pollock, "many of the units are now unused and, of course, the killer chose the most isolated and abandoned part of the site. Unfortunately for Mrs Corcoran, although it offers a shorter route to her home from the hospital it's not a shortcut favoured by many; certainly not in the early hours of the morning."

"Did you find anyone who could offer even the slightest help? Maybe someone arriving early for work spotted our killer leaving.

Of course, there would be no obvious signs that he was a killer but he certainly would have been in a hurry to get as far from the place as he could."

"Afraid not, Sir. None of the units starts work before eight o'clock so none of the employees had any reason to be there at the time of the murder. And no-one I asked could remember seeing anyone loitering around the place so if the killer did go there beforehand to check it out he did so in a very subtle way. And, needless to say, there are no cameras in that part of the site. Something, I imagine, the killer was well aware of."

"I suppose I suspected as much," Pollock spoke with a definite air of resignation, "but it was worth a try. How about the truck driver – Colin Molloy? Anything on him?"

Once again Geoff Hughes had nothing useful to report.

"I checked the files as you suggested, but I'm afraid there's nothing there. He appears to be as clean as a whistle."

"Ah well," Pollock sighed, "it would have been a useful starting point if he already had a criminal record. Still, it doesn't rule him out of anything yet."

Bridget Corcoran's fellow workers had also been of little help. Having got their names from the cleaning agency contracted to carry out all the hospital's laundry work Noel Lawson had visited the various women leaving it, as he'd suggested to Pollock, until early afternoon before disturbing their much-needed rest. They were understandably shocked to hear of the violent death that had greeted their colleague on her way home.

"I can't believe it," Esther Wilson had sobbed. "She was so cheerful when she left us this morning."

"What time was that?" asked the detective.

"Just after six as usual," replied another, younger woman as she put a comforting arm around the sobbing Esther.

"To think it must have happened only minutes after she left us," gasped Marjory Griffin. She lived in the small side street that led to the industrial estate. "A murderer so close to home." She shuddered at the thought and glanced instinctively at the windows as if checking their safety value.

Similar reactions came from each woman as she was given the news. Similar fears were expressed. Similar concerns about the safety of the area and the need for extra policing were voiced. And, together with these responses, a clearer picture of the victim herself began to emerge.

Bridget Corcoran, Lawson learned, had worked in the hospital for the past fourteen years. She was, by all accounts, a cheerful, lively woman with what one workmate described as a "devilish sense of humour". No-one had a bad word to say about her. She always did her fair share of the work without complaint and was always willing to lend a friend a hand when needed. No-one could think of a reason for such a violent death.

Strangely, in Noel Lawson's opinion at least, they were able to tell him very little about her private life. Open and friendly she may have seemed but she'd always evaded questions about her family. As a result her colleagues could offer little information on that score.

"I know her daughter and son-in-law lived with her," Marion Hayes reported, "because I met them once when I had to go to her house to deliver some Avon stuff to her. I used to be an Avon rep. and, since she'd wanted the stuff in a hurry, I took it straight to her, rather than waiting till I saw her at work.

"Funny thing that," she added as her memory became clearer. "You'd have thought that she'd have been glad that I'd taken the trouble but I got the distinct impression she didn't really want me there. Still, I suppose as far as she was concerned work was work and home was home and she didn't want to mix the two."

"So you didn't socialise then?" Lawson asked.

"Not really," Mrs Hayes replied. "She didn't mind coming out with us when it was just a girls' night but she never joined us if husbands or boyfriends were included. We never asked but we got the impression that her husband was no longer around. But whether he was dead or had left her we never knew."

Phil Coady and Margaret Power had a similar story when the team gathered once more in the incident room.

"No hint of a husband," Coady reported. "Apparently the next-door neighbour – the one in the adjoining semi – has lived there for almost thirty years. She was there when Mrs Corcoran moved in. She says there's never been any permanent man in the house, at least not until the daughter got married. There have been a few male guests, as she called them, over the years but none stayed for longer than a few months."

"Chris," Pollock turned to his inspector, "did Angela Corcoran – sorry, Angela Molloy – have anything to say about her background?"

"As I told you yesterday after I'd spoken to her," said Murphy, "she really wasn't in any fit state to tell me anything. She only answered those couple of questions about her mother's work routine before she broke down completely. I did call over to the house this morning but, as you know, she was far too heavily sedated to talk to me."

"I daresay another day won't make much of a difference and it's probably not important anyway but it's strange that no-one seems to know anything about the family background."

"There's something else, Sir," said Coady. "Miss Greer - that's the neighbour – said that Mrs Corcoran arrived with two children."

"Two children?" Pollock's interest was instantly aroused. "That's the first we've heard of another child." He turned to Inspector Murphy. "She didn't mention a brother or sister to you, Chris?" Murphy shook his head. "What about you, Mags? Do you know anything about this mystery sibling? Did she tell you anything?"

"Not at all, Sir. She just said that she'd lived in that house with her mother for as long as she could remember and when she got married it seemed sensible – and cheaper – for her and her husband to go on living there. I got the impression it was so that her mother wouldn't be left on her own. There was certainly no mention of anyone else living in the house."

"How long has she lived there?" Pollock asked Coady.

"About twenty years or so. Miss Greer couldn't be more exact. But she was definite about there being two children – a girl and a boy – even though she rarely saw the boy. Not only that but it seems he only left home a couple of months ago. There was a huge row apparently. Miss Greer said that she could hear a lot of shouting and banging going on, although that wasn't unusual by all accounts. The walls between those semis are very thin it seems. Anyway, noisy arguments were common in the Corcoran household although they had got worse in recent years. This one, however, was quite frightening as far as Miss Greer was concerned and she was even thinking of calling the gardai. Then she heard one final bang – the front door slamming as it turned out – and when she looked through her window she saw young Corcoran heading off down the street."

"You say 'young Corcoran'. How old is he?"

"According to Miss Greer he was scarcely more than a toddler when the Corcorans moved in so that would put him in his early twenties"

"And has anyone seen him since he left home?"

Pollock's hopes rose. Here was a possible suspect; especially if there had been a major family row resulting in the young man being forced out of the family home. Murders, he knew, had been committed for less. Not only that, there was definitely something very odd about the fact that he had not been mentioned at all. This didn't seem like normal family behaviour. Certainly this was a good line of investigation worth following up.

"When did this row take place?" Pollock now asked.

Coady consulted his notes. "About eight or nine weeks ago as far as Miss Greer could remember. Unfortunately she couldn't be more accurate than that. And she certainly hasn't seen him since. Nor have any of the other neighbours I spoke to."

He looked questioningly at Margaret Power.

"Same here," she replied. "However, I did speak to the man in the local shop – it's just on the corner of Holly Avenue, about ten houses down from the Corcoran home. Anyway, he said he's surprised the young man put up with his mother for as long as he did. Like all the others we spoke to, he hardly ever saw the lad – and he's been working in that shop for over twenty years – but whenever he did he was always with his mother and it appears she gave him dog's abuse. Treated him like dirt by all accounts."

"That fits in with what the neighbours witnessed," Phil Coady agreed. "It would appear that the daughter, Angela, could do no wrong, even as a child. The son was always the whipping boy."

"I presume you got a name for this unfortunate young man," observed Inspector Murphy.

"Richard," Coady replied. "Richard Corcoran."

"Richard Corcoran," Chief Superintendent Pollock repeated. "Right, I want him found. Now. As quickly as possible. Jump to it, people."

Chris Murphy added the name to the white board then turned to Pollock.

"We might have just got lucky," he said. "This could be easier to solve than we'd expected."

"Don't build your hopes up too quickly, Chris," warned Pollock. "We could have a long way to go yet."

It was at that moment that the door opened and a young uniformed guard walked in. She was carrying a small plastic envelope which she handed over to Chief Superintendent Pollock.

"Forensics asked me to bring this to you, Sir," she said. "It was found in your murder victim's hand. They told me to tell you that they've checked it for fingerprints but although they found some they can't identify them at present."

Thanking the young woman Sean Pollock opened the envelope and shook the contents onto the table in front of him. He'd been so caught up in the discovery of the mysterious Richard Corcoran that he'd almost forgotten this equally mysterious piece of paper. Elizabeth Mason had phoned him earlier in the day to tell him that they had found it in Bridget Corcoran's hand though it was almost certainly put there after her death. That meant it had been put there by the murderer for some reason and Pollock, anxious that there be no damage to any forensic evidence it might yield, had instructed the doctor to send it to the forensic department first. This was, therefore, his first opportunity to see what mysterious message the killer might be wanting to send.

His curiosity changed to bewilderment as he looked closely at the piece of paper.

"What the hell?" he muttered.

In his hand was a small piece of plain white paper which, he could tell from the crease marks, had been carefully folded to a size that would fit neatly into the dead woman's hand. On it someone had carefully typed out what looked very much like crossword clues. He read them carefully.

1 Across: Eve and Hilary were two such ladies

6 Down: A fly-by-night, hesitating.

Grimly he handed the paper to Inspector Murphy.

47

"As I said, Chris, we could have a long way to go yet. This case has just taken a very strange turn."

****

"Any ideas anyone?"

Chief Superintendent Sean Pollock looked hopefully at the team of detectives gathered in the incident room.

He'd just shown them the intriguing scrap of paper carefully prised from the victim's hand. A copy of that particular piece of evidence had been added to the white-board in the hope that it might inspire someone to come up with an explanation.

"They're crossword clues."

Geoff Hughes was the first to speak.

"Well I'd got that far." Pollock's voice was full of sarcasm. "What I need is someone to give me the answers."

"Or for that matter," added Inspector Chris Murphy, "any explanation as to why it was left in the victim's hand."

"That, I think, could be fairly obvious," Pollock replied. "The killer is presumably sending us some kind of message. The trouble is we don't yet know what it is. But it's quite likely to be something important so get your thinking caps on. Fast."

While the others quietly discussed the two obscure clues and the possible reason for them being left with the body Noel Lawson stood in front of the white-board, carefully studying this strange message.

"Well, Sir," he said eventually, "it's actually very straightforward."

"You think so?" Pollock didn't sound convinced.

"It is – for anyone like me, anyone who's interested in cryptic crosswords. It's a bit of an addiction of mine," he continued, grinning. "My only vice."

"Oh yeah!" Coady raised his eyebrows sceptically.

Lawson ignored him, focussing, instead, on the two clues.

"One across," he explained, "is very straightforward. Eve was the first woman created. Hilary Clinton was one of America's first ladies. So the answer, the thing they have in common, is most probably the word 'first'."

48

Pollock's hopes began to rise.

"I see that now," he said. "It's quite obvious when you explain it. But what about the other one?"

"Ah."

Noel hesitated for just a moment before nodding, more to himself than the others. They had ceased their various conversations, intrigued, now, at the way he was opening up this particular lead for them.

"That's quite a clever one. A fly-by-night usually – in crosswords, at least – is either a bat or a moth. In this case I'm certain it's '*moth*' and the whole word is '*mother*'."

"'*Er*' being a sign of hesitation," put in Geoff Hughes. "I can see it now."

So did Sean Pollock and he wasn't happy.

"*First mother*," he said. "Bloody hell! He's telling us that she's just his first victim. He intends killing the whole family." He turned abruptly to the others. "We've got to find Richard Corcoran. Fast. And we've got to warn Angela What's-her-name, immediately. If he really means that, this is only the start of a killing spree. God only knows why, but whatever the reason we must find him and stop him."

IV

"So, Mrs Molloy," Inspector Murphy began once they were settled in the cluttered front room of number seventeen Holly Avenue. It was still as cluttered as ever, as far as Mags Power could see. There had been no major changes, no concessions to the tragedy which, only yesterday, had struck the family. "Tell me about your brother."

Angela Molloy was caught off guard, but only momentarily, as was shown in her answer.

"I have no brother."

"Come now," said Chris Murphy, sternly. "We've learned that you do have a brother. We've been told that when your mother first came here she came with two children, a girl – you – and a boy. So, I repeat, tell us about your brother."

"Ah." There was a pause. "The nosey old cow next door, I suppose. Been spouting her mouth off as usual. It's like this, Inspector. I don't have a brother. I had a half-brother. He's gone. End of story."

"Why didn't you mention him before?" Murphy demanded, his patient tone covering the irritation and frustration he was beginning to feel. But only just. If Richard Corcoran was their killer then it was essential that they find out as much about him as possible. And as quickly as possible.

"I didn't see the need," Angela Molloy replied, casually. "After all, he was never important in my life and now he's gone. There's nothing else to say."

Margaret Power had a fleeting image of her own brothers, all four of them. They were a huge part of her life, each of them special in his own way. She couldn't understand how anyone could be as cold towards a brother as Angela Molloy obviously was.

"Mrs Molloy," she said gently, with a quick glance at her senior officer.

Murphy nodded almost imperceptibly. Over the past three years that she had been part of the team he and Pollock had both come to appreciate the true worth of this particular colleague. She seemed to have a special knack for dealing with people in sensitive situations like this one. That was why Pollock had insisted that she accompany Inspector Murphy for this particular interview. Chris's nod signified that he was happy to let her continue.

"Mrs Molloy. It is essential to our investigations that we know as much as we can about your mother's family and friends. Tell us, why do you say you have no brother?"

Angela Molloy hesitated for a moment or two then seemed to reach a decision. Flicking her dull brown hair back off her face she began speaking. It seemed to both Power and Murphy that a lifetime of experience was coming out in what she had to say.

"My mother didn't have it easy," she explained. "When she became pregnant with me my father left her, abandoned the two of us leaving her to cope alone. She decided to keep me and, hoping to find a man who would take care of both of us, she ended up with Richard, my brother's, father. It resulted in exactly the same situation. My mother was deserted yet again. Another man had betrayed her. So when she gave birth to a little boy she already had a strong dislike for males. She had, or at least she believed she had, a very good reason for doing so. Not only had she been betrayed in her relationships but as far as I know her own father left her mother in very similar circumstances. They do say these things sometimes run in families. Clearly they have in my mother's.

"She had very little to do with my brother," continued Angela. Now that she had started explaining it seemed almost as if she wanted to unburden herself completely. "Apart from the basic needs that is. And I must say I felt pretty much the same. I was nearly eight when he was born. I'd got used to it being just Mum and me and, I suppose, I resented his intrusion in our lives. But I soon realised things weren't going to change much. My mother saw to that. So, he was there but that was about it. At first he spent most of the time either eating or sleeping – he didn't cry much as I remember – and then, as he grew older, he spent a lot of time in his room. I daresay he learned at a very early age that, as far as Mum was concerned, it was better if he could just keep out of the way and amuse himself. So I didn't know him. And, thanks to my mother probably, I didn't really want to know him. I agreed with her. Look what had happened. Men had always let her down so why should she trust a son to be any different?"

"So what changed with you?" Margaret Power pressed as the other woman fell silent at last. "How come you got married? And happily so, from what I can tell."

"Oh Colin's different," came the immediate reply. "Colin will do whatever I ask. He knows exactly what his role is and we're happy that way."

Inspector Chris Murphy winced. Somehow he couldn't imagine being in that sort of relationship: nor could he imagine his wife, Fiona, being happy with it. Once the novelty had worn off, of course.

"And your brother?" persisted Mags. Another quick glance at Murphy reassured her that she was doing the right thing. "When did he stop doing whatever was asked?"

There was hesitation again before Angela told them, "My brother left."

Power and Murphy waited.

"There was a row," she continued. And then it seemed almost as if a light had come on in her mind. She began to sense where their questions might be leading. An expression of horror filled her eyes.

"You don't think ...." She stopped abruptly.

"We don't know anything yet, Mrs Molloy. Please go on with your story." Margaret continued to speak gently but she could see the alarm growing on the woman's face.

"Richard wouldn't have done this," she protested. "There's no way ...."

"We aren't saying that he did," Inspector Murphy interrupted her. "But we do know there was some sort of a row and that your brother hasn't been seen here since. Tell us what exactly happened."

"You know there was a row then?"

The two officers nodded.

"They came home, my mother and Richard. They came home from the dole office. About six, seven weeks ago I think. Something serious had happened because the row seems to have started as soon as they came through the door. Colin and I were already here, out back, in the yard. We wondered what on earth was going on, my mother was screaming so much. And Richard was so cold and calm with her. Eventually he stormed upstairs and into his room. I thought that might be an end of things but minutes later he was back down. Said he was leaving. And that was that. He went out, slamming the door. And I've not seen hide nor hair of him since. That's the honest truth."

"And you don't know where he went."

"No. I have no idea."

"Does he have any friends he might go to?"

The laugh which greeted that particular question was totally lacking in humour.

"Friends? Richard? Where would he make friends? He kept to his room the whole time. When he wasn't in school or doing a few chores here, he was in his room. And when he left school and couldn't get a job he spent even more time there."

"So you've no idea where he could have gone? This is important, Mrs Molloy," Inspector Murphy added. "Very important."

"You think he did it, don't you?" Angela Molloy finally faced the truth. "You think Richard killed our mother."

"Do you think it's possible?" countered Murphy.

"You and I both know, Inspector, that anything's possible." Angela gave a sigh before continuing. "I loved my mother. I loved her very much. But if I'm honest she wasn't fair to Richard. Who knows what went on in his mind? None of us did because he never talked to us. Could be that she pushed him over the edge. I don't know. I don't want to believe it but you've asked me the question. And yes, I do think my brother could have killed my mother."

"So you can see why it's so important that we find him," said Murphy.

"There's more to it, isn't there?"

She suddenly sensed something but whether it was in his words or his manner Murphy didn't know. He paused, trying to decide how to explain the threat to her that they thought might exist without alarming her too much.

"We have received some information," he began carefully, "which suggests that your mother might have been the killer's first target – but not the only one."

She turned pale.

"You mean me!" she gasped. "You mean I might be next. Could he hate me that much too?"

"We don't know," Murphy hurried to reassure her. "We don't even know if he's the guilty party. But that's why it's so important that we find him."

The fear in her face underlined the truth of her next words.

"Honestly, Inspector, I have no idea where he might have gone. I can't even think where he'd start looking for a place to stay. I wish I did. Especially after what you've just said."

She shivered despite the warmth of the room; the stress of the whole situation making itself felt more and more. It was clear to both officers that Angela Molloy was fighting hard to remain in control of herself. It was a losing battle.

"What must I do? What shall I do if he comes back here? Will he come back here?"

She looked round fearfully as if searching for somewhere to hide from the terror that had just entered her home.

"First things first, Mrs Molloy. I'd like to see your brother's room; see if I can find any clues there." Chris Murphy started to get to his feet. "We also need a photo of your brother. The most recent one you have."

Angela looked distressed.

"Oh, Inspector," she said "I only wish I could help. But we have no photos of Richard." Almost involuntarily she looked at the many photos adorning the walls; apart from a single wedding photo of Angela and her husband not one of them showed any men. "No-one ever wanted one."

Chris Murphy was shaken by an overwhelming sense of sadness as he thought of the miserable life this young man must have had to endure with these two bitter women. He could, at that moment, feel very little sympathy for either the victim or her daughter.

"Never mind," he said, quickly masking his thoughts. "We'll just have a look in his room, if we may."

Once more Angela Molloy shook her head, her dejection increasing.

"I'm afraid that's not possible either," she said. "The day he left Mum gathered up all his possessions into a couple of big black sacks and got Colin to take the whole lot to the dump. There is absolutely nothing of his left in this house."

Chris Murphy sat down abruptly. This interview was getting more frustrating by the minute.

At that moment the three of them were startled by an unexpected sound from the hallway. Someone was trying to unlock the front door.

"Colin. Thank God," breathed Mrs Molloy, jumping to her feet and heading from the room, only pausing when she saw the look of alarm on the faces of the two detectives. "It's O.K.," she said. "Richard doesn't have a key."

She disappeared for a moment or two and they heard the sound of subdued voices. Clearly, Angela was trying, very hurriedly, to explain the situation to her husband.

"Angela says you think she might be in some danger," Colin Molloy declared as he strode into the room, his wife close behind him. "She says you think her brother killed Bridget."

"We don't know that," replied Murphy, "but it is a possibility. One of several," he added.

This was a complete falsehood but the Inspector didn't want Colin Molloy jumping to too many conclusions. He was a big, tough-looking man; one who, Chris Murphy was sure, wouldn't hesitate to take the law into his own hands if he felt he or his wife were in any way threatened. Or, for that matter – Murphy smiled grimly to himself – if his wife told him to.

"However," he now continued "I was just about to suggest to your wife that it might be a good idea for you two to move out for a day or two. If Richard Corcoran did kill his mother, for whatever reason, he may feel the same hostility towards his sister."

"He'll never lay a finger on her," snarled Molloy. "Just wait till I get my hands on him. Murdering bastard!"

"Mr Molloy," Murphy was anxious to defuse the increasingly tense atmosphere, "as I've told you, we have no evidence that your brother-in-law is in any way guilty. But we do need to find him. Have you any idea where he might be? Your wife tells us there was a major row between him and Mrs Corcoran a few weeks ago and he hasn't been seen since. Do you know anywhere he might have gone?"

"How would I know?" Despite the harshness of the question Colin Molloy sounded calmer now. "I've hardly spoken to the guy. In all the time I've lived here I doubt if we've exchanged more than half a dozen sentences. I haven't a clue where he'd go but I can tell you this ...."

Angela Molloy put her hand on his arm, that small gesture enough to halt his returning aggression.

"That'll do, Colin," she said. "Leave it to these detectives to sort out. I don't want you getting into bother over that toe rag."

She turned to Inspector Murphy. She was calm now and very much back in control. Her husband's presence, it seemed, was all that was needed to restore her sense of equilibrium. Indeed it appeared that, as far as she was concerned, the interview was now at an end.

"Don't worry, Inspector," she said. "I've friends who'll put us up for a few nights."

She'd been sitting on the arm of the easy chair but now she got to her feet, a clear signal that, as far as she was concerned, it was time for the officers to leave.

"You have my mobile number," she continued. "You can give me a call when you think it'll be O.K. for us to come back."

So saying she headed out of the room leaving Murphy and Power with no choice but to follow her. Their brief goodbye to Colin Molloy was received with just a curt nod.

"Thank you, Mrs Molloy," said Inspector Murphy as they reached the front door. "And if you do think of anything else or anywhere where we might try looking for your brother let us know straightaway."

The door was already closing.

"Don't worry. I will."

****

"Well," said Inspector Murphy once they were back in the car. "What do you make of that then?"

"I think it's very sad," was Margaret Power's immediate response. "What a lonely life that young man must have had. Do you think he did it?"

"It certainly sounds as if he had plenty of reason. I imagine those two women gave him dogs' abuse. And all because his mother was abandoned. Talk about the sins of the father!"

He was silent for a few moments, concentrating on the often strange antics of other road users. One driver in particular appeared to be taking the inner city speed limit to extremes; Chris was not surprised to notice that pedestrians were travelling faster than he could. He wasn't sorry when the annoying driver finally pulled up at the kerbside – without indicating, of course.

"Didn't get us any closer to finding him though, did it. And that's what worries me. More-so now we've heard the kind of life he had with his mother."

"Do you think his sister was telling the truth? Do you think she knows where he is?"

"I doubt it. She seemed genuinely shocked at the thought that he might be after her. I think, in view of that, that if she knew where he'd gone she'd certainly have told us." Murphy sighed. "I'm afraid Chief Superintendent Pollock isn't going to be too happy. Trouble is, we don't have any other leads to follow."

Margaret Power said nothing. She was well aware of the importance of finding Richard Corcoran as quickly as possible but she also realised, as did the rest of the team, that without any clear leads it was like looking for the proverbial needle in the haystack.

"Maybe the others will have a little more success, Sir," she eventually suggested.

They had still been in the incident room when Chief Superintendent Pollock had ordered Phil Coady and Geoff Hughes to follow up other possible sources: Coady had returned to the Holly Avenue area in an attempt at discovering whether anyone in the neighbourhood might have known Richard Corcoran and possibly helped him while Hughes was visiting the local school in the hope that the staff there might know something.

"We definitely need some sort of help," agreed Inspector Murphy. "If Lawson's right about those crossword clues and we've got the message right then there could be another murder very soon. Unless we can find Corcoran and stop him."

"No-one's tried the dole office yet, have they?" Margaret Power asked suddenly.

"We've only just found out that he was drawing the dole," Murphy pointed out. "How do you think they'll help?"

"Well," she said, "since the row started after he and Mrs Corcoran had been to sign on for his dole we have to assume that something unusual happened there to spark the argument. Maybe someone working there saw what happened. Added to which," she went on, "since, as far as we know, he's unemployed and claiming dole, he'd have to sign on regularly in order to get money."

"So there's a good chance he's still doing so." Chris Murphy seized the glimmer of hope this suggestion provided. "I imagine it could still be his only source of income. It didn't sound as if he was particularly employable, especially not in the current climate. And that means they could well have a record of his new address. You could be on to something. Maybe our visit wasn't a total waste of time after all."

Sean Pollock decided to give Noel Lawson the task of visiting the city's Social Welfare Office. Lawson was glad of the chance to get out of the garda station. He'd felt somewhat redundant when the other team members had all been sent off on various lines of enquiry. Added to which he found the paper work he'd been left with especially tedious. This was one part of the job that had never held much appeal to Noel Lawson. Computer research was fine; reading, writing and filing reports certainly wasn't.

There were fewer people in the Social Welfare Office than he'd expected but it was after midday by the time he got there; lunchtime was about to begin and public service offices, he knew, often closed during the lunch hour. As a result Lawson didn't think he'd get much immediate help but orders were orders – and it was worth a try.

"Can I help you?"

It was obvious that the young woman at the reception desk was just getting ready to leave for her own lunch break. She looked very young, in Noel's eyes at least, probably just out of school, her enthusiasm not yet destroyed by the daily procession of unfortunate cases which passed through these offices.

Noel Lawson smiled and showed her his warrant card.

"I'm looking for some information," he explained. "We're trying to track down someone we think has been signing on here in recent months."

"Name?" she asked, all eager efficiency, anxious – or so it seemed – to impress the detective with her ability.

"Richard Corcoran."

She turned quickly to the computer, the indispensable tool of all government offices as Noel was well aware. A few clicks of the buttons and she was able to provide at least one answer. According to the records Richard Corcoran of 17 Holly Avenue had been attending that office regularly in order to claim unemployment benefit.

Lawson's face fell. This, he felt sure, was going to prove yet another dead end. The receptionist had told him nothing they didn't already know. Still, he felt compelled to persevere. Just in case. He soldiered on.

"I need to speak to someone who might have dealt with him."

She checked with the computer again.

"You probably need to talk to Mr Moroney," she informed him. "He's been dealing with Mr Corcoran's claim."

"And where will I find Mr Moroney?"

She glanced at her watch and then, as if to double check, at the wall clock behind her.

"I would think," she told Lawson, "that he'll be having his lunch. Just a moment. I'll go and check."

So saying she disappeared through a door to the right of the reception desk.

Lawson gazed around him. The reception desk was in a small entrance hall beyond which was a large room which he took to be the main public area of the building. It was empty now and Noel found it hard to picture the stories he'd heard about daily queues in this room, so great that they stretched through the main door behind him and beyond. It was hard to imagine so many people jobless in a city where trade and industry had once flourished so much. Not for the first time he thanked his lucky stars that he'd chosen his particular career and that, for the moment at least, job security was one problem he didn't have to worry about.

The young receptionist returned.

"Mr Moroney is on his lunch break at present but he's in the staff-room so if you'd like to come with me I'll show you the way."

She led Lawson through the door, down a corridor and into the small room which served as the staff's rest room. Half a dozen easy chairs and as many occasional tables provided the only furnishings, apart from a very old water heater on top of a cupboard unit in the corner. The room's sole occupant, was a middle-aged man in his forties, Lawson guessed.

Henry Moroney was a pale man in every respect. His fawn-coloured jumper, his light grey trousers even his beige shoes echoed the paleness of his features. His wispy blond hair and almost opaque blue eyes gave him a distinctly colourless appearance. In fact, he looked almost ghostly.

He was seated in one of the easy chairs engrossed, or so it seemed, in his newspaper which, Lawson observed, was open at a familiar crossword page. Beside him, on the table, was a mug containing the remnants of a drink – but whether tea or coffee it was impossible to tell – and a plate, the crumbs on which gave evidence that this was, indeed, where Mr Moroney had enjoyed his lunch. It was also clear from his pre-occupied manner that, although his meal might be over, he was determined to enjoy the remainder of his lunch break to the full.

"I'm sorry to interrupt you," Lawson began, producing his warrant card once more.

Henry Moroney seemed unimpressed, indifferent, almost, to the fact that his lunch break had been interrupted by a member of the gardai.

"We need your help," Lawson persisted. "In a murder case," he added.

Still there was no apparent response from Mr Moroney. Noel Lawson decided to try a different approach.

"I see you're like me," he said. "Hooked on crosswords."

There was the slightest flicker of a reaction; hardly huge encouragement but enough to make Noel think this was, perhaps, the correct approach.

"It's the cryptic ones which always fascinate me," he continued, "though I must admit that I'm not actually very good at them. I do find though," he struggled on, fully aware that his efforts seemed to be increasingly in vain, "that if you do crosswords set by the same person regularly, like, for example, you with that newspaper, you do eventually learn their little tricks and get to recognise the various hints."

To his surprise this was the first comment to earn a response. Mr Moroney lifted his head from the paper and stared directly at the young detective.

"So which one do you do?" he asked.

Noel was not surprised to learn that Mr Moroney had a very quiet voice. Indeed, if a voice could be described as being pale this was certainly Henry Moroney's.

"When I get the chance," he replied, "I tend to do the Irish Times one although I've found it's changed a bit since that old fellow died. You know, the one who made up their crosswords for so many years."

It was as if Noel Lawson had suddenly found the key to a magic box. Henry Moroney smiled at him – a not unfriendly smile – and handed him the folded newspaper.

"Well in that case, young man," he said, "see what you can make of ten down."

At last Noel Lawson understood. The man's attitude had nothing to do with a dislike of the gardai or even any great displeasure at being interrupted during his lunch-time. The man had simply been racking his brains trying to solve the final and, it seemed, the most frustrating clue in his daily crossword.

Noel took the paper and studied the clue. It was definitely as difficult as any he'd seen lately and it took him a moment or two to start figuring it out. There was complete silence in the room until, at last, he felt able to present an answer.

It was a nine letter clue: '*To the French are thick clouds for panickers.*' Mr Moroney had already filled in four of the letters and this helped.

"I think," Noel said, slowly, "I think I've got it." He paused then nodded. "Yes. *Alarmists.* It has to be '*alarmists*'. '*Mists*' could be '*thick cloud*', '*to the*' in French is '*a la*' and the letter '*r*' often replaces the word '*are*'. And, of course, alarmists could be seen as panickers."

Satisfied, he handed the newspaper back to his companion.

"Well done," said Henry Moroney. "I think you're right." He gave a contented sigh. "I hate it when that thing defeats me. Always try to get it done in my lunch hour. Now," he was all business, "how can I help you?"

Relieved that he might finally be getting somewhere Noel Lawson began to explain.

"We're looking for a young man by the name of Richard Corcoran," he explained. "We need to contact him urgently."

"Ah." Moroney gave a knowing grunt. "This will be about his mother, I take it. I read about her in the paper. Mind you," he continued, "I wouldn't be a bit surprised if the young fellow didn't kill her himself."

Lawson was both shocked and excited by this reaction.

"Could you explain?" he said, settling into the opposite chair and taking out his notebook.

"I suppose I shouldn't have said that," Henry Moroney apologised, "but I really did feel sorry for the lad. Especially that last time."

"Why? What happened?"

"Well now, this recession has been very bad for a lot of people, especially the youngsters. It's not so bad for us older ones – not that I include you in that group," he hastened to add. "But people my age and older, we've been through this sort of thing before. At least we've got some idea of how to cope. But the youngsters, straight out of school and never knowing what it's like to go without, well, they haven't a clue. Spoiled Celtic Tiger brats, that's what they are."

"And you think Richard Corcoran was one of them."

"Oh no. His situation was far worse. Not only did he have no real qualifications – just a couple of Leaving Certificate passes if I remember correctly – and no experience, he also had his mother."

"I don't understand." Lawson sounded perplexed.

"Well, it seemed to me that she just never gave him a chance. Do you know, he's probably been signing on here for over three years now and not once, in all that time, did she let him come here on his own."

"You mean she came with him every time." The young detective was astonished.

"Yep. She didn't quite hold his hand but she certainly was making sure he showed up. That's probably why the last time was so awful."

"What happened?"

"Well, I don't know if you're aware of the fact but during the recession we had to change the rules here. There were just too many people all showing up to sign on at the same time. The queues were horrendous."

Lawson nodded. "So I've heard."

"Anyway, now we work on an appointment system. Everyone doesn't just have a particular day when they sign on; they also have to come at a set time. And, for some unknown reason, poor Richard Corcoran got it wrong.

"Well," Mr Moroney continued, warming to his subject, "you should have heard the carry-on. In front of everyone. His mother began shouting at him, calling him all sorts of names – not all of them lady-like, I might add – and really showing him up."

"What did he do?"

"That's just it. He did absolutely nothing. Mind you, I daresay he was well used to it. She never spoke kindly to him. Not that I ever heard, at least. Never had a good word for him. But on that particular day she really went mad. I half expected her to start hitting him she was so angry but no, she obviously thought vicious words could do just as much damage."

"And this was when exactly?" Lawson asked.

"I'd have to check the records but off the top of my head I'd say it was about seven weeks ago. It's got to be at least that because he was due to sign on again during this past month but I've not seen him at all since that particular upsetting incident."

Noel Lawson couldn't help feeling disappointed. Here, it seemed, was more evidence of a motive but it already sounded as if Mr Moroney would be no help in helping them discover the young man's whereabouts. Still, it was worth a try and he wasn't going to give up just yet.

"We know," he began, "that there was a major row between Richard and his mother round about the time you've been talking about. It was probably caused by what went on here. We also know that, as a result, he moved out of the family home. The trouble is we don't know where he's living now. I had hoped you might be able to help us with that."

Henry Moroney sighed.

"I'm afraid not," he said. "If we were notified of it any change of address would automatically appear on the computer. I take it young Sharon at reception has already checked that for you."

Noel Lawson nodded gloomily.

"The only address on the computer is his mother's house."

He closed his notebook, now containing several pages scrawled with his own particular brand of shorthand, and stood up.

63

"Anyway, sir," he said, "thanks for your help. And, once again, I'm sorry to have disturbed your lunch break."

"Oh, don't apologise." Henry Moroney laughed. "After all," he waved the folded newspaper, "you were at least able to solve one problem."

Noel Lawson grinned and walked to the door. As he opened it Mr Moroney called after him.

"I hope you find that young man," he said. "But you can take it from me, if Mrs Corcoran behaved to others the way she did to him then, much as it might be wrong to say it, she probably got just what was coming to her."

Noel Lawson pondered this as he made his way back to his car. Chief Superintendent Pollock would certainly be disappointed that the Social Welfare people hadn't come up with a more recent address for Corcoran. On the other hand, from what Henry Moroney had said, it seemed even more certain that the young man was, indeed, the killer. Now, all they had to do was find him.

VI

As expected Sean Pollock was less than happy when the team members reported back later that afternoon. Foolishly, he now realised, he'd pinned a lot of hope on Noel Lawson's visit to the Social Welfare Office arguing, reasonably enough, that, whatever other problems Richard Corcoran had, "He's still got to eat. And that takes money."

At least Henry Moroney's story had strengthened their view of a possible motive for the killing.

"She sounds like the mother from hell," Pollock commented when he heard Lawson's account. "Although, from what everyone else says about her, the son was the only one to suffer."

"And according to Angela Molloy, Mrs Corcoran seems to have felt no remorse in taking out all her resentments over the men who betrayed her on the son one of them left her with," added Inspector Murphy. "No wonder the poor guy snapped eventually."

"If he did," Pollock reminded them. "In spite of what appears to be a very strong motive we still have no real proof the Richard Corcoran is the killer. And we're still no closer to finding him."

Phil Coady had returned to Holly Avenue to see if he could get any further information from the neighbours. They were all aware that this was probably just a shot in the dark but there was always the outside chance that someone might have befriended the young man, offered him a room or at least have some idea where he had gone. It had, however, proved a vain hope.

"No-one had much to add to what they told us yesterday," Coady reported to his colleagues. "Bridget Corcoran, it seems, was considered a pleasant enough person. Not particularly neighbourly – she didn't go in for this business of having coffee in her neighbours' homes – but friendly enough when she met them in the street. Of course, they didn't really see that much of her, what with her working nights. She spent most days catching up on her sleep."

"What about the son?" asked the Chief Superintendent. "Did they have much to say about him?"

"Very little," Phil Coady replied. "Mainly because they hardly ever saw him. In fact quite a few people in that street told me they didn't even know she had a son. And those who did told me that, apart from when he was going to school, it seems he rarely went out. Certainly not on his own. Even Miss Greer, the woman who lived right next door to the family, hardly saw him at all. And when she did it was only a fleeting glimpse. There was never a time when he'd stop and talk. In fact," he concluded, "she didn't even know his name."

"How about that shop on the corner?" Chris Murphy enquired. "Could they tell you anything?"

"Not really. I got the impression that Bridget Corcoran didn't use it very often. Probably preferred one of the big supermarkets. The man I spoke to could only remember two occasions in recent months when Richard Corcoran was in the shop. Both times he was with his mother and both times, in spite of the fact that he said or did nothing wrong, she was – in the shop assistant's words - 'quite abusive to him'."

"Just what Mr Moroney said," agreed Noel Lawson.

"And," added Geoff Hughes, "pretty much the same as the school had to say."

Hughes had visited St Saviour's, Corcoran's former school, in the hope that they might be able to supply him with names of friends the lad might have had during his time there; friends who might now be willing to give him a place to stay for a while. It had proved a fairly pointless exercise.

"Did they tell you much about Corcoran?" Pollock asked the young detective.

"Not really," Hughes replied. "I got the impression that no-one there really knew him. Of course, it's four years since he left but I think he was probably like hundreds of kids up and down the country. Not particularly smart or cheeky or disruptive or anything like that. He wasn't especially clever – didn't do spectacularly well in exams – but, on the other hand, he wasn't in what the principal termed the 'special needs' category."

"In other words," said Murphy, "as far as the school was concerned he was a bit of a nobody."

"Absolutely," Hughes agreed. "It seems he had no friends ...."

"None at all?" Margaret Power interrupted, her sympathy for the young man growing all the time, despite the fact that he could be a murderer.

"None that any of the teachers knew about. In fact he was the victim of some bullying when he first started at the school. As far as the school counsellor could make out the other lads took the Mickey out of him because he made up some outrageous story to explain why his father was never around: but since he never fought back the bullies eventually gave up."

"And you say they had a similar story about his relationship with his mother," Pollock prompted.

"Oh yes. It seems she only came to one parent-teacher meeting the whole time he was there and I got the distinct impression they were very glad she never returned. The students accompany their parents to these meetings in that particular school so Richard had to stand there and put up with total humiliation each time a teacher said he wasn't doing particularly well in a subject. According to the principal it became highly embarrassing for everyone concerned – everyone except Mrs Corcoran, that is."

Margaret Power sighed. "He really does sound like a very pathetic young man," she said.

"But don't forget, Mags," Chris Murphy warned her, "this pathetic young man may well be responsible for the brutal murder of his mother and could be planning a similar attack on his sister. Sad or not he could still be a vicious killer."

They were all agreed on that. Richard Corcoran, from all they'd learned about him, had every motive for committing this otherwise senseless murder. What they now needed was proof. And, of course, the young man himself.

"What about the place where the murder happened?" Lawson's voice broke the silence. "Was there nothing there to give us any clues?"

Sean Pollock shook his head.

"The forensics people went over the place with the proverbial fine tooth comb. They found absolutely nothing. And the post-mortem was equally unhelpful. Bridget Corcoran's death was murder, pure and simple. No sign of sexual assault, no sign of robbery – her handbag and the couple of bits of jewellery were untouched – no hint of any motive other than simply ending her life."

"But surely it's not a particularly salubrious part of the city," Phil Coady remarked. "Isn't it just possible that she just rubbed someone up the wrong way? Especially if she was walking through there early in the morning when some of the regulars who haunt the place might have been beginning to feel the unpleasant after-effects of their particular fix. "

Geoff Hughes had revisited the murder site the previous afternoon. It was certainly an unsavoury place. What had once been a thriving estate of small, up-and-coming businesses was now the meeting place for drug addicts and drunks.

"Most of the units are closed now," Hughes told his colleagues," thanks to the recession. But I did get to talk to a few people who still work there. A couple of them even remembered seeing Mrs Corcoran occasionally – when they had to go in early for some reason and she was on her way home. It was after all, her regular route, according to her workmates, and she'd never shown the least concern about walking through the place in the early hours of the morning."

"If she treated all men the way she treated her son most of the drunks and druggies would run a mile rather than tangle with her," Phil Coady remarked.

Although the ensuing laughter eased the tension in the room Inspector Murphy remained serious.

"That's the awful thing," he said. "All her resentment was directed solely at her son. By all accounts she was reasonably pleasant to other men."

"And not averse to bringing one home occasionally, according to the neighbours," Coady added.

Chief Superintendent Sean Pollock stood up and began to pace the room. The others watched him in silence. They all knew from experience that he was now weighing up all the information they had given him in the hope of seeing a clearer path ahead. Finally, he halted in front of the whiteboard, studied it carefully for a few moments then turned to face them. A few scribbled words had been added during the course of the day as the detectives reported back on their various interviews. Cause of death and probable time were also there.

"There are," he said, "a few discrepancies in all we've heard so far. We all seem convinced that Richard Corcoran had a very strong motive for hating his mother and, from what Noel has told us, that incident in the Social Welfare Office may well have been the last straw which finally pushed him over the edge.

"We know – both from the next-door neighbour and from the sister – that he and his mother had a major row, probably as a result of that incident, which resulted in him leaving home. And, although we don't have an exact date for that event, everyone seems agreed that it was probably about seven weeks ago."

The others nodded but said nothing, waiting to see where Pollock's musings would lead them.

"Now," he continued," the first question I would ask is: why did he wait so long to kill her? If this was the final straw; if he spoke to his mother in a way his sister had never heard in their whole lives; if he stormed out of the house in a boiling rage then how come he waited for seven weeks before taking his revenge?"

The silence continued. No-one had a clear answer to that particular question. After a while Pollock spoke again.

"On the other hand, if he's innocent why hasn't he come forward? No matter how spiteful his mother was to him wouldn't you think that he'd put in an appearance – if only to gloat at her passing?"

"And to proclaim his innocence," added Geoff Hughes. "After all, he must realise that we'd be asking questions and we'd soon discover that he had a definite motive for killing her."

Sean Pollock nodded but said nothing.

"Of course, we could be barking up the wrong tree," said Chris Murphy. "We could be off on a wild goose chase trying to find Richard Corcoran and our killer could be someone completely different. Someone who, perhaps, also had a motive that we don't yet know about."

"Don't think I haven't thought of that," Pollock admitted. "But, from what we've learned so far about our victim, the only person she ever hurt was her son. According to everyone else she was a pleasant, affable, ordinary person with no apparent enemies."

"So could it be a random killing?" suggested Coady. "You don't think we've got some lunatic on the loose who gets his kicks from strangling middle-aged women."

Pollock glared at Coady. Unusually, he wasn't in the mood to appreciate the young man's rather flippant tone.

"The trouble is," he pointed out, as Phil Coady sank back into his seat, "if this was some random killing it doesn't really explain that piece of paper. There's definitely a message there and, assuming Noel's right – and I don't see why he shouldn't be – it seems that the killer has a definite programme lined up. First the mother, Mrs Corcoran, and then ..." He let the sentence trail off. They were all thinking the same thing. Angela Molloy could certainly be the next target.

VII

Wednesday. Two days after the discovery of the body and it seemed they were no further on. Of course they knew how the victim had met her death. And if what they'd heard from Angela Molloy and Henry Moroney, from the school, the neighbours, the local shop – if all this were true they quite likely had the motive for the killing. As a result they were even fairly confident they knew who the killer probably was. But of their suspect there was absolutely no sign. Every area of enquiry they'd tried had led to a dead end. Richard Corcoran, it seemed, had vanished into thin air.

They weren't helped by the fact that they had no recent photograph of him. The only photograph they had was the one taken when he'd started secondary school ten years earlier so it was of little use, although there were some noticeable similarities to the victim.

Descriptions on the other hand, even from his sister, varied so much they were of scant use.

"Could fit any number of young men," was Pollock's scornful comment when he heard them.

His hair was anything from dark brown to dull blond. He was 'quite short for his age' or 'fairly tall' depending on who was being questioned. He was also 'quite skinny', 'well built' or just plain 'ordinary'. In short, no-one could give them a really accurate picture of the elusive Richard Corcoran.

By five o'clock the previous evening Chief Superintendent Pollock had decided to dismiss the team, urging them with a tired sigh to try and come up with a new angle when they met again the next morning. He didn't sound particularly optimistic.

A quick pint in the Seanachai with Chris Murphy at the end of a frustrating day had done little to help his mood.

"I don't like it, Chris," he said, glumly. "It's just too simple and yet there's no other possible candidate. And until we find Corcoran I don't see where we go from here."

"I agree," Murphy replied, downing half a glass of cider in one gulp. "We've looked at all the obvious explanations. There's no evidence of Bridget Corcoran doing anything drastic enough to bring about her murder. And you're absolutely right, that weird crossword clue makes it seem highly unlikely that we're dealing with a random attack."

"So everything points to the son." Pollock sighed. "I still think it's just a bit too obvious."

Chris Murphy studied his senior officer in silence.

"I certainly don't want to end up barking up the wrong tree ," Pollock muttered, as if he'd read the Inspector's mind. "And, as a result, leaving some nutcase free to kill again. And there's no need to tell me we'll get it right in the end. We might not if we're fooled by what seems to be the obvious conclusion. Whatever happens," he downed the last of his pint, "I don't want Richard Corcoran suffering for our carelessness." He paused and held up the two empty glasses. "Time for another?" he asked.

Inspector Murphy shook his head. "No thanks. I'd better be getting home. I promised Fiona I'd try and be early if I could. Matthew has a school project that he's a bit stuck on and I said I'd give him a bit of a hand." He got to his feet. "I'll see you tomorrow then." He moved away then, turning back. "And don't spend the whole evening brooding over this one," he said. "You never know what might turn up tomorrow."

With that he was gone.

Sean Pollock sat alone for a few minutes debating with himself whether to have another pint of Smithwick's before he, too, went home. The he stood up.

"No," he said, to no-one in particular. "It's not worth the risk. Not when I'm driving."

****

For Sean Pollock there were two bad times of the day and they had existed for him ever since his wife's premature death.

Even after more than ten years, waking up was still a nightmare. That awful transition from sleep to wakefulness still brought with it the painful awareness of the empty space where his beloved Claire had once slept. Although she'd only shared his bed for a mere twelve years he'd had no inclination to find someone to fill that empty space.

Oh, there had been odd times when he'd thought about it. Urges, he knew, didn't always die just because a beloved partner did. He'd even invited women out to dinner occasionally with the vague idea that maybe it would lead somewhere. It never did. Even Elizabeth Mason – his last date, if he could call it that – even she, good-looking and interesting though she was, couldn't fill the void left by his wonderful Claire.

If mornings were bad homecomings were often even worse. A legal secretary by profession Claire had always been there when he got home, ready to welcome him with a relaxing drink, a good meal and a sympathetic ear. It was a ritual he still missed. Now, as he unlocked the front door, he felt that the empty house was more than usually laden with the echoes of happier times.

"I must be getting old," he said aloud. "Old and maudlin."

As he took off his coat and hung it up on one of the hooks at the foot of the stairs he hesitated for a few moments, torn between a glass of whisky and a more sensible cup of tea. In the end discretion won over desire. After all, he could always have the whisky later on in the evening.

He made his way into the kitchen – spartan and masculine in a style he knew Claire would never have recognised – filled the kettle and

71

began the process of preparing a light meal for himself. He didn't want or need much. Since he'd been living alone he'd taken to having his main meal at work whenever possible. The canteen's meals weren't too bad and, when they did appear less appetising than usual, An Seanachaí just down the road produced a reasonable carvery lunch – and at a reasonable price. Nonetheless, he mused, in either case it was probably just as well that he was no gourmet when it came to food.

Cheese and pickle on toast along with a large mug of tea would, he decided, fit the bill this evening and, as soon as it was ready, he carried it into the sitting room. With Claire he would have sat at the kitchen table, lingering over his food while he discussed with her the various difficulties and intrigues which his working day had produced. Now the television provided his only company, though it was a poor substitute.

The central heating was already on, providing a gentle background warmth; however, he still lit the gas fire – more for the comforting effect of its artificial flames than for more heat – and turned on the television. Then, finally, he flopped into his favourite easy chair, loosened his tie, kicked off his shoes and settled down with the newspaper to study his viewing options for the evening ahead.

A quick glance at the paper's headlines convinced him that he had no desire to read about the woes of the country or the world. Nor did he want to go on reading the book he'd started at the weekend. He was, he knew, far too distracted by the frustrations of the current case to lose himself in the deeper interpretations of life offered by Buddha, fascinating though he might have found them in other, less stressful circumstances. No, it would have to be the television.

He'd discovered soon after Claire's death that the television had one major advantage over the radio: it brought a sense of people being in the room. Many evenings this wasn't really a big issue and he was quite content to sit back and listen to his favourite Lyric FM but on occasions like this, when his mind was so unsettled, the distracting – and often strange – antics of the men and women of TV- land provided the only remedy.

He scrolled through the channels commenting to himself on the lack of what he considered good entertainment – too many soap operas, too much so-called reality television – and finally settled on a repeat of the excellent Sharpe series. Decision made he sat back to enjoy his tea and was soon lost in the dangerous world of the Napoleonic Wars.

Only when the programme was over – two episodes back-to-back, in fact, which had provided a pleasant bonus – did he decide to indulge in the whisky he'd promised himself earlier.

He crossed to the drinks cabinet, drawing the curtains as he passed the window to hide the now-dark street outside, and poured himself a good two fingers of Jameson's finest.

Once more he settled himself in his chair, having decided to watch the main evening news followed by a documentary on the so-called victory over the recession – a notion which, he suspected, might still be somewhat premature. Slowly he sipped his drink.

The room was warm, the whisky relaxing, the chair comfortable. It had been a long and difficult day. Gradually his eyes grew heavy, his head began to droop and he escaped from the drama of more tension in the Middle East into a peaceful, carefree slumber.

****

He had no idea what woke him but something had nudged his sleeping brain back into consciousness. What was it?

He listened carefully but there were no unusual sounds, either in the house or in the street outside. Had a car back-fired? Had a couple of courting tom cats engaged in a loud battle over the local available females?

Nothing. No hint of what had brought him so abruptly back to this fully alert consciousness.

He glanced at the television as if it might provide the answer. The documentary was well underway. And it was then that he discovered what had stirred his resting mind and roused it back to wakefulness. Employment opportunities.

The programme's presenter had been talking about the gradual increase in employment opportunities which had led to a slow but steady decline in the number of unemployed and a corresponding increase in consumer spending – both important factors in the war against inflation.

"Of course," she now declared, "the situation has been greatly helped by the fact that we not only have several government initiatives for job seekers, there has also been a noticeable increase in the number of recruitment agencies in towns and cities throughout the country."

Chief Superintendent Sean Pollock was now wide awake, a big grin spreading across his face. That was it. That was what had filtered through the sleeping officer's mind and struck a chord. They'd assumed that the only place Richard Corcoran would go for help was the Social Welfare Office since that was what had been familiar territory to him ever since he'd left school. But supposing he'd gone to one of these recruitment agencies: as far as Pollock knew there were several in the city.

Gone the despondency, gone the frustration. By sheer chance a new lead had suddenly opened up. Could this be the opening they'd been waiting for? Was this a way of tracing Richard Corcoran? He could do nothing about it tonight but first thing tomorrow morning he'd get the team working on it.

Smiling he poured himself another small whisky, in celebration, and settled down to discover just how the country had defeated the recession.

VIII

When Chief Superintendent Sean Pollock entered the incident room at exactly eight forty-five on Thursday morning he was well pleased to observe all the team already present, eager to try and wipe out the disappointments of the previous two days. He'd already been working at his desk for over an hour, catching up on paperwork and, more importantly as far as he was concerned, finding out all he could about the city's various recruitment agencies.

"There are seven," he informed the group. "I've a list of them here, complete with all the relevant details. In the next hour or so I want all of them visited and questioned as to whether or not Richard Corcoran is or ever has been on their books.

"I don't care how you divide up the job," he went on, "but I want it done as quickly as possible. It could provide our last – our only – lead to this fellow's whereabouts."

"Why don't we just phone them?" Phil Coady asked.

"Because it's quite possible that they'll be anxious about considerations of client confidentiality. And that means they'll want assurances that your enquiries are genuine. Better to go in person and show them your credentials. Could save time in the end."

With that he left the room, disappearing into his office where he buried himself once more in the seemingly never-ending volume of

74

paperwork his job now demanded and trying desperately hard – and not altogether successfully – to curb his impatience and suppress the bubble of optimism which had been slowly growing inside him since the previous evening's brainwave.

It was Margaret Power who burst that bubble.

"Excuse me, Sir," she said, having knocked and entered.

Her expression warned him that the information she was bringing was not what he'd hoped for.

"I take it I'm not going to like this," was his only comment.

"I'm afraid not, Sir," she replied, almost apologetically.

"Go on."

"Richard Corcoran can't possibly have murdered his mother. He wasn't even in the country when she was killed."

"You'd better explain," Pollock ordered the young woman. "And," he indicated the chair opposite him, "you might as well sit down while you're doing so."

She sat before resuming her report.

"Well, Sir, the receptionist at the recruitment agency – Phoenix Partners on Collins Street – remembered Richard Corcoran. A very intense young man, according to her, and clearly very desperate to get a job – any job, anywhere – as quickly as possible. It seems he looked both hungry and uncared for, so much so that she had the distinct impression that he was homeless, living rough. I think that's the main reason he stuck in her memory.

"Anyway," she went on, while Pollock listened in silence, "as it turned out that very day they'd had word from CSAC – that's a computer help-line centre out on the south ring road – that they were looking for operators to man their telephone services. So, taking pity on Mr Corcoran she sent him out there to see if they'd take him on straightaway."

"And did they?"

"She assumed that they did since he never came back."

"I take it you've contacted this company."

Pollock knew that Mags Power wouldn't hesitate to act on her own initiative. As with the other members of the team this was one of the main reasons why he'd been so pleased to have her working for him - and why he'd miss her when she left.

"I went straight over there," she replied. "The Human Resources officer was more than helpful. He told me that demand was so great that they were willing to take on pretty much anyone – within reason, of course."

"And Corcoran fitted the bill," was Pollock's comment.

"So much so that he was literally taken on there and then."

"Did he give an address? Do they know where he's living?"

"Strangely enough he gave his mother's home as his address. And, naturally, they saw no reason to question it so they had no other address to give me."

Chief Superintendent Pollock's disappointment was very apparent.

"So we're no closer to tracking him down," he said.

"It wouldn't have mattered anyway," she replied.

"How come?"

"As Mr Mitchell explained to me, the first thing any of their new recruits have to do before they can start working here is undergo an intensive six week training course at the parent company's headquarters."

"And?" There was clear resignation in Sean Pollock's tone.

"The headquarters are in Glasgow. Richard Corcoran started the course just over five weeks ago and has been there ever since. And," she added, snuffing out the last glimmer of hope," "I've just phoned the man who supervises the trainees. He confirmed the story. What's more, he also told me that they provide a twenty-four hour help-line service which means there's a certain amount of shift work and at the time his mother was murdered it would appear that Richard Corcoran was working a night-shift in Glasgow. So you see ...."

She got no further. The door was flung open and Geoff Hughes burst in.

"Sorry, Sir," he said, panting from the exertion of running up two flights of stairs, "but I've just been talking to Larry O'Dwyer downstairs. He was about to call you. They've just had a frantic

phone call from a couple of very upset young lads. It seems they've
just discovered a body."

$$* * * * * * * * * * * *$$

THE SISTER

My situation might have been easier if I could have shared it but my sister, my one surviving sibling and therefore my only real ally, was part of the conspiracy. My mother might have had reasons for hating me; my sister did so merely to keep in favour. And only I knew why.

My sister was five years old when I arrived on the scene. My brother was born less than two years later. My father had already left by then and in the months following his departure she had, surprising though it might seem in one so young, already formed an unholy alliance with my mother which I found impossible to break. And my brother's death within a few months of his second birthday made me even more vulnerable.

Not that I was aware of it to begin with. As far as I knew, all older sisters treated their kid brothers in the same ill-tempered manner. It was only as I became more conscious of the unfairness of my mother's treatment that I also began to realise how deliberately cruel my sister actually was. I'd had very little chance to mix with other children but, on the odd occasions when I did, it began to dawn on me that there was usually a level of affection underlying the way brothers and sisters behaved towards each other. This was never the case with my sister and me.

She'd use any excuse as a reason to torment me and, gradually, the cry 'He did it, it was his fault' became so common in my life that I began to believe in my own hopelessness. I was blamed so often and described as a useless waste of space so regularly that, eventually, I decided it must be true. It had to be my own fault. There was no other explanation. I'd obviously committed some great misdemeanour at some stage in my life that had earned the clear dislike and obvious distrust of both my mother and my sister and there was nothing I could do to change things.

The early years weren't too bad. There was little I could do – whether right or wrong – and, as a result, little my sister could do to satisfy her resentment. I quickly learned to bear the sly pinches, the odd thumps when no-one was looking although, looking back on it, I don't think my mother would have cared in any case. It was my fault and I deserved everything I got.

It got worse by the time I reached my teens. Knowing why my mother resented me made little difference to the way she treated me and none at all to the way my sister behaved. And when my mother died – too many cigarettes, too much alcohol or worse - just a few months after my fifteenth birthday things became really bad.

My sister had passed eighteen by then and, consequently, was seen – by law at least – as a responsible adult. This meant she could become my legal guardian, a situation I had to accept as there was no real alternative. No-one else wanted me.

I don't think my sister ever called me by my name. If she did it was such a rare event that it slipped from my memory completely. To her I wasn't a person: I was the whipping boy, the laughing stock, the butt of all her jokes. I'm sure she used to invite her friends to the house just so they could get a laugh at my expense. I was made to look a fool and, worse still, I was made to feel a fool. More than that I became, in many respects, her obedient slave, for to do so was usually easier, safer and wiser than trying to protest.

By the time I'd finished school she'd decided that I was to blame for all that was wrong in her life. It was my fault when she didn't get a particular job she'd wanted. It was my fault when she failed her driving test. And when boyfriends broke up with her that was my fault as well.

The trouble is, when you know that however hard you try you can never do right you eventually give up trying. Nonetheless, by the time I reached my late teens I resolved to begin the struggle to achieve some sort of normal situation and, more importantly, win back my self-esteem.

It was, I confess, a complete failure.

The day I came home and announced that I'd found myself a job and that I'd be leaving home was a total fiasco. She laughed in my face; called me all kinds of a fool, pointing out that no-one in their right mind would really want to employ me for any length of time because no-one would employ an idiot. And, fool that I was, I started to believe her. All my resolve crumbled. The following day I telephoned the man I'd hoped would be my new employer and told him that, for reasons I was unable to disclose, I could not, after all, take up his kind offer. I was seventeen and, once more, I'd cracked under my sister's ridicule.

This time was different, however, and, even as I bent to her will once more, something deep within me snapped. This would be the last time. Never again would she wield such total power over me. It was at that moment that I knew that one day I'd get my revenge. I didn't know how or where or when but I did know that sooner or later someone was going to have to pay for the wrong I'd endured.

****

MICKEY

I

Mickey Connolly often wondered what love was like. He'd even settle for affection. For, throughout his seventeen years, he'd never felt either loved or even wanted.

He couldn't really remember his father, although in his mind were vague images of a vicious, angry brute who thought his fists were the answer to every wrong, real or imagined. In those same images he always saw his mother as the main target for such violence although, as he grew older, he discovered that his older sister hadn't always avoided the odd punch. He even had very dim memories of himself being at the hospital and wondered if this, too, was the result of his father's brutality.

His father had finally left them when Mickey was three years old. Mickey never discovered why or where he went; nor did it ever bother him. He still had plenty to cope with.

His mother had found her own escape from her unhappy existence. Her particular route was through a bottle and she soon reached the point where alcohol dominated most of her waking hours. Eventually, of course, the consolation drink had once provided began to fade so she turned to drugs as a new way out. It was a lethal combination, one which eventually killed her.

Mickey was fifteen at the time and he clearly remembered the day when he came home from another miserable day at school – a place he really hated and one which, he felt sure, hated him just as much – and found his mother sprawled across the settee, the empty syringe still in her arm, the empty vodka bottle on the floor beside her. Mrs Connolly's battle with life was over: Mickey was forced to continue his.

His sister, Maureen, was not quite twenty when their mother died but, since she was deemed by law to be an adult, no-one saw any reason why she should not act as Mickey's guardian. It suited the already over-burdened authorities since it saved them the task of finding suitable foster parents for a young lad who, it was believed, was already a difficult case to say the least. In a way, he soon discovered, it suited his sister – although for all the wrong reasons.

It might have suited others. It certainly didn't suit Mickey.

If he disliked the memory of his father as a vicious bully and resented his mother's withdrawal into an oblivion of her own creating, his feelings against his sister were even stronger since it was here that he felt the lack of affection most strongly. They should have been friends at least, allies bound by the common burden of their ineffective parents. It didn't work that way. Maureen, he discovered at an early age, had inherited all of their father's viciousness but in a far more subtle way. Whereas Mr Connolly had resorted to his fists as a way of showing his power, his daughter used words. In Mickey's case they proved far more lethal. The old rhyme, he often thought, wasn't true. Sticks and stones could certainly break bones but harsh words could cause just as much harm. The damage they did might not kill the body; they could certainly destroy the spirit.

By the time he was ten Mickey had already become so used to being ignored by his completely ineffective mother, so used to being called all kinds of a fool and being treated as little better than a slave by his sister that he began to accept it as almost the normal way of life. Unfortunately, when his sister became his guardian, things became much worse.

****

Mickey had few friends; none that he could call a true friend, although Sammy Ferguson who lived two doors away from him in the row of terraced houses where he grew up could, perhaps, fall partly into that category. The trouble was it wasn't a friendship of equals nor was it a beneficial friendship as far as Mickey was concerned. Sammy used him when there was nobody else around, used him for entertainment, used him as his fall guy. For Sammy had begun the life of a petty criminal at the tender age of seven. He was delighted to recruit Mickey as his accomplice and Mickey, desperate to feel wanted, was only too happy to comply.

The exploits were never major: some articles lifted furtively from the open counters of one or two of the city's large department stores – although the dangers posed by the alarm systems usually far outweighed the profit; the occasional successful raid on a jacket or handbag carelessly left hanging on the back of a cafe chair while the owner ordered a drink; one or two failed attempts at breaking into cars. For the most part, however, they confined their criminal activity to the local corner shop. It was easier.

Mickey would provide a distraction for Mrs Goggin, who owned the shop, or for Betty, her middle-aged assistant, a role he could play with unfailing success. With his almost angelic looks – blond hair and bright blue eyes were, in this instance, a huge advantage –

and the not uncommon neighbourly awareness of the life the poor boy had lived neither Mrs Goggin nor Betty could imagine his conversations with them as being anything but completely innocent. So, while he smiled and chatted and beguiled, Sammy was able to help himself at leisure.

There were drawbacks to this arrangement. For a start, Mickey never got what he thought was a fair share of the spoils. More importantly, for Sammy the spoils soon didn't seem worth the effort.

"What's the point," he'd say, "in goin' through this for a couple of bags of sweets, some crisps and, if we're really lucky, the odd magazine?"

Sammy wanted more and he wanted Mickey to help him. Soon Mickey's world was split between home – and the abuse that held – and the streets where Sammy led him into further and further outrageous exploits.

There was, however, a third dimension to his life, one which might have given him the understanding and the help he so desperately needed but one which, instead, caused him to feel even more alienated.

School.

At primary school he'd been quiet and disinterested and, in spite of his teacher, Mrs Casey's, best efforts he never truly opened up to the care and attention which she so willingly gave. He progressed through the school, moved on to different teachers and withdrew further and further into himself.

"How's young Mickey Connolly doing?" Mrs Casey would sometimes ask in the staffroom, still anxious about a little boy she felt certain was crying out for help.

"He's O.K, I suppose," the answer would come back. "Sits there, doesn't make much noise, causes no trouble. Doesn't do much work either."

But at least having him quiet in a class of thirty young lads was an advantage and his very silence meant he would, for the most part, be ignored. His education suffered accordingly.

By the time he got to second level he'd fallen out with the whole notion of learning and, under the guidance of an increasingly bold

Sammy Ferguson, non-attendance at school became more and more frequent.

The two boys would set out together under the watchful eye of Sammy's mother – no-one in Mickey's house had ever cared enough to see him off – but as soon as they'd rounded the corner they'd make their way to an abandoned warehouse where they'd made for themselves their own secret hide-out. It was here that Mickey tried his first drink, reluctant though he was since the experience of his mother was vivid in his mind. And it was here that he tried his first cigarette, an experiment which quickly became an addiction.

He did draw the line one day when Sammy, very excited, turned to him as soon as they'd reached their den.

"This is great," he told Mickey. "Now we'll have some fun. Look what I've got. And there's plenty more where they came from."

The 'fun' , as Sammy saw it, took the form of two spliffs, strange smelling cigarettes which, he assured Mickey, would let him relax and view the world through spectacularly rose-coloured glasses.

Mickey knew enough about drugs to know that this could well be the road to ruin. And this was one road he wasn't prepared to travel, not even for a few minutes of contentment. So, while Sammy drifted into a world where all was peace and light Mickey made do with a few cigarettes and a couple of gulps of vodka.

II

This became the pattern of Mickey's life – evenings of constant persecution from Maureen at home and, whenever possible, days of freedom with Sammy. The fool's paradise in which Mickey had sought refuge might have lasted for months, especially since it appeared that no-one seemed to be aware of his truancy. At least that's what he told himself. Until the letter arrived.

He knew it was bad news as soon as he saw the plain white envelope lying on the mat when he arrived home one Thursday evening. It looked far too formal to contain anything good. The fact that the address was typed and that it was addressed to his sister did nothing to allay his fears.

Resisting the temptation to destroy it he picked it up along with the electricity bill and a postcard – presumably from one of Maureen's friends since no-one had ever sent him anything like that – and placed them on the small hall table. He'd find out soon enough what misfortune that letter might be bringing him but there were jobs to be done and he'd be in even more bother if they weren't done properly by the time Maureen got home. In any case he was in no doubt that he was likely to suffer no matter what the letter's contents might be. He was right.

"You little bugger! You rotten, skiving little bugger!"

Maureen's voice rose with every word until she was soon screaming at him.

"So stupid you can't even make do with just skipping a couple of classes. Oh no, not you. You have to miss whole days, weeks even. You bloody eejit! What the hell do you think you're playing at? Do you think I want to waste my time trailing into that school just because you can't sit in a classroom for a few hours?"

She paused. Mickey didn't bother saying anything. He knew she was just drawing breath, ready for the next onslaught. It soon came.

"You do realise I'm going to have to take time off work in order to go and sort this out. Thanks to your stupidity I'm going to lose pay. And how do you think I'm going to feel asking my supervisor to let me have time off because my idiot brother has been playing truant? You worthless waste of space. You never think of anyone but yourself. God knows why I agreed to keep you here. I should have insisted that they put you into care. You're just ruining my life, that's what you're doing."

Another pause. Mickey knew what was coming next. It was always the same when Maureen found fault in him. First there were the screams of abuse and then ....

"So, for a start you can get the bucket and brush and scrub that back yard till I could eat my dinner off the ground. And I don't care how long it takes."

It was the same old pattern: a lot of abuse then another long, arduous and, to Mickey's mind, pointless task as punishment for the trouble he'd caused. He'd lost count of the number of times the yard had been scrubbed. For some reason that was Maureen's favourite punishment, closely followed by cleaning the windows. That, he now realised, would probably come next. Not that it made much of a difference to Mickey. There were very few jobs in the house which he didn't do. Cleaning, washing, he did them all. He was even expected to iron his own clothes although Maureen drew the line at letting him touch her things, telling him he was so useless he'd probably ruin them all.

"You know something, Mickey," Sammy Ferguson used to tease him. "You'll make someone a wonderful wife one of these days."

Now he sighed, went slowly into the kitchen and began filling the bucket, wondering, as he did so, what he'd ever done to deserve such unfair treatment.

****

Maureen's appointment with the school principal was such a humiliating experience that Mickey resolved never to do anything that might lead to a second visit.

Maureen had been charm itself when she first arrived, greeting the principal, Mr. Collins, with a winning smile and completely hiding her resentment over the enforced meeting under an air of polite and caring interest. It hadn't lasted.

"I've asked Mrs Fitzgerald, the guidance counsellor to join us," Mr Collins announced, shaking hands with Maureen and ushering her into his office. Mickey was expected to wait in the outer office until he was called. "And I've also asked Mr Morrissey, Michael's class tutor, to come along."

The inclusion of Mr Morrissey surprised Mickey. Everyone knew that old man Morrissey was as weak as water and would simply agree with whatever the principal suggested. Expecting him to have any opinion on Mickey's conduct or how to deal with it was, to Mickey's mind, a complete waste of time.

"However," Mr Collins went on as Maureen settled herself into one of the two easy chairs in the room, revealing, as she did so, far more leg than Mickey later thought appropriate, "I'd like a bit of a chat with you first, Miss Connolly. If you don't mind. Just to see if we can put a few things into perspective before we try to find a solution. Helen," this to his secretary as he pushed the door closed, "could you get us some coffee, please. Is coffee alright, Miss Connolly, or would you prefer tea?"

"Coffee's fine," replied Maureen, smiling sweetly.

It was an act Mickey recognised very well. His sister would be as nice as pie as long as he wasn't around; letting everyone see what a wonderful thing she'd done in taking on her difficult young brother. On the other hand, as he knew from bitter experience, it was only an act. He dreaded to think what she'd be like once he was in the room with them. He doubted if anyone had ever waited in the outer office with greater trepidation than he felt during those ten minutes while his sister and Mr Collins discussed him behind the closed door of the principal's office. Then the door opened.

"Helen, could you ring through to the staff room and ask Mrs Fitzgerald and Mr Morrissey to join us, please," said Mr Collins. Then he turned to Mickey. "Michael," he said solemnly, "you'd better come in now."

He'd never been inside the principal's office before having, until his truancy was discovered, kept a very low profile as far as the teachers were concerned. Now, as Mrs Fitzgerald and Mr Morrissey came in and shut the door, all he could do was stand near the window, as instructed, and wait for the inevitable explosion.

It came, as he'd known it would, in a sudden torrent of abuse which, he was sure, took everyone else in the office completely by surprise. One moment Maureen Connolly had been the charming,, caring sister, the next she was a screaming harridan, her voice rising the angrier she got.

For fifteen minutes he had to endure the embarrassing attack. She called him every name under the sun to describe his laziness. She criticised his lack of effort in all things, described him several times as a 'complete waste of space' and left no doubt that her life was being ruined because of what she termed 'the millstone round her neck' that he'd become.

She didn't allow either the guidance counsellor or the principal a chance to say anything, interrupting as soon as either of them tried to ask a question or make a point. And finally, she looked at her watch and stood up.

"I can't hang around here any longer," she announced. "I have to get back to work. You deal with him as you think fit. Do what you like with him. And you, you worthless piece of shit," she glared at Mickey, "don't you ever do anything like this to me again."

With that final outburst she departed, leaving Mr Collins and his colleagues open-mouthed and speechless. Mickey couldn't remember ever feeling as embarrassed as he did at that moment. Nor as helpless.

"Well, Michael," said Mrs Fitzgerald eventually, taking up her appointments diary. "I think the best thing is for you to make an

87

appointment so that we can discuss your behaviour. How about Thursday morning, nine fifteen?"

Mickey nodded. The way he felt he'd have agreed to anything as long as it meant he'd never have to endure such a public humiliation again.

"And, of course, you'll have to do a detention," added Mr Collins. "Maybe you'll arrange that, Mr Morrissey. I think the next scheduled detention is on Tuesday afternoon. I think we can take it that your sister will have no objection to us keeping you behind for an hour as punishment."

Mickey said nothing. There was, after all, nothing he could say.

III

Things certainly didn't improve for Mickey after that. The jobs he was expected to do increased while there was no let-up in the spiteful words Maureen regularly hurled at him.

"I wish you'd never been born" was one of the more frequent jibes. "You should never have been born."

It was a sentiment with which he increasingly agreed wholeheartedly. More than once he considered taking the easy way out. He knew, or thought he knew, that it was quite easy. Just a handful of pills – and he was sure any household painkiller would do – and a bottle of vodka – and if he couldn't get that, Sammy certainly could. And then the endless sleep. No more spitefulness, no more bullying. Nothing.

Strangely enough it was the nothingness which scared him. He was, after all, only sixteen. In theory, he had his whole life ahead of him and, surely, once he was legally an adult he could break the chains of his current awful existence and make a life for himself. It was something to work towards and, he hoped, a much better solution than the bottle or the pills.

His response, therefore, was to withdraw into a world of his own creation where the shouts of his teachers and the verbal assaults from his sister could not reach him. He went through the motions of daily living both at school and at home – doing the minimum of work in the former and almost all the work in the latter. And, whenever he had a spare moment, freed from the many petty little chores which Maureen found for him to do or when she was out with any of her friends, he'd retire to his room where he found a whole new refuge. He began to write.

It wasn't necessarily good writing but it quickly became a way of releasing all the pent-up resentment inside him. He wrote short stories, sordid little tales full of anger and violence and in each case the central character, himself, triumphed over the forces of evil – usually in the form of his sister. Often he let his imagination carry him away as he wrote of dire punishments which he – or at least his character – would inflict on her. At least in fiction. Whether he would ever have the courage to stand up to her in real life remained to be seen.

He wasn't much of a scholar although, after the truancy episode, he made sure that he did enough work to avoid drawing too much attention to himself. The trouble was that very little at school really interested him. The only subject he actually liked was English and even that not all of the time. Some of the books and stories they were expected to read thrilled his imagination and there were one or two bits of poetry that caught his attention but it was essay writing that he liked best and, in that, even his teacher, Mr Morrissey, had to admit he excclled.

To Mickey's surprise Mr Morrissey even went so far as to offer him some extra coaching, helping him improve his spelling and grammar so that his essays could gain more strength.

The additional help proved very effective and there was no surprise when he passed the Junior Certificate English examination with flying colours. More importantly – and to his own amazement – he managed to pass all of the eleven subjects taken, although only English was at the Higher Level.

When he collected the results from the school he felt a sense of triumph such as he'd never experienced before and, as he made his way home, carrying the precious slip of paper on which his marks were recorded, he hoped that, just for once, it would prove to his sister that he wasn't such a fool or an idiot after all. Vain hope.

"I don't know what you're making such a fuss about," was her scathing response when he showed her his grades. "Everyone knows that the Junior Cert is dead easy and any fool can pass it. Even a dumbo like you. It means absolutely nothing. Just wait till next year. You'll see then how hopeless you are."

Even the A in English didn't impress her.

"Probably cheated," she muttered to her friends. They all laughed at him. "Silly fool," she added as Mickey retreated to the kitchen, his delight in his achievement killed, his resentment fuclled. And, while his classmates were out celebrating, he stayed at home to scrub the kitchen floor and wash the windows.

Not for the first time he thought about packing a bag and just running away. Sometimes he'd considered it seriously as an option but he'd seen a documentary on television about kids like him who ran away from home in the hope of finding something better. There had been pictures of these youngsters sleeping in doorways, under bridges, in bus shelters, wrapped in newspapers or cardboard boxes, scrounging or begging, not knowing how they were going to survive.

"So many of them," the presenter had told the viewers, "end up being easy prey to drug pushers, pimps or paedophiles. Kids like this are just looking for love or affection, for someone to care. They become easy targets."

No, that wasn't what Mickey wanted.

He couldn't even consider going to family for, as far as he knew, he had no family other than Maureen. His parents, his sister and he had lived in a complete vacuum where, so it seemed, relatives just didn't exist. There'd never been any talk of aunts or uncles, no family get-togethers at Christmas, no reunions with cousins at birthdays. For all he knew he might have lots of cousins – or he might have none. It made no difference. There was no-one he could go to.

As for friends, still the only friend he had was Sammy Ferguson and Sammy had already led him into bother once. Sammy, he firmly believed, was heading towards a life of crime and that was something Mickey didn't want. So he stuck it out, buried himself further in his writing, watched television when he was allowed, read a bit and waited, continuing to endure the hard work and abuse which Maureen poured on him. And all the time he had just one ambition: to reach a stage where he was no longer dependent on his sister. He looked forward with ever-increasing relish to the moment when he could tell her that she'd never see him again.

He often wondered why Maureen hadn't asked him to leave long ago if she hated him so much, although he thought he probably knew the answer. He'd once overheard a conversation in the corner shop, one which for him, provided the obvious reason.

"It's that sister of his you have to admire," Mrs Goggin had told one of her regular customers, unaware that Mickey was still in the shop, hidden by a stand full of birthday cards. "I think it's wonderful the way she's sacrificed so much of her time to take care of him. I don't think young Mickey would be a particularly difficult child but it can't be easy for a young woman like that. She should be having a life of her own, not tied down to a younger brother all the time."

The customer had been cautious in her agreement.

"Of course she'll get quite a bit of state help. Money, anyway. That would always come in useful."

"Oh I don't think she'd get a lot. And no matter, I still think she's a remarkable young woman. It's a pity there aren't more like her."

So that was it. The money she received as his guardian – although what she did with most of that he had no idea since he never seemed to get any benefit – perhaps more than made up for the bitter sense of sacrifice she felt. But, of course, there was also that wonderful public image she'd acquired. That probably mattered as much as anything else. If only they knew!

IV

The final straw for Mickey came not long before his eighteenth birthday. He'd found school-work increasingly difficult. Even English, which had once been his only real interest, no longer held him in quite the same way, despite Mr Morrissey's continued efforts. So, as his schooldays began to draw nearer their end, he began to focus more and more on his future, a future which probably wasn't going to include great examination results and a wonderful college course but a future which would definitely not include Maureen.

She had, in recent times, become even more difficult; so much so that Mickey started to wonder whether she feared his future independence as much as he longed for it. The fact that her own life had taken a couple of turns for the worse certainly didn't improve her temper and, as always, Mickey got the blame.

"It's all your fault," she'd screamed at him one night recently, starting her attack almost before she'd had time to close the door behind her following an evening out with her boyfriend.

She'd seen her eight months' involvement with Nicholas as the basis for a permanent relationship. As Mickey was soon to discover, Nicholas had simply viewed it as a passing fancy.

"You put him off," Maureen went on, her eyes full of hatred as she turned on the one person she always blamed for all her ills. "How could I ever bring anyone here when you're always slouching around, always in the way. And you never keep the place up together properly. No wonder Nicky didn't want to come here any more. How can I ever have a chance of happiness with you always in my way?"

With that she'd stormed tearfully off to her room leaving Mickey to reflect, not for the first time, that it was more likely Maureen herself who had damaged the relationship. For years he had wondered why any young man would want to spend time with her, although Sammy Ferguson's comment that it was probably because she was generous with her affections in every way didn't convince him. It didn't matter. Another romance had come to an abrupt end and, as far as Maureen was concerned, Mickey was to blame. So he got what he now cynically referred to as 'the treatment' – complete silence and a further twist in the number of tasks he was expected to do.

As if the collapse of her romance wasn't bad enough Maureen received a further blow less than twenty-four hours later and, once again, it was Mickey who got the blame.

She arrived home much earlier than usual and one look at her face was enough to warn Mickey that he was in for another attack.

"That's it," she yelled at him, taking off her dark blue coat and throwing it onto a chair. "You've really done it this time. You've been a cross I've had to bear for years. And now, after all I've done for you, what thanks do I get. None. Quite the contrary in fact. Because, thanks to you I've lost my job."

He couldn't understand how he'd caused her to lose her job but he also knew it was pointless trying to ask for an explanation. She had used him as the root of all her ills for so long it was now such a habit that he sometimes wondered if she ever realised how stupid some of her accusations were. Probably not, he decided. He accepted her accusation and, as so often in the past, resigned himself to yet another pointless task.

Over the next few weeks Mickey was, for the first time in his life, glad to be going to school. Not only that, he was beginning to take an interest once more. Much of this was thanks to Mr Morrissey, whose enthusiasm for Mickey's ability in English had never waned and who was now more than willing to give the young man the extra help he would need if he was to have any hope of leaving school with at least one exam pass. Added to which, at least school got him out of the house and away from Maureen's constant sulking and complaining.

She complained about not having any money, then she complained that the Social Welfare payments were far too little for her to manage. She complained that there was no-one to spend her days with since her friends all had jobs and couldn't keep her company. She complained that there were no jobs available and then that those on offer weren't suitable.

Fortunately she'd already got a part-time evening job – one which kept her out of the house a couple of evenings a week, frequently until the early hours of the morning. She always dressed especially carefully on these occasions but, unfortunately, was often even more dissatisfied the following day. Mickey began to wonder what kind of job it was that could have such an effect on her. He didn't dare ask.

He knew she'd started the job a couple of weeks before her former employer had sacked her and had even speculated that that might be the real reason why she was dismissed. Again, he never questioned her about it. Instead he used the freedom it provided to go to Mr Morrissey's house for those much-needed extra lessons. And since he never left the house until after she had gone and he was always back long before her return there was no need to tell her about these visits. It was, he knew, better that way.

It was after one of her evenings out that Mickey finally reached a decision which was to change his life forever. Maureen had been out late the previous evening and was in a particularly bad mood; so much so he began to suspect that she'd spent the evening drinking and was, as a consequence, suffering from a hangover.

"It's your fault we can never afford any luxuries," she told him. "The measly amount I get for taking care of you certainly doesn't cover what you're costing me. No wonder I can never get any nice things for myself. The sooner you get out and get a job the better, though," she added spitefully, "I doubt if anyone in their right mind would be daft enough to employ you."

It was this final comment which decided Mickey. In a couple of months he'd be eighteen and soon after that he'd be leaving school. And unless he took some drastic action he'd be forever stuck in a situation he hated so much. It was time he got his act together and began to sort out what kind of a life was available to him. There must be some way he could get help – at least until he got himself organised. He'd spoken a little about this to Mr Morrissey. Now he

93

made up his mind. The next chance he got he would visit the Social Welfare Office and try to find out exactly what they could do to help him in his bid for freedom.

His chance came two weeks later. There was a parent-teacher meeting scheduled at the school and, since this meant that teachers would not be available to teach their classes, the school day ended at twelve-thirty. For once he didn't mention this to Maureen who would undoubtedly have found plenty of useless tasks with which to fill his free time. Instead he waited until two o'clock by which time he was fairly confident the Social Welfare Office would have reopened after lunch.

He was right but, more importantly, the help and advice which he got proved to him that he could begin walking away from his current existence almost as soon as he wanted. His school career was almost at an end but there were several training courses available for young people like him. It was simply a matter of deciding which one he wanted to do. And, best of all, he would get paid while he was doing it.

Smiling, triumphant, he walked out of the office and into the large room which formed the main public area of the building – and straight into Maureen. She turned on him instantly, regardless of who was watching or listening.

"How dare you laugh at me!" she shouted, completely misunderstanding his cheerful expression. "How dare you come here and mock me. Isn't it enough that you made me lose my job in the first place? This is just typical of you. All my life you've been in the way, making a fool of me and ruining any chance I might have of getting on. I hate you for it. I hate you."

And with that, for the first time in his life, she raised her right hand and slapped him hard across the face. Apart from one or two gasps from people nearest to them there was total silence throughout the large room followed, seconds later, by a hum of conversation as the onlookers tried very hard to cover their embarrassment over what they'd just witnessed.

To his surprise Mickey had never in his life felt calmer nor more in control than he did at that moment. He didn't so much look at his sister as through her.

"I'm going home now," he said, quietly, coldly, cutting across any further comment she was about to make. "I'm taking my things and

I'm leaving. And I'll never see you or do another thing for you. In fact, I'll see you dead first."

The sense of freedom he felt as he walked away from her was all he needed.

TWO DOWN, FOUR ACROSS

I

It took just over fifteen minutes for Chief Superintendent Pollock and Inspector Murphy to reach the disused building site where the latest body had been discovered. There were similar sites in several parts of the country, mute witnesses to the fairytale property boom which had suddenly turned sour. This particular site was surrounded by a high fence which had obviously been put there by the site owners in the hope of deterring any unwanted visitors. Clearly, as the broken panel proved, it had been in vain.

Two uniformed gardai stood beside this illegal entrance accompanied by two very pale and very shaken-looking young boys. They were, Pollock guessed, in their early teens and their rather scruffy school uniforms explained much. Apparently school was not high on their list of priorities and they were, to use the common teenage slang, 'on the duck'.

"Probably came here for a quiet fag – or worse," Sean Pollock muttered to his Inspector.

Chris Murphy gave a grim laugh. "Maybe this will teach them a lesson," he said. "In future school might seem preferable."

Pollock shrugged. "Somehow I doubt that," he murmured.

They paused long enough to confirm that the two gardai had made a note of all the relevant details from the boys.

"Yes, Sir," replied the younger of the two officers. "Once they'd stopped throwing up, that is," he couldn't resist adding with a slight smile.

Sean Pollock turned to the boys, took in their rather sheepish expressions and realised that the pair were going to be in trouble no matter what happened next. He decided to give them the choice.

"Well now," he said, "you two seem to have got more than you bargained for this morning. That's the trouble with skipping school: you never know what trouble it might lead you into."

"Yeah," remarked the older of the two, a lot of his bravado now apparently restored. "But then that corpse might not have been found for months. So, really, we've helped you in a way."

He was silenced by a sharp nudge from his friend and, more effectively, by a stern glare from Pollock.

"I might remind you," the Chief Superintendent warned them, "that breaking and entering – which is clearly what you've done, not to mention trespassing, - are all crimes. Now, since you're probably going to be in a bit of bother both at home and at school I might be prepared to overlook that this once. But not," he added, "if I have any more of your cheek. Do you get my meaning?"

Both boys nodded, their eyes now firmly fixed on the ground.

"So," Pollock continued after a short pause, "where's it to be – home or school?"

The pair, suitably cowed for the moment at least, exchanged glances and then, as if a silent message had passed between them, announced in unison: "School."

"It would seem that the terrors of the school principal are somewhat less daunting than those of parents," remarked Chris Murphy, as one of the uniformed men led the pair towards the waiting squad car."

"Oh no," said Pollock. "I would have thought that, as the father of two lads, you'd realise the amount of prestige this will give them among their classmates. It'll certainly be worth having to put up with a lecture from the principal on the evils of skipping school."

Murphy laughed. "And, of course, it delays the hour when they have to face their parents. Without a gang of excited admirers," he added.

"Anyway," Sean Pollock clambered through the gap in the fence, "let's see what they found."

****

The crumpled, lifeless body of a young woman lay just beyond the boundary wall of what should have been a small, luxury bungalow. She looked, Pollock thought, in her early twenties, certainly no more than twenty-five or twenty-six. He sighed. Sudden, unnecessary death was always hard to accept but, somehow, it seemed far worse when the victim was a young person..

"I take it Dr Mason has been contacted?" he asked the remaining guard.

"Yes, Sir. She's on her way."

'Not that we really need the pathologist to tell us how she died,' Pollock muttered to himself.

The dark green tie pulled tightly round the girl's slender neck could do that.

"Same as before?"

It wasn't really a question. Like his colleague Inspector Murphy could see the similarities between this body and that of Bridget Corcoran.

"Looks that way," agreed Pollock. He knelt down beside the body, careful not to disturb anything. "Her clothes don't seem to have been disturbed too much so I think we can probably rule out any sexual attack."

"She looks as if she was dressed for a night out, though," Murphy pointed out.

It was true. The smart, dark blue coat the girl had been wearing had fallen open to reveal a short, stylish black dress of the sort worn at cocktail parties. The sheer black tights and solitary, high-heeled, black shoe reinforced the impression that she had, indeed, been involved in some special occasion. For the time being, however, they had no clue as to whether she'd met her death before or after that event – whatever it might have been.

The forensic team arrived and quietly and efficiently began their work, searching the site inch by inch in the hope of finding some clues both to the identity of the girl and that of her killer. The missing shoe was soon found as, too, was a possible explanation of how the young woman had come to be in the disused building site.

"Over here, Sir," one of the team called to Pollock.

He held the second shoe in his hand, pointing to scuff marks on the back of it and then to a series of tracks on the sandy ground.

"It looks as if she was dragged backwards from that opening in the fence. It's quite likely her assailant was behind her, the murder weapon already tightening round her neck. She was probably already fighting for her life as he pulled her backwards. If you look here you can see how the sand and gravel has been scuffed about suggesting that she was struggling to free herself even as she was being dragged further in. Whereas here," he moved nearer to where the body lay, "these two lines would suggest that she'd given up the struggle. These marks fit in with the notion of two motionless objects being dragged in a straight line – and that's how her feet would be once she was dead. You'll probably find that the heel of her" – he glanced at the shoe he was still holding – "left foot is scraped and torn."

Sean Pollok looked down at the dead girl once more.

"Poor kid," he muttered, then he looked up as Dr Mason approached. "Ah, Elizabeth," he said. "Thanks for getting here so quickly."

The doctor, already wearing the familiar white protective suit, nodded briefly to the detective before kneeling down beside the body, ready to begin her preliminary assessment.

A sudden thought occurred to Chief Superintendent Pollock.

"Can you do me a favour?" he asked the doctor. "I know this might seem strange but before you do anything else can you check her hands first? See if she's holding anything."

Elizabeth Mason regarded him curiously for a moment then did as he asked. Gently she uncurled the fingers of the young woman's left hand, the one nearest her. It was empty. Moving carefully to the other side of the body she repeated the process with the right hand.

"Is this what you were looking for?" she asked, holding up a small, folded piece of paper.

Sean Pollock sighed deeply.

"Yes," he said. "Listen, I don't want to touch it" – he indicated his bare hands – "as we'll need to get the experts to check it for evidence but can you open it up and tell me what it says."

Slowly Dr Mason unfolded the paper. Although they left her puzzled the contents didn't really surprise Sean Pollock.

"*2 down*," read Dr Mason, "*a relative in the hospital. 4 across: more than enough, as well.*"

II

Sean Pollock stared at the piece of paper in Dr Mason's hand. There was no way of avoiding the fact. This crime was so similar to the murder of Bridget Corcoran it had to have been the work of the same person. And that person quite obviously intended playing games with the gardai through these annoying crossword clues. They were, in effect, the killer's chosen trade-mark but why, or what they might all mean, was still unclear. Not only that but, as

Pollock had feared, the evidence already suggested that this was another carefully selected victim.

The young woman's clothes appeared undisturbed and, although they would obviously have to wait for the pathologist's report, this made it unlikely that this was a frustrated sexual attack. Nor did it seem to be a mugging gone wrong. Although there was no sign of a handbag the latest victim's jewellery, such as it was, had not been touched.

"But then," Chris Murphy pointed out, "from the look of it it's only cheap bling."

"That's not the point," Pollock replied. "A mugger would probably have taken the lot and checked it out later. Anyway, it's quite possible she didn't have a handbag with her."

There was some evidence to support this. In one pocket of her coat there was what looked like a house key and a few odd coins while in the other was what turned out to be the first clue towards discovering her identity. It was a simple white business card with clear black lettering: '*Harmony Escorts*'. It gave the name of the manager – Martina McDonagh – an address in the centre of the city, a telephone number and even an e-mail address. So, while Inspector Murphy returned to the incident room to begin organising the team Chief Superintendent Pollock decided to make his way to the address on the card.

"If nothing else," he told Murphy, "someone there might be able to tell us who she is."

****

'*Harmony Escorts*', he discovered, operated from a small office comprising two rooms on the fourth floor of one of the city's older but renovated buildings. The outer room appeared to be a waiting area for it contained just three easy chairs, a small coffee table on which were scattered a few trendy magazines – or, at least, what Pollock considered trendy magazines – and, on the walls, several photographs of remarkably attractive young women. The room was empty.

Carefully Pollock took his smart phone from his coat pocket and scrolled through to the photograph of the dead woman which he'd taken before leaving the crime scene. Slowly he compared it to the faces on the wall but, though there were some vague similarities, he didn't find an exact match. Satisfied, he turned to the only other door in the room, knocked and was promptly greeted with a brisk "Come in".

This second room, clearly the centre of business, was equipped with a large, dark-wood desk on which sat a computer, telephone and the usual accoutrements of a modern office while against one wall was an elegant unit on which were a few books and several very unusual ornaments. Behind the desk sat a rather severe-looking woman of, Pollock guessed, late thirties or early forties.

"Can I help you?" she asked, an artificial smile replacing her initial stern expression.

Introducing himself Pollock produced his warrant card and the photograph of the victim.

Not wishing to alarm the woman he simply said, "I need to know if you can identify this young woman."

Martina McDonagh, for that was who Pollock assumed her to be, studied the photograph for a moment or two with a puzzled expression.

"Well," she said at last, "I'm almost sure it's Maureen Connolly but it's certainly not a good photo. In fact ...." she stopped abruptly then, as her suspicions grew as to the possible explanation for both his presence and the poor quality of the picture, demanded: "Is there anything wrong, Chief Superintendent?"

Pollock could see no reason for hiding the truth.

"I'm afraid," he said, "that her body was found this morning. There was a business card giving this address in her pocket."

The stern expression dissolved as tears appeared in the woman's eyes. These, Pollock noted, were far more genuine than the earlier smile.

"The poor girl," she cried. "Was it an accident? How did it happen?"

"She was murdered," Pollock replied.

There was, he'd decided, no point in beating about the bush. It was important now to get as much information as he could as quickly as possible, before Ms McDonagh was overcome by the enormity of the situation.

"We need to know anything you can tell us about her. I assume from the card in her pocket and from the fact that you recognised her that she was connected to this business. In that case can you give me any information you have, not only about her but also about the person she might have been meeting last night. From the way she was dressed we imagine she had probably been on a date of some sort. It's possible that there is a connection between that person and her death."

"Well, yes. Of course." The woman sounded a little confused. The notion that one of her clients might be involved in murder had proved more unsettling that the detective had intended. "Let me think."

She turned towards the computer and, after a few moments' hesitation, typed in a couple of words. Within seconds Pollock had both a name and an address for the victim and, more importantly, details of the person she was supposed to have met the previous evening.

'It's just possible,' Sean Pollock mused as, having thanked Ms McDonagh for her assistance, he made his way back to brief his team. 'that we've not only got details of the last person to see her alive. He might also be the killer.'

III

 "Maureen Connolly, aged twenty-six with an address at 17 Murdoch Street in the south of the city."

While Chief Superintendent Pollock gave the details to the team Inspector Murphy stuck a photograph of the victim to the whiteboard, next to that of Bridget Corcoran.

"Strangled," Pollock continued. "It looks as if both women met their deaths the same way. Obviously we have to wait to see what Dr. Mason's post-mortem report has to tell us but, as Inspector Murphy has already told you, there was no sign of sex or robbery as a motive. We have evidence to suggest that whoever killed Miss Connolly was acting in the same way as the person who killed Mrs Corcoran and that must lead us to the conclusion that we're dealing with one and the same person.

"We need," he went on, "to get full details about Miss Connolly – family, friends, work, and so on. Ms McDonagh was only able to give me the basics. We also need to follow up on this person – John

Martin. He's the man who made an appointment to meet her last night.

"Geoff," he began giving orders, "get along to Murdoch Street. I'm afraid you'll have to be the one to tell them about the girl's death. Mags can go with you. We'll need someone to come in and formally identify the body as soon as possible. And, if they're up to it, see what her family can tell you about her friends. Especially boyfriends," he added, as a sudden thought occurred to him. "It's always possible we could be dealing with a jealous boyfriend who couldn't stand the idea of her escorting other men, although I can't see how that would fit in with Mrs Corcoran's death."

"Phil," Pollock continued, "I want you to go with Inspector Murphy to find this John Martin person." He gave them the address that Martina McDonagh had given him – 14 Elm View, on the north side of the city. "It's quite possible we might have to bring him in for formal questioning at some point but let's start with an informal chat first. See how that goes. You'll possibly get a better idea as to whether or not he's the man we're after that way."

"Noel, you can try a background search on the computer. Let's see if our man's got form. But first I've got another job for you."

As they all departed on their various tasks Pollock turned back to the whiteboard for a moment.

'These,' he thought, 'are always the worst cases.'

Murder was never easy to deal with but at least most of the ones in recent times were either gangland killings, of which there seemed to have been a growing number, or some breakdown in family relations which had led to a violent solution. It was the apparently motiveless murders like these that were always the hardest to solve. These two killings were clearly connected, of that there could be little doubt, and – he picked up the small plastic envelope containing the piece of paper which had been found in Maureen Connolly's hand – solving these two clues seemed at least one way of figuring out how.

"This," he said, turning back to Noel Lawson, "is a link between these two cases so come on, get that cryptic mind of yours working on this."

****

3 DOWN:.11 ACROSS: 4 DOWN:

14 ACROSS, 7 DOWN, 17 DOWN

I

As the two men studied these latest clues there was a knock on the door and a young guard entered.

"Chief Superintendent Pollock," he said, "this was left at the front desk for you."

He handed over a plain white envelope and then left the room, carefully shutting the door behind him.

Sean Pollock looked at the envelope. There was no address, no stamp, just the four typed words –*Chief Superintendent Sean Pollock.* He paused for moment or two, remembering past stories he'd heard or read about, stories of unexplained envelopes and packages being delivered mysteriously to people in authority. On more than one occasion, as he now recalled, such unsolicited mail had been found to contain anthrax or, even worse, an explosive device. They were, in fact, deliberate and callous attempts to kill the recipient.

He held the envelope up to the light then carefully he shook it. Neither action told him anything further about the envelope's contents; in fact, it was so thin he wondered if it contained anything at all.

He glanced at Noel Lawson, already deeply engrossed in the two new clues. If the envelope did contain anything dangerous was he about to harm the young man as well as himself? Then common sense took over. He really wasn't that important. He couldn't remember any criminal he'd sent to jail ever uttering wild threats against him. There was no reason why he should suspect the contents of this envelope.

Curiosity got the better of him. Taking a deep breath he opened the envelope. The single sheet of paper it contained only deepened the mystery.

"Noel," he said, tapping the young man on the shoulder, "I think you're going to be here for a while. Take a look at this."

Lawson's eyes widened as he read the contents.

3 Down: Origin of a parent, says Wordsworth.

104

11 Across: How angry changes when put into action.

4 Down: Old-fashioned you stretches into a notion.

14 Across, 7 Down, 17 Down: Very similar to one of ten in tablet form.

"Well, Sir," he said eventually, "he's certainly chosen a novel way of sending us a message."

"The devious bastard," was Pollock's response. "As if we haven't enough to do in this case without having to play silly games. Anyway, see what you can make of it while I head down to the front desk. See if anyone there saw whoever left this for us. It'd certainly make things a lot easier if we could get a description but," he shrugged, "I'm not holding my breath."

****

When Sean Pollock reached the front desk there were several people milling around and a rather harassed-looking young guard trying to deal with them. He recognised the young man straightaway: it was Peter Hynes, only recently part of the force but, or so Pollock had heard, with neither the confidence nor the initiative to progress very far in his chosen career. He would obey orders without question and do his duty as diligently as he could, Pollock knew that, but he lacked that extra bit of grit and tenacity. Certainly it didn't seem likely that Hynes would ever make a detective.

He wasn't without certain skills, Pollock realised as he watched how the young man dealt skilfully and politely with the group of people, satisfying them with the information or forms which they needed. Only then did he turn his attention to the senior officer.

"Chief Superintendent, Sir," he said. "Can I help you?"

"Have you been on the desk all morning?" Pollock asked.

"Yes, Sir. Ever since I came on duty at nine o'clock. And, for some reason, it's been very busy this morning. But did you get that letter, Sir?"

"That's what I've come about. You don't by any chance happen to remember how it got here."

Hynes shook his head.

"I'm afraid not, Sir. As I say, it's been a bit hectic this morning. Silly little things – form signing mostly – passports, lost driving licences, that sort of thing."

Pollock knew only too well what Hynes meant. He'd done that particular job many times during his years in uniform. It was the other public side of the gardai, often forgotten but usually just as important as solving crimes

"I'm sorry," Hynes went on, "but I was concentrating too much on them so I didn't actually notice anyone deliver it. It must have just been left there at some stage."

It had been a forlorn hope, Pollock knew, and he wasn't surprised that it proved unsuccessful. Whoever they were dealing with in this particular case had, as was already perfectly clear, quite a devious mind and certainly a cunning brain like that would not be foolish enough as to be caught out so easily.

"Not to worry, lad," he now reassured Peter Hynes. "It was worth a try."

And with that he made his way back to the incident room.

There he found that Noel Lawson had made some progress; not as much as Sean Pollock would have liked though he was fascinated by the complicated thought process involved. He'd never been one for crossword puzzles – or puzzles of any kind, for that matter – as detective work was usually puzzling enough in itself and, as far as he was concerned, attempting any other kind as a leisure pursuit was a bit like taking work home. However, the younger man was clearly fascinated by the whole process.

"What's this?" Pollock asked, leaning over Lawson's shoulder to look at the sheet of plain paper the young man was working at. On it he had drawn a blank crossword grid and he was trying, cautiously, to fill in the solutions they had so far managed to solve.

"Most basic crosswords," he told Pollock "have a bit of a pattern and a lot are based on a grid of thirteen squares across and thirteen down. If we then take the clue numbers we've so far been given and then leave a couple of blanks to mark the end of a word we've got something like this."

And, sure enough, he'd written in the two words from the clues found in Bridget Corcoran's hand.

"Now, Sir," he continued, "I think I've sussed out possible answers to the next two, though it would help if he'd told us how many letters are in each word. Of course, I daresay the killer thinks that would make it too easy."

"So what have you got so far?" demanded Pollock. To be honest he didn't always want long explanations, preferring instead just a straight answer.

"Well, I think the latest – the ones in Maureen Connolly's hand – are probably these." He pointed to the first word running down the grid. "A *sister*," he went on to explain, "is a relative but a sister also works in a hospital. That seems to make the most sense. I was a bit stuck on the second clue but the hint is in the comma. The answer must surely be one word but with both these meanings. And the only one I can come up with that fits the bill is the word '*too*'".

"So," Pollock murmured thoughtfully, "we now have a message which reads '*Mother first, sister too*'. That's always assuming you are correct. And that he wants us to read it as a message." He shook his head. "That makes no sense, at least not to me. As far as we know there's absolutely no relationship between the two victims. Certainly not mother and daughter."

"I've been thinking about that, Sir," began Lawson, tentatively. "Is it possible that Maureen Connolly was Bridget Corcoran's natural daughter but was given away at birth? We know she had two children by two different fathers so perhaps there was a third. That would certainly give us a link."

Sean Pollock looked doubtful but, following the younger man's theory, he asked: "And who would be the killer in that case? The obvious answer is Richard Corcoran who, if your idea is correct, is both son and brother to the victims, but we know it can't be him. He wasn't even in the country when these murders took place and has a rock-solid alibi to prove it.

"And," he continued, further destroying Lawson's theory, "if, by any chance, Maureen Connolly does have a brother I don't see why he should want to kill Bridget Corcoran. This is getting bloody stupid."

He swore, his frustration showing more and more. Then he looked back at Lawson's crossword grid.

"Have you made any progress with the latest messages?" he demanded. "Maybe they'll give us an idea. Though," he concluded, bitterly, "I very much doubt it. I think our killer's having far too much fun tying us up in knots. He doesn't plan to make things easy."

Noel Lawson shook his head.

"I'm afraid there's not very much I can tell you yet. I think I might be onto something with this group" – he indicated the last line of the message – "but I'm somewhat confused. When you get a clue referring to several spaces on a grid it usually suggests that the answers belong together to form a particular phrase."

"And?"

"Well, whenever I've come across a clue which refers to ten in tablet form before it's always referred to the Ten Commandments which, of course, were given to Moses ...."

"All right." Pollock was in no mood for a scripture lesson. "I get the point. Just give me what you've got."

"Sorry, Sir. Anyway, as you know several of the commandments begin with the words 'Thou shalt' which would probably fit in with the first two spaces. The trouble is, if that is the case, I cannot figure out which of the commandments he's referring to. I thought it might be '*Thou shalt not kill*' but that really doesn't make sense, does it, Sir. Added to which the clue suggests only three words but the commandments all have at least four."

"Oh, to hell with it!" Pollock straightened up, rubbing his back where it had stiffened from bending too long over the desk. "For all we know these clues have absolutely nothing to do with any of it. It's just as likely they are all just red herrings deliberately intended to mislead us."

He sighed and headed off towards his office. At the door he paused and turned back.

"Any word from the others yet?" he asked.

"Not yet, Sir," replied Lawson.

"Well with any luck they shouldn't be much longer. Maybe they'll have something useful to report."

With those words Chief Superintendent Pollock disappeared into his office and closed the door, unaware that his hopes were doomed to further disappointment.

When Chris Murphy and Paul Coady arrived at number fourteen Elm View it was no surprise to discover that John Martin was not at home. It was, after all, only early afternoon and therefore quite likely that he would still be at work. His wife, at least they assumed the weary looking woman who opened the door – child on her hip, two more clinging to her skirt – to be his wife, was.

"No wonder he fancied a bit on the side," muttered Coady under his breath receiving, in response, a stern glare from the inspector.

"Mrs Martin?"

The woman nodded.

Chris Murphy introduced himself. "I'm Inspector Chris Murphy and this is my colleague, Detective Coady. We're looking for your husband. He isn't home by any chance?"

The woman's weary look turned to one of alarm.

"No. No, he isn't. What's wrong? Nothing's happened has it?"

"No, no," Murphy hastened to reassure her. "We just think he might be able to help us in one of our investigations. Could you tell us where we might find him?"

She hesitated, not totally comfortable with the fact of two gardai arriving on her doorstep looking for her husband.

"He should be at work," she eventually replied. "He works in the city. Blair Imports on the Mall. He doesn't usually get home till six but you could catch him here then. Or," she seemed to sense some of the urgency of the situation, "he should be in his office now. I don't think he was going out anywhere today although he does have to travel about quite a lot."

She was talking too much, too fast, clearly distressed by a situation which she didn't yet understand but which, she apparently feared, could have a huge – and possibly terrible – impact on her family.

"Are you sure I can't help?" she said at last, shifting the youngest child to a more comfortable position on her hip and drawing the other two even closer to her.

It was obvious that she was anxious to be told what trouble, if any, her husband might be in but at that moment a piercing wail from inside the house distracted her.

"Sorry, it's the baby," she apologised. "He's teething."

She turned, torn between good manners, a desire to know what had happened to her husband and the needs of her infant.

"Don't worry, Mrs Martin," said Chris Murphy, soothingly. "I understand. I have a family of my own and I know what it can be like at times like this. You go and see to the little one. I'm sure we don't need to trouble you any longer. We'll go and see if we can find your husband at work. We can always come back later if we need to."

Was it relief or fear that crossed her face? They didn't know,, but as the door closed behind them Murphy couldn't help saying: "I hope for her sake that he isn't involved in all this. She's got enough on her plate as it is."

Phil Coady shrugged. He was still single and had often made it clear to anyone who would listen that he had no intention of getting caught in what he saw as the trap of marriage and children. Not for a good while yet, anyway. He was having far too much fun for that.

****

They made their way back into the city centre, easily locating the offices of Blair Imports where they were shown into a large room which, they assumed, was usually reserved for meetings.

"Mr Martin should be with you in a moment," said the smart young woman who had greeted them on their arrival, "although I know he's very busy at present.. If you don't mind waiting in here I'll try and contact him for you. Can I get you a cup of coffee or something while you're waiting?"

She was definitely full of curiosity over these unexpected and very official-looking visitors who, although they had not identified themselves, had made it clear that they needed to speak with Mr Martin at once on a matter of the greatest importance and urgency.

"No thank you." Inspector Murphy refused for both of them.

Phil Coady would have accepted – if only to gain a further opportunity of admiring this very pretty and rather desirable young female. He'd already made eye contact with her and was confident that further progress could be made. He was between steady girlfriends at present and, despite that fact that he'd already arranged a date for this evening, was always on the look-out for a new companion. Pity. This young receptionist might have filled the gap very well.

"We'll just wait here," Murphy added, looking around the room.

Realising that she wasn't going to get any more information from the two men the girl withdrew – much to Coady's disappointment – and closed the door behind her.

Inspector Murphy had hoped that a visit to John Martin's place of employment might give them some idea of the kind of man they'd come to meet but this particular room gave them very little to go on. Everything was neat and tidy. A large, oval-shaped mahogany-looking table (for some reason Murphy doubted that it really was solid mahogany) dominated the room and placed around it, at regular intervals, were ten chairs of a similar make, their seats covered in dark green leatherette. The rest of the room was, for the most part, bare although a small bookshelf stood in one corner, the few books which it held all dealing with marketing, and on the wall opposite the room's single window there was a collection of certificates, each one celebrating the various achievements of Blair Imports' more important employees.

Fortunately they did not have long to wait. Within a matter of minutes the door opened and in walked a short, plump man. His appearance came as something of a surprise to Chris Murphy; for some reason, though he couldn't explain why, he'd expected more of the modern yuppy-type character so common in television dramas. Instead here was a very ordinary-looking middle-aged man with thinning reddish hair, a slightly podgy face and quite nondescript features. At this precise moment he looked very flustered to say the least.

"Gentlemen," he said, "our receptionist tells me that this is urgent but unless that really is the case I'm afraid I'm going to have to ask you to make an appointment. I really am very busy. We're up to our eyes here. We were expecting an important delivery this afternoon and I've just learned it's stranded in Rotterdam. Some kind of customs technicality. It's not now likely to get here till the middle of next week. You've no idea of the knock-on effect that's going to have.

"So," he didn't bother to sit down, choosing instead to remain standing close to the door, his body language clearly expressing his great desire to be rid of these uninvited visitors as quickly as possible, "who are you and what exactly do you want?"

Both officers produced their warrant cards, identifying themselves as they did so. John Martin's expression changed instantly from one of anxiety about his work to concern over his personal life.

"What's wrong? Nothing's happened has it?" he asked, unconsciously echoing his wife's words.

"There's no need to get alarmed, sir," Chris Murphy assured him. "We've just been to your house and spoken to your wife. She told us we'd find you here. However we do have a very serious matter which we must discuss with you. I appreciate that you are a very busy man but I'm afraid this is too important to wait."

Clearly worried now, John Martin moved to the nearest chair and sat down, indicating that the other two should do the same. Inspector Murphy sat near him: Phil Coady remained standing beside the door.

"I understand," the Inspector began, "that last night you were in the company of a young woman, one Maureen Connolly, an employee of Harmony Escorts."

It was hard to tell whether John Martin's expression was one of fear or relief but his reply soon provided the answer.

"Well, yes," he said, giving a small laugh, "though, to be quite honest, I didn't realise that enjoying the company of a pretty girl was against the law – especially since my wife was well aware of it and approved wholeheartedly."

This wasn't quite the reply they'd expected and it was Phil Coady who promptly demanded a further explanation.

"You say you've been to my house," Martin began. They nodded. "You'll have seen then that my wife has her hands full. Four youngsters all under five is enough to keep anyone busy and it certainly wears her out. She has neither the time nor, to be honest, the inclination and certainly not the energy to accompany me to the various business functions which I have to attend as part of my work.

"At the same time," he continued, "since many of these meetings are of a social nature and for me they are pretty much compulsory, I've got into the habit of contacting Ms McDonagh at *Harmony Escorts* for a suitable companion. Last night was, in fact, the third time that Miss Connolly has accompanied me. However," he concluded, "I still fail to see how this can be of any interest to the police."

Inspector Murphy ignored that remark pursuing, instead, his own line of questioning.

"Would you mind telling us where you went with Miss Connolly and how long you were with her?"

There was now definite concern on Mr Martin's face. He'd realised that something serious had happened and was now clearly anxious to discover just exactly what it was.

"It was a dinner," he said "with some of our overseas contacts at the Carlsworth Hotel. I met Miss Connolly in the foyer there at seven, we joined the others in the bar, had dinner in the restaurant and she left me just after ten o'clock."

A sudden thought seemed to strike him.

"But surely you already know that," he exclaimed.

"What do you mean?" Coady demanded.

"Well didn't one of your fellows ring her?"

Chris Murphy and Phil Coady exchanged glances.

"We were all in the hotel bar having a final drink," Martin went on, "when her mobile phone rang. She moved away to answer it and then announced that the caller was from the gardai, that something serious had happened at home and they needed to see her straightaway. I must admit she didn't look best pleased about it."

"Did she say anything else?" Murphy persisted. "The name of the caller, perhaps? Or where she had to meet him?"

"Nothing. Just the usual apologies and thank yous and goodbyes to the people we'd been with. Then she excused herself and left."

He paused for a moment trying, it appeared, to remember every part of that final conversation.

"There was one other thing, I think," he said eventually.

"Go on."

"Well, I can't be absolutely sure but as I was helping her on with her coat she muttered something to herself. It sounded like '*bloody brother*' or '*blood brother*'. I really don't know."

"And what did you do after she left?" Coady asked.

"Nothing. Well, naturally I finished my drink but the evening was pretty much over by then anyway and the group was breaking up so I got a taxi and went home. I was home before eleven o'clock which, to be quite honest, suited me down to the ground. Some of these evenings can go on into the small hours which is not so good if you have to be at work first thing the next morning."

"And all this can be vouched for," insisted Chris Murphy.

John Martin looked even more alarmed.

"Well yes," he replied, "if it has to be. But I do wish you'd tell me why ...."

Inspector Murphy cut across him, deciding that there was nothing further to be gained in hiding the truth. In any case, it was information which, thanks to the usual ghoulish media attention, would soon be public knowledge.

"I'm afraid sir," he said, "a woman's body was found on an abandoned housing estate project over on the east side. She'd been murdered. We've reason to believe it's Maureen Connolly."

John Martin gasped, an expression of sheer horror on his face.

"And apart from the murderer," Murphy went on, "it would seem that you and your colleagues were among the very last people to see her alive."

Martin's naturally pale complexion turned even paler.

"You don't think .... You can't think .... I couldn't .... I didn't ...."
As the terrible thoughts rushed through his mind he stumbled towards some fact, some reassurance to cling on to.

Chris Murphy spared him further anguish.

"It would appear, sir, from what you've told us – and I see no reason to doubt that we can very easily verify those facts – that you had nothing to do with her death. We would like it, however, if you could give us any more information about Miss Connolly that might help us in our investigation."

Mr Martin frowned.

"To be honest," he said, recovering himself slightly after the Inspector's reassuring words, "I don't know very much else. We were scarcely, if ever, alone in a situation that required conversation between ourselves. On each of the three occasions I was with her we met wherever the function was being held – *Harmony Escorts* insist on that as a precaution for their girls – and we were always in company. From what little I did gather I understand she had no family apart from a younger brother and I got the impression he was something of a trial for her. As for her parents I've no idea what happened to them. I assumed they were dead but I don't know. I'm sorry, Inspector, I don't even know where she lived, or if she had another job, or anything like that."

There was panic in his voice now, as if he finally understood the reality of his situation. He, a married man, had been out in the company of a pretty, younger woman and now she was dead. Murdered. Just, it seemed, a few hours after she'd left him. No wonder the gardai had wanted to see him so urgently. He was, without doubt, at the very top of their list of suspects.

"Listen, Inspector," he exclaimed, "I'm very sorry but I really don 't know anything more. She seemed like a nice girl just trying to earn a little extra money and I'm quite sure she didn't deserve whatever fate she met. But there really is nothing more I can tell you."

The two officers agreed and, thanking him for his co-operation and urging him to contact them without delay if he thought of anything else which might be useful, they took their leave.

****

"Do we check out his story straightaway?" asked Coady, once they were back on the street.

"Might as well," Murphy replied, "though I'm pretty certain he's on the level." He paused, considering their next move. "Tell you what. I can walk to the Carlsworth from here. I'll go and check out his story there while you take the car and get back to his wife. Get her to confirm what time he got home."

Phil Coady began to protest, convinced, as he was, that Chris Murphy, the family man, was far better suited to deal with the unhappy Mrs Martin.

"Of course," he said, "he could always ...."

"Oh I know," interrupted Murphy. He was only too well aware of the way Phil Coady's mind worked and although the younger man was certainly a good officer he certainly wasn't going to give him any excuse to spend the rest of the day in one of the city's plushest hotels searching for non-existent evidence. "He could be on the phone even as we speak asking her to confirm his story. But I don't

115

think so. I think he's told us everything he knows and I don't think he's involved.

"What worries me far more," he went on, more to himself than to his colleague, "is this story of the phone call. Who could possibly have fooled her enough not only to convince her that it was official police business but also to get her to meet them at that hour of the night in such an out-of-the-way place? If that brother of hers is as no-good as John Martin seemed to think then the sooner we track him down the better. He could play an important part in all of this."

III

There was no reply at number seventeen Murdoch Street when Geoff Hughes and Margaret Power arrived. Nor was there any sign of life.

"O.K.," said Hughes. "I suppose we start with the neighbours. See what they can tell us."

He looked at Mags, a twinkle in his eye.

"What do we do? Left or right?"

"Right," she said, smiling and already moving towards the right-hand property.

Still their luck was out and Hughes' firm knock was met with total silence.

"It's not your day, is it," grinned Mags.

"Oh I don't know," he replied. "I could be stuck in the incident room with Pollock. Instead of which I'm out here with a pretty girl." He laughed. "Just think. It could have been Chris Murphy."

"With me or with you?" she teased.

"Don't go there," he warned, although he was smiling as he turned to knock on the next door.

He recognised Sammy Ferguson immediately, having come across this particular young man on more than one occasion in the course of various investigations. The recognition was mutual as Sammy's look of shock turned swiftly to a cheeky grin.

"Well, well. Officer Hughes," he said. "What can I do for you?"

He was addressing Geoff but his interest was immediately taken by Mags Power whom he eyed with unashamed admiration.

116

"Now there's a good question, Sammy."

"Come on now, Mr Hughes," said Sammy looking sheepish. "I ain't done nothin' wrong."

Instead of answering Hughes turned to his colleague.

"Detective Power," he declared, "may I introduce Sammy Ferguson, slippery as an eel but quite certainly part of this city's criminal community. I'd forgotten he lived in this neck of the woods."

"Now then, Officer," Power spoke out indignantly, "you can't say that."

"Oh, I may not have proved anything yet but I'm quite convinced you've had more than your share of knowledge of several of the crimes I've asked you about over the years. Anyway," he continued, "that's not what we're here for."

Sammy Ferguson looked relieved. Hughes was right. The two had met on three separate occasions in what were, for him at least, rather awkward circumstances, although each time he'd managed to convince the gardai of his innocence. He'd been lucky. Hughes' words were a bit too close for comfort: he had been involved but each time he'd wriggled his way out of any formal charge. "No proof, no crime," was what he'd cheerfully told Geoff Hughes the last time and his mother had obligingly backed him up. As a result, as on previous occasions, he'd escaped with a warning.

"Next time we catch you," Geoff Hughes had told him, "you won't talk your way out of trouble so easily. You can bet your life on that."

With this in mind – and in light of his activities earlier in the week – it wasn't really surprising that the appearance of two members of the gardai on his doorstep had been, to put it mildly, unnerving. The sooner he got rid of them the happier he'd feel. Apparently, they didn't yet know about the nice little raid on a tobacconist''s which he and his mate, Richie, had carried out. He wanted very much to keep it that way.

"So what do you want then?" he asked Hughes

"Maureen Connolly," Hughes began before Mags Power interrupted him.

"Maybe," she said, "it would be better if we stepped inside for a few moments. After all, I get the distinct impression, Mr Ferguson, that you're not the kind of person who likes it to be seen that you're being visited by the authorities – any authorities."

Geoff Hughes was amused: Sammy Ferguson was impressed.

"You're right," he agreed, stepping back. "You'd better come in here."

He led them into the front room of the small terraced house. He didn't invite them to sit down but they did so anyway – Geoff on the black, imitation-leather settee, Mags on a matching recliner chair – nor did he offer any refreshment. Hughes wouldn't have expected it.

"So," said Sammy. "What's this about that cow, Maureen Connolly?"

"Oh, you do know her then."

"Of course I know her. She only lives two doors away. Everybody in this street knows everyone else – and most of their business. That's the trouble. Can't do a thing without someone spying on you."

He directed his complaint at Mags Power and sounded quite bitter, so much so that she began to understand why he'd been so nervous when he'd found them on his doorstep. There was more, she realised, to Sammy Ferguson than they had either the time or the authority to follow up on this particular visit. Their job was to learn more about the latest murder victim.

Geoff Hughes continued speaking. "Can you tell us a bit about her and her family?"

"Why?" Ferguson persisted. "What do you want to know about her for? What's she done?"

Hughes sighed. "We found a body this morning. We have reason to believe it's Miss Connolly. And we need to notify the family,"

"Bloody Hell!" Sammy exclaimed. "Murdered was she? I wouldn't be surprised."

"Why do you say that?" asked Margaret Power.

"Ah, she was a right bitch. Gave poor Mickey a rotten time always no matter what he did."

"Mickey?"

"Her brother. Only family she'd got and she treated him like a slave. Gave him dog's abuse."

Both Hughes and Power regarded him sharply on hearing this.

"Tell us more," said Hughes quietly.

"Not much more to tell. There's no family. I think the father buggered off when Mickey was about three or four. Never been seen again. Not round here anyway. As for the Ma, she was no use to anyone. When she wasn't on the booze she was drugged up to the eyeballs. 'Course it did for her in the end. But then, that's what happens when you lead a bad life." Sammy Ferguson was clearly enjoying himself. "Tough on Mickey, though. It was him what found her. Don't know that he ever got over that."

"And this happened when?" asked Mags.

"Hell! It must be at least ... let me think ... seven or eight years ago."

At that moment the door opened and in walked a thin, grey-haired woman of, Mags reckoned, about fifty. She looked as if she'd had a hard life, one which had drained her of any colour or cheerfulness. Her mouth seemed set in a permanent downturn while her shoulders were slumped as if the burden of the life she led was becoming heavier the older she got.

"What's all this, Sammy?" she asked, in a voice as miserable as her appearance. "Who are these people?"

Apparently she didn't recognise Geoff Hughes in spite of the fact that she had met him on each occasion that her son had been involved with the gardai.

"It's alright, Ma," Sammy assured her with surprising gentleness. "Just the gardai asking a few questions about Maureen Connolly. It seems someone's done her in."

The news of her young neighbour's violent death appeared to leave Mrs Ferguson totally unmoved, causing Mags to wonder about their young victim who, it seemed, despite the violent nature of her death, could not arouse any sympathy from this older woman.

"We're trying to find out as much as we can about her, Mrs Ferguson," Mags explained. "We're sorry to disturb your morning but we do need to find out about her family. They haven't yet been told but your son was just telling us that both her parents are dead."

"Well now," said Mrs Ferguson, "I can't say anything about the father. He could be anywhere. Alive or dead. Not that it would make any difference to those kids. He gave up on them the day he left and I'm pretty sure they've not seen hide nor hair of him since.

"And the mother?" Mags persisted. "Mr Ferguson was just telling us that she died several years ago."

While his mother thought about this for a moment or two Sammy positively glowed at the manner in which Margaret Power had referred to him.

"Aye," said Mrs Ferguson, finally. "I suppose it would be round about ..." another pause while she carried out some calculation in her head, "eight years ago. Yes, that would be it. Just before my man went."

Mags felt she now could begin to understand why this woman seemed so beaten down by life. Sammy, she reckoned, would be about eighteen or nineteen which meant that Mrs Ferguson had been left to raise what was quite likely an already troublesome son on her own. However she didn't like to ask where Mr Ferguson had gone – whether he was dead or whether, like so many men it seemed, he'd just found marriage and family life too difficult.

"Yes," said Mrs Ferguson, almost as if she'd read the young woman's mind, "it'll be seven years come Christmas that Liam died. Cancer. Gets so many, doesn't it." And, as if to underline that thought, her remark was followed by a hacking cough which seemed to go on forever.

"You go and rest, Ma," said Sammy, his solicitous attitude at odds with his reputation. "Get yourself a cup of tea. I can deal with this. After all, Mickey and I were good mates. I knew more about that family than anyone, I daresay."

Mrs Ferguson shuffled out of the room, gratefully it seemed, leaving her son to continue his role – an unexpected one – of assisting the gardai with their enquiries.

Geoff Hughes had not spoken during the exchange with Mrs Ferguson. Like his colleagues he recognised that Margaret Power was far better than he was at dealing with people like Sammy's mother and she usually got far more information from the women they dealt with than the others ever could. He was also very much aware of the effect she was having on Sammy. Clearly impressed by her looks – and who couldn't be? – Sammy was enjoying both the limelight and the chance to show off in front of what was, after all, a very beautiful woman.

Now, however, he decided to speak.

"So you know Mickey Connolly well."

"Mickey and I have been friends for years," Sammy explained. "Well, makes sense don't it, living so close to each other and being the same age. Grew up together pretty much. Got into some scrapes too, I don't mind admitting. Nothing serious," he hastened to add, seeing the doubtful expression on Hughes' face. "No. A bit of drink and a few fags when we were younger. And there was a bit of skiving off school, although when Maureen found out about that she soon put a stop to it. But then that was her way."

"So what happened when the parents died?" Geoff asked.

"That was probably the worst thing. Maureen was already over eighteen and an adult so the authorities decided it was O.K. to leave Mickey with her. Big mistake. She'd never been very nice to him but once she was in charge she really made his life hell. Just 'cos she was working – to get enough money to keep him as she never stopped telling him – she made him do everything. And if he dared to step out of line she'd find more jobs for him to do. Poor sod. Never had a life of his own. I think that's why he started skipping school. Just to have some time of his own.

"Mind you," Sammy was really warming to his subject now, "it was bad enough when she was workin' but she lost her job a few weeks back and that made her ten times worse. I'm not surprised he finally reached the end of his tether."

"How do you mean?" asked Hughes sharply.

Was Sammy Ferguson about to tell them something which would make solving this crime a whole lot easier?

"Well, when I last saw him – a few days ago – he told me he was finally moving out. At long last he'd got the balls to leave her. Sorry, Miss," - he suddenly realised that this might not be the kind of talk used to impress such a lovely woman – "that just sort of slipped out."

Margaret Power favoured him with one of her charming smiles.

"It's alright, Sammy," she said. "I have heard far worse."

"I suppose so," he mumbled, utterly ensnared by her.

121

Hughes could understand the feeling. His colleague was one of the loveliest women he'd ever met. Robert Lane, her fiance, was a very lucky man. However, they still had a job to do.

"Did he say where he was going?" he asked.

"Not exactly. Only that he needed a bit of money – enough to rent a room in some hostel or other for a couple of weeks till he could get himself sorted out. He'd only come back here to get his stuff and to see if I could help him out."

"Did he say which hostel?"

Sammy thought for a moment or two then shook his head.

"I don't think so. No, I'm pretty sure he didn't. Hey," – a sudden thought struck him – "you don't think he did it do you? Killed her, I mean. Not that you could blame him. Not after the way she's treated him all these years. Hell! No-one could blame him."

"Thank you, Sammy." Hughes avoided giving any response to this suggestion by standing up, signifying an end to the interview. Margaret Power followed him out of the room. "We appreciate all the help you've given us. We'll get back to you if we need to."

By this time both detectives had made their way through the front door but Geoff suddenly turned back.

"There is one more thing," he said. "You say Maureen Connolly lost her job recently."

Sammy nodded.

"Do you happen to know where she was working?"

"Oh yes, Sergeant." Sammy grinned, delighted, it seemed, to give yet another example of his usefulness. "She worked at the hospital."

IV

The team had all returned; their reports had been presented and, in spite of their best efforts, they were not much further forward. The fact that their number one possible suspect – for the Connolly murder at least – was not involved at all had done little to improve their mood and an air of frustration was steadily growing.

"His story checks out completely," Inspector Murphy informed them. "Phil spoke to his wife and she was certain he was at home before eleven. That, apparently, is when the baby gets his final feed and Martin was definitely home to help her with that."

"I bet you enjoyed all these intimate little details of family bliss," quipped Noel Lawson, receiving, in return, a glare from Phil.

Chris Murphy silenced the ensuing laughter.

"Now I know that she could have been lying to cover for him but it so happens that when I checked at the Carlsworth where he claims to have spent the evening they were able to confirm everything he told us. The doorman even recalled helping Miss Connolly into a taxi and he was adamant that that was at about ten o'clock last night and, more importantly, that, at that stage, she was on her own."

Even more troubling was Inspector Murphy's other piece of information. The fact that Maureen Connolly was probably lured to her death by someone claiming to be from the gardai was alarming to say the least and, at first, no-one dared even consider that the caller could have been genuine.

"I'm getting it checked out even as we speak," Pollock informed them. "Larry O'Dwyer has been asking around but so far with no success. Of course, we'll have to wait till the night shift arrives to be sure but as far as both he and I are concerned there is no-one on this force who would be in any way involved with murder. I'm absolute certain of that."

He glared at them, almost daring anyone to contradict him. Nobody did.

"Now," Pollock continued after a pause, "there's still plenty to do. Mags, Geoff, get going on your search for that hostel. Phil, you can take a look at what Noel's been working on. We've now got those extra clues and we still can't make head nor tail of them."

While Pollock and Murphy went into the chief's office to review all the information so far gathered in the various reports and Coady and Lawson got together over the crossword clues, Margaret Power and Geoff Hughes, each armed with a telephone directory, began contacting the various hostels in the city trying to locate the one in which, according to Sammy Ferguson, Mickey Connolly was now staying. They eventually traced him to the Boston Street Hostel for Men only to discover that he was not there at the time. The less than helpful manager had, as he put it, no idea when he'd be back.

"I run a hostel not a prison camp," he informed Hughes testily, "and I certainly don't expect the residents to report to me every time they leave the building. Not even if they are wanted by the police."

"He's not wanted by the police as you suggest," Hughes pointed out, struggling to control his growing irritation at the man's rudeness. "However, we do need to speak to him on a personal matter of some urgency. That's why we'd appreciate some help from you."

The man's manner didn't change.

"The only thing I can tell you," he announced brusquely, "is that, since he didn't ask for a late key, he'll be back by eleven thirty. That's when we lock up."

And with that he hung up.

"Thanks a lot, you helpful bugger," muttered Hughes as he replaced the receiver. "There are some people ...."

He didn't need to finish the sentence. The others knew exactly what he meant. In every investigation, no matter how serious, there were always some members of the public who begrudged any assistance requested by the gardai. As always, it made their job just that little bit more difficult.

There seemed at this point very little more that either Mags or Geoff could do to push the case forward. As Pollock had reminded them at the briefing, they had two victims and they knew how they'd died. They were pretty sure the cases were connected and that they were dealing with a single male killer. But who and why remained a complete mystery.

"Unless," Mags told Geoff, "those clues are actually going to tell us."

With that possibility in mind but less than hopeful of success she and Geoff joined their two colleagues and began studying the new crossword clues. It was no good. The combination of weariness and frustration plus, for three of them, a total lack of understanding of the mindset involved in devising and solving cryptic crossword clues left them more annoyed than ever.

They agreed with Noel that the multi-word clue was probably connected with the Ten Commandments. He was, after all, the only expert among them and his reasoning did make sense. However, a quick check on the Internet – "You mean none of you know them

124

by heart," Coady quipped – showed them that, if that were the case, their choice of which one of the ten was the correct answer was very limited.

"Supposing," said Mags, at last, "if this is all part of the killer's devious mind, we're expected to take a different interpretation of the clue. What exactly does it say?"

"Very similar to one of ten in tablet form," Lawson read out to her.

"Well," she spoke slowly, as if trying to organise her thoughts even as she was speaking, "supposing the words 'very similar' in the clue are telling us that the answer isn't exactly word for word as it appears in the Ten Commandments. Supposing our answer is a slightly altered version. Surely that gives us something more to go on."

The three men watched her in silence as she concentrated on the computer screen. According to the information in front of her there were two versions of the Commandments: one in the book of Exodus, the other in Deuteronomy. The wording in each was slightly different but the meaning was, naturally, the same in both cases.

"We're presumably looking for one which has three words," Mags went on. "According to this the nearest gives us 'You shall not murder' – which, according to this website at least, is exactly the same in both books – and 'You shall not steal'. And as you can see, they are almost the same."

"I take it coveting your neighbour's wife and all that doesn't really fit," said Coady, with a grin. "Although murder over an ox or a donkey would certainly be different."

"Shut up, Phil," said Hughes. "Mags could be onto something here."

"We might even, at a stretch, include the one about false witness," Mags continued, the smile she gave Coady taking the sting out of Geoff Hughes' words, " since all that means really is telling lies."

"Or possibly even, in our terms, committing perjury," Lawson put in.

They were now seized with renewed enthusiasm. If Mags were right there was a whole new set of possibilities to explain the two murders.

"Maybe," added Geoff Hughes, "the killer is telling us that these murders are in some way connected with a past crime; one which somehow involved both victims. Let's get the boss in here. See what he thinks."

"Hang on a sec," cautioned Phil. He still had one or two doubts about the whole thing. "Let's talk to Murphy first. We don't want a rollicking from Pollock for going off on a wild goose chase."

"What wild goose chase?" They hadn't noticed Sean Pollock and Chris Murphy coming back into the incident room, not until Pollock spoke. "What are you all getting so worked up about?"

Briefly Noel Lawson explained Mags' theory. Pollock smiled

"It definitely makes sense," he said eagerly, "and we certainly ought to look into the possibility that both Bridget Corcoran and Maureen Connolly were connected with some previous crime. It should be easy enough to check that out. Noel?"

"Already onto it, Sir," said Lawson, his attention totally focussed on the computer screen in front of him.

"If you're right," Pollock continued, " this would give the case a whole new dimension.   If that's the link between the two women it's just possible it might give us a better idea of the motive if not the actual identity of the killer.

It didn't take Noel Lawson long to dash their hopes.

"Sorry," he said, shaking his head, "there's absolutely no record of either woman having any connection to any crime."

Pollock tried not to let disappointment get them down. They'd all faced frustrations like this before: it was almost an accepted part of the job.

"Well," he told them, "apart from that there's little more we can do at present so I suggest that you start writing up your reports. Geoff, give me the address of that hostel and I'll go and find Mickey Connolly later this evening. Maybe he'll be able to shed some light on why his sister died in such a tragic way."

So saying he left them and returned once again to his office.

V

It was a disappointing end to a miserable day and each of the frustrated group of detectives was more than happy to take Inspector Murphy's advice and finish early for once.

Chris Murphy, the family man, headed straight home – much to his wife Fiona's delight – and was able to distance himself from the day's events by relaxing for a while with his three boisterous children.

Phil Coady was as pleased as anyone to be finishing earlier than he'd expected but before leaving the incident room he used his mobile phone to conduct what was clearly an important piece of business. Following this, although he left with the others, when it was suggested that they make a brief stop at the Seanachai he refused, informing them that he had what he termed a 'hot date' for the evening.

"So much for his notion of important business," murmured Geoff Hughes as, together with Mags and Noel, he crossed the road to the nearby pub which had become for them, and for many of their colleagues, the local.

Despite its name the Seanachai was not what Geoff Hughes termed 'Hollywood Irish', all shillelaghs and leprechauns, but a modern bar with comfortable seats and several alcoves which gave the customers a certain measure of privacy. This was one of the reasons why it suited members of the gardai so much.

They settled down with their drinks – the two men with pints, Mags with a glass of white wine – and, not surprisingly, began discussing the day's events. Not for long, however. After just one drink they were joined by Mags' fiance and the conversation turned to more general topics.

****

For Sean Pollock it was a very different story. Left alone in his office, long after the others had gone, he returned again and again to the information they'd got so far. It really wasn't very much.

Two women, apparently unrelated, both murdered in isolated places late at night or early in the morning – he had yet to see the final post-mortem report on the second victim. Forensics had turned up very little at either crime scene. There was evidence of a slight struggle in both cases but not enough, as far as he knew so far, to leave any traces from the killer himself. Nothing that could lead to either fingerprint or DNA identification. Although the first weapon – that pretty scarf – was hardly a normal item for a male wardrobe it was definitely the kind of thing a man might buy for a wife, girlfriend or female relative without any questions being asked. Even more frustrating neither it nor the perfectly ordinary tie used to strangle Maureen Connolly appeared to hold any clues whatsoever.

As far as Pollock could tell there was no apparent link between the two murder sites – apart from their isolation – and, in fact, although not quite at opposite ends of the city they certainly weren't within easy walking distance of each other. It was therefore unlikely, though not impossible, that the killer lived near either place. Did this mean he had a car? Pollock wrote the word '*car?*' on the notepad in front of him with the vague idea of getting someone to go back to the murder scenes and ask if anyone might have seen any unfamiliar or suspicious-looking vehicle in the area. But even as he looked at the word he knew that this was almost a pathetic idea.

"You idiot, Sean Pollock," he muttered to himself. "No-one's likely to have been in either place late at night to have noticed anything. The only people prowling round either of them after dark would be too drunk or too far gone on drugs to even know their own name let alone notice anything out of the ordinary."

No: the killer, he knew, was far too clever to be caught out like that. Still, he left the word there. After all, if they did get as far as finding a suspect it might be worth checking out any vehicle he might own.

Another thought occurred to him. Was it possible that there was some link between the Connolly children and Bridget Corcoran's son and daughter? He didn't really accept Lawson's idea that Maureen Connolly was Mrs Corcoran's daughter, given away at or soon after birth and he realised that the age difference between Angela Molloy and Maureen Connolly was too big for them to be friends. But what about Richard Corcoran and Mickey Connolly. Had they known each other at school? Was it possible that both boys had attended St Saviour's? Given the city's excellent bus service and the free choice parents had over their children's education it was quite common for children who lived in two widely separated areas of the city to end up in the same school. He was, he knew, clutching at straws but he also knew there were odd occasions when straws could be very productive. This might be one of them. He made another note to himself.

He looked once more at the two victims. Bridget Corcoran, mother of two, worked at the city's regional hospital; Maureen Connolly, single woman, worked for an escort agency. However, Sammy Ferguson had told Geoff Hughes that he thought Maureen Connolly had previously worked in some kind of hospital, although he was very vague about any details. Perhaps that was the link.

Pollock had already arranged for Inspector Chris Murphy to follow up on that particular lead first thing the next morning.

"Take Margaret Power with you," he'd told the Inspector. "She's usually very good at getting information out of people who don't normally like talking to the gardai. According to Hughes she had that rogue Ferguson eating out of her hand. He even apologised to her for using language she may have found offensive."

Chris Murphy had laughed. "Having seen her with some of our previous suspects while she's been with us nothing would surprise me. She really does have a way with people."

'Hopefully,' Pollock now thought, 'she can get someone to show us if there really is any connection between our two victims.'

Apart from that he couldn't think of any other direction in which to take the case. The forensic report was on its way; the fact that there had been no major struggle on the part of either victim, once confirmed in the report, would only serve to reinforce his opinion that the killer was a man. Although both women were quite slightly built he was still convinced that the strength needed to strangle them would be more likely to come from a man than a woman. He doubted that the post-mortem reports would differ much and since Bridget Corcoran's death was definitely caused by strangulation it was practically certain that Maureen Connolly's was as well.

On a sudden impulse Pollock picked up the phone and dialled a number though, glancing at his watch, he was fairly sure his call would go unanswered. For once, luck was on his side and after the fifth ring the receiver at the other end was lifted and he heard the familiar sound of Elizabeth Mason's voice.

"Elizabeth," he said. "Sean Pollock here."

"You're lucky to have caught me," came the reply. "I was just putting on my coat ready to leave. What can I do for you? Not another body, I hope."

"God forbid!" exclaimed Pollock, with absolute sincerity. "No, it's just that there are a couple of things about these two murders that I want to sort out with you and I wondered," he paused, feeling for an instant ridiculously like a tongue-tied teenager, "if you're not in a rush, that is, whether you could meet me for a drink."

"Certainly," she said to his immense surprise. "I've nothing planned for this evening. Where do you want to meet? The Seanachai?"

He hesitated. The Seanachai was close to where they both worked so it would certainly be convenient. At the same time that was its main drawback. He didn't want to set tongues wagging by showing up there with Dr Mason, even though they were only meeting in an official capacity. At least, that was his excuse.

"How about the Merlin in town?" he suggested. "In about half an hour? I've some business to attend to in that part of town later and, if I'm not mistaken, it's on your route home."

"That's fine," she replied. "See you in half an hour."

The call ended but, for a while, Sean Pollock sat in silence just thinking.

He thought about his team. Chris Murphy, family man, home now and probably enjoying a relaxing evening with Fiona and the children, unwinding after the tensions of the day. Phil Coady, the exact opposite, still playing the game of devil-may-care man about town. Without doubt he'd have some female lined up for this evening, willing to help him relax and forget the stresses of the job. Noel Lawson, he knew, had a steady girlfriend – Ruth, he thought she was called – and though there'd been some talk of them splitting up a year or so back there'd recently been a suggestion that they were getting back together. Pollock hoped so: it was good to have someone to go home to after a hard day like the one they'd just had, someone who represented normality, far removed from the horrors of a murder case.

Margaret Power was already looking forward to married life in a new country. Even solid, dependable Geoff Hughes, as far as he knew – and the station's grapevine was usually pretty accurate when it came to such matters - was rumoured to be happily involved in a relationship, although no-one seemed to know any details.

He sighed.

'And what about me?' he thought, then stood up abruptly.

"None of that, Sean, my lad," he said out loud. "Let's just go and meet the lady. And, don't forget, after that there's still work to be done."

He picked up the piece of paper with the address of the hostel on it and slipped it into his pocket. Then, putting on his coat, he switched off the lights, carefully locked his office door and headed off to meet Dr Mason.

VI

The Merlin was a quiet pub on Spring Street, just off the main shopping precinct. The lounge bar was not very big and was dimly lit by small table lamps each with a red lampshade which gave the place a warm, rosy glow. Although, perhaps, not as private as the alcoves in the Seanachai could be, the fact that it was less popular and that the tables were well spaced out made private conversations very easy. That was one reason why Sean Pollock had chosen it. Another, equally important, was that he was far less likely to be recognised here. Too many of the city's pubs were used by men – and women – involved in the law, both criminals and the people who represented them in court. The Merlin would not, he hoped, present the same problem.

He was correct. Only two of the tables were occupied – three women at one and a young couple at the other – and although the occupants all looked towards the door when he entered this was simply an automatic response and they all swiftly returned to their conversations. No-one showed any further interest in him.

Dr Mason, he noted, had not yet arrived so he bought himself a pint of Smithwicks and settled at a corner table near the window from which he could watch her arrive. He didn't have long to wait. Within five minutes he saw her hurrying across the street towards the pub.

She was certainly a good-looking woman; not beautiful in the accepted sense but, with strong features framed by a mass of dark brown curls, she was definitely quite striking. Her height added to this impression. She was, Pollock guessed, about five foot seven or eight and, although it was currently hidden beneath a heavy beige overcoat, her slim, shapely figure made her look younger than the mid-forties that he knew her to be.

Watching her now Sean Pollock began to regret his decision to go and speak to Mickey Connolly and, for a brief moment, even wondered if he could postpone the meeting or, at least get one of the others to take his place. An evening with Elizabeth Mason was a far more appealing prospect. But no, work was work and he had an important and unpleasant task to perform which, he knew, could not wait. He sighed but by the time Dr. Mason had come through the door he was already on his feet, ready to help her off with her coat and get her a drink.

"I'll have a glass of Guinness, please," she said, smiling at his surprised expression. "And you needn't look like that," she added. "Why is it that these days everyone expects women to order 'girlie' drinks like wine or these alcopop things. Why can't a woman enjoy a glass of the black stuff?"

"Why indeed?" he laughed as he made his way to the bar.

For a few minutes, once he'd returned with her drink, they made idle conversation about trivial things – the weather, the awful build up of traffic in the city, the fact that, if the shop windows were to be believed, Christmas was approaching – and Sean was surprised at how relaxed he was beginning to feel. Normality was, he realised, a truly wonderful thing and once again he felt that he could quite happily have spent the rest of the evening in the company of this rather attractive and very charming woman. Unfortunately, as he reminded himself, this was not an option on this particular occasion.

She must have sensed a change in him – although he did not know how – for, all at once, she became quite business-like. He feared he might have offended her.

"Now, Sean," she said, "you said on the phone you wanted to discuss one or two things with me so tell me, what's on your mind?"

"Well," he replied, troubled by the sudden change in mood, "I hate to bring up work when your day has officially ended but it's about these two murders."

"I realise that." She smiled, taking away any sharpness suggested in her words. "How can I help? I've the second post-mortem report ready – apart from all the usual toxicology results – so that will be on your desk in the morning."

"Time of death was as we suspected?"

Like her, Chief Superintendent Pollock was all business now. In a murder case, he reflected somewhat ruefully, time off was a rare commodity – not only for those in charge of the case but also for the many others whose work contributed so much to finally reaching a solution.

"She'd probably been dead about twelve hours when we saw her which means she was killed between ten thirty and midnight. Certainly no later."

"No sign of this being a sexual attack?"

"None at all. She was sexually active but there were no signs of recent intercourse. Rape was definitely not a factor."

"And death was by strangulation. No indication of any other cause like drugs or a very heavy blow."

"Nothing like that. The killer simply put that tie around her neck and pulled hard. It seems to have been quite quick since there are no signs of any real struggle."

"Tell me, Elizabeth," said Pollock, when she'd finished, "in your expert opinion is our killer a man or a woman?"

She didn't hesitate.

"I'd say without any doubt at all you're looking for a male suspect. The ligature marks correspond with the weapon used in each case so we know both women were strangled and, as I say, there is no evidence that either victim was sedated in any way prior to death. Now, without getting too technical, one of the things we check for is signs of obstruction to the carotid arteries; another is to see how much damage has been caused to the thyroid arteries. Each of these can tell us a great deal about the amount of pressure or force used by the killer. In the case of both your victims there was a great deal of pressure which, given that they don't appear to have struggled much and yet weren't sedated, suggests to me that not only is your killer a man he's probably a very angry man."

"You think his anger gave him extra strength in some way."

"Absolutely. I am certain no woman could have exerted so much pressure so fast that the victims couldn't at least make some attempt to resist."

Their conversation drifted to a halt as each considered the implications of all that had been said. Sean Pollock, glad to have his own view endorsed, had been thrown straight back into the complexities of the case while Elizabeth Mason, aware that, for this evening at least, she had lost him, wondered where she should go from here.

She'd admitted to herself some time ago that she felt very attracted to this lonely, self-contained man. She was fully aware of his history – especially the tragic early death of his much-beloved wife – and had heard comments from various sources that he was the original 'one-gal-guy' yet surely they could become friends. Close friends who could share evenings out together, day trips, holidays even and who knew what else. What harm could that do?

She sighed deeply and stood up. Pollock had been so lost in his own thoughts that she'd already put her coat on before he realised what was happening.

"Elizabeth," he cried, leaping to his feet and almost overturning the table in the process, "I'm sorry. I was just ...."

"Don't apologise, Sean," she said gently. "You have a job to do and, if I know you, you won't really relax until this crime is solved and the killer is safely behind bars. However," she warned, putting her hand on his arm," when it is over I shall insist on cooking a meal for you. A kind of celebration if you like. And I won't take no for an answer."

Impulsively she leaned towards him and kissed his cheek then, before he could utter a word, she was gone.

He stood for a moment or two watching her cross the road and disappear into the multi-storey car park which served the shopping precinct. Yes, there was no doubt about it, she was a good-looking woman. For the first time in over ten years Sean Pollock felt stirrings of an emotion he'd long believed had died with his dear wife, Claire.

'A meal with Dr Mason,' he said to himself, suddenly grinning. 'That might not be a bad idea at all."

With that thought in mind Chief Superintendent Pollock decided it was time to try his luck and see if he could track down Mickey Connolly. They were almost certain of the identity of their latest victim but it would certainly help to have this confirmed by what seemed to be her only surviving relative.

VII

Boston Street Hostel for Men was not far from the Merlin pub but the building itself, and those surrounding it, couldn't have been more different. It was a narrow, five-storey building painted in a drab olive green and, as he walked through the front door and approached what he took to be the reception desk, Pollock saw that the outside colour was simply a reflection of the drabness within. There was nothing homely, comfortable or welcoming about the entrance hall and he very much doubted if things improved further inside. Not for the first time he found himself wondering what had caused Mickey Connolly to wind up in a place like this rather than stay at home with his sister.

"Yeah?"

The word came abruptly from the lanky youth seated in the corner behind the reception desk. He seemed, at least in Pollock's opinion, to be far more interested in whatever was playing through his earphones than in dealing with any member of the public. It never paid to judge by appearances although this young man's long, stringy, black hair and stained T-shirt made it very hard to follow that particular rule. Nonetheless, Pollock decided that the situation called for maximum use of his authority and, producing his warrant card, he introduced himself.

"Chief Superintendent Sean Pollock. I'm looking for someone I understand is staying here."

The effect on the young man wasn't quite what Pollock expected. Normally, playing what he saw as the official card created rapid responses – fear, curiosity, respect, any or all of those. Yet, in this case it didn't.

"Name?" the young man asked, still plugged in to whatever machine was producing the tinny sound that Pollock could make out as he drew closer.

The Chief Superintendent got annoyed. It had been a long day and not a particularly good one and the last thing he needed was an insolent lack of co-operation from this particular young fool. He'd had enough. He thumped his fist on the desk and glared at the young man.

"This is an official garda enquiry," he snarled, "and I need to speak to Mickey Connolly. Now. If he's here. And unless you get up off your backside, turn that bloody thing off and give me the information I want you'll find yourself being hauled out of here and charged with obstruction."

This time the effect was almost instantaneous. Without bothering to turn anything off the young man snatched the plugs from his ears and stuffed them in his pocket.

"Yes, Sir," he mumbled. "Connolly you say." He flicked through the registration book. "Ah. Mickey Connolly. Room number six. Been here just over a week."

"Is he here now?" asked Pollock, his anger subsiding a little.

"I'm not sure. I only came on duty at six. I don't know whether he came in before that but I haven't seen him."

"Well can you check?" The tone showed just how fragile Pollock's patience had become.

The youth hesitated.

"Strictly speaking I'm not supposed to leave the desk," he muttered.

"Police. Business." Pollock uttered each word very slowly and with careful emphasis.

"Yes. Right. Of course."

It was very clear that the young man was now torn between the anger of this rather irate officer and that of his boss but in the end there was no competition. Struggling to his feet he moved out from behind the desk and, murmuring "I won't be a minute", disappeared through an inner door which Pollock assumed led to the guest accommodation.

The Chief Superintendent waited, pondering again as he did so what kind of home situation and what relationship with his sister Connolly must have had that had driven him to seek refuge in a place like this. He was still wondering about this when the door opened and in walked a tall, thin youth probably, Pollock guessed, in his late teens. There was something about his looks that was vaguely familiar; so much so that the detective decided to take a chance.

"You wouldn't be Mickey Connolly, by any chance?" he asked.

The young man looked startled and, flustered, didn't reply.

More confident now Pollock continued. "I'm Chief Superintendent Pollock from the Criminal Investigation Bureau. I'm looking for someone called Mickey Connolly and if, as I believe, that's you then I have to talk to you. It's a serious matter I'm afraid."

Mickey, still looking bewildered, nodded slowly.

"Yes," he said, "I'm Mickey Connolly but I ...."

At that point the inner door re-opened and the scruffy young receptionist slouched back into the hall.

"He's not in," he declared and then, noticing that the officer had company, added: "Oh, I see you've found him."

Pollock nodded coldly, reluctant even to offer a word of thanks for a task performed with such ill-grace. He glanced around and made a quick decision. Knowing how sensitive his conversation with Connolly was likely to be he realised that neither this entrance hall nor Mickey's room – which, in any case, he probably shared with others – was ideal.

"I think, Mickey," he said, quietly, "it might be an idea if we talk in my car. It's just outside."

Without waiting for an answer he moved to the front door, opened it and led the way to his waiting Renault. Somewhat reluctantly, Mickey followed him.

He wasn't at all what Sean Pollock had expected although, now he came to think about it, he wasn't even sure just what he had expected. Certainly not this smart, clean-cut young man, tidily dressed in jeans and a sweater, dark blond hair cut short and combed back neatly and blue eyes that squinted slightly behind narrow-framed glasses. As he'd noticed already, the lad was tall though not particularly well-built and was, in fact, the kind of young man who could easily be lost in a crowd. He was so, for want of a better word, ordinary.

They climbed into the car.

"I thought," the Chief Superintendent began "we'd get more privacy here though I fear," he tilted his head in the direction of the hostel, "I may have damaged your reputation in there. However, I'm afraid I've bad news for you."

There was no response.

"We found a body earlier today in one of those half-finished housing developments on the east of the city," Pollock went on without hesitating. There was, he knew from experience, no easy way of imparting such bad news as that which he now had to give the young man sitting silently beside him. "We have reason to believe it's your sister, Maureen."

During his many years of service Pollock had had to perform this unpleasant duty on several occasions. He was used to the variety of reactions such news usually aroused but he certainly wasn't prepared for this one.

"That's it then," said Mickey Connolly, solemnly. "Now I have no-one at all."

Sean Pollock found himself at a loss for words. There was no shock, no horror, no grief in the lad's tone. In fact, there was no emotion at all. It was a plain statement of fact uttered in the same way he might have described the weather or the time of day.

Pollock decided that the shock at the news was such that, for the moment at least, the reality of the affair was just too great for young Mickey Connolly to absorb. He felt obliged to continue.

"I'm sorry to put it so bluntly," he explained, "but we found a business card in her coat pocket and it was through that that we got an initial identification."

Aware that he was rambling Pollock stopped, deciding that what the boy really needed was a little time in silence in order to let the news sink in. They sat quietly in the car, each lost in his own thoughts. Finally, Mickey Connolly spoke.

"How was she killed? Was she murdered? Like that woman the other day?"

There was an awful calmness about the lad which Pollock found slightly unnerving.

"Strangled, I'm afraid."

Mickey nodded. "Like that other woman," he repeated calmly. "The one the papers reported a couple of days ago. Do you think it's the same killer?"

Once more Pollock was taken aback by the young man's cool attitude. In fact, Mickey Connolly seemed so unaffected by the news of his sister's death that an awful suspicion began creeping into his mind.

"It might be," he now conceded. "We don't know. However, as Maureen's next of kin we do need you to identify the body for us. And I'm afraid I also have to ask you where you were last night."

Mickey Connolly's laughter was the biggest surprise of the evening and Pollock began to wonder whether he was, in fact, dealing with a severe case of hysteria. The young man's next words showed how wrong he was.

"Listen, Chief Superintendent. I admit I hated my sister. She has made my life pretty difficult for as long as I can remember. That's why I finally moved here. I just couldn't take any more. But kill her? No way. And, in answer to your question, I spent most of yesterday evening at the home of one of my teachers getting extra tuition for my Leaving Cert exam. And because regulations here are very strict I was back in my room by eleven thirty. And since I share that room with four other people I have no shortage of people to support my story."

Pollock was startled not just by the young man's words but also by the reference to school. He thought at first that the lad looked too old to still be attending but appearances were obviously deceptive in this case. He also realised, when he thought about it, that what he'd just heard fitted in with all that Sammy Ferguson had told Geoff Hughes earlier in the day. He knew that, as a matter of form if nothing else, he would have to follow up on Connolly's story but he was already quite sure that what he'd just heard was the truth. It appeared that this was another dysfunctional family in which there had been so little love or affection that even violent murder had no real impact.

"So," Mickey now said, his hand already on the handle of the car door ready to take his leave, "if there's nothing else you need to know I'll go on in. What time do you need me to come in tomorrow morning? I've a couple of free lessons first thing – the Irish teacher is away – so I could come in then, if that's O.K."

Sean Pollock nodded slowly, almost at a loss for words. He'd faced the death of people close to himself and he simply could not comprehend this young man's total indifference. Maybe, in spite of both his words and his manner, this really was the result of shock. Perhaps, in the morning he'd see a very different side of young Mickey Connolly. For some reason he found himself hoping very much that this would be the case.

"If you can call at the police station at quarter to nine tomorrow morning and ask for me," he said, "I'll get things organised. And perhaps we'll have time to talk a bit more then."

Without another word Mickey Connolly climbed out of the car and pushed the door closed. Pollock reached out to stop it from shutting completely.

"And Mickey," he called to the young man, "I'm sorry for your loss."

He couldn't be sure but the words he though he heard in reply sounded very much like:

"I'm not."

****

"Let me explain something, Chief Superintendent," said Mickey Connolly, in the same detached tone he'd used ever since Pollock had first met him.

They were now sitting at opposite sides of a bare table in one of the various small rooms used as interview rooms. Although most often used as somewhere to question possible suspects of crime, these rooms were also very useful for private conversations such as this.

"You seem surprised at what I think you see as my total lack of reaction to my sister's death. Am I right?"

Sean Pollock nodded but said nothing. It was true. He had become increasingly suspicious of the young man's behaviour and, although he still didn't think that Connolly was personally responsible for his sister's death, he was quite glad he'd ordered Geoff Hughes to St Saviour's School to check on the lad's story about having extra tuition with one of the teachers.

Connolly's attitude was a totally new one in Pollock's experience. The previous night he'd put the absence of any sign of grief down to shock, assuming that the news had been such that the boy had been unable to absorb it fully and therefore unable to respond in what Pollock would have considered a more appropriate manner. Yet this morning, at the mortuary, Mickey had displayed exactly the same almost callous disregard for his sister. He'd looked at the body, identified it as that of his sister and then walked away with no more emotion than if he'd been studying an unwanted bargain in a city store.

"For as long as I can remember my sister hated me," Connolly now informed the detective. "I don't know why; she never explained. Obviously I wasn't important enough to deserve an explanation. I imagine, however, that the fact that our father left when I was three had something to do with it. Until I came on the scene she'd had five years of being, I suspect, a cherished only child so when our father found he could no longer cope in the role of family man and upped and left she would obviously see me as the cause. Unfortunately, my baby brother died young, before he could share the blame.

140

"My mother was no help. She consoled herself first with drink and then with drugs and finally died of an overdose when I was fifteen. At that point my sister, who had already - in her mind if not in reality - lost both her parents because of me, was over eighteen and, therefore, was considered an adult. So the authorities decided that she was the obvious choice as my guardian.

"What they didn't realise," he continued, "was just how much she hated me. She'd been spiteful to me for years. Now, as far as she was concerned, she'd been given a legal right to treat me exactly as she wished."

"So what exactly did she do?" Pollock wasn't just interested in the young man's story for its own value. Here, he realised, was a possible link between the two victims. He scribbled two words on the notepad in front of him. *'Spiteful women'.*

"She never hit me if that's what you're thinking; at least, not since I grew taller than her. Except," Connolly added ruefully, "for the last time I saw her." He hesitated for a moment, remembering. "No. Her methods were far more subtle but just as hurtful. I had to do everything for her – all the household jobs, all the shopping, everything. And when she was particularly annoyed by something or just feeling especially mean she'd find extra jobs like scrubbing the back yard on my hands and knees or cleaning out all the drains."

"You never told anyone about this?"

"What was the point? My mate Sammy Ferguson – he's the one who told you where to find me – he had some idea but we were both just kids. Who was going to believe us? And anyway, as far as the neighbours – and everyone else for that matter – as far as they were all concerned she was little short of a saint to look after her younger brother the way she did."

"And no-one ever considered that you were being badly treated?"

"Why would they? Few people actually saw us together. When she was on her own – at work or out with her friends – she was probably as nice as pie. She must have been, since she had plenty of friends and even a couple of fairly serious boyfriends. It was as if my presence lit some kind of fuse in her that she just couldn't control.

"I'll give you an example. Not long after I started at St Saviour's Sammy and I started playing truant from school. Eventually, of course, the school realised what was going on and Maureen was asked to go in and talk to the principal about it. At first she was on her own in the office with him and was her usual pleasant self. But as soon as I was told to join them she turned on me with that vicious tongue of hers."

"And how do you know that she changed so dramatically if you weren't in there to begin with?"

"Mr Morrissey told me. He was my class tutor at the time so, of course, he was also called in to the office to join in the discussion. He's the man I was with last night, giving me grinds in English."

"All right then, Mickey. If it was so bad why didn't you leave earlier? Why wait until now?"

"Tell me, Chief Superintendent, where would I go? I've no family that I know of and few, if any, friends. In fact Sammy's about the only one and, to be quite blunt, since I've realised what a bad influence he could be I've seen far less of him. Added to which, what would have been the point in going to him? He only lives two doors away."

"Was there a final straw?"

Once more Pollock's mind was working overtime. Two young men, two bullying females. In Richard Corcoran's case it had been that final row that Angela Molloy had told them about which had eventually driven him away. Could it have been the same in Mickey Connolly's case? He couldn't see where such a link might lead but his gut instinct told him there was one - and one definitely not to be overlooked.

"As a matter of fact there was," admitted Mickey. "About five weeks ago she lost her job. She used to work at the hospital but I guess you already know that."

Pollock nodded.

"Anyway, ever since then she's been like a demon. It didn't help that her boyfriend broke up with her a couple of days earlier and, naturally, she blamed all her troubles on me.

"It had actually got so bad that I decided it was time I really started thinking about my own future. I turn eighteen in a couple of months so I decided to go to the Social Welfare people and find out how I'd be fixed financially if I decided to leave home."

Again Pollock realised he was on the brink of yet another connection between the two cases.

142

"Unfortunately, I happened to choose the same day that Maureen went to sign on for the dole. She saw me there and promptly hit the roof. Called me every name under the sun. In front of all those people. You've seen the size of her. You know how tall I am. How do you think I felt being treated like that in front of everyone?"

It was a question that didn't require an answer. Sean Pollock's imagination did the job just as well.

"So I told her there and then that I was leaving. And that's exactly what I did. Went straight home, packed a few things, borrowed a bit of cash from Sammy and left. And I haven't seen her since. Until now."

The room fell silent. Pollock's heart went out to this poor young man who, through no fault of his own, was as much a victim as his sister had been. He wasn't her killer, the Chief Superintendent fully believed that, but he was also sure that, if he had been, a clever lawyer and a sympathetic jury would have let him off with the smallest of punishments.

He stood up. Mickey followed suit.

"I suppose it's up to me to make the arrangements for the funeral," he said.

His voice sounded far less confident now as if, having related his sad story and released all the pent-up hurt he must have felt for years, he was unsure what to do next.

"That's usually the way," Pollock agreed. "I'll let you know when we can release the body though I doubt it will be too long. Meanwhile, maybe you can find someone to help you. Sammy Ferguson's mother, perhaps, or one of the other neighbours."

Mickey nodded and opened the door. There he paused, his hand on the door-knob.

"There is one other thing." His voice faltered. "The last thing I said to her. I told her I'd never see her or do another thing for her. I'd see her dead first." A pause. "I didn't really mean it."

Head bowed to hide the fast-approaching tears Mickey Connolly hurried away.

Chief Superintendent Pollock remained in the interview room for a while. He knew that the last thing Mickey Connolly needed was an audience. The poor lad had more than enough to cope with as it was.

'I should be used to all the rotten things that happen in this world,' he told himself, 'and yet there are still some things that can surprise me.'

Still he had, he was quite certain, a useful couple of new leads in this particular case. He shrugged, picked up the notepad and made his way upstairs to the incident room, eager now to discover how the rest of the team had got on.

VIII

Maureen Connolly had worked in the administration department of the hospital as Chris Murphy and Margaret Power found out when they arrived there first thing on the morning following the discovery of the second victim. Having obtained this information they began to make their way to the relevant section of the building – not an easy task as it turned out.

The Regional Hospital was a little like Topsy in Harriet Beecher Stowe's nineteenth century novel. Like her it had just 'growed' from a small public clinic into a sprawling mass of buildings struggling to serve the needs of the city. Over the years several additions had been made to the original two storey building creating such a maze of corridors that one almost needed a map in order to find the relevant department.

"We could spend years wandering these corridors, joked Murphy. "Imagine Sean Pollock's face if we have to call for a search party!"

Mags smiled at the comment knowing that both she and Murphy had had enough experience of the hospital – him with the birth of his children, her with the deaths of her family – to know that appearances were, as is often the case, very deceptive. The hospital was, they both agreed, highly efficient and was, in fact, recognised by many as the finest in the country.

"At least," she reminded him, "the people working here know their way around and that's the main thing."

By now they had finally reached the administration section where, until quite recently, Maureen Connolly had been an employee. It was in one of the many prefabricated sections attached to the hospital, scheduled for renewal in the earlier part of the century but, in the end, yet another victim of the recent recession. At one stage, Murphy thought ruefully, they couldn't stop building in this country. Now they couldn't even afford a new administration wing to an important city hospital. Ah well, such things were not his concern. Not today at least.

They were greeted at the door of the administration block by a sharp-featured woman with an angular body and steel-grey hair, all of which created an impression of severity betrayed only by her red-rimmed eyes. Clearly she'd recently been crying and the reason for her tears was made apparent as soon as Chris introduced himself.

"Oh, Inspector," she cried, tears forming once more in the corners of her eyes, "you've come about poor Maureen Connolly. That poor, poor girl."

"I'm afraid we have," Murphy agreed, as gently as he could. He glanced at Mags Power, his look implying that this could be a situation in which she might well play the better role. She understood.

"Perhaps," she said softly, "in the circumstances, there's somewhere we might go and talk, Mrs ...."

She left the sentence hanging, awaiting the introduction which, she was sure, the woman's in-built efficiency would soon provide.

"Kennedy," replied the woman, regaining her composure slightly. "Emily Kennedy. I'm the department supervisor."

So saying she led the two officers further down the corridor and into a small room which, she informed them, served as a kind of common room for those working in the department.

"Of course," she explained, her composure quickly restored by the need to play hostess to these two officers, "it's only a temporary place. Certainly not big enough to hold the number of people now working here. Still, it's useful. Some of the girls find it more convenient to come here during their breaks rather than trailing along to the main canteen."

She moved towards a corner of the room where, they noticed, there was a small cupboard on top of which stood an electric kettle, a jar of coffee and a bag of sugar.

"Can I get you some coffee?" Ms Kennedy asked. "There's no milk yet, I'm afraid. Kelly usually brings it in with her and she doesn't start until ten thirty. But, if you don't mind it black ...."

"That will be fine," Mags hastened to say, cutting off not only Ms Kennedy but also the refusal she already sensed would come from

145

Inspector Murphy. As a matter of fact she hated black coffee – didn't even like coffee very much, to be honest – but she'd learned through her own experiences that a shared drink, no matter what it was, often relaxed people and made them more inclined to talk. Maybe it was just the comfort of sharing something that made people open up to each other. Whatever the explanation she hoped it would work in this case as the more they found out about Maureen Connolly the greater the chances of finding some lead to her killer.

It appeared that Chris Murphy was, for the moment at least, quite willing to be led by his subordinate. He quickly settled into one of the half dozen chairs in the room and observed the two women. Sean Pollock was right. Margaret Power really did have a knack when it came to dealing with people. Emily Kennedy already looked more relaxed than when they'd first met her and although she still maintained her somewhat severe appearance at least, to his great relief, she no longer appeared to be on the verge of tears.

"I imagine everyone here has heard the news of Maureen's death," Mags said quietly.

She and her colleagues were well aware that it had been headline news on the local television channel the previous evening and in the morning newspapers. To the great disgust of those carrying out the investigation the more sensational tabloids were already using terms like *'serial killer'* and *'murdering rampage'*, which might help sell newspapers but certainly did little to help their enquiries.

"Such a terrible thing to happen," agreed Ms Kennedy. "Of course, she hadn't worked here for about," - she paused to consider the length of time since the young woman's departure -"about five weeks but that still didn't make the news any easier. And I know for a fact that some of the girls have met up with her a few times since she went. They'd become quite good friends while she was working here and, of course, there was no need for that to end just because she'd left."

"Why exactly did she leave?" Murphy asked as the two women carried the mugs of steaming coffee over to where he sat. Emily Kennedy put one mug on the table beside him, adding the bag of sugar and a teaspoon and indicating that he should help himself.

"I'm afraid that was my decision," she admitted, almost shamefacedly, as she settled into the seat opposite him. "From what I'd gathered from some of the other girls she'd found herself another job. Not that there was anything wrong with that," she

146

hastened to add. "Not in itself, at least." She sighed. "The trouble was it seems to have been some sort of night work. Well, maybe not night work as such but certainly something which took up a large part of the evening. Unfortunately she also planned to continue working here during the day but, as a result of the hours she was keeping, she soon started oversleeping and coming in late for work.

"Of course, the first couple of times I said nothing hoping that she'd realise that, no matter how young you are, you just can't keep burning the candle at both ends. It made no difference. She still arrived late on several occasions and even when she did get here on time she was often too tired to do her work properly. And," Emily Kennedy was eager to stress, "you must understand that this is one place where we simply can't afford clerical errors. Of course, all the consultants have their own secretaries and there is a separate financial department but people would still be amazed at how much basic administration has to be carried out in a large hospital like this. And with far too little funding."

Inspector Murphy sensed that, her shock at Maureen Connolly's death now sufficiently overcome, Emily Kennedy was about to mount a particular hobby horse about economic cutbacks and financial restrictions which could lead them far from the point of their visit. He decided it was time to intervene.

"Have you any idea what this job was?" he asked.

He already knew the answer but it would be interesting to find out what, if anything, Maureen had told her colleagues.

"I don't know exactly, but," she looked both embarrassed and sheepish, "I was beginning to think it might not be, how shall I put it, the right sort of job for a young woman."

Mags Power knew what she was trying to say and wanted to help her out of her awkwardness. There was, however, no easy way.

"Why did you think that?" she asked.

"Well," replied the older woman, her face growing red, "she'd come in with all this talk of fancy restaurants and expensive places she'd been to the night before – and it was quite obvious she'd not been alone. I know it's wrong to speak ill of the dead but I've an awful feeling Maureen had started working as," she hesitated, unwilling, it seemed, to voice the one word uppermost now in all three minds.

"As a prostitute," she concluded, the final word no more than a whisper.

Mags was quick to reassure her.

"Don't upset yourself, Ms Kennedy," she said, kindly. "From what we've found out so far you can rest assured that it certainly wasn't that."

"Oh, thank goodness." The relief was genuine. "She wasn't a bad girl, you know. And certainly she was wonderful to take care of that brother of hers the way she did. That's what makes the whole thing so awful."

The tears were back and this time both Power and Murphy decided to allow them to flow for a moment or two before continuing. It didn't take long for the supervisor to recover her self-control.

"You say she had friends among the girls here," Inspector Murphy said at last. "Was there anyone in particular?"

Emily Kennedy thought for a moment or two before replying.

"I suppose," she said eventually, "that Margaret O'Neill would probably have been the closest. From what I've heard they've met up a few times since Maureen left."

"Is Margaret here this morning?"

"She is. Though, to be honest, I was already thinking of sending her home again. She's so upset I don't think she'll be fit for much work today."

"That might not be a bad idea," agreed Murphy, "but we would like a word with her first."

"Of course," agreed Emily Kennedy, rising to her feet. "I'll go and get her. That is," she paused, "unless there's anything more I can do to help."

Margaret Power gave one of her bewitching smiles.

"You've been very helpful," she said, "and we know if we want any more information we can certainly call on you."

Emily Kennedy blushed at the compliment and blossomed under the smile.

"Thank you," she said. "I'll send Margaret to you straight away."

"So," said Murphy while they waited, "not much to go on so far."

"Not really," the younger officer agreed. "At least we know why she lost her job. Although," she added, "I must say this is a very different picture of the victim than Geoff Hughes and I got from Sammy Ferguson. I wonder why."

"Perhaps," Chris suggested, "it's the usual male-female thing. Her girlfriends saw her as a genuinely good person, her brother's friend saw her as a pain in the neck. Happens all the time, I suspect."

Before Mags could reply there was a timid knock on the door which then opened to admit a small, slender young woman of, Murphy guessed, no more than twenty-two or twenty-three. Her expression spoke volumes. If Emily Kennedy had been upset by the news of Maureen Connolly's death, Margaret O'Neill was clearly devastated. This, Murphy decided, was definitely a matter for his colleague. At least to begin with. He looked at her, nodded, then moved to the far corner of the room where, to outward appearances at least, he soon became engrossed in the small selection of magazines he found there.

Mags moved forward, recognising the necessity of steering the distraught girl into the room.

"Hi, Margaret," she said, settling the girl into a chair. "I'm Mags. I know this must be very hard for you but I do need to talk to you about Maureen."

Margaret stifled a sob but she was so obviously struggling to regain control that it was clear that, for a while at least, they would get very little useful information from her. Mags decided on a different approach.

"The worst thing about losing someone we know and someone we care about," she began, "is the awful guilt we begin to feel. We're sure there must have been something we could have done to prevent this awful thing happening. And, of course, that's not always true. Certainly not when someone is killed like this.

"I know," she went on. "When I was eleven a friend was killed by a drunken hit-and-run driver while we were playing outside his home. For months afterwards I kept asking myself if there was anything I could have done to prevent it. And, of course, there wasn't. It was only much later that it dawned on me that, while I could have done nothing to prevent poor Tommy's death, I could try and stop other people's young brothers from being killed in the same way. And that's why I became involved in our local neighbourhood's campaigns both for safer roads and stricter drinking laws. And," she hoped the lie would be forgiven, "that's why I eventually joined the gardai."

She'd got the girl's attention now. The tears had stopped and Margaret O'Neill was beginning to show much more interest.

"And it's exactly the same for you. At the moment I expect you're still in the guilt stage but, for Maureen's sake, you must not stay there. You've now got to make sure that no-one else has to go through the same awful feelings you're going through now."

"But what can I do?" the girl asked, timidly. "I don't know what I can do. They say there's this awful man going round strangling innocent women like Maureen. How can I stop him?"

Inwardly Mags cursed those members of the media who saw nothing wrong in sensationalising crimes such as this and spreading panic among the population. Outwardly she remained calm.

"You can't. Not on your own. That's our job," she told Margaret. "The best thing you can do is tell us all you know about Maureen Connolly. That way we can build up a picture which, along with the information we have on the other victim, could lead us to find the person who did this dreadful thing."

"But I don't really know anything," Margaret objected.

"That's not true," Mags pointed out. "As Maureen's friend you certainly know things we don't. You can tell us, for example, who her other friends were. And her boyfriends. And her family. And maybe you can tell us a bit about this new job she had – the one that she did in the evenings."

Inspector Chris Murphy listened in amazement as, slowly but surely, Margaret O'Neill began to talk. It wasn't what she said that surprised him; it was the way in which Mags Power had got this seemingly completely overwrought young woman to talk so coherently.

She told them a lot of things. She told them about the group of friends, herself included, who used to meet regularly for nights out and, less regularly, for weekends and holidays away. She talked of the occasions – not too many, she seemed glad to admit – when she'd visited Maureen at the house in Murdoch Street. Those visits, she admitted, had made her feel rather uncomfortable.

"Why was that?" Mags asked softly, not wishing to disturb the flow of information that Margaret was giving her.

"It was alright when it was just us girls," Margaret replied. "Then we'd have a bit of a gossip and a laugh. But, somehow, when her brother was there, she changed completely. It was as if she became a totally different person. You've got to understand: Maureen was a lovely person, a real friend. But when she was with her brother she could be – well, to be honest she could be a real bitch."

"Did she ever say why?"

"I never asked her. But it was just as if his presence set off some kind of spite in her that she just couldn't control. I think it had something to do with their past, when their Mum died or maybe even when their Dad left. I don't know."

"What about boyfriends?" Mags decided to change the subject. Margaret was beginning to look distressed again and she didn't want to lose her just yet. "Was there anyone serious?"

"Not really." Margaret paused. "Although, come to think of it, she was really hung up on the last guy. Nicholas. I think she thought he was getting serious about their relationship. In fact, I think she was probably beginning to see it as a permanent thing. So, naturally, she was very upset when they broke up."

"Nicholas who? Do you know his other name?"

Margaret thought for a while.

"If she told me I can't remember it. But I don't think .... Wait a minute. Yes. Yes, she did. One time at her house we were talking about the future – you know, silly girl talk about how we saw ourselves in five or ten years' time. And she saw herself as Mrs....What was the name? Oh yes. Mrs Kearns. So. Nicholas Kearns. That was his name. But," she finished, lamely, "I don't know anything more about him."

"And he was the one who ended the affair?" Mags asked. "Not her?"

"That's right. She was terribly upset at the time. Couldn't understand what had gone wrong. And then a couple of days later she got the sack here. It was awful. I'm sure she felt the whole world was against her."

Again emotion threatened to overcome Margaret O'Neill and bring the interview to an abrupt end. Mags Power knew she was now probably beginning to run out of time.

"Margaret," she said, her voice full of compassion, "we've suggested to Ms Kennedy that you be given the rest of the day off. You need time to come to terms with the news. But, if you can, there's one more question I'd like you to answer."

Margaret nodded but said nothing.

"The other victim, Mrs Corcoran, also worked here in the hospital. She worked at nights here in the laundry. Is there any way she and Maureen might have met?"

The question was so unexpected that it lifted Margaret from the well of misery she was about to sink into.

"I doubt it," she replied, her voice firmer that Mags had expected. "We finish here at five and Maureen was never one to hang around once it was time to go home. Added to which there'd be no real reason for them to meet, either here or in the laundry." She paused before continuing. "In fact the only places they could possibly have met – here at the hospital at least – would be in the shop or in the staff canteen. To be honest, I doubt they met in either but you can ask."

Chris Murphy and Margaret Power agreed. Maureen Connolly had worked in the administration section of the hospital at one end of the jigsaw of buildings that the hospital had become; Bridget Corcoran had worked in the laundry – not only at the other end of the complex but in the basement. Maureen Connolly worked by day, Bridget Corcoran by night. The chances of them meeting were remote indeed.

"On the other hand," Chris pointed out once Margaret O'Neill had left the room, "people both in the shop and the canteen might have known both women. There's no harm in wandering along there and finding out. That's if we can find our way back," he added, with a smile.

They said goodbye to Emily Kennedy, thanking her for her help and promising not to hesitate to return if they had further questions. Unlike Margaret O'Neill, she appeared to have regained her composure completely: work came first, grief could wait.

****

As they made their way back along the various corridors following, for a while, a series of signs intended, Murphy was sure, to confuse as much as to direct, he pondered on the conversation, as he'd heard it, between the two young women. Curiosity eventually got the better of him.

"You did very well in there," he began. "Was it all true?"

"About my friend?" she asked.

"I was thinking more about the rest. Is that why you joined the force?"

She smiled and there was only the slightest hint of regret in her smile.

"The truth, Inspector? As I once told Geoff Hughes, I was always a great fan of TV detective shows. The trouble was the heroes – the detectives themselves – were almost always men. Only one or two were women. I was determined to redress the balance."

She laughed and, after a moment or two of surprise, he joined in. They were still laughing as they entered the hospital's main foyer where, they'd been told, the shop was situated

It was obvious as soon as they walked into the fairly large retail area that not only might Bridget Corcoran and Maureen Connolly never have met – whether here or elsewhere – but that, even if they'd frequented the shop separately, they were unlikely to be remembered. Although it was still quite early in the morning – and certainly well outside the strictly imposed visiting hours – the place was still busy. Service staff buying their morning paper, flexi-time workers just arriving and grabbing a drink or a snack before facing into the day's labours, people arriving for outpatients' appointments, relatives of those about to be admitted – all ended up in this shop seeking attention. And there was, both officers knew, very little chance that the two rather harassed-looking women behind the counter would ever recognise any of them again if they met them in the street twenty-four hours later.

"Let's try the staff canteen," Murphy suggested. "We might have more luck there."

This time his hopes appeared much better founded. Having followed the directions of two porters – and got lost both times – they were eventually led by a third to a large barn of a room which served as the staff canteen. Not surprisingly, considering the time of day, it was completely empty save for a bald-headed, middle-aged man at a corner table contentedly engrossed in a large mug of something, a Danish pastry and a copy of a tabloid newspaper. He looked up as Murphy and Power entered.

"At a guess," he said, "I'd say you could be officers of the law."

He spoke in a quiet voice but in a very precise tone. He was, Murphy was tempted to believe, the product of some minor private school although, as he acknowledged to himself, this could be a complete illusion.

"Absolutely right, sir. Inspector Murphy and this is Garda Power." They both produced their warrant cards. "And you are?"

"Hugh Mellor," was the reply. The identification cards were totally ignored. "General Manager of this canteen and, as you can see, for the moment at least, its sole occupant. How can I help you?"

They sat opposite him at the table and, as they did so, Mags noticed that the paper was open at the puzzles page but whether that was simply because, when they'd arrived, he had been skimming through the paper or whether he had any particular interest in that page there was no way of knowing, especially since the first thing he did when they sat down was close the paper and move it, his mug and the plate to one side.

"You probably know," Murphy nodded towards the now-folded paper, "that two women have been found murdered in the city in the past few days. Both, it transpires, worked here. So we're questioning various likely people to see if they knew either of the two and can tell us anything about them. The staff canteen seems a likely spot for Maureen Connolly, the second victim, but I don't know whether it's open to night workers like Mrs Corcoran, the first victim."

"No, is the answer to your second point. The canteen closes at nine so although we might see one or two of the night staff when they first come in and before they go on duty that doesn't happen very often. And since we don't open again till eight-thirty in the morning we don't see them then either. However, in answer to your first point yes, I actually knew both women."

"You seem very definite about that, Sir," said Murphy. "How can you be so sure? This hospital must employ – how many people? Over two hundred at least. Surely you don't know every single one."

"I'd like to contradict you," Mellor replied, "but, sadly, you're absolutely right. And the only reason I know those two – or at least why I know who they were – is because of the way they behaved."

He regarded the two officers' faces with some amusement. Already they were wondering just what to make of this rather eccentric character. His appearance – rather rotund figure and slightly protruding brown eyes, together with the totally bald head – gave him the look of a cartoon character. In fact he reminded Chris Murphy very much of Elmer Fudd, a character in one of his daughter Maeve's favourite cartoon shows. Now, Inspector Murphy had the feeling that Mr Mellor was, in some indefinable way, poking fun at them. It was not a comfortable feeling.

Margaret Power sensed the inspector's mood and, fearing that he might become angered and thus alienate this rather awkward man, decided to speak up.

"In what way, Mr Mellor?" she asked.

Hugh Mellor gave her a strange look.

"Tell me again," he said. "Which of you is the inspector?"

"I am," Murphy confirmed, "but my colleague's question is a very pertinent one. In what way did the behaviour of Mrs Corcoran and Miss Connolly make them so memorable to you?"

Again Mellor regarded the younger officer for a moment, his unblinking gaze making her feel increasingly uncomfortable. Then he directed his full attention back to Chris Murphy.

"There are," he began, somewhat ponderously, "some people – including many of this hospital's employees – who are memorable simply because they are nice people. That's a description I hate but it sums up people who have good manners, are thoughtful, don't try to pull the wool over your eyes, don't look down on you. You must know the kind of people I mean."

Murphy nodded. He'd realised that Hugh Mellor was one of those people who chose only to speak to the senior officer. Margaret Power was reduced to the role of observer. He knew it was a role she'd readily accepted and one she'd play well.

"Then," went on Mellor, "there are those who are memorable for exactly the opposite reason. The pompous oafs who think they are doing the world a favour simply by being here. Sadly we have quite a few of those, too."

"And which group did Mrs Corcoran and Miss Connolly belong to?"

"Well, now, that's where it gets interesting. Take the younger woman, Connolly they say her name was though I get to know surprisingly few names here. She was usually one of the nicer people. Had a lovely smile. She was quite a good looker, too. And she knew how to behave. At least that's what I'd thought."

"So what changed your mind?"

"It's a strange thing, Inspector, but you'd think that working in a place like this people would get to know you and, more importantly, to recognise you."

Murphy was about to interrupt, certain the man was beginning to wander away from the question, but before he could do so Mellor resumed speaking.

"It doesn't happen. They see you outside the familiar confines of this place," he looked around, "and they simply don't recognise you. That's what happened with Miss Connolly.

"I was in a supermarket out near Easthall, near where I live, some time ago – it must be at least three months, since it was before she stopped working here and someone told me that she left a few weeks back. Anyway, I was wandering up and down the aisles looking for various necessities – I live on my own you see so I have to do all my own shopping; although I'm well used to that – when I heard this dreadful uproar.

"Not for a long time do I remember so much shouting and I'm sure the only other place you'd hear the kind of language being used would be on some of these modern television programmes. I'm only human, I'm afraid, and curiosity got the better of me. I made my way to the source of this outburst and there was Miss Connolly – good-looking, nice Miss Connolly – giving out to some young fellow like an old fishwife. Eventually, of course, she was asked to leave. The interesting thing is that the lad went with her as if they'd been together all the time. Imagine being humiliated by someone in public like that and then going off with them. How embarrassing!"

He paused, his own anger at the memory appearing, for a moment, to get the better of him.

"And it's because of that that you remember Miss Connolly," Chris Murphy said.

"Absolutely. Just think. She couldn't even call him by his name. Just kept using all these terrible words instead. I couldn't look her in the face after that. I left one of the others here to deal with her whenever I could."

"And Bridget Corcoran? What about her? What made her stick in your memory?"

"Now that's what will make this all so interesting for you, Inspector. You must understand that, as I told you, normally we don't see the night staff workers in here. And even if they do come in – to get drinks or sandwiches from those machines over there – we're not here. But I remember Mrs Corcoran for exactly the same reason that I remember Miss Connolly."

"How's that?" demanded Murphy.

"The way she treated someone," was Hugh Mellor's firm reply. "You see, I was going home one evening - I'm sorry, I can't for the life of me remember when but it was quite some time ago. I know it was late spring because the clocks had gone forward so I didn't need a lamp on my bicycle. Anyway, I was adjusting my cycle clips and the same thing happened. Right there in the Accident and Emergency Unit. The ambulance men let me store my bicycle in their office there. There's plenty of room and it's far more convenient for me than trailing across to the other end of the car park. So, where was I?

"Ah yes. There were lots of people around – as there always is in that place – and there was Mrs Corcoran yelling and screaming like a banshee at some poor young chap, despite the fact that he was clearly in some sort of pain. Turns out, as someone told me later, it was her son, though you'd never have suspected it to hear the names she called him. He'd damaged his arm in a fall but to hear her you'd have thought he'd done it deliberately just to cause her bother.

"I don't know what you think, Inspector," he concluded, "but to my mind some women just aren't fit to be mothers. And Bridget Corcoran was one of those women."

Silence descended. Hugh Mellor had, it seemed, finished his speech and was now ready to step down from his particular soap box.

"I take it," Inspector Murphy said at last, having, for a little while, been lost for words, "that, apart from those two occasions, you didn't actually know much about either of these women."

157

"Certainly not!" Mellor answered. "As I said, there are some people who are really nice. A lot of them work here. But those two? Absolutely not."

****

"He didn't actually say that they got what they deserved," Margaret Power noted as the two detectives, having taken their leave of Mr Hugh Mellor, made their way back to Inspector Murphy's car, "but I got the distinct impression that's what he thought."

"Definitely," agreed Murphy. "And he wasn't very taken with you, either. Pushy young thing – that's what he saw you as. And," he laughed, "he's right, of course."

"Thank you, Sir." She laughed with him. "But don't you think there's more to him than meets the eye?"

"Very much so," replied the Inspector, "and I'm quite sure Chief Superintendent Pollock will be more than a little interested in what we have to report. This, I feel, has proved to be a very worthwhile exercise."

IX

Geoff Hughes didn't believe in coincidences so the fact that, only two days after entering the modern glass doors into St Saviour's school seeking information about one murdered woman's son, he was returning to ask about another murdered woman's brother was certainly cause for concern. Two dead women: two young men, both students of the same school. There must be a link somewhere.

He was still considering what he believed to be a highly relevant turn of events as he knocked on the wooden hatch-way labelled 'Enquiries'.

At first there was no response although there was certainly someone inside the general office. He could hear a voice and soon recognised this as one side of a telephone conversation. That explained the delay. He didn't mind waiting. He'd deliberately chosen to arrive early even though he didn't expect to meet up with Howard Morrissey until the school break-time. And that, he'd been informed when he'd phoned to arrange the visit, was not until eleven o'clock.

He looked around, thinking to himself that schools really didn't change much. They might have fancy entrance halls like this one, liberally decorated with modern paintings, photographs of past students and, in one long glass case, various cups and medals, witnesses to the school's sporting prowess. Or they could be like the Victorian monstrosity he'd attended, where the public office was situated just inside the heavy main door at the start of a long, gloomy corridor with neither painting nor photograph to relieve the monotony of the dull green walls.

"Boys," his school principal used to declare, "are here to learn not to waste time looking at pictures."

Still, in the end it made no real difference what the building looked like. All schools, or so Hughes believed, had the same smells, the same sounds, the same feeling so that, even blind-folded, you would always know you were in a school. The distant sound of a recorder group practising, not altogether successfully, and the nearer chanting of German verbs from the light treble voices of first year students, new to both the school and the subject, obviously provided the biggest clue but there was something more, some indefinable aura which ....

"Can I help you?"

He was roused from his reverie by the sound of a woman's voice and, looking round, he saw that the wooden hatch door was now open and a smiling, grey-haired woman was observing him rather curiously.

"Sorry," he said. "It's being here – always stirs some sort of memory. I suppose it does for most people, one way or another."

The woman laughed.

"You're not the first one to tell me that," she said, "and I'm quite sure you won't be the last. It's Sergeant Hughes isn't it." She smiled at his surprise. "I recognise you from your last visit."

"I'm a bit early, I'm afraid, but I was hoping I might get a chance to talk to Mr Collins – if he's not too busy – before I see Mr Morrissey. I know the principal is probably up to his eyes but if he could spare me a little of his time I would be grateful. It is important."

"It's about the Connolly girl isn't it," the secretary said. "I read about it in this morning's paper. What a terrible thing to happen! And poor young Mickey. To have something like this happen – after everything else that's happened to him in his young life. Some children seem to be born to sadness, don't they."

She stopped, aware that she was talking too much, the enormity of Mickey Connolly's tragic young life distracting her for a moment from her usual efficiency.

"If you'd like to wait over there," she now said, pointing to four easy chairs grouped around a low table to one side of the entrance hall, "I'll see if Mr Collins will be able to talk to you."

Geoff walked over to the chairs as directed but, before he could sit down, his attention was caught by the four photographs on the wall. They showed, according to the carefully printed legend underneath, photographs of the entire school – one taken for each of the past four years. He looked carefully at the oldest one. Was it possible that, if he looked closely enough and for long enough, he would find both Richard Corcoran in his final year and Mickey Connolly in his first year? Coincidence? No way.

"Sergeant Hughes." Mr Collins was standing at the open office door, welcoming him forward. "Do come in. My secretary tells me you'd like a few words. I'm afraid I can't spare you as much time as I'd like but I will try to help if I can."

Hughes followed the principal into the inner office and sat, as directed, in one of the easy chairs. Mr Collins took his seat behind the large desk that dominated the room.

"I presume this is to do with Mickey Connolly and his sister's untimely death. It's a terrible thing. You can't imagine how upset the whole school is by the news. Especially coming so soon after another student – or at least former student – suffered a similar tragic loss. Such an awful coincidence."

Hughes decided not to voice his opinion about coincidences. This was neither the time nor the place.

"What can you tell me about Mickey Connolly?" he asked instead.

Collins thought for a while, steepling his hands under his chin as he did so and causing Geoff Hughes to wonder why it was that so many people in authority chose that particular pose when considering their answers.

"He's a quiet lad. Not especially bright, I don't think, although Mr Morrissey, his English teacher, thinks he has great talent in that subject. I couldn't tell you exactly, not off the top of my head, but I don't think he did too badly in his Junior Certificate exams. However, I doubt if he's university or college material."

"Did he ever cause any bother in school? Get involved in bullying, anything like that?

Knowing that Sammy Ferguson was one of Connolly's friends and knowing the kind of troublemaker Ferguson was reported to be, Geoff believed this was quite possible. Collins' answer surprised him

"Goodness no! Nothing like that. In fact he was only ever brought before me once and that was for playing truant. As a matter of fact that was the only time I met his poor sister."

"How long ago was that?"

"Oh, that was not long after his mother's death. What with all the trouble he'd had at home – I assume you know about his mother's death?" Hughes nodded. "Well, young Mickey just didn't seem to recover. I think he'd lost interest in studying long before but now he began skipping school altogether.

"We found out, of course, called his sister in and that was the end of it. Mind you," Collins frowned at the memory, "the way she spoke to him that day I'm not surprised he didn't dare make the same mistake a second time."

"Tough on him was she?"

"Tough isn't the word for it. In fact I found the whole thing acutely embarrassing which is probably why I still remember it so clearly. Still, she was only young and having to rear him by herself cannot have been easy."

"Is there anything else you can tell me – either about Mickey or his sister?" Hughes asked, though not very hopefully.

"Not really. As I told you, I only met Miss Connolly the once and as for Mickey, apart from his lack of great ability – and he certainly can't help that – he's been a model student."

Geoff Hughes nodded. Then a final thought occurred to him.

"One other thing, sir. Do you know, by any chance, whether Mickey Connolly and Richard Corcoran knew each other? I know Corcoran was a few years ahead of Connolly but they might have shared a common interest – sport, debating, something like that."

"I'm afraid I don't know, although I think it's unlikely. As far as I can recall neither of them had any interest - or talent for that matter – in any sports and, to be honest, they never seemed to have any time for after-school activities. In fact ..." he paused for a moment as if to clarify a thought which had only just struck him "now I come to think of it that's something the two lads did have in common. According to their class tutors over the years they always seemed in a hurry to get away from here. It's strange. I can't think they hated school that much."

He sighed then, looking at his watch, got to his feet.

"I'm sorry, Sergeant, but I must leave you. I've a meeting with the Board of Management in a short while to discuss a couple of promotions before we interview the candidates. I understand you want to talk to Howard Morrissey. It so happens that he's one of the staff members in line for promotion so he'll be free after break; although, strictly between ourselves, I don't think the Board will keep him very long. His chances are not very good.

"Anyway," he moved quickly to the door as if suddenly aware that he might have said too much, "you are welcome to wait in here until he's free. It won't be too long before the bell goes for break-time. Meanwhile," he added, as he opened the door, "I'll get Helen to get you something to drink. Which would you prefer – tea or coffee?"

"Tea, please," replied Hughes absentmindedly, his thoughts still on the two young men whose lives had been dogged by tragedy. From what he'd learned both had suffered a far from happy home life and yet school, it appeared, had offered no consolation either.

The door opened again, this time to admit Helen, the secretary, carrying a tray on which Hughes saw a small tea-pot, milk and sugar and even, he was pleased to see, a plate bearing half a dozen biscuits. She placed the tray on Mr Collins' desk then, having checked that there was nothing more she could do and promising to send Mr Morrissey in to him when the bell rang, she left him to his musings.

****

It was less than ten minutes later before, outside, echoing along the three floors of the school, a shrill bell rang to be followed, almost immediately, by the raucous din of over one thousand boys and young men eager to enjoy fifteen minutes of freedom after their enforced confinement.

It was only moments later that the door opened and in walked Howard Morrissey. For some reason he immediately reminded Geoff Hughes of Robert Donat in *'Goodbye Mr Chips'*, a film he

162

had seen many years ago but one which he remembered with a certain nostalgia. Here before him, in grey trousers and a tweed jacket, was a similar mild-looking man of about fifty with thin, sandy-coloured hair, receding at the forehead, and pale blue eyes – a combination which made him appear almost colourless. His was an ordinary face made almost weak by a narrow, pinched mouth and what Hughes imagined, judging by the lines on his brow, was probably a permanent worried expression. He was quite short, barely five foot six; certainly shorter than many of his students. With memories of his own school days now very clear in his mind Geoff was quite sure that Mr Howard Morrissey didn't always have an easy time in the classroom.

"Sergeant Hughes." Morrissey's quiet voice seemed to confirm all Hughes' suspicions. Surely this man lacked the firm authority needed to deal with a roomful of teenage boys. "I believe you want to talk to me about poor young Mickey Connolly."

"That's right, sir," Geoff agreed. "I'm sorry to disturb your break-time. I understand that these interludes are very important for teachers. Gives them chance to catch up on bits and pieces and prepare for the next onslaught."

"Oh, don't worry about that," replied Mr Morrissey, settling himself into a chair opposite the officer. "As a matter of fact I have my own special routine and although this is a hiccup it certainly doesn't put me out that much."

He tapped his jacket pocket from which protruded a carefully folded newspaper. It was folded open, Hughes noticed with surprise and more than a little interest, at the puzzle page.

"Crosswords."

Geoff Hughes' mind made the link. He didn't realise he'd voiced the thought out loud.

"Yes," said Morrissey. "A little foible of mine. Call it a discipline if you like. I always try to start the daily crossword first thing, in the ten minutes or so before school starts. Although I never do more than six clues then. I do another six at break-time and then I aim to finish the whole thing during the lunch-hour. You might think it's a strange routine," he shrugged, a little shame-faced, "but I do find that both the discipline and the mental stimulus are a wonderful escape from the inevitable pressures here."

As if to emphasise the point their conversation was briefly interrupted by a group of teenage boys, all dressed in sports gear, who slouched past the window nudging, calling and blaggarding as only schoolboys can.

Mr Morrissey winced. Geoff Hughes grinned sympathetically.

"I see what you mean," he said. "So," getting down to business, "what can you tell me about Mickey Connolly?"

The next few minutes revealed a great sympathy towards the young man whose sister had just been murdered. It was clear that Howard Morrissey had a lot of interest in the boy, one which was certainly based on what his English teacher described as outstanding literary talent. However, Geoff Hughes couldn't help wondering if there was anything more to it than that.

When Howard Morrissey finally paused the detective took advantage of that pause to ask an obvious question.

"What about his sister? Did you know her at all? Did you ever meet her?"

"I only saw her once. I don't know if you'd even call it meeting her since she ignored me completely. In fact, she seemed to ignore everybody on that occasion. Everybody except Mickey, that is. And I imagine that he'd wished she'd ignored him too."

"How do you mean?"

"Mickey wasn't a happy child. That was obvious to anyone who took the trouble to notice," Morrissey explained. "I was his class tutor when he first came here and I did make the effort to try and get to know him. I even talked to his last primary school teacher to see what I could find out. Not that I found out much. Mickey, apparently, was a quiet lad who behaved. That doesn't tell you anything. Trouble is, Detective, there are a lot of Mickey Connollys in our schools; children who, for various reasons, don't want to draw attention to themselves. And, since classes are often large and teachers are under pressure, these kids are usually ignored. Mind you, I don't think Mickey particularly liked school. He'd probably tell you that himself.

"Anyway, to cut a long story short he began to play truant. We found out and Mr Collins called his sister in to see if we could find out where the problem lay. I'll tell you this, the day I saw her I knew where the problem lay.

"Later Mr Collins told us that she had been extremely pleasant and sympathetic until we – myself, the school counsellor and Mickey – were asked to join them. To use Mr Collins' own description, it was almost a Jekyll and Hyde transformation. The verbal abuse she gave the poor lad was nothing ordinary. And he just had to stand there and take it. The embarrassment for us was bad enough. I would think that for him it was almost unbearable. I've never met her again and I can't say I'm sorry."

"I understand that's the only time he was in trouble in school."

"Oh yes. He wasn't going to risk a repetition of that particular outrage. I can't say I blame him. He settled down, tried to do his best and that's when I discovered his flair for writing. Superb pieces of work. Wonderful stories, although with an edge of bitterness which, having seen his sister in action, I found quite easy to understand. That's when I began to encourage him. It's not often in this job that you come across real talent in your particular subject. I've been determined to help Mickey Connolly ever since I struck this particular genius."

"I understand you give him extra lessons. Is that why?" Hughes asked.

"Oh most definitely. He sailed through his Junior Certificate English – didn't do too badly in the other subjects, I don't think – but he's found the Leaving Certificate courses difficult. And, for some reason which I don't understand, he began to lose interest in his studies. That is until a few weeks ago when he came to me at the end of a lesson and asked if he could talk to me. You see, although I'm no longer his class tutor I'm still his English teacher and I've kept an interest in him. I think he must have been aware of that."

"So what did he want to talk about?"

"Well: he knew that he wasn't going to do brilliantly in his exams but he also knew that he'd have to do something about preparing for his future. So he wanted to know what advice and help I could give him. I suggested that he talk to Mrs Fitzgerald, the counsellor, but he seemed reluctant to do so. Sometimes boys find it hard to talk to a female counsellor. It's not an ideal situation in a boys' school, of course. Anyway, I suggested instead that maybe the people in Social Welfare could help him. I don't know much about these things but presumably they'd have a better idea than I would about the kind of help a boy like that might be entitled to. Courses, financial help, that sort of thing.

"However," he continued, "as far as I was concerned – and whatever about his other subjects – I told him he'd certainly do well in English, if he was prepared at this late stage to make the extra effort. And if he was willing to do that then I would certainly be happy to give him some extra tuition."

"His sister," Hughes pointed out. "She didn't object to this?"

"Oh she didn't know. At least, as I understand it she didn't know. Apparently she'd got some sort of evening job. I don't know what. Mickey never said and I didn't ask. Anyway, whenever she goes out – sorry, went out - he comes to my house and I give him all the help I can. And I must say, he's making great progress. I have high hopes for him in the exam."

"And when was the last time he had one of these lessons?"

"He was with me both yesterday evening and the evening before. He has quite a lot of work to do to catch up on the set texts so we're kept busy."

"That's all well and good, sir, but, if his sister didn't know, where did he get the money to pay for all these extra lessons?"

"You don't understand. I meant what I said. I give him these lessons. And I'm more than happy to do so. You see, Mickey Connolly has the potential to be great. And, you mark my words, now that he's free he will be."

There was little or nothing Geoff Hughes could think to say in response to such a strong outburst, although he couldn't help wondering about the true nature of Howard Morrissey's interest in Mickey Connolly. For the moment, however, he felt that he'd probably got as far as he was going to get with this particular interview. He looked at the clock above the door. It was ten past eleven."

"What time does break end?" he asked.

"Quarter past eleven," was the reply.

"Well, Mr Morrissey, thank you for your time and your help. I won't keep you any longer. You might just have a few moments for a couple of clues before the bell goes."

"Oh, don't worry about that," said Morrissey. "Mr Collins has arranged for me to be free next lesson. There are some promotions in the offing and, since I might be in line for one of them, I have to meet with the Board of Management. They should be here by now."

He stood. Hughes, also getting to his feet, hadn't the heart to tell him that – if what Mr Collins had implied was true – Howard Morrissey's hopes of promotion were doomed to failure.

The two men shook hands and Hughes was a little taken aback at the strength of the other man's grip. For such a seemingly weak and insignificant individual he had a very firm handshake. It was another small fact to be filed away for possible consideration later.

The last thing he saw as he watched the English teacher walk through the outer office was the newspaper being drawn from the jacket pocket and the mind being focussed on the crossword.

<u>X</u>

Sean Pollock was in a much more buoyant mood when he entered the incident room which, rather to his surprise, was empty. Clearly Hughes, Coady, Murphy and Power had not yet returned from their various missions but Noel Lawson's absence puzzled him. He knew that the young man was still battling with the various crossword clues so it was possible that he was carrying out some particular research in connection with them. It would be useful to get some sort of lead from the damned things, as Pollock well knew, but he wasn't holding his breath. Their killer, it appeared, clearly had no intention of making things too easy for them.

He crossed over to the white-board, picked up the red marker and, in bold print, added several words. '*Spiteful women, hospital, dole office, school*' and put question marks beside each. Then, as a final question, '*Who knew about both women*?' Stepping back he surveyed his handiwork and then, satisfied, withdrew to his own office. There was, he knew, plenty of work waiting for him there.

****

The meeting in the incident room, when it finally began, was an interesting one. Inspector Chris Murphy related, briefly, what they'd learned at the hospital and Geoff Hughes followed suit with his meeting with Howard Morrissey. Noel Lawson had meanwhile been searching various records to see if anything could be found which might link Bridget Corcoran and Maureen Connolly. Following his interview with Mickey Connolly Pollock was pretty sure this was a line of enquiry which was going to lead nowhere, but he appreciated Lawson's determination to leave no stone unturned.

The only other person with almost nothing to report was Phil Coady. The fact that Maureen Connolly had been lured to her death through a call on her mobile phone had troubled Pollock, not only because the caller had claimed to be a member of the gardaí but also because, according to the forensic team, no trace of the phone had been discovered at the murder site.

"There are," he'd told Phil Coady, "two possible explanations. Either those two lads found it and decided to keep it or, more likely, the killer took it away with him. Still, you'd better track down those lads and see what they have to say. You never know, we might get lucky."

They hadn't. Phil had tracked down the two boys who'd found Maureen Connolly's body and questioned them about any mobile phone they might have found at the crime scene. However, each was adamant he'd seen no trace of any such phone.

"They were such angels," he laughed as he made his report, "you'd swear they'd never done anything wrong in their lives. Of course they were telling the truth: of course they wouldn't have taken anything. And even though I suggested to them how much they'd be helping stop a further crime and maybe catch a murderer by telling the truth if they had taken it, they still stuck to their story. As far as they were concerned they certainly hadn't touched the body and they'd seen no mobile phone."

Pollock nodded. "I didn't think it was much of a lead," he said. "After all, I think we're dealing with someone who's far too clever to make such a simple slip as to leave a mobile phone behind. He'd know it could provide evidence against him.

"So," he stood up and looked round at the team, "what sort of man are we dealing with? And I can confidently suggest that, after a chat with Dr Mason yesterday evening, we are dealing with a man. I needn't go into details but as far as she's concerned – and she's the expert – all the signs point that way. As you can see, while you've all been busy I've not been idle."

He smiled as if to make light of his words but they all knew that, in a case like this one, no-one gave more than Chief Superintendent Pollock.

"It strikes me that we have three areas in common to these two women." He indicated the words on the board beside him as he spoke. "The hospital where they both worked and where, according to Inspector Murphy's report, at least one member of staff knew them – not directly through work but because of incidents involving unpleasant treatment of, in the Corcoran case, a son and, in Connolly's case, a brother.

"We then have the dole office where we know, from Noel's report the other day, that Bridget Corcoran was overheard having a major row with her son, Richard, and where, as Mickey Connolly himself told me this morning, he suffered a huge verbal attack from his sister. How likely is it that Mr.....What was his name, Noel?"

"Moroney, Sir."

"Yes. Thank you. That Mr. Moroney overheard both attacks? And then at the school, as Geoff has told us, Howard Morrissey was witness to the kind of behaviour from Maureen Connolly that her brother described to me earlier. Did Mr Morrissey ever have any dealings with Bridget Corcoran, I wonder. Given that he has been a teacher at St Saviour's for some years it is quite on the cards that he taught Richard Corcoran and so might well have met the mother. Indeed, he may well have witnessed the same kind of cruel attack on her son that he saw from Maureen Connolly.

"So, where am I going with all this?"

He pointed to the first two words: '*Spiteful women*'.

"I think," he declared, "that this is our motive. And I also think, although it may take some time to prove, that one of these three men" – he scribbled two names on the board – "What was the third fellow's name, Chris?"

"Mellor. Hugh Mellor."

Pollock added that name to the board before continuing. "It might sound completely off the wall but in my opinion one of these three may well be our killer."

He paused, waiting for the comments and protests that he was sure would follow such a dramatic statement. He didn't have long to wait. It was Inspector Murphy who raised the most obvious objection.

"But why?" he demanded. "Why would these three apparently respectable men with no connection at all to the two women suddenly start on a killing spree?"

"After all," put in Geoff Hughes, "even if they did witness some rather unpleasant behaviour from these two it hardly seems a reason to go out and kill them."

"Surely, if that was the case," protested Margaret Power, "there would be a whole host of random killings daily. Throughout the country."

"Starting with the politicians," added Phil Coady, bringing a smile to their faces.

"You may well be right," Pollock agreed. "However, I think whichever one it is could be trying to gain some weird kind of revenge for similar treatment he himself received from the various women in his life. Mind you, if I'm right, proving this certainly won't be easy."

He then perched on the edge of the desk and looked at his team, waiting for the discussion which he knew he'd just set in motion to continue. He considered this one of the best things about this particular group of detectives: they weren't afraid to argue both with him and with each other. And although there were times when different points of view could be a drawback and slow down an investigation, most of the time such debates were more than helpful.

It was Phil Coady who took up the challenge.

"I take it, Sir, you're no longer looking for a family link to the killer. You don't think it was either Corcoran or Connolly who, even if they couldn't have committed the murders themselves, might have arranged to get the killings done."

"In the first place," answered Pollock, "they both have alibis. We've checked them and they're valid. Secondly, it seems to me that, even if they did know each other in school – and I don't know if they did – how likely is it that these two young lads, probably already embarrassed by the treatment they were enduring, would seek to confide in each other? My understanding is that Connolly kept most of what went on to himself and what little Sammy Ferguson knew came from living nearby rather than from being told about it."

"Not that you'd dare tell Sammy Ferguson much," murmured Geoff Hughes. "He'd likely use it in some scam or other."

There was a ripple of laughter through the room. They'd all come across Sammy Ferguson or his type in the course of their work.

"So," Pollock caught their attention once more, "to answer Phil's point, I think we can rule out the family connection. And we can definitely rule out either a botched rape or a botched mugging. And, as we all know, random attacks by sociopathic or psychopathic serial killers are far less frequent than some of the more lurid film makers or writers would have everyone believe. No: I think it comes back to these three. So do we have any clue which might lead us to one in particular?"

At that moment Noel gave a cry of triumph.

"Got it!" he said. "I'm sure that's it."

They all looked at him and he turned red at being the centre of attention.

"Sorry," he apologised, "but I think I've finally cracked the last of these damn clues. And I'm almost certain they give us a message – one which may very well fit in with what the Chief Superintendent has just been saying."

"Come on, then," said Pollock eagerly. "Let's hear what you've got. But," he warned, "no long explanations, please. Just give us the answers and the message you think it holds."

Noel spoke slowly, mindful of the Chief Superintendent's warning.

"I think," he began, "that the order in which he put those latest clues is important. I think that, although we got the ones from the victims first, the ones he left here are actually the start of the message. It definitely makes more sense that way."

"So what is this message?" Pollock was already getting impatient.

"Putting them together the answers to those clues should read *'child angrily thought thou shalt commit murder'*. I'll explain why later, if anyone wants," Noel couldn't resist adding; eager to show the clever brainwork which had not only created the clues but had also finally led him to the answers. "If we then add the other answers – *'mother first, sister too'* – we have what I think is a definite message."

"It looks quite possible," agreed Chris Murphy, "but who was the child and why did he come to that conclusion?"

"Spiteful women," said Mags Power. "That's why he's killed these women. As a child he had two spiteful women in his life – a mother like Richard Corcoran's and a sister like Mickey Connolly's."

"And when he witnessed another poor sod going through the same experience," Geoff Hughes took up the idea, "he felt compelled to do something. What we don't yet know is why he's only now decided to get his revenge – if that's what he's doing."

"There's something else, Sir," said Noel Lawson eagerly. "When I met Henry Moroney the other day he was busy doing a crossword puzzle. In fact, I had to help him complete it," he added rather sheepishly, "before he would answer any of my questions. He refused to have his concentration broken. Apparently the crossword was part of his daily routine and he wasn't going to break that routine – murder or no murder."

"And you think" - Pollock's interest was growing – "that someone as, shall we say, addicted to crosswords as he is would be quite capable of posing the kind of clues we've been given."

"I think it's highly likely," Noel agreed. "He has the right kind of mind to solve these complicated clues. And he told me that cryptic clues were his favourite so I'm sure he'd have no difficulty in using patterns he's come across before to devise clues like these."

"I'm sorry to burst your balloon," declared Hughes, "but there's one drawback to that."

"Go on." Sean Pollock already felt the beginnings of disappointment.

"Well, our friend Howard Morrissey is also a crossword addict. Same kind of discipline – although he spreads his puzzle solving over three sessions each day – and the same interest in the more complicated ones."

Even before Superintendent Pollock could reply to that Margaret Power piped up.

"You're not going to like this, Sir, but I'm afraid that when we sat down opposite Hugh Mellor I noticed that his paper was open at the puzzle page, although I didn't find out whether that was by chance or habit. Still, there's no reason to think that it couldn't be the latter."

Pollock managed a weary grin.

"So," he said, "are we agreed that we might have a possible motive and three quite likely suspects?"

They all nodded.

"In that case what we now have to do is start a detailed investigation into each man's background. We need to know their family history, especially how they were treated as young men. And we need to see if we can find something which separates one of them from the other two. It's just possible that, if our killer is one of these three and was abused in the same way, something in him has snapped and led him on this killing spree. If that's the case we need to find out if one of them has just suffered a recent blow of some kind – probably involving a woman - which might have pushed him over the edge. Our only trouble is ...."

Timing, Pollock thought afterwards, was everything. If ever a scene appeared stage-managed for dramatic effect it must surely have been this one. He hadn't had chance to finish speaking before Sergeant Harry Overton hurried into the room.

"Sorry, Sir," he announced, "but I thought you'd want to know. We've just received a report about a missing woman."

****

THE WIFE

I only met George Kadarijc on two occasions yet I felt I owed him a huge debt of gratitude. Like so many, especially from Eastern Europe, he'd decided to take a ride on the Celtic tiger in the hope of finding the leprechaun's pot of gold. And when that tiger had collapsed under the strain he'd chosen, like so many other so-called newcomers, that there was probably just as much wealth at home. The big thing for me was that, when he did go home, he took my sister with him as his wife. I've not seen nor heard from her since although this is not really surprising since she was already in her mid-teens when I was born.

My mother had died two years earlier and gone to plague other souls in torment for all eternity. So, at long last, I was free – or so I believed. I should have known better. I should have realised that the harridans from hell pick their targets well and rarely let you go once they've found you. It takes courage to destroy them and, at that time, although I didn't realise it immediately, I didn't have that kind of courage.

I'd never had a social life. Thanks to my mother and my sister my time had been caught up first in school, then in work and when I wasn't in either of those places I was almost literally confined to the house, restricted to doing only what they wanted.

Freedom was therefore a novelty for me and therein lay the seeds of future disaster.

I really didn't know how to socialise but, listening to colleagues, I soon learned that there were places in the city where a young man like me could go, meet people, make friends. I don't think I was looking for more than friendship, companionship, possibly with people who shared my interests, few though they were. Certainly the notion of finding any long-term female companion, let alone promising to share my life with her, never crossed my mind. With me it was truly a case of once bitten, twice shy when it came to living with women. Fate, to use the old cliché, had other plans.

I'm not sure that my colleagues really took me seriously. Let's be honest, I have no illusions about their opinion of me. As far as they were concerned I was a total recluse, completely naive and, quite possibly, the object of some ridicule – behind my back, at least. However, when it was suggested I join them to celebrate someone's engagement – I don't recall whose – I think I was so excited at the prospect of being out with people my own age, people having fun, that I really didn't want to look too closely at anyone's motives. In my innocence and my ignorance I certainly did not appreciate that nightclubs can be one of the many roads to hell. In my case that was almost literally true.

At first she only wanted a drink. Then she wanted to dance and later still she wanted to talk. How my ego blossomed under such attention! For the first time in my life here was a woman, my own age or perhaps slightly older, who was actually interested in me. More than that here was a woman who - unlike my mother and my sister for whom I was 'you idiot' when they were at their gentlest but by whom I was usually called far worse – was actually using my name. Little did I suspect that this was a situation which would not last long.

I'd heard of whirlwind romances but had never been too sure exactly what that meant. I soon found out. We saw each other every day for two months after which she decided we should get married. She organised everything giving me very little choice. She didn't want a big fuss; a small, local church suited her fine. She had no family living in Ireland – or none that I had ever met – but her parents and two of her brothers travelled over from Scotland and there were plenty of her friends who were perfectly willing to join us for the celebration. A fairly miserable honeymoon followed before we returned and moved immediately into my home and the door closed once more on my own personal prison cell. I'd escaped from my mother, escaped from my sister – and found a wife.

In the end it was exactly the same.

****

ZAC

I

Zechariah Enoch Muldoon could never understand his mother's choice of name nor, in his heart of hearts, could he forgive her for it. He asked her once why and she told him that, in her youth, she'd spent many hours studying the Bible – for reasons which she never explained – and that these were two of the names she'd found particularly appealing. As a result she had been determined that, if she were ever to be blessed with a son, these were the names she would give him.

When he was eight years old - and already suffering the misery of two such unfortunate names, especially in a class full of Seans and Marks and Andrews and ordinary names - curiosity got the better of him and he'd taken the large family Bible - a wedding present to his parents some twenty years before his birth – and found that Zechariah was one of the writers in the Old Testament. The discovery was of little help although, when he looked at some of the other names of the preceding books, he realised that things could have been worse. There was, as he'd already experienced, a dark, spiteful side to his mother's nature; a side which might easily have persuaded her to call him Habakkuk or Zephaniah.

Yes, things could have been worse although, even as he got older, he continued to lack the courage to tell her of the misery her unfortunate choice caused him. On such small things do lives revolve.

He managed, away from his mother at least, to get away with Zac. But, as every school child knows, there were certain times of utter torment when names had to be read out in full in front of the whole class. 'Zechariah Enoch Muldoon' was inevitably met with hoots of scornful laughter leaving the holder of that name to squirm in his seat in a valiant but vain effort to disappear completely from view. To his lasting shame and embarrassment he lacked the personality of Florence Matthew O'Hara who, on hearing his full name called out, would half rise from his seat and perform a formal bow of acknowledgement – to the delight of the others in the class. Zac simply couldn't do that: he lacked the necessary bravado. Florence was a hero, Zechariah a nobody.

Being a nobody meant that very few people wanted to mix with him. Other nobodies – and there were one or two in his class – tended to keep very much to themselves, frightened, as they had become, of committing themselves to any personal involvements which might ultimately lead to hurt and humiliation. It soon became a lonely life for Zac and one which left him vulnerable, as he was to discover.

He left school at eighteen with enough qualifications to go to college where life became easier and where he did make one or two friends. It was also where, for the first time in his life, he began to socialise with people of his own age. Sadly, all this came to an abrupt end when his mother fell ill towards the end of his third year. She was a widow already in her mid-sixties: his sister had left the country following her marriage leaving him as the only other member of the family. There was no question. He would return home to care for her: his studies would simply have to be shelved.

He managed to get a job in one of the offices of the local city corporation but it was, nonetheless, a depressing few months for him. The cancer which had attacked his mother refused to be defeated, in spite of vast quantities of chemicals which were pumped into her body, and in little over a year Zac found himself alone.

He could have returned to college to complete his four year course; there was no doubt that he had done well in his studies and his tutor had promised him that the college authorities would certainly be sympathetic in view of the tragic circumstances surrounding his abrupt departure. Yet, somehow, the life of a student no longer held any appeal for him. He felt that, during the months of his mother's illness, he'd aged quite a lot – or at least he'd matured – and now would have little or nothing in common with his fellow students. Instead he gave up all ideas of a professional career and settled into a lonely life which revolved almost entirely around his job and his home. There was nothing else.

Many of his colleagues seemed much younger than him, although this wasn't actually the case. In manner and lifestyle he appeared to have more in common with older employees than with the youngsters so it came as both a surprise and a bit of a shock when he was invited to join them in celebrating the engagement of one of the girls from his office.

After some hesitation he decided to accept the invitation. After all, he could see no harm in it. Although a stranger to the nightclub circuit he was assured by the other young men in the office that it would be a great night out, a good laugh and even the opportunity to pull a few females and get laid. He could, he knew, welcome a bit of fun and the laughter and entertainment which might be involved but what the others didn't know was just how much the rest both appalled and terrified him. He couldn't tell them. He wouldn't tell them. He believed he'd left weak Zechariah behind. He was Zac; he was twenty-five; he'd go along with the others and hope that he could handle whatever the evening brought.

It brought, among other things, Siobhan – sharp-witted, sharp-featured and, as he was later to learn, sharp-tongued. She was small and slightly built with shoulder-length dark brown hair and light brown eyes flecked with gold. Her smile lit up her thin face and gave her slightly ordinary features a certain beauty. As the evening progressed she seemed, much to Zac's surprise, to show a growing interest in him, joining the table where his friends were now happily engrossed in their own female conquests and engaging him in conversation in which politeness if nothing else forced him to participate.

She didn't seem a bad sort and, certainly, she didn't appear in any way put out by his obvious awkwardness with women. In fact, at one stage, she told him quite bluntly: "I like that in a guy. It makes me feel so much safer."

For the first time in his life he'd had praise from a woman. He loved her for it and, his ego stroked, his heart swelling, he asked if he might see her again. She acted coy and he didn't notice the glint of triumph in her eye.

"I don't know about that," she said, smiling. "I tell you what though. Why don't you give me your mobile number and maybe I'll ring you in a day or two. When I've thought it over."

It was the best he could expect, he knew that, and was surprised to have even got that far. So his delight knew few bounds when, two evenings later, his mobile rang.

"Zac?" The voice at the other end sounded quite shy. "Is that you? It's Siobhan here. I was wondering - if you're still interested - whether we could meet this evening."

Happiness comes in many forms and, for Zechariah Enoch Muldoon, that was one of the happiest moments of his life so far.

They met regularly after that and if she dictated more and more what they should do, where they should go, who they should see, he probably never noticed and certainly didn't mind. No longer was he a nobody. He had a steady girlfriend. He was, as far as he was concerned, in love. To his delight his new girlfriend seemed to share his growing belief that they were meant to be together and before long he became convinced that she was as committed to the relationship as he was.

Siobhan had played the game very skilfully and picked her target well. She'd lied when she'd told him she was a year younger than him and, with her thin features and small, slim body, she was easily able to get away with taking more than ten years off her true age. She wasn't, as she had told him, twenty-four: she was, in fact, thirty-five and, to her mind at least, heading rapidly towards a place on the shelf. She had a very strong reason to want to avoid that at all costs.

Zac's joy knew no bounds when, one evening, Siobhan announced that they should get married. He never thought to question the fact that, contrary to tradition, it was she who did the proposing. Nor did he protest when she took over the entire organisation of the event. He was just so happy to have found his soul-mate, someone with whom, he was certain, he could live happily ever after.

II

Although Irish, Siobhan's parents had decided, many years earlier, to leave their native home choosing, instead, to move to the north of Scotland where first her father then later two of her five brothers found work on the North Sea oil rigs. Siobhan had hated it there and had moved back home, as she never ceased to call it, as soon as the opportunity arose. As far as she was concerned home was Ireland. As a result she was determined to celebrate her marriage in her homeland no matter how much it might inconvenience her family. Added to which, as she was quick to point out, all her friends lived nearby so it made perfect sense that she and Zac get married in her local church.

Zac had no say in the matter. In fact he had no say in any of the arrangements and, before he knew it, he was seated in the front pew of the small church – one he didn't know – surrounded, for the most part, by strangers to take part in an event which he was no longer sure he wanted.

He glanced round. A few – a very few – of his colleagues had agreed to attend but that was all. Not really surprising since, apart from the sister he'd not seen nor heard from for several years, he had no immediate family, very few friends and no-one particularly close. Still, one of them had agreed – although reluctantly, Zac sensed – to act as best man and for that he was very grateful.

179

Siobhan, on the other hand, had plenty of guests, crowded into the left-hand section of the church and making it even more obvious how few friends he had. Her parents looked both proud and, strangely, relieved to be attending their daughter's wedding while the two of her brothers who'd decided to attend looked, Zac thought, slightly sceptical about the whole thing. And, in the rows behind them, sat so many of her friends in a glorious peacock array of wedding finery and with a mixture of expressions which Zac could not fathom.

The organist began to play and, for the next hour, Zac moved, puppet-like, through a show in which he felt he had almost no role. It had only one real moment for him and that one he found truly unpleasant.

It came when the priest began the exchange of vows. Father Cullen was an elderly man, unused to and unhappy with many of the new ideas and a stickler for the old church traditions. He was insistent, therefore, on using the old – and to him proper – form of marriage liturgy. Zac had been totally indifferent to this until the awful moment came when he heard the priest intone the familiar words.

"Repeat after me. I, Zechariah Enoch Muldoon ...."

He cringed, sensing, real or imagined, the stifled laughter of the congregation. In his nervousness and embarrassment he stumbled, not only over that but over the remainder of his vows. He was very much aware of Siobhan's annoyance, a certain stiffening of her slim form as she stood beside him in an unusual yet elegant, tailored, white trouser suit. Her own responses were clipped and efficient, a sure sign of her growing irritation. She was clearly put out at his weakness and determined he should know it.

She'd organised a reception at a local GAA clubhouse. It was a lavish buffet affair – an eating arrangement which Zac had never found comfortable having failed, on the few occasions he'd attended such things, to find a way of coping with a plate in one hand, a glass in the other and still manage to eat. As a result he spent most of the reception standing there, hungry, longing for a drink and listening to shallow conversations with, for the most part, complete strangers. His colleagues – his so-called friends – soon abandoned him. Even the best man, after a brief and meaningless speech, had made an excuse and left. Siobhan had told Zac that he would have to make a speech but her orders were very precise.

"Keep it short. Just a few brief thank-yous. And absolutely no ridiculous jokes."

180

He'd certainly had no intention of making a long speech and definitely had no plans for comedy but he had still been ill-prepared. All he had managed was a few mumbled thanks to her parents, to the lovely bridesmaids and, of course, to his beautiful new wife. Even as he had spoken those words Zechariah Enoch Muldoon had begun to realise what an awful mistake he might have made.

The honeymoon, again arranged by Siobhan, had lasted a week, spent in the heat of southern Spain. They were booked into a large hotel full of package holiday-makers and honeymooners like themselves. It was mid-July; temperatures soared to reach the high thirties during the day making only a small drop at night. Any movement was uncomfortable although Siobhan seemed to have no difficulty spending hours stretched on a sun-lounger beside the hotel pool, drinking – to his eyes at least – endless glasses of sangria and chatting , laughing and, in some cases, flirting with anyone who took the time to talk to her. Zac, fair-skinned and freckled like so many red-heads, found the constant heat and blazing sun far too unpleasant to be able to join her. After the first unfortunate occasion when he'd sat with her beside the pool and - despite liberal quantities of high factor sun screen – had suffered the misery and discomfort of angry, red, sun-burned skin he'd been compelled to spend most of the time in any shaded area he could find or confined to their hotel room. This did not go down well. Apart from meals he'd spent his time, alone, on one of the hotel's sheltered terraces reading, dozing or just watching the world go by and musing on the dramatic way his life had changed. And not necessarily for the better.

They met as a newly-married couple for their meals which soon were being eaten in an almost unbroken silence interrupted only when one of her many new friends stopped at their table for a chat. If they thought the continuing silence between Mr and Mrs Muldoon was odd they were too polite to refer to it.

Strangely enough the one part of the whole honeymoon he'd really dreaded became the easiest of all. He'd not realised, certainly not until it was too late, that Siobhan had probably married him for one reason only: to be married. She had no other interest in him; definitely nothing of a sexual nature. That became apparent when, on checking in, he discovered that she'd booked a twin bedded room for them in the hotel. She made no demands and he certainly made no advances. This was, it was becoming increasingly clear, just a marriage of convenience.

On the last night of the honeymoon he lay awake long after the steady, rhythmic breathing from the other bed told him she was asleep. He couldn't sleep, his mind too busy contemplating the future. He had a home, he had a wife and he had a job. He was luckier than many, he knew that, yet still he worried.

****

The house was his, left to him, as the only son, following his parents' deaths. His wife was a complete mystery to him but he knew that marriage was something which took quite a while to understand. As for his job, he was happy with it: it was a permanent position – something very important in the current economic climate – and certainly wasn't arduous in any way. Yet somehow he doubted whether it would be good enough for Siobhan. She had a very good job herself in the offices of an investment company in the city, so they certainly weren't going to be short of money, but he sensed that she might not be satisfied with that. He was twenty-six and, if he were honest, he had no great ambition. Siobhan, he felt certain, would have enough for both of them.

He was right. They hadn't been home many weeks before she launched her initial attack.

"Is that the best you can do?" she'd demanded one evening over dinner.

At first he'd thought she was talking about the meal he'd prepared for it had been tacitly agreed that he would do all the cooking.

"How can I face my friends," she'd continued before he had chance to reply, "when they ask me what my husband does? How will I feel when I have to tell them that you're just an office boy?"

"At least it's a job," he'd pointed out, resignation strong in his tone.

"And that's your excuse is it? I don't know how you can call it a job. It's the sort of thing school-leavers do if they've no qualifications or old men nearing retirement with nothing else to hope for. But then, that just about sums you up doesn't it. No ambition. No drive. And certainly no sense of how I might feel."

Strangely enough, she hadn't tried using the same excuse when she left more and more of the household chores to him. She seemed to have simply assumed that he would do them and, if he were honest, he didn't dare argue. Ever since she'd moved into the house with him he'd been the housekeeper and he didn't think he'd done a bad

182

job. They were sitting in the kitchen, a bright, airy room which, as anyone could see, was spotless. All the surfaces were clean with everything in its place, the floor tiles were sparkling, there wasn't a speck of dust anywhere, not a crumb nor any sign that anyone ever used the room let alone that he'd prepared a tasty meal there for them less than two hours ago.

He did the housework, she complained; he did the cooking, she complained; he did the shopping, she complained. He did the washing, that wasn't right. He did the gardening, wrong again.

He didn't change his job but over the next few years he discovered that complaining and criticising was to become the pattern for their life together. Indeed the longer he was with her the more he began to wonder just why she had ever bothered to marry him or, for that matter, why she stayed. Even more to the point he soon began to wonder why he stayed with her although that was a much easier question to answer. This was his home and although he hadn't been born there he'd spent almost his entire life in it. It hadn't always been an easy life, of course, not for an only son of older parents. Yet it did have one or two very happy memories. It was part of his world and he had no intention of giving it up.

On the other hand he knew his own limitations and simply couldn't see himself either telling Siobhan to change her ways or ordering her to leave. He had never been a strong character; certainly he wasn't strong enough to deal with his very difficult wife.

He couldn't even persuade her to call him by his name. He might have loathed his mother's choice, it might have been the cause of much misery, especially during his teenage years, but at least it made him a person. Being referred to as 'you' at best and far worse names when Siobhan was in a really bad mood did much to undermine any self-confidence he might have been able to develop.

Sometimes he wondered if life would have been different had he been christened John or Liam but, in his heart, he doubted it. He had grown to understand that his was an inner weakness and his awkwardness and lack of personality had very little to do with his mother's strange choice when it came to naming her son. It was that weakness of character which made him sure that he could never tell Siobhan to leave; in the same way that he couldn't argue with her; in the same way that he simply put up with all her criticisms and name-calling. As the old saying went: he'd made his bed and he'd just have to lie in it.

All of this soul-searching might have given him some answers but it still left one very important one. He knew why he refused to leave and he understood that he lacked the emotional strength needed to ask Siobhan to leave. But why didn't she leave him? Even if only half of what she said to him were true then she couldn't possibly be happy with him. So why did she stay?

The answer – and there was one – so shocked him that, for a while, he really did not know what to do.

She'd invited a couple of friends round to visit one evening - her friends, of course; and, while he'd been expected to get the house tidy and prepare a light supper, he certainly wasn't invited to join them. Instead he was relegated to the study upstairs where at least he could watch television in peace.

He'd been there for about an hour, engrossed in a documentary about global warming, when he realised that if supper was to be served at precisely nine o'clock, as Siobhan had demanded, then he should go down immediately and turn on the oven ready to heat the sausage rolls and vol-au-vents. As he reached the foot of the stairs he noticed that the door to the sitting room was slightly ajar, making it easy to overhear the conversation. He wouldn't have stopped; he wouldn't have dared to eavesdrop had it not been that, at that precise moment, one of Siobhan's friends asked the very question he'd been asking himself for several years.

"Why do you stay with him if he's so dreadful?"

Wild horses couldn't have dragged him away after that and he just prayed that no-one would try to leave the room until he'd heard the answer.

Siobhan gave a sly laugh, a horrible sound and one which he could only remember hearing once before. That had been on their wedding day when he'd overheard one of her brothers say to her that he'd never have believed any man would be foolish enough to take her on. She had made no reply, simply given that same laugh. At the time he'd believed her brother's comment to be just another of the typical tongue-in-cheek remarks people made at weddings while her strange laughter he had put down to typical 'wedding nerves'. Although she'd not laughed like that again until now he'd long since discovered what a misunderstanding that had been.

"It's simple," she now told her unseen guests. "I was brought up - the only girl with five older brothers – by a mother who was, in all respects, a traditional Irish mammy. Nothing was too good for her sons and they had to be waited on hand, foot and finger. And that, in her view, was pretty much the only role for a woman.

"So, when I came along, there was never any question about it. I would at first assist and later take over that particular role. And my brothers revelled in it. I became, for them, a non-person – or near enough. Someone they could order about; someone they could expect to do all their chores for them. And when I tried to rebel I was disciplined – verbally by my mother, physically by my father."

There were muted gasps of horror at this revelation and Zac had to restrain himself from any audible exclamation.

"So," his wife continued, "by the time I was fifteen, sixteen, I knew exactly what I was going to do when I left home. Sooner or later I would find the ideal man. Not the perfect Greek god type with lots of money and a wonderfully romantic nature. No my ideal man is exactly the one I married."

He smiled at that until he heard her next words.

"I married somebody that I could treat in exactly the way I'd been treated for the first eighteen years of my life. Revenge, they say, is a dish best served cold and I'm enjoying every single mouthful of it."

Zac wished he could see the expressions on her friends' faces. Surely they must be as appalled as he was at this callous explanation. It appeared not, for the room was suddenly filled with girlish laughter and a voice said:

"Well fair play to you. You've really got it made."

Sad, hurt and sickened he moved on into the kitchen. He didn't want to hear any more. He now had his answer. He was too weak to leave her and she was far too strong to want to go. It was, in many respects, a tragic state of affairs and one which, surely, could only get worse.

****

Strangely enough, for a while, knowing what he now did, Zac found it easier to put up with the snide remarks and bullying comments. They had become a part of his life; not a very pleasant part, admittedly, but one which he found he was increasingly able to turn off in his mind.

Of course there were times when this was more difficult: usually when they were in public. He could endure her scorn and abuse at home but in front of an audience it always took him back to those humiliating schooldays when the teacher, with the hint of a grin, would call out 'Zechariah Enoch Muldoon' and Zac – head bowed, face bright red – had to stand up in front of thirty or more grinning and laughing teenage boys and admit that this was indeed his name. Remembering how he'd felt all those years ago he began increasingly to avoid situations when he might be in public with his wife. Although it wasn't always possible it was self-preservation in a big way.

One of his worst humiliations had happened quite recently when there was a phone call to his work-place telling him that Siobhan had had an accident and had been admitted to hospital. He'd been genuinely concerned and, having explained the situation to his supervisor and arranged to get off work, he'd hurried to the sprawling hospital building, stopping only to buy some flowers and to enquire in which ward he would find his poor, injured wife.

He'd first thought how fortunate it was that he'd received the news in time to get there during the official visiting time: it wasn't long before he was to regret that fact. As soon as he walked into the ward Siobhan spotted him and her spite, fuelled now by the pain from her injury – a broken leg caused when she fell down the stairs at work – erupted immediately.

"You're late," she shouted at him causing several patients and their visitors to cease their conversations and turn to stare at him. "And what do you call those?"

She pointed at the bunch of white roses he was clutching tightly. Even he had seen the possible irony if he'd chosen red roses. There was no chance to explain: the tirade continued.

"Why on earth did you buy roses? You know how I hate them. Put them down somewhere or give them to someone else. I don't want them."

He placed them carefully on the nearest bedside locker but that was a mistake.

"Not there, you idiot. That's not mine."

He cringed as he moved the offending flowers to a table and then sat in the one of the chairs beside her bed. For a few precious moments she remained quiet and the other people in the ward resumed their individual conversations, believing the show to be over. They were wrong.

For over fifteen minutes she abused him, making no effort to lower her voice or control her choice of words, until at last – and to Zac's great relief – a nurse arrived and suggested that it might be better if he left as he was clearly upsetting not only his wife but the other patients in the ward as well. Glad of the excuse he wished her a hurried goodbye and left, trying hard neither to run nor, more embarrassingly, to cry like a little boy. As he made his way back to his car he was convinced that he'd never hated her as much as he did then.

****

He always kept hoping that things might improve but they never did. Even when they were at home it wasn't always possible to keep her abusive nature private. Even in their own garden she became so worked up at what she saw as his failure to keep the lawn tidy and weed-free that windows began opening in neighbouring houses as people tried to identify the source of such alarming shrieks.

He sought escape in his work in spite of the fact that she frequently complained at what she saw as his failure to achieve any position of importance. Naturally he took great pains to avoid any situation in which his colleagues might witness his utterly abject acceptance of her abuse and although this saved him a great deal of embarrassment it also prevented him from attending those social functions where promotions could often be won or lost. Far preferable to him were her scathing attacks in the privacy of their own home than in front of any audience.

IV

Unlike Zac, Siobhan was doing very well at work and held quite a senior position. She loved both the work and the occasional perks which came with the job. One of these was the fairly frequent dinners arranged by the manager whenever the company had to entertain visitors. She was usually invited to attend these dinners and had, as a result, eaten in some of the city's finest restaurants and hotels.

187

A visit from some of the staff from their sister company in Birmingham was always entertaining. She'd got to know many of the staff there and nights out with them were always good fun. So, when Paul Roche, her boss, informed her, one morning in late October, that five of the Birmingham team were arriving unexpectedly that afternoon and he was planning to take them to dinner at the Carlsworth Hotel she was delighted to accept his suggestion that she join them. She was well aware that Roche had more than a passing interest in her and though she had no intention of damaging her marriage – or his – she'd often contemplated a mild flirtation with him. There had been several discreet affairs since she'd married Zac Muldoon but she had always followed two very strict rules. She drew the line at any involvement with a colleague and she always made sure that Zac never found out about any of them. She was having far too much fun at his expense to ever risk losing him.

She'd been allowed to finish work early and had made arrangements to go to the hairdresser, the only drawback being that her car was in the garage having a faulty clutch repaired. A quick phone call told her that, unfortunately, the vehicle would not be ready until at least six o'clock so, to her great annoyance, she had to turn to Zac for help.

"Collect me at four o'clock," she ordered when he answered the phone. "I'll be at the hairdressers' in Tower House. Don't be late."

She hung up giving Zac no time to question or object to her instructions. Instead he had to invent a very painful toothache in order to convince his boss that he'd have to leave work early.

He arrived at the Tower House Shopping Mall near the city centre in plenty of time to park the car in the basement of the underground car-park and make his way up to the second floor and Hair Flair, the hairdressers' Siobhan always claimed was the best in the city. He thought he'd timed things to perfection. Not so. When he reached the door she was already waiting, wearing her coat and a very irate expression.

"I don't ask much," she began loudly, "but I'd have thought even a disaster like you could manage to get here on time. Couldn't you even get that right?"

She made no attempt to lower her voice, forcing the stylists to turn away in awkward embarrassment. This had no effect. Neither did his mumbled apology.

"I'm sorry," he said as they walked towards the lift. "My watch must be wrong. I thought it was four o'clock."

"Well you were wrong, weren't you," she snapped. "Why don't you ever check things? Or is that too much to ask? You're so bloody incompetent. Talk about a complete waste of space."

She continued in this vein, with no modification of either tone, volume or language, as the lift made its way – painfully slowly as far as Zac was concerned – to the basement. Only as the doors slid open and Siobhan strode majestically out did he become fully aware of the other two occupants of the lift.

Both were male and both were staring at him with that combination of embarrassment and disgust that he'd become so used to over the years. That was bad enough but this time there was an extra - awful - familiarity about one of the men. It was the area manager from his office. The other man, too, looked vaguely familiar and there was something about the man's cynical grin that reminded him of someone from his past. He couldn't for the life of him think who.

He didn't dare speak, not even to acknowledge either man's presence. He chose instead to hurry - head bowed, face burning - towards his wife who was now waiting with toe-tapping impatience to be let into the car.

****

Later that same evening he sat in the study enjoying a time of peace and quiet. Only then did he remember where he'd last seen that cynical grin. It had been on his wedding day, on the face of his best man when he'd said, with bitter humour,

"Zac, we wish you all the luck in the world. If Siobhan's outfit is anything to go by you're going to need it. Looks like she's already decided that she'll be wearing the trousers in your house."

He couldn't help seeing the irony in that particular memory since Siobhan had left some time earlier beautifully dressed in a deep pink trouser suit. With her dark hair – skilfully coloured and styled as always - framing her small face and giving her that certain elfin appearance, she still looked younger than her years and still very attractive. Watching her as she climbed into her car he was surprised by a sudden sense of pride. She was, after all, a woman any man might be proud to call his wife. In looks at least.

He didn't know for sure where she was going; only that it was an important dinner for some of the people from work. She never bothered to give him any details whenever she went out so, as usual, there had been no mention of what time he could expect her home. One thing was certain though. He knew, without being told, that it would not be in his interests to go to bed until she was safely home – no matter how late that might be. He settled down to watch television.

****

He'd been dozing. The film he'd been watching on television had been disappointing, far less exciting than he'd hoped and, he realised, he must have nodded off. He looked at his watch. It was two-twenty. He knew that must be right since, following the outburst at the hairdressers' earlier, he'd made a point of checking his watch both with the clock in the car and the electric clock in the kitchen. Two-twenty. That seemed very late for a dinner party, even an important business one. The first vague stirrings of concern moved slightly in his mind.

By three-thirty concern had turned to anxiety. She knew he'd wait up for her. That was one of her many unwritten rules. Even if - and, troubled though he was, he couldn't resist a small smile at this unlikely thought – she was being unfaithful to him she'd still make a point of coming home.

Five o'clock saw him pacing through the house, dogged by an ever-deepening fear. He didn't know what to do. He had no idea who to call. The dreadful fact hit him. He had no idea where his wife had been, where she now was nor who she was with. And if he followed his growing instinct and called the hospital or the police how could he explain that. Even in an alarming situation such as the one in which he now found himself his wife had still managed to make him appear foolish. Some things just never changed.

****

190

TEN DOWN, FIVE DOWN, THIRTEEN DOWN

I

The house on Church Road bore what Chief Superintendent Sean Pollock had always considered a most uninspiring name. St Jude's. He could never understand this need some people had to name everything in any case; but there certainly seemed, to his mind at least, something very odd about naming a house after a saint – especially the saint in charge of hopeless cases, the one you were supposed to turn to when all else failed.

'Still,' he thought, 'we're all different and I suppose that's not a bad thing.'

Two uniformed gardai were already at the house. He didn't recognise either of them.

"In here, Sir." It was a young guard who opened the door. "We've only just got here ourselves so we haven't really much information yet. Sergeant Overton radioed us to say you were on your way so we thought it best to wait till you got here."

It was clear that this young man felt quite uneasy in the presence of the Chief Superintendent, a fact which made Sean Pollock feel both old and a little nostalgic. He could still remember his own sense of inferiority when, many years ago, as a newly enlisted member of the force he'd been in a similar situation. Much as he'd always wanted a career in the gardai he'd never imagined that one day he'd be the one the new recruits were nervous of. Still, at least these two had had the sense to wait until his arrival before asking any questions. It saved a lot of unnecessary repetition and time-wasting. If this woman really were missing time was of the essence – especially in the current circumstances.

"This is Mr Zac Muldoon, Sir," said the second young guard. "It's his wife, Siobhan, who's missing."

The man perched on the edge of the large, chintz-covered settee looked wretched. He obviously hadn't slept all night and there were dark rings under his eyes, made even more pronounced by what Pollock thought was probably the natural pallor of his skin. His fear was very apparent and, Pollock thought grimly, quite possibly justified. If Mr Muldoon had read the papers or watched the local news on television his imagination would, in all probability, already be struggling with the awful fact that two women had already been murdered in the city following a late night out. The dread that his wife may have met the same fate would surely create a particularly agonising hell for the man; one which Sean Pollock hoped would soon be brought to a satisfactory end.

"Mr Muldoon. Chief Superintendent Sean Pollock." He introduced himself before taking a seat in the opposite chair. "I take it you've done all the usual things – checked the local hospitals, contacted Mrs Muldoon's friends. All that sort of thing."

Zac Muldoon nodded but said nothing.

"And you don't think she might have decided that it was too late to come home and chosen to stay with one of her friends instead?"

A negative shake of the head this time.

"Right. So I need you to tell me all you can about your wife's movements last night: where she went, who she was with. I need everything you can give me."

Mr Muldoon now looked, Pollock thought, extremely awkward.

"That's the trouble, Chief Superintendent," he finally admitted. "I don't know where she was. She told me she was going to an important dinner with some people from her work but I don't know whether it was in someone's home or in one of the city hotels. Although," he added, "I believe it's more likely that a business dinner would be in a hotel or a restaurant. Don't you think?"

Pollock nodded in agreement.

"And where does your wife work?"

"She works at Global Investment Company in Glenning Street," Muldoon informed him. "I phoned there as soon as I thought there'd be someone there. They just told me she hadn't arrived yet. I didn't know what to say to that. You see ...."

He paused, looking extremely uncomfortable. Sean Pollock said nothing, just waited.

"You've got to understand...," Zac Muldoon said eventually, then hesitated once more, struggling to find a way to explain the strange relationship he had with his wife.

He was still hoping with all his heart that this was all just a big misunderstanding and Siobhan would arrive home, safe and well, sometime during the day. At the same time, however, he dreaded to think what her reaction would be when she discovered what an unnecessary fuss he had made. He tried again to find a way of explaining the situation.

"My wife," he said at last, "tends to be a very private person. She keeps things to herself a lot and, to be honest, Chief Superintendent, she'd hate all this fuss. I just didn't know who I should speak to or how to explain to them that she hadn't come home. She'd be most upset if she thought I was talking about her behind her back, especially to her colleagues."

Warning bells began to sound in Sean Pollock's head. Just watching the man opposite him as he made his faltering explanation Pollock began to realise that here was yet another victim of a dominant female. In the light of what they'd begun to surmise about Bridget Corcoran and Maureen Connolly's killer this might not bode well for Mrs Muldoon. He knew he had to be extremely careful dealing with Mr Muldoon. The man was already verging on a state of panic: the detective didn't want to push him right over the edge.

"Perhaps, Sir," he said eventually, "if you called them just to find out where the dinner was last night. Maybe," he went on, seeing the growing unease of the man opposite, "you could just tell them that she left something behind – a scarf, a purse, something like that. You can just say that she's on her way in. and she asked you to collect it but you've forgotten which hotel. I don't think there'd be any problem with that, sir."

Zac Muldoon thought for a moment then nodded slowly and got to his feet.

"I'll do that straightaway," he said and hurried out of the room.

Sean Pollock took the opportunity provided by the other man's departure to study his surroundings. The room in which he found himself was at the front of this detached house and looked out onto a quiet road of other, similar properties. Each was separated from the road by a fairly large area of garden and given a good measure of privacy by a high, well-tended hedge.

The room itself was tastefully decorated, the walls papered in a textured cream paper on which was a random pattern of pale pink roses. The dark wooden floor was covered with a deep-pile rug, dusky green in colour and large enough to leave only a small border of wood showing. The three piece suite was covered with a bold chintz fabric and, apart from a glass-topped coffee table the room's only other furniture was a large, old-fashioned sideboard on which were arranged several framed photographs.

Chief Superintendent Pollock got to his feet and wandered over to study these photographs. Apart from what appeared to be a wedding photograph and one of an elderly couple – Mr Muldoon's parents he guessed, seeing a definite family resemblance – they were all of the same person. Pride of place was given to a large studio portrait of an attractive, dark-haired woman - Siobhan Muldoon he assumed. There was no denying her good looks caught, as they'd been, by the skill of the photographer, yet something about her eyes made Pollock wonder what kind of person she really was. There was, he thought, a certain cunning glint in them which she'd failed to disguise, even for the camera. Or maybe that was just his imagination.

"The Carlsworth," Zac Muldoon said, as he came quickly back into the room. "The dinner was at the Carlsworth."

Pollock turned and smiled, hiding, he hoped, the dismay which that name had caused him. Maureen Connolly had been dining at the Carlsworth the night she was murdered. He hoped this really was just a coincidence: he was, however, not so sure.

"Well, sir," he said brightly, "I'll tell you what I'll do. I'll call over to the Carlsworth now and see what they can tell me about your wife's movements. It'll be better," he went on, sensing that Mr Muldoon was about to insist on accompanying him, "if you wait here. In case Mrs Muldoon phones or comes back."

Zac nodded. That, he realised, made sense although he wasn't sure he could cope with much more waiting. Still, the Chief Superintendent was right. It would be best if he stayed where he was. Just in case.

"A couple more things, sir, before I leave. How did your wife get to the hotel? Was she collected? Did she drive there herself?"

"She took her car. It had been in the garage earlier getting the clutch fixed but Paddy Johnson, the mechanic, brought it back for her at about six yesterday evening. He's very helpful that way."

"I see. And what was she wearing when she went out? I've looked at the photos over there," he nodded towards the sideboard, "but I'll probably need to give a fuller description to the hotel staff. Especially if they were busy last night."

Pollock hoped he sounded both plausible and reassuring. Until his growing fears were proved other than groundless he owed that to this very unhappy man.

"A trouser suit," Muldoon replied after a moment or two's thought. "Pink. Dark pink."

"Did she have a coat? It gets quite cold these nights."

Mr Muldoon shook his head. "She wasn't wearing one but I know she always keeps a warm jacket in the car. Black, I think. Or maybe very dark blue."

"Right, Sir," said Pollock, with as much optimism in his voice as he could muster. "I'm sure we can get this sorted out very quickly. We'll have your wife back here in no time. I hope," he added under his breath.

'But,' he thought to himself as he climbed back into his car, "I'm not happy with this. Not happy at all."

II

Sean Pollock never actually reached the Carlsworth Hotel. Within minutes of leaving St Jude's, Church Road, a message came through on his car phone. A woman's body had been discovered by a security man in the new, and so far unused, business park out on the Stewarton Road. There was more.

"Another of those envelopes arrived, Sean." Pollock recognised Chris Murphy's voice. "I took the liberty of opening it. It's another clue. Lawson's dealing with it now."

In the confines of his car where no-one could hear him Pollock cursed loudly and violently. There was no excuse for murder at any time but the game which this man was now playing was beneath contempt.

As he made his way towards the site of this latest killing his pity for the man he'd just left grew enormously. Zac Muldoon, he felt sure, had probably been as much a victim as Richard Corcoran and Mickey Connolly; perhaps even more-so since they had youth on their side and the chance – as both had proved – to leave the source of their misery and start a new life. Muldoon, Pollock felt certain, had possibly been trapped in a difficult marriage from which, his upbringing had taught him, there could be no escape.

****

The Stewarton Road Business Park had been planned as yet a further demonstration of the dynamic growth of the city during the years of unbridled prosperity. With developers receiving more money, almost, than they could use, in the form of bank loans, it seemed there would be no end to the colossal building boom which had swept the country. Unfortunately this had not proved the case and an economic crisis in the United States had rapidly cast its long shadows throughout much of the world. The Celtic Tiger had been doomed to a swift and painful death.

For the people behind the Stewarton Road complex the final blow had come when the major American medical research company which was going to be the anchor for the whole business park had decided to relocate in the far cheaper economic environment of eastern Europe. Other businesses had soon followed suit even before the various buildings which were to house them had been completed. The result, as Pollock now saw as he drove in through the ornate entrance, was a series of empty buildings and half-completed shells resembling not the glories of prosperity but a ghost town peopled by dead illusions. The only visitors to the business park now were the security men who patrolled the grounds regularly.

'And a cold-blooded killer,' thought Pollock grimly. 'But God only knows why Siobhan Muldoon would be here. How on earth was she tricked into coming here alone so late at night?'

Presumably they'd get an answer to that question sooner or later.

The presence of Inspector Chris Murphy's car and two garda vehicles, one of which he hoped would have brought the forensic team, guided him to where the body lay. One glance confirmed his fears. Less than fifteen minutes earlier Zac Muldoon had described – with a certain amount of pride, Pollock recalled – the elegant woman with her freshly styled hair, immaculate make-up and smart deep-pink trouser suit. Indeed, the detective had seen for himself in that large studio portrait the attractive woman whose cunning eyes were now glazed over in death.

"I take it," said Chris Murphy, reading the Chief Superintendent's expression, "that this is the missing woman."

Sean Pollock sighed.

"Yes," he said. "This is Siobhan Murphy."

****

196

Neither Sean Pollock nor Inspector Murphy stayed long at the murder site. There were, they knew, enough experts there, people who knew exactly what needed to be done.

However, Elizabeth Mason had arrived before they left and, even without being asked, the first thing she had done was to remove from the dead woman's hand yet another of the terrible clues. It lay on the table in front of Pollock now, alongside the latest envelope to have been left at the front desk an hour earlier. As before his name was clearly printed on the front but otherwise there was no clue as to its origins. He read the first set once again.

10 Down: Confused small father

5 Down: Football Union initially mixed with law and became terrible

15 Across: Spratt's was prone to cholesterol perhaps

The clues meant nothing to him but, hopefully, it wouldn't take Noel Lawson too long to work out the answer. The rest of the team had also looked at them but were, as yet, as bewildered as he was.

****

7 ACROSS, 15 ACROSS, 19 DOWN, 16 DOWN

I

Back in his office Sean Pollock picked up the envelope that had been left for him. As before his name was carefully typed on the front but otherwise there was no hint as to who might have delivered it. He knew there was no point in bothering to test it for finger prints nor was there any reason to go to the front desk and see if anyone had seen the person who had left it for him. He already knew the answer. He just wished he knew the answers to the mysterious clues it contained.

7 Across: Endless pulp mixed in fits with added E is nasty

15 Across: Females win twisted new Order of Merit initially

19 Down: Lincoln and us together do wrong

16 Down: Merry with the outlaw in green

In all his years as a member of the gardai he thought he'd witnessed all the peculiarities of human nature but this kind of taunting by the killer was something completely new to him. And, although he agreed with the others that the answers to the clues did indeed contain a message, he was no longer sure that it was going to be of much help in tracking down the killer. It seemed to him that they only gave information after the event. Certainly, even though Lawson had managed to solve the earlier ones, it had not saved poor Siobhan Muldoon.

The team had listened in shocked silence as he described his meeting with Zac Muldoon. He went on to explain his own theory – that this was, once again, the murder of someone the killer saw as a spiteful woman.

"That's it." Noel Lawson's shout was an automatic response and one for which he apologised immediately. "I'm sorry, Sir, but I wouldn't mind betting that's the answer to the clues left for you this morning. I've figured out three of them but I haven't worked out the first one. I still can't see how but I'd lay odds that the first word is '*spiteful*'."

"And what do you think the others are?" asked Pollock, pleased that at least one small part of the riddle might be explained.

"I'm pretty sure the second one is '*women*', the third is '*abuse*' and the last one almost has to be '*men*' as in Robin Hood and his merry men."

"If that's the case you're right in your theory," said Inspector Murphy. "What we now have is the message '*Spiteful women abuse men*' which is what we think was happening to Richard Corcoran and Mickey Connolly. And you tell us you got the same impression of Mr Muldoon."

Pollock nodded but he seemed a little distracted.

"I think we're on the right lines," he said "but I'm not sure things are going to be quite the same for Mr Muldoon as they might be for the other two. We will, of course, go through the usual motions. Obviously Mr Muldoon will have to come in and identify the body. I'll see to that. And I think I've got to be the one to tell him about his wife though God alone knows how he's going to take it."

"You don't think he'll be as relieved as the other two seemed to be," Hughes suggested.

They had all heard about Mickey Connolly's reaction on hearing of his sister's death while the fact that Richard Corcoran still hadn't returned from Scotland appeared to speak volumes about his response to his mother's death.

"I think it's different." Pollock was slow to answer. "I was thinking this earlier. I don't know how long they were married but it doesn't matter. Marriage is a very different relationship and although she quite possibly made his life misery there must have been something that kept him with her. If you think about it, the other two eventually had enough and left. We don't yet know if there was a similar public outburst for Mr Muldoon but what I can tell you is that there were absolutely no signs that he was thinking of leaving."

"In that case you don't think he's the killer?" Phil Coady asked.

"Definitely not," Pollock replied. "Mr Muldoon struck me as a very weak man and I don't for a moment think that he would have the strength – not physical but mental – to have murdered his wife. In some strange way and in spite of everything I actually think he loved her. And I think that, for a while, this is going to break his heart."

There was silence in the room for a moment or two. They all knew that this was a situation in which the Chief Superintendent had far more personal experience than any of them. He knew how it felt to lose a wife to a tragic death.

Sean Pollock roused himself and became business-like once more.

"So," he said, "this is what we're going to do. We're going to have to talk to our three suspects at some stage and find out if they knew Mrs Muldoon. And if they witnessed anything untoward between her and her husband.

"Before we do that, however, I want to start looking into their backgrounds. Mags, I want you to come with me when I go back to Muldoon. Two heads are better than one and you might pick up on things I may miss.

"Phil, Geoff, get out on Church Road. Canvass the neighbours. See what they can tell us about Muldoon. I think this is probably just going through the motions but nonetheless it has to be done. And you never know what you what you might turn up.

"Chris," he turned to the Inspector, "I'll get you to go to Global Investment Company. They're in Glenning Street. Speak to Mrs Muldoon's colleagues. We need to know what happened last night. And if they know nothing about her or saw nothing out of the ordinary get to the Carlsworth – that's where the dinner was apparently. See what they can tell us. I really don't like the fact that Maureen Connolly was lured to her death from the same hotel in very similar circumstances.

"Noel, I know you'll keep hammering away at those clues, although, to be honest, I think they're only telling us what has happened not what will happen. And I'm really beginning to think they have very little value. So what I also want you to do is start looking into the background of these three." He indicated the names on the board. "I want to know all we can about them – their family background, where they work, where they've lived, anything you can find that might point to one of them as our killer. And since you're the computer expert you'll know better than any of us where to look."

Lawson grinned at that comment. This was the kind of police work he really enjoyed. He was far happier dealing with technology than with the public and had been more than happy to discover, on joining the team, that this was as much an important part of detective work as hunting clues and interviewing suspects.

The meeting broke. They all knew what had to be done. The sooner they got started the closer they might get to their killer.

Zac Muldoon had been expecting the worst. Pollock had been right: he had read the papers, he had watched the local news and, no matter what explanations the Chief Superintendent had tried to give, Zac knew that Siobhan would not have stayed out all night.

He couldn't have said how he knew. After all, what better way to hurt him, especially in view of these murders? It might have appealed to the cruel side of her nature though he didn't believe this to be the case. He knew she was a spiteful woman, had known that almost since the day they married. And, having overheard that conversation with her friends, he knew why she was like that.

However, he also understood that hers was the kind of spite that liked to see the effect of her harsh words and cruel deeds. She would never be able to witness the terrible effect that staying out all night would have on him and so she wouldn't do it. He was quite sure he understood his wife enough to know that it simply wouldn't make sense. It was for that reason above all others that he was positive that something bad had happened to her, although this was something he just couldn't explain to the gardai.

In the end when Sean Pollock returned to give him the news it was almost a relief. At least now he knew.

He'd had time during the long, wakeful hours of the night to consider how he would feel if something had happened to her but theory and practice, as he now discovered, could be very different. He'd expected the news. He hadn't expected the agonising, heart-wrenching pain which shot through him. Since the early days he hadn't thought he loved his wife. Now, in some strange way, he knew that he'd actually loved her quite a lot. He couldn't stop the tears and, for once, there was no embarrassment. Siobhan had gone.

Pollock waited quietly, allowing grief to slowly give way to anger and the familiar need to know the details, however painful they might be.

"Was it the same as the other women?" Zac asked at last.

"I'm afraid it looks that way, sir. Obviously we can't say for sure yet, but there are some similar signs."

"And you think it's the same person."

"I think ...." Pollock hesitated, torn between the knowledge that, professionally, he mustn't say too much and the human side which felt that this man deserved at least part of the truth. "I think there's quite a strong possibility that it's the same person."

Muldoon's anguished look changed to one of anger.

"And you still haven't found him. You still don't know who it is," he accused.

"We are following several leads, sir," was all Pollock could say.

"It's not good enough," said Muldoon, with a force he'd never known he could possess. "If you'd done your job properly and caught the bastard my wife would be alive now. You must have had some clues. What about finger prints, DNA, police records?"

He was running out of steam as the violence of his misery subsided and the fire of anger died almost as swiftly as it had begun.

Sean Pollock watched and said nothing. He understood better than most – and certainly more than Mr Muldoon realised – how much despair and grief and frustration could fuel such an outburst. He'd felt the same when Claire had died, had turned on the doctors with similar rage, cursing them for their inability to find the magic potion which would have saved his wife. And just as he'd finally apologised so, too, did Muldoon.

"I'm sorry, Chief Superintendent. You're doing your best. And now, of course, I must help you all I can. That would be far better than shouting at you."

Margaret Power came into the room, a mug of tea in each hand. Not for the first time it struck Sean Pollock as remarkable how, in times of sorrow and stress, the cup of tea was always the first remedy. There was, he knew, something very comforting in the hot drink.

"I need you to tell me exactly what happened yesterday," he began, once he thought Muldoon had calmed down sufficiently. "Was there anything different about the day? Did you or your wife go anywhere different or meet anyone different? Anyone who could have found out where your wife was going to be and taken advantage of that knowledge?"

Zac Muldoon thought for a while.

"I don't think there was anything different," he said, "apart from the fact that Siobhan had this dinner last night. I did finish early. We

202

both did. Siobhan was going to get her hair done and, since her car was in the garage being fixed, she asked me to collect her."

"Which garage did she use?"

"Paddy Johnson. He's got a garage two streets away from here. We've always taken our cars to him."

Pollock was not surprised to note that Margaret Power was already discreetly taking notes. 'Good,' he thought.

"So what time did you collect her?"

"Four o'clock. Or a minute or two after."

"And the hairdressers' is?"

"It's in the Tower House Shopping Mall. I think it's called Hair Flair or something like that."

"And you didn't see anyone, anyone you knew?"

There was a pause as Zac Muldoon recalled the two men in the lift. Even the memory caused him to blush a little. Sean Pollock noticed this and realised that whatever Mr Muldoon had just remembered it was certainly enough for even the memory to make him feel awkward and embarrassed.

"Yes, Mr Muldoon?"

"Well, there was someone in the lift that I did recognise. But only when we were coming out. That's when I looked at one of the other people in the lift and realised who it was. The other man looked vaguely familiar but it was only much later that I realised who it was. We didn't speak to them and they didn't say anything to us, either of them."

"And who were these two people?" Pollock persisted despite the other man's obvious discomfort.

Zac Muldoon shifted uncomfortably in his seat.

"One of them," he admitted eventually "was Robert Grant. He's area manager at work. And, as I say, I thought I recognised the other man from somewhere but it's so long since I've seen him that it was only much later that I realised who it was."

"And who was it?"

"A fellow I knew many years ago. As a matter of fact he was best man at our wedding, although we lost touch after that. He went abroad for a while, if I remember rightly."

"And what's his name?"

"Mellor. Hugh Mellor."

Chief Superintendent Sean Pollock's face betrayed nothing. Nor, he was glad to note with grim satisfaction, did his colleague's..

"And you say," he went on, "that you didn't actually talk to either of these men."

Zac Muldoon was visibly uncomfortable for reasons which were not, as yet, clear. Pollock waited. He knew the wisdom of waiting and letting the man answer in his own time.

"Like I've said, Chief Superintendent," Muldoon muttered eventually, "I didn't really take much notice of them and it was only when Siobhan ..." a look of pain crossed his face as he said her name, "and I were leaving that I recognised the one and only much later that I figured out who the other was. In fact, if I think about it, it might not have been him at all. Just someone who looked a bit like him. After all, it's fifteen years since we got married and I haven't seen him since. So no, we didn't speak."

Sean Pollock knew he'd have to approach his next question very carefully. He didn't wish to cause any further heartache to an already very unhappy man but, at the same time, the question had to be asked. Hugh Mellor was one of the three men he was considering as a potential suspect. Obviously if his theory about the motive behind the murders were correct and if one of his suspects had witnessed any scene between Mr and Mrs Muldoon he needed to know.

"I hope you done mind my asking but was there anything about you or your wife that might have attracted their attention. You say, for example, that your wife had just come from the hairdresser so I imagine she was looking particularly attractive. Only," he went on hastily, "we may want to speak to them and it would be useful if I could give them something to jog their memory."

In spite of tears welling up at the memory of just how lovely his wife had looked, less than twenty-four hours ago, Zac was feeling increasingly embarrassed. There was a long pause before he finally decided how to answer Pollock's question.

"As a matter of fact, Superintendent," he began, cautiously, "I had unfortunately been delayed and so was a little late arriving to collect my wife. Naturally enough, since she had an important appointment and she really needed plenty of time to get ready, my wife was a little irate. It's just possible they might have been aware of that."

It troubled Pollock to see how carefully Zac Muldoon had chosen his words. If the stories they'd heard about Bridget Corcoran and Maureen Connolly were true – and there was no reason to doubt that – and if his theory about the motive for Siobhan Muldoon's murder were accurate – and he believed it was – then 'irate' was probably not the word to describe what Pollock felt sure would have been quite an angry scene in the lift. It was even possible that this scene had led Mellor to somehow pursue Siobhan Muldoon and finally kill her. However, as with so much about this case, thinking that was one thing; proving it would be a different matter altogether.

He felt they'd questioned Zac Muldoon long enough. What the poor man now needed was time to come to terms with his loss.

"I m afraid, sir" he said, getting to his feet, "I have to ask for a photograph of your wife. It will be useful as we make our enquiries."

Mr Muldoon winced but said nothing. Instead he got to his feet, walked over to the sideboard and picked up one of the smaller photographs. Slipping it out of its frame he handed it to Pollock

"Unfortunately, sir, I also have to ask you to make a formal identification of your wife. Not immediately if you don't feel up to it," Pollock was quick to add, "but perhaps you could meet me later this afternoon. In the meantime is there anyone Garda Power can contact, someone who could perhaps come and keep you company for a while."

Muldoon shook his head. "It's alright," he said quietly, "I'll be O.K. on my own. And yes, I'll come and see you at about four if that's alright. I just can't ...."

Grief overcame him once more and he buried his face in his hands. Pollock nodded to Mags . There was nothing more they could do for Zac Muldoon at the moment, nothing except find the man who had brought him such misery. Quietly they left the house.

****

"I don't know about you," Pollock said, settling himself behind the steering wheel of his car, "but, as I've probably said before, I'm not a great believer in coincidence and the fact that Hugh Mellor's name has cropped up twice and, more important, that he's one of our possible suspects makes me very wary."

Margaret Power agreed and added, "There is one other thing, Sir, that I didn't think of at the time but I'm wondering now if it might be relevant."

"What's that?"

"When Inspector Murphy and I spoke to him yesterday and I asked him a question he came back with a very smart answer, something about who was in charge or who was the Inspector. At the time I just thought it was the fact that he only wanted to deal with the most important officer. But now I'm wondering if there was more to it. Whether it was actually the fact that I was a woman questioning him that annoyed him."

"You could be onto something there," Pollock acknowledged. "We're definitely going to have another chat with him. But before we do, let's get back to the station, see what Noel's found out. And see what those damn fool clues mean."

III

Chicf Superintendent Sean Pollock didn't believe in coincidences. Neither did Geoff Hughes. And, like the his boss, he was in for a surprise.

Having been given the rather tedious task of questioning Siobhan Muldoon's neighbours and trying to get some picture of the dead woman's life and her relationship with her husband, Hughes and Coady had so far visited three houses with very little success. At the first two there was no reply while at the third the door was answered by a very young woman, seventeen or eighteen Coady guessed, whose use of the English language was so limited it very quickly became apparent that she would be no help to them at all.

"An au pair, I assume," said Hughes, as they moved on to the next house. "There must be money in this part of town still."

"I'm glad to see someone's still got some," muttered Phil. "The way things are going I soon won't be able to afford anything other than the basics."

"I'm sure you'll still find enough to take your various lady friends to all those fancy restaurants you like to frequent," laughed Geoff.

"You can talk. A little bird told me you were dining at Les Oliviers the other night. And that doesn't come cheap. And you were with a very beautiful young lady, so I'm told."

"That's the trouble with this place," his colleague muttered gloomily. "Or maybe it's the job. Whatever it is you can't do anything without someone seeing you and deciding they have to report it."

"Don't worry. I happen to be on very good terms with the head waiter there and he recognised you. He used to work at McCauley's and you and I have been there on more than one occasion. But what I find far more interesting," he grinned as he spoke, "is the company you're keeping. Is this a new romance you're hiding?"

To Geoff Hughes' immense relief they'd been moving during this increasingly unsettling conversation and the fact that they were now at the door of the next house in the street meant he could avoid the necessity of a reply. Hughes wasn't like Phil Coady, who seemed to take great delight in boasting about his many conquests. Geoff was, in fact, a very reserved person. What went on in his private life was nobody else's business and he was determined to keep it that way.

Unlike the Muldoon's the owner of this house appeared to have made few concessions to individuality. No imaginative garden, no fancy house name, just a well-kept lawn on either side of a gravel path and a small, brass number eight on a solid wooden door. There was no answer when Coady rang the bell but a couple of sharp raps on the simple door-knocker proved more successful.

"Alright, alright. I'm on my way," called a voice and the two officers then heard the rattle of a door safety chain.

The door opened to reveal a short, slight man in a fawn-coloured jumper and trousers that were only a shade darker. He had wispy, blond hair and almost opaque blue eyes. He was, Hughes thought, in his late forties or early fifties but was one of those people whose appearance was so nondescript that it was very difficult to decide exactly what age he was.

"Gentlemen," he said, when they'd shown him their warrant cards and introduced themselves, "do come in. How can I help you?

207

You're actually lucky to catch me in. Normally I'd be at work at this time but I was owed a couple of days off so I decided I'd treat myself to a bit of a break."

"We won't keep you long, sir, but we're making enquires about one of your neighbours."

"No problem. Come on in," he repeated, ushering them into a room at the rear of the house which appeared to serve as both sitting and dining room.

It was dominated by a large, flat-screen television; there was only one comfortable chair, near a flame-effect gas fire, but next to the dining table were two straight-backed kitchen chairs. Coady and Hughes each took one of these while their host settled back into the easy chair which, if the newspaper on the floor beside it was anything to go by, was where he'd been sitting previously.

"So," he now asked, "what exactly is it you want to know?"

"I'm afraid," began Hughes, "the body of one of your neighbours – Mrs Muldoon from St Jude's, four houses along – was discovered earlier this morning on the outskirts of the city. She appears to have met a violent death and, as is normal in these cases, we're making a few house to house enquiries in the hope that someone might have some information which might shed some light on why she died . Did you know her or her husband at all?"

"I wouldn't say I knew them," came the reply, "but I do know who you're talking about. I think he's always lived in that house. I've been in this house for nearly thirty years now and he was certainly there when I first moved in. His parents were still alive at that time and he was living with them. I always thought he was an only child although someone told me that there was, in fact, another child. A daughter. However, it seems she was quite a bit older. Married some foreigner and went off to live with him. Certainly I never saw any other young person at the house and the parents looked quite elderly so the son might have been born quite late in their lives. I daresay he inherited the house when they died and saw no point in moving, even when he got married."

"Did you talk to him or his wife much?" Phil Coady wanted to know.

"Oh no, no. I'm afraid they weren't the type of neighbours you would stop and chat to. In fact, to be honest, they weren't the type of neighbours you would really want anything to do with."

"What do you mean?" Coady demanded.

"Well, for a start, you rarely, rarely saw them together and when you did they seemed to be always arguing. Quite noisily too."

"As you say," Hughes agreed, "not the type of people who would encourage neighbourliness. Was that always the case or had they only started arguing recently?"

"Oh, I think they've always been like that. Don't get me wrong, though. I didn't see or hear them that often but it just struck me that, whenever I did, they didn't seem particularly affectionate towards each other. And I'm not the only one. Mrs McLoughlin next door to them has commented on it to me more than once. She should know, living where she does. And like me and several others she was shocked at the carry-on the other week."

"Why? What happened?"

"It must have been a Saturday or Sunday since there were a lot of people at home. Anyway, I was in the kitchen getting myself some lunch and I heard this awful noise outside. It seemed to be coming from the back of the houses. I tell you I thought some kind of accident had happened, or a robbery, something like that. There seemed to be so much screaming and shouting."

"So what did you do?" asked Hughes, automatically glancing through the window to his right.

He imagined the gardens of these houses would be quite large although this one, he suspected, was probably all lawn, if the front was anything to go by. He couldn't see much from where he was sitting apart from a fine mountain ash tree still clinging to the last few bright red berries. Plenty of berries meant a harsh winter: the memory of his grandmother's old saying came to mind, utterly irrelevant in the present circumstances

"Well obviously I thought I'd better take a look and see what was going on. I went outside and could see nothing but the noise continued and seemed to be coming from the direction of the Muldoon's house – or Mrs McLoughlin's. I couldn't really tell. Other people had heard it, of course, and windows were opening in various houses. Anyway, I must confess that, by now, my curiosity had got the better of me so I went up to look out through my bedroom window. See if I could discover what was happening."

"And what did you see?" Geoff Hughes asked, although he was beginning to suspect what the answer would be.

209

"The two of them – Mr and Mrs Muldoon – were in the garden. I think he must have just mown the lawn; the weather's been so mild that we still need to do that even though it's so late in the year. Certainly the lawn-mower was still there. Anyway, I don't think she was pleased with what he'd done. She was screaming at him like a fish-wife. I only caught a few words but, believe me, they definitely weren't the kind of thing a wife should call her husband. But the poor man, he must have been aware that there were people listening and yet he seemed helpless. He certainly made no attempt to stop her or to move away."

"And this was how long ago?" asked Hughes, aware that this was all now fitting into a very familiar pattern. Chief Superintendent Pollock was right. These deaths were definitely connected and the very public vicious abuse these women gave their men-folk was the key.

"I couldn't give you the exact date but I would say it was probably three weeks ago. Maybe four. Mrs McLoughlin might be able to tell you although she's away visiting her sister at present and I'm not too sure when she's due back."

He had little else to tell them and, after a few more questions to which he had no answers, the two detectives got to their feet.

"Thank you for your time," Hughes said as they made their way along the hall to the front door. "You've been most helpful, Mr ...?"

"Moroney. Henry Moroney."

IV

Glenning Street was a narrow side street about a hundred yards from the large pedestrianised precinct which dominated the city centre. The offices of the Global Investment Company, on the second floor of number seventeen, were situated towards the rear of the building and seemed to consist of one large room containing a series of individually partitioned areas each with its own desk, phone and computer. All but one was occupied by apparently very busy men and women of various ages. A further look round showed Inspector Murphy that his initial observation had been faulty. There were in fact two more rooms to the left of the entrance: according to the signs on them one was a general meeting room while the other was the private domain of Paul Roche, Manager. He knocked on this second door.

210

After a very brief wait the door opened to reveal a tall, dark-haired man in shirt sleeves in spite of the fact that neither the day nor the room was particularly warm. He was, Murphy guessed, in his mid-forties.

"Can I help you?" he asked, trying, the Inspector thought, to hide his impatience at being disturbed.

"I hope so, sir," Murphy replied. "Inspector Chris Murphy from the Serious Crimes Unit. I'm afraid I have some bad news."

Mr Roche looked startled. It was not hard to imagine the thoughts a bald statement like that from a police inspector would inspire, especially if, as was quite possible, the man had a wife and family. Chris Murphy cursed himself for this rare lack of tact.

"It's about one of your employees," he was quick to add. There was an instant look of relief on Paul Roche's face.

"I don't imagine that any of my employees can have got into trouble with the law?" It was a question not a statement.

"No, sir. I'm afraid it's nothing like that. It concerns Mrs Siobhan Muldoon."

"Oh, I'm afraid you're unlucky, Inspector. She's not here this morning, although it's most unlike her not to have phoned in if she's sick. She's rarely absent and never fails to let us know...." He stopped abruptly as if Murphy's earlier words had only just sunk in. "Bad news you say."

Chris sighed. "I'm afraid I have to tell you that Mrs Muldoon's body was discovered earlier this morning."

Not surprisingly, Paul Roche looked shocked by this and he sat down abruptly on the nearest chair, covering his face with his hands as he tried to take in the awful news.

"But how can that be?" he asked at last. "She was out with us last night at a business dinner. She was fine when we all left. I don't understand. How did she die?" Realisation suddenly dawned and, before Chris Murphy could speak, he answered his own question. "She wasn't another victim of this serial killer the papers are full of, was she?"

Inspector Murphy gave another sigh, of exasperation this time. The tabloid press was already spreading panic through the city with its lurid tales of a new 'Boston Strangler' stalking any woman out on her own late at night. Such media hype seldom made his job any easier.

"It looks as if she was murdered, sir," he told Roche, "and yes, it does appear similar to the other two killings.

"But this is dreadful," the man protested, his distress at the news finding strange comfort in an angry outburst. "Have you no clue, no idea who's doing this? No woman is safe at the moment and what are you doing about it?"

Such hostility towards the gardai for appearing unable to do their job correctly was familiar to Chris Murphy. People never seemed to realise that catching a killer was difficult enough, proving guilt was often even harder. And the gardai had to be sure of that proof before they could make an arrest.

"We have various leads we're following, sir," he said, very politely. "Maybe you could answer a few questions for me which might help us even more."

"Yes. Of course." Paul Roche seemed almost ashamed of his outburst and now was more than willing to perform his public duty. "What exactly do you want to know?"

"I understand that you dined at the Carlsworth Hotel yesterday evening. What time was that?"

"We met in the bar at seven thirty. Dinner was served at..." He thought for a moment. "I suppose it was eight fifteen when we all sat down."

"How many of you were at this dinner exactly?"

"Ten of us altogether. Five from this office – including Siobhan and myself – and the others from our sister office in Birmingham. The Birmingham lot were staying in the hotel overnight but planned to take an early flight home so they'll have left by now."

"And how did Mrs Muldoon seem?" Murphy's questions continued. "Was she troubled by anything or out of sorts at all? Was there anything unusual in her behaviour?"

"On the contrary, Inspector. Siobhan Muldoon is, sorry, was one of my most reliable staff members. That's one of the reasons why I was so keen for her to join us. She was a most diligent employee and very adept at dealing with any visitors we might have to entertain. She was definitely in very good form and there was nothing about her manner that would make me in any way

212

complain. But then," he finished, sadly, "she was far too professional to allow any private problems to interfere with her work so I can't really say whether there was anything upsetting her."

"Tell me, what time did you leave the hotel?"

"It was probably close to eleven thirty when we finally decided to call it a night. Like I say, the people from Birmingham had an early start planned for this morning so they felt it was late enough. We'd finished our meal and had a couple of drinks in the bar and then went our separate ways."

"Did Mrs Muldoon leave with you?" the Inspector wanted to know.

"We all left together and .... No. Wait a minute. She started to leave but then decided she needed to visit the Ladies before going home. So we said goodnight and headed on out."

"And you didn't see her leave the hotel."

"No. I already had a taxi waiting and two of the others shared it with me. Angie, she was the other one from this office, was being collected by her boyfriend and he was actually waiting at reception for her."

"So no-one saw Mrs Muldoon leave?" Paul Roche shook his head but Chris Murphy had another question. "Did she receive any messages during the evening? Did anyone phone her or give her a message in any form?"

Roche considered the question for a moment or two before answering. "As far as I remember someone's mobile did go off while we were eating." He paused again, considering this memory. "But, come to think of it, it wasn't hers. It was one of the Birmingham crowd."

"And she didn't talk to anyone else except your group for the whole time you were there?"

"Apart from the waitresses, no. And I'm sure they didn't give her any message."

Both men fell silent, each wrapped up in his own thoughts. Paul Roche was still struggling to come to terms with the news he'd received, wondering how best to report the sad fact to Siobhan's colleagues. She'd been a very popular member of staff and would be missed very much. It was indeed a sad day.

Inspector Murphy was weighing up the answers he'd just been given. He didn't doubt their accuracy for a moment but was frustrated at how little he'd actually learned. They were no nearer to knowing who lured Siobhan Murphy to her death nor how it was done. Perhaps the answer would be found at the Carlsworth Hotel. He got to his feet.

"I think that's all, sir," he said, reaching for the door handle as he spoke. "I'm sorry to have been the bearer of such sad news but thank you for your help."

Paul Roche looked at him and nodded but didn't reply. He seemed, Chris Murphy noted, quite close to tears.

V

The Carlsworth Hotel was probably the finest hotel in the city: it was certainly the best-known. Its central position, elegant decor and fine cuisine made it a popular venue for locals and visitors alike, both as a comfortable place to stay and as a consistently good place in which to enjoy a meal whether it be a carvery lunch in the bar or a full dinner in the beautifully decorated restaurant. It had the added advantage of always delivering value for money and Chris Murphy had enjoyed several meals here, usually when celebrating some special family occasion with Fiona. They'd even brought the children here a couple of times and, thanks to the kind attention of the staff, that had not proved the ordeal that eating out with young children could sometimes be. In fact, now he came to think of it, they'd come here after Matthew's First Holy Communion service a few years ago and that he remembered as a particularly happy event.

The reception area of the hotel was impressive and as he walked in Chris Murphy thought it no small wonder that so many of the city's business people used it as a venue for entertaining important guests. The revolving glass doors opened onto a large area with pale cream walls and dark woodwork. Large modern paintings brought splashes of vivid colour and though they weren't to Murphy's taste he could appreciate their effectiveness. A sense of opulence was created by a deep red carpet and several armchairs, with plush velvet seats of a similar colour, discreetly placed around the room. All the wooden furniture – the trim on the chair arms, the low occasional tables and the reception desk itself – was mahogany and rounding off the impression of style and taste was the single large Waterford Crystal chandelier.

Behind the reception desk a young woman was busy attending to some paperwork but she raised her head and greeted the Inspector with a bright smile as he approached. It was, he realised, the same girl that he'd spoken to little more than twenty-four hours ago.

"Inspector Murphy," she said, "I didn't expect to see you again so soon. Is this another official visit?"

"I'm afraid so," Chris answered, ridiculously pleased to have been remembered by her even if it was only a day since his previous visit. "Is Mr Keane in?"

He noticed that efficiency and curiosity were battling within the young woman but efficiency won and she lifted the phone and spoke briefly into it.

"He'll be with you in a moment," she informed him, as she replaced the receiver. "Perhaps you'd like to take a seat while you're waiting."

Murphy chose, instead, to walk across to the glass doors which led into the dining room. Through them he could see various staff members busily clearing up after the few lunchtime guests who preferred the more formal arrangement of the dining-room to the far more popular and much more casual carvery lunch served in the bar. He considered the fact that it was in this dining-room that two of their victims had eaten what turned out to be their final meal. Was there a connection? Did someone in the hotel lure them to their deaths? That might undermine the Chief Superintendent's theory of the three suspects. Or it might simply add a fourth to the list? But if so,who? He had no time to ponder this further, his thoughts being interrupted by a voice behind him.

"Hello again, Inspector. How can I help you today?"

Chris Murphy turned and recognised the same small, round, silver-haired man he'd spoken to on his earlier visit. Patrick Keane had, he knew, been manager of the Carlsworth Hotel for over twenty years and it was under his careful guidance that the hotel had become so successful. He would, Murphy knew, give all the help he could – and with the utmost discretion.

"Shall we go into my office," the manager continued. "It might be easier to talk there."

"There's no need for that," replied Murphy. "Not yet at least. I first need to speak to some of your staff about a group who were here for dinner last night."

"Oh." The surprise was evident in Patrick Keane's voice. "I assumed it was something connected with that tragic business the other evening. Have you made any progress on that, might I ask?"

"We are making progress," Murphy acknowledged, "but I'm afraid there was a similar incident last night and, once again, this is the last place where the victim was seen alive.'"

"Not another murder!" Keane sounded and looked shocked, especially when he was struck by an even more distressing thought. "You surely don't think the hotel is involved in any way. You can't believe there's any connection between these deaths and anyone in this hotel."

Murphy was quick to reassure him.

"That's not what we're looking at," he said. "What I do need to know is exactly when this latest victim left and, more importantly, who, if anyone, she left with. I also need to know whether any message was left here for her and whether she met with anyone other than her colleagues. I do know that she remained behind for a couple of minutes after the rest of the group had left and it's possible that one of your staff might have seen something."

Keane considered this for a moment or two before answering.

"Unfortunately, as I told you before, several of our dining-room staff only come in to work in the evenings so I doubt if there's anyone here now who would have served the particular group you mention. Still, the restaurant manager should be around somewhere so you can have a word with her. She may be able to answer some of your questions.

"You'll probably have more luck in the bar," he went on. "Our regular bar staff are here every day and, since most people go to the bar for a final drink before leaving, they might have been the last to see this poor woman. If you like I can make my office available and send them in to you."

Chris Murphy shook his head.

"I don't think there's any need for that. Not at the moment. It's often the case that people remember more when they're actually in the place where the incident occurred so, if I may, I'll go into the restaurant first and have a word with the manager there. If you could perhaps find her for me."

Patrick Keane led the Inspector into the restaurant and they went over to where two young girls were finishing setting one of the tables.

"Is Mrs Watson around?" the manager asked.

"Yes, sir," answered the taller of the two girls. "She's in the kitchen. Shall I go and get her?"

The manager nodded and the girl disappeared, returning a short while later followed by a plump, blonde woman of, Murphy reckoned, thirty-five at the most. He felt a brief moment of guilty surprise. He'd not met the restaurant manager on his last visit – there had been no need – and, despite the manager's words, had automatically assumed that he would be meeting a man.

The woman laughed, recognising his look.

"You aren't the first man to show surprise that a woman has this job," she said, holding out her hand. "Miriam Watson, restaurant manager."

Murphy shook her hand, noting the firm grip.

"Inspector Chris Murphy," he said. "I have a few questions for you if you don't mind."

"I'll leave you to it," said Patrick Keane, as he turned to leave. "I'll be in my office if you need me, Inspector."

"I appreciate your help," Murphy replied. "I'll probably go straight to the bar next but I will see you again before I leave."

He watched the manager leave before turning to Ms Watson.

"Shall we sit down for a moment," he said, pulling out a chair for her before seating himself, "and I'll explain why I'm here."

The two young girls, he noticed, had tactfully and quietly left the room. They now had the place to themselves.

"As you are surely aware," he began, "we're involved in a murder investigation and, unfortunately, two of the victims appear to have been lured to their death after attending a dinner here. I'm particularly interested in a group which was here last night. A group from Global Investments."

"That's right," Miriam Watson agreed. "They were certainly here. Ten of them. They sat over there."

217

She indicated a large table almost in the centre of the room.

"Were there many other diners in here?" Murphy asked.

"Actually we were very quiet last night. There were only two other tables occupied all evening. A young couple over there by the window and a family of three in that corner."

It was clear that, among other things, the Carlsworth respected the privacy of their diners and tried, when possible, to seat them far enough apart that conversations could be enjoyable without being intrusive. Unfortunately, this meant there was no chance that any of the other diners would have seen or heard anything out of the ordinary as far as Siobhan Muldoon's party was concerned.

"This particular group of ten, did you have much to do with them?

"Not really, Inspector. Obviously I welcomed them, showed them to their table, introduced them to their waitresses; all part of my normal routine. And a couple of times during the evening, as is my habit, I went over and checked that everything was to their satisfaction."

"And what about the end of the evening?" Chris persisted.

"As usual I thanked them for their visit and their kind words. I reminded the five who were staying here about the breakfast times – although, as it turned out, they were taking an early breakfast as they had a flight to catch. Then, while the others went on into the bar for a final drink, I think, Mr Roche stayed behind to deal with the usual paperwork. He often brings business guests here so it's a familiar routine."

"And, as far as you could tell, there was nothing out of the ordinary and they all left together."

Like I say, they all seemed to enjoy the meal and everyone seemed happy. You'd probably be better talking to Anton the barman. He might be able to tell you more. As far as I know that's where they were headed when they left here."

The room fell quiet as Inspector Murphy considered what he'd been told and tried to decide if he had any more questions for the restaurant manager. He could only think of one, although he was pretty sure he already knew what the answer was going to be.

"One last thing, Ms Watson, and then I'll let you go. I know yours must be a busy job and I really am grateful to you for sparing me the time to answer my questions."

"Look, Inspector," she replied, "as a woman living in this city at the moment I will certainly do all I can to help the gardai find this maniac that's on the loose. I might not believe all the nonsense you read in some of our papers but I can see that the sooner he's caught the better it'll be for everyone. So what's your last question?"

Chris couldn't help smiling at her, warmed by her sensible attitude. It would make the job so much easier if everyone had the same approach to garda investigations. Sadly, quite a few didn't.

"Did you notice if anyone in the group – any of the women in particular – received any message during the meal: either on a phone or written down?"

Miriam Watson shook her head.

"I'm sorry, Inspector. As I say, I wasn't in here all the time but, when I was, I saw or heard nothing like that."

There was, Murphy realised, little more to be learned and certainly no need to take up any more of this woman's time. He stood up, thanked her once more and made his way into the bar to try and find Anton.

****

The bar of the Carlsworth Hotel often surprised people. In complete contrast to the elegance of the entrance, the Old Oak Bar, as it was called, (for no obvious reason as far as Murphy could see), seemed to be some designer's attempt at recreating a traditional Irish bar. The experiment had not been a successful one. The room was full of posters, knick-knacks, the inevitable copy of the 1916 Declaration of Independence, all thrown together with no apparent pattern whatsoever. The tables, chairs and stools were all so close together it was hard to move among them. Certainly they would make any private conversation utterly impossible. Chris had only been in this part of the hotel a couple of times and couldn't understand how the manager could accept the unbelievable difference between the elegance beyond the bar and the disorder within. He knew, however, that it worked: this was one of the most popular places in the city for tourists and residents alike.

All evidence of the carvery lunch had been cleared away and, apart from three middle-aged women lingering over a cup of coffee, the place was empty. There were two men behind the bar, the younger of the two restocking the shelves, the other wiping glasses. Murphy

219

recognised the younger one; he'd spoken to him only yesterday. The older one, he assumed, was Anton.

"Excuse me. I'm looking for Anton. Is that you?"

"That's me," the older man replied. "You must be the policeman they tell me is here asking a load of questions. So. What can I do for you?"

He spoke with a really broad Irish accent, a fact which surprised the Inspector. It soon became clear that he wasn't the first to be taken by surprise.

"Don't worry," said the barman. "You'd be amazed how many people look exactly the way you did when I tell them I'm Anton. That's what comes of having a German mother and an Irish dad. You end up being called Anton O'Brien."

He laughed and Murphy was perfectly happy to join in despite the serious nature of his visit. It helped break the ice.

"Anyway," the barman went on, "just what do you want to know?"

Chris Murphy introduced himself and went on to give the reason for his visit.

"There was a group of people in here, ten of them, quite late," he explained. "They'd eaten in the restaurant and I'm told some of them were staying here overnight. I understand they probably came in here for a final drink after their meal. It was a business dinner involving Global Investments. I believe the company entertains here quite regularly."

"Oh yes," Anton agreed. "Paul Roche and his colleagues. They were here until, oh, I suppose it was about half eleven before they finally left."

"Did they all leave together?"

"I think so." The barman pondered for a while. "No, wait a minute. They called their goodbyes to me and they all moved towards the door but then one of the women said something to the others. There was some laughter and the usual hugs and then she made her way over there," he nodded to a door in the far corner, "to the toilets. She must have left about four or five minutes after the rest."

"Can you describe her to me?"

Murphy had a copy of the photograph of Siobhan Muldoon taken at the crime scene but he was reluctant to use that until necessary.

"Good looking woman. I suppose late thirties, early forties. Small, dark hair, slightly sharp features but that didn't take away from her looks. She's been here a few times with Roche and his people so I presume she works for them."

Murphy nodded.

"And what was she wearing?" he asked, just to be completely certain it was Siobhan Muldoon that the man was describing.

"Oh heavens. My wife always tells me I'm hopeless when it comes to women's clothes. But then," he added with a grin, "I'm far more interested in what goes into them. Anyway I'm almost sure she was wearing what they call a trouser suit. Sort of pink or red. That sort of a colour."

Inspector Murphy finally showed him the photograph.

"Would this be the woman?" he asked.

"That's right. That's her. Although that's a terrible photo. Like I told you she's quite a looker."

Murphy could see that the barman was beginning to get suspicious, probably putting two and two together and coming up with the right answer. Before having to deal with too many unnecessary questions from the man he continued with his own.

"And you didn't see her meet up with or talk to anyone else?"

"Nope. She said goodnight as she went past and that was it. She was almost the last to leave. There was a couple of residents in the corner but they were far too engrossed in each other to pay anyone else any attention."

"O.K.," said Chris. He could see that this was getting nowhere. "Thanks for your help."

He moved away but after a moment or two turned back.

"This is probably a long shot," he said, "but she didn't by any chance get any phone call while she was here? Or any message of any kind?"

Anton shook his head. "To be honest, Inspector, I couldn't say. We were fairly busy last night and ...." He thought hard. "No. No I don't think she did but I really can't say for certain."

Chris Murphy repeated his thanks and walked through the bar and back to the reception area. He was beginning to feel all this had been a complete waste of time. They were no further on in finding out why Siobhan Muldoon should have chosen to go out to that abandoned business park rather than going home. Even if she were having an affair and had arranged a late night assignation it still seemed a very strange place to meet a lover. There was, he realised, one more possible way of discovering what happened in this hotel. Once more he made his way over to the reception desk.

"You weren't by any chance on duty last night were you?" he asked the young woman.

"No, sir," she replied. "I started at eight o'clock this morning. But if it's any help I think Mr Keane did part of the late shift. Sue took ill at short notice and couldn't come in so he took over."

Chris thanked her and returned to the manager's office; he knocked and, in response to the call, entered the small room. Patrick Keane was seated behind his desk talking on the phone but he indicated that Chris should take a seat. Within a matter of moments the call had ended and Mr Keane could turn his attention to the Inspector.

"Any luck?" he asked.

"Not really," Murphy admitted, "but you might be able to help me. I understand that one of your receptionists fell ill so you were on duty at the reception desk late last night."

"That's right. It was the easiest thing to do. They're good girls and usually reliable and it does me no harm to keep an eye on that side of things once in a while."

"Would you have been there at about eleven thirty?"

"Oh yes. It's fairly quiet by then. Gave me a chance to catch up on a few bits and pieces."

This time Inspector Murphy decided to waste no time. He handed over the photograph.

"You didn't by any chance happen to notice this woman leaving? She'd been with the rest of her group of diners in the bar but decided to make use of the toilet before leaving."

Patrick Keane glanced at the photograph but only briefly.

"As a matter of fact I can do better than that," he said. "I not only saw her, I spoke to her."

"Oh. So you knew her."

Murphy's hopes began to rise, only to be dashed by the manager's next words.

"No. Not at all. I'd seen her a few times when Global Investments brought people here but I didn't even know her name. However," he went on, "at about, I don't know, maybe an hour before they left, a youngster came in. Didn't look much older than my Rachel and she's only thirteen. Shouldn't have been out at that time of night. Anyway, she came in, handed me an envelope and asked if I'd give it to the lady in the dark pink trouser suit when she came out. That was all. She'd gone before I could ask any questions."

"And you don't know what was in the envelope, what the message was."

"It was nothing to do with me, Inspector. We're often asked to give messages to guests so even though it was late and the messenger was younger than usual there's no way I'd read other people's private messages."

"So you gave it to this woman," said Inspector Murphy, trying hard not to let his disappointment and frustration show.

"Yes. Mrs Muldoon. That was the name on the envelope. Siobhan, I think."

"Did you see her open it? Did she open it straightaway?"

"She was already moving away when she did but I could tell that whatever it said didn't please her. She crumpled it up and threw it into the bin." Murphy's looked hopeful but his hopes were soon dashed. "And I'm sorry, Inspector, but all the small wastepaper bins are emptied first thing each morning and, as we have a private arrangement to get the big hotel bins collected every day, it's probably in an incinerator somewhere at this stage."

"And you didn't see her after that?"

"No. And unfortunately there's no-one on the door at that time. Most residents are in by then and, with cutbacks being what they are, we've had to stop the doorman service at ten thirty. It's a pity: it takes away from the traditional standards of service we've tried to maintain in this hotel but that's the sort of thing we have to do to stay in business these days."

A thought occurred to Inspector Murphy as he turned to take his leave of Mr Keane.

"I understand she drove here," he said. "After she'd seen the note did she go straight to the hotel car park?"

"Oh no. I understand she'd already made arrangements to leave her car here overnight. As far as I know she left by taxi."

Thanking Mr Keane once more Murphy made his way back to his car. It was possible that they now knew a little more about how Siobhan Muldoon had been lured to her death. Disappointingly, however, it seemed they were no closer to discovering who'd done it.

VI

"It looks," said Chief Superintendent Pollock, "as if we might be able to reduce our suspects to two."

They were all back in the incident room, late that Friday afternoon, making their reports and discussing their next moves. The fact that both Henry Moroney and Hugh Mellor had a connection, however slight, with the Muldoons certainly put them at the top of the list.

"I take it we've found nothing so far to connect Siobhan Muldoon or her husband with either Howard Morrissey or St Saviour's school. Certainly Morrissey's name never came up when we were talking to Muldoon. And since they don't have children I can see no way there could be a link. Unless Mr Muldoon himself was a pupil there. But that would surely not give much of a link with Mrs Muldoon and I can't see how it would create any situation in which Morrissey would see the two of them together."

All were agreed that this seemed unlikely.

"O.K., Noel, so what have we got on these three men?"

"Not very much I'm afraid, Sir," Lawson replied. "But, if you don't mind, before I go into that I can tell you that I think I've solved the remaining clues. And you're right, Sir; I'm pretty sure of that now."

"Go on then. Tell us what they are."

"I believe the last three, the ones in Siobhan Muldoon's hand, are '*add awful wife*'. So we've now got a fairly logical message. '*Child angrily thought thou shalt commit murder. Spiteful women abuse men. First mother, sister too. Add awful wife*'. It seems he's telling us why he's taking this action and what he's done so far."

"Which, sadly, is no great help," Sean Pollock pointed out. "It still doesn't give us a lead on who he is. So now, Noel, what else have you got for us?"

"I haven't finished following all lines of enquiry yet, Sir, but here's what I have found out. Henry Moroney," Lawson began, "is a native of the city. As far as I can find out he was born here in 1966. He had at least one sister and a brother but so far I haven't been able to trace either. It may be that they've left the city or even the country. Curiously enough there's no mention of the father on his birth record which might possibly fit in with our idea of a dominant mother. Educated in the city – not at St Saviour's – passed the civil service exams and has been there ever since. Started in the Ministry of Transport but moved to the Social Welfare Office eighteen years ago, where, as we know, he still works.. No criminal record. There is record of him being married but I can't yet say whether his wife is still around or if they had any family."

"There was no sign of a wife at the house," Hughes pointed out. "And I didn't see any pictures of family either, although, of course, we were only in one room."

"But," Coady added, "it struck me he spent most of his time in that room, especially what with that big television, and you'd have thought if there were family photos that's where they'd be."

"Anything else about him?" asked Pollock.

"That's about it, Sir. Doesn't own a car. At least, if he does he hasn't taxed it. Nothing else I could get through the particular channels I've tried so far."

"I'm amazed you even got that much." Chris Murphy was impressed. He was, he knew, a complete novice when it came to computers.

Noel Lawson grinned. "It's surprising what you can find out if you know the right buttons to press."

"What about our next man? Hugh Mellor?" asked Pollock.

"Hmm," was Lawson's initial response. "He proved far more difficult to track down. Like Moroney he was born and educated here – again no link to St Saviour's – but PRSI records show nothing for him from the time he was twenty-eight until three years ago so it's quite possible that he was out of the country during that time."

Pollock thought back to what he'd heard earlier in the day.

"That would fit in with what Zac Muldoon told us," he suggested. "He said he'd been married fifteen years and Mellor was his best man so the time-span would probably be about right. You say he comes back onto the radar three years ago?"

"That's right and as far as I can make out he's been working at the hospital ever since."

"Family?"

"Again, not very much information although it looks as if his mother may have claimed some sort of single parent allowance so it could well be that the father wasn't around. Two siblings as far as I could find: a sister and a brother. Now, here's where it gets interesting because that's how he features in a police report.

"Oh?"

More than one voice reacted to that piece of news. Everyone in the room had been taking in every word of Lawson's report.

"Yes. It transpires that Hugh Mellor's brother died in somewhat suspicious circumstances. Nothing was ever proved – to be honest I don't see how it could have been – although the driver maintained throughout that the child was actually pushed in front of his car. Trouble was he couldn't see who might have done it. And given that it was a bunch of kids, nine or ten year-old, it's quite possible that they were larking about as kids do. Whatever. The driver had no chance to stop, all the evidence showed that this was the case, and it was put down as an accidental death. Although it seems Mrs Mellor never accepted that. She wanted the man punished.

"I found all this out from Inspector Kinsella. He remembered the case although it's almost thirty years ago. Told me he'd never heard a woman carry on so. He's heading off to Canada on Monday but said to tell you that, if you want, he'll come in and talk to you a bit more about it tomorrow."

"He's surely not missing us that much already," joked Coady and the others joined in the laughter.

"What strikes me," said Chris Murphy, as the moment of humour faded, "is that, if we take this idea of the spiteful mother, Mrs Mellor might well have blamed Hugh for his brother's death. And perhaps that's when she started ill-treating him."

"It's certainly an idea," agreed Pollock.

226

"What if," added Margaret Power, "it was actually his sister who was the guilty party? Knowing, as I do," she grinned at them, "how devious young girls can be, it's equally possible that she followed her mother's example in order to transfer the guilt she might have been feeling onto her brother."

"You definitely paint a very plausible picture," Pollock acknowledged. "Any evidence about a wife, Noel?"

"Couldn't find anything, Sir. He might have got married while he was away. There's certainly no record of one living with him now."

"Same goes for children, I suppose."

"Yep."

"O.K. It looks like we might be able to put Hugh Mellor at the top of our list. There are certainly signs that he might have had a fairly unpleasant upbringing. Did you get anything on Howard Morrisson?"

"Morrissey, Sir. He was the one I got least about, despite my best efforts. He was born in England so I've very little on his family, though I'm pretty sure his parents were Irish. He came here to finish his studies, as far as I can make out, got the job at St Saviour's and has been there ever since. It appears he was married but not for long as his wife died only a few years after the wedding. There were no children and I don't know about any other family. In fact, as far as I could tell, he has only one relative living here. An elderly aunt. So I decided to chance my arm and I actually tried ringing her. Thought I could make up some excuse about how he's been very helpful to us but we didn't think it right to keep pestering him at work so could she tell us when would be the best time to catch him at home. It seemed worth a try."

"Now that's what I call initiative," said Inspector Murphy, a comment which caused Noel Lawson to turn red with embarrassment.

"Don't know about that, Sir," he mumbled, "but anyway, it didn't work. I talked to some kind of housekeeper. Turns out the aunt has a lot of trouble with arthritis and has been in and out of hospital over the last six months or so. And that's where she is at the moment."

"Is that it?" asked Pollock.

"Apart from the fact that, according to the motor taxation office, both Mellor and Morrissey own a car."

"On that basis alone," Pollock declared, "Henry Moroney is the least likely and we should maybe focus our attention on the other two, concentrating on Hugh Mellor in particular. Now, how do we set about that?"

"It would help," muttered Geoff Hughes, gloomily, "if we could at least get into his mind. We know he's clever – those crossword clues show that. And we know he's devious. But it would be so good if we knew just exactly what game he's playing."

The phone rang. There was total silence as Sean Pollock answered it, each of them holding his breath, fearful that this might be yet another victim. There was an audible sigh of relief as the Chief Superintendent relaxed. It was simply the front desk telling him that Mr Muldoon had arrived to make the formal identification of his wife's body.

Pollock got to his feet.

"This'll take about an hour at most," he told them. "Meanwhile, let's get everything written up, all the information we have. We need really solid fuel when we approach any of these men. We have to be one hundred per cent certain we can back up our suspicions. And, in the meantime, if any of you come up with any further ideas keep them in mind and we'll discuss them when I get back."

He noticed more than one of the team risking a quick glance at the clock on the wall behind him.

"Don't worry," he said, irritation clear in his tone, "I don't intend keeping you too late tonight. But this being a murder investigation you can all expect to be working for at least some of the weekend. That's how it goes."

So saying he left.

VII

It was, as everyone in the room knew, pure formality. Zechariah Muldoon looked at his wife's body, nodded briefly and mumbled: "That's her: that's Siobhan" before breaking down completely. Sean Pollock withdrew a distance, leaving the man chance to recover himself alone.

228

"It never gets any easier, does it," he said to Elizabeth Mason. "No matter how many times we go through the ritual."

"And, hopefully, it never will," she replied. "Because if it does that's a sign that you're beginning to lose your humanity. And that's when it's time to quit."

"You're right, of course," Pollock admitted, then changed the subject. "Nothing unusual in the post-mortem I suppose."

"Nothing so far. She seems to have been a fit and healthy woman with no bad habits. No sign of drugs or anything like that. In fact, there's only one sign of any physical problem; she suffered a broken leg not too long ago. But I very much doubt if that's connected to the murder in any way."

It probably wasn't but that didn't stop Sean Pollock mentioning it to Mr Muldoon as the two of them walked back to his car.

"Your wife broke her leg quite recently, didn't she," he said. "How did that happen?"

Zac Muldoon was surprised by the question, lost, as he'd been, in a world of his own.

"What? Oh, that happened at work. About four months ago. She fell down some stairs. It must have been quite a bad break as she had to stay in hospital for a couple of days. I can tell you, Chief Superintendent, she wasn't too happy about that."

He stopped abruptly as if suddenly remembering some unpleasant incident connected with his wife's accident. Sean Pollock began to wonder just what it was and then, as he remembered something he'd heard earlier, a small suspicion began to grow in his mind. It was probably nothing but he'd have to check it out – if only to satisfy his own curiosity.

He had to wait until he was back in the incident room. Everyone was still there, busily working on their reports or discussing all they'd learned, trying to find that one small clue which would break the case wide open. Seeing their determination he felt a flicker of remorse for his earlier irritability. They were, he knew, every bit as determined as he was to find this man and stop him, once and for all.

"Noel," he called, as he walked into the room, "did you say that Howard Morrissey's aunt had been in hospital during the past few months?"

"Yes, Sir. On and off for about six months, so the housekeeper said."

The others looked at the superintendent expectantly, aware that he must have found another link to follow,

"Phil," he went on, with a slight grin, "given that you have so many female connections in the city" – they all laughed at this, including Phil Coady – "is there by any chance a nurse from the Regional Hospital among them?"

"Three actually, Sir," replied Phil, looking very pleased with himself although a little bemused by the question. "Why do you ask?"

"I need you to use all your charm and powers of persuasion and get one of them to find out if there was any way that Ms Morrissey – I take it that is her name, Noel?"

Lawson nodded.

"If there's any way," Pollock continued, "she might have been in hospital at the same time as Siobhan Muldoon. It appears Mrs Muldoon fell and broke her leg a few months back. If both women were in for orthopaedic treatment there is an outside chance their visits coincided."

He refused to say more, retiring instead to his office where he began a series of telephone calls, the last of which appeared, as the others glanced at him through the window separating his office from the incident room, particularly difficult. Phil, his own phone calls completed, joined him ten minutes later.

"What have you found out?" Pollock demanded, as soon as the younger man had knocked and entered. "Something interesting to judge by your expression."

"Definitely," Coady answered. "My, er, friend remembered that occasion very clearly. Actually, to use her words, she doesn't think she'll ever forget it."

"How come?"

"Apparently there was quite a carry on. Poor Mrs Morrissey was very upset. It seems she's a dear, sweet old lady who wouldn't hurt a fly. Anyway, there was this huge row on the ward one time when she was there. One of the other patients really tore strips off her husband for no obvious reason by all accounts. It was so bad in fact that Carol, my friend, had to ask the man to leave, even though, as

230

far as she could make out, it was his wife who was causing all the trouble. That's why she remembers it so well."

"Do I get a prize for guessing who the wife was?" asked Pollock, wearily.

"I doubt it, Sir. I think you'd already thought of it. Siobhan Muldoon. And what are the chances that Howard Morrissey was visiting his aunt at the time and so witnessed the whole thing?"

"Let's just say we're back to three suspects. Thanks, Phil. Go and tell the others. And ask Inspector Murphy to join me. Oh, and Phil," he had a twinkle in his eye as Coady paused at the door and looked back, "I hope you get your – how shall I put it? – just reward for this."

****

So," said Chris Murphy, a few minutes later, "Howard Morrissey may well have witnessed Siobhan Muldoon abusing her husband. So where do we go from here?"

"I'll tell you exactly where I'm going," Pollock informed him. "Derry."

"Derry?"

Murphy was completely taken aback. In all his years working with Sean Pollock he'd never known him to go far from the centre of things while an investigation of this size was ongoing. He knew, therefore, that this decision must have something to do with the case but, for the life of him, couldn't imagine what.

"Derry," he repeated. "Why Derry?"

Sean Pollock didn't answer the question directly; instead his comments surprised the Inspector.

"I've been thinking a lot lately about this whole notion of profiling in cases like this. Don't worry," he added, seeing the look of amazement on his colleague's face,. "I know I've said on more than one occasion that I think it's a lot of mumbo-jumbo but I know - well, sort of know - a fellow in Derry who is supposed to be particularly good at understanding and interpreting human nature. And, given that, as we all agree, these cases are probably all based on some sort of psychological issues and, more to the point, we've got three potential culprits, I'm wondering if he might be able to give us some sort of insight into the mentality of our killer."

Chris Murphy couldn't understand this. They were in the middle of a very bizarre case. There seemed to be no reason at all for Chief Superintendent Pollock - the most cynical of officers when it came to alternative approaches to police investigations - to spend time visiting some little-known psychological expert. Nevertheless, he trusted his boss enough to wait for the explanation before judging him.

"I think it was Geoff who said something about getting into the mind of our killer. It struck me that an expert psychologist perhaps knows as much as any of us about the mind of a person who's been a victim of abuse. And I happen to know that this particular person lived as one for many years."

"Did he realise that at the time though?" Murphy wanted to know.

"I don't think so. But he's had a lot of time to think about it since he managed to break free. Anyway, he's agreed to see me and I'm hoping he can give us some professional advice on how we should proceed. Perhaps he can suggest ways in which we can eliminate two of our three suspects. Damn it all, Chris, I'm not sure any of us can understand the complex motives of this particular killer."

"But surely," Chris protested, "there are perfectly able psychologists here in the city. Why bother trailing all the way to Derry?"

"Because," Pollock replied, wearily, "I knew this man many years ago and, without going into any unnecessary detail, I feel I owe him something. More to the point, I'm pretty sure I can trust him."

Inspector Murphy wasn't completely happy with this answer. He could see the logic in getting professional advice. After all, police forces in many countries were using so-called profilers more and more to help them track down murderers. He also understood what Sean Pollock was trying to do. However, he still wasn't altogether sure this was the right way to do it. Still, it was clear that Pollock had made his decision: Chris would just have to go along with it.

"When will you go?" he asked.

"I'm going this evening. Now, in fact. I'll dash home, throw a couple of things in an overnight bag and drive up there. It's not such a big journey, especially now the roads have improved so much. This fellow's agreed to see me first thing in the morning, even though it's Saturday, so, with any luck, I'll be back here by mid-afternoon at the latest. To be quite honest, Chris, I don't think

232

we can do much more here at the moment, short of dragging those three men in for questioning. And I just don't think we have enough hard evidence for that. And, you never know, it could well be that my trip gives us just the lead we're looking for."

"Do you want the others in here tomorrow then?" Murphy resigned himself to accepting the decision.

"Not first thing. They can come in tomorrow afternoon. I'll aim to be back here by four so they should be here by then. Who knows? I might come back with the whole case solved."

Chris Murphy was still highly sceptical and doubted this very much. He was concerned that this particular journey had more to do with Pollock's need to get rid of some kind of weird sense of responsibility, guilt even, towards this psychologist rather than with identifying a killer. He chose to say nothing. It was, he felt, better that way.

VIII

Eugene McPhillips had changed greatly since Sean Pollock had last seen him, although that wasn't really surprising since, as the Chief Superintendent now realised, it was more than thirty years since the two had last met. It appeared that the psychologist had lost weight and his once-brown hair, though still wavy, was almost completely grey. Gone was the thick moustache he'd once sported; gone, too, was the air of uncertainty which had surrounded him when they had first met. None of this was surprising considering all the man had been through.

'And all my fault,' thought Pollock, miserably. 'I should have found out sooner. I should have known. I should have seen.'

He hadn't said a lot to Chris Murphy but he'd first known McPhillips when they'd shared a dormitory in the rather exclusive boarding school they'd both attended. As a young lad he'd not fully understood his schoolmate's reluctance to share stories of home life. Nor had he appreciated the utter misery his young friend had suffered at every occasion involving a visit from parents. In fact, if he were honest, it was many years since he'd even thought about Eugene: only the thought of certain similarities, late the previous evening, had brought to mind the misery his schoolmate had tried, usually unsuccessfully, to share.

It was these memories which had driven him to his computer in the early hours of the morning. These same memories which had led

233

him to search for his friend on various websites. And these same memories which gave him no surprise when his research revealed that Professor Eugene McPhillips was an eminent psychologist, specialising in the trauma of childhood psychological abuse.

This, he'd realised, might be the ideal person to give them the insight they so desperately needed to break open the case. Perhaps, also, the visit could help him personally, removing some of the guilt he's felt over the years. He could but hope.

"Sean Pollock," said McPhillips when he opened the door of his office, a single room in an old terraced house about five minutes from the city centre. He didn't offer to shake hands. That was, perhaps, understandable as far as Sean Pollock was concerned. "I must be honest, I didn't expect to see you again."

"I can understand that," replied Pollock. "In your shoes I'd feel exactly the same, which is why I appreciate you seeing me like this. Hopefully it will help both of us; perhaps even go some way towards making amends for the past."

"Chief Superintendent, let's get things clear straightaway," said McPhillips, his voice hard. "I agreed see you because I can understand your guilt. I thought we were good friends, close friends. Perhaps you should have been able to spot what was going on. On the other hand, we were both little more than children so maybe that was too much to expect. Only later could I begin to understand. Only now, through my profession, have I been able to see why things happened the way they did. And when I read her diaries, after her death, I realised how devious her mind was. She left me damaged for most of my youth. I tried to tell you but you couldn't understand or believe what was happening. After all, she was my mother. So, in the end, we both suffered as a result. I'm not sure either of us is ever going to recover fully from that and I don't blame you any more than I blame myself."

Sean Pollock was relieved to hear this but before he could say anything Eugene McPhillips went on speaking.

"Having said that, I escaped. I was accepted at university where my choice of subject was obvious. By the time I was eighteen I'd realised that the only way I could come to terms with my mother's behaviour was to try and understand what was going on in her mind. As I daresay you've found out - since I doubt you came here on spec, so to speak - I did several years of study in various countries and finally came here. And I've made a good life for myself. I've agreed to see you, to help you, because it might put

234

your mind a little bit at rest. But that's all. I don't want any kind of analysis of what happened when I was young: that part of my life is now a closed book. I want to continue to go on and so, Sean, should you."

He sat down behind the desk and indicated that Pollock should take the armchair facing him.

"So," he concluded, "I will help you in this case if I can but I want nothing from you. And I don't want to see you again. Ever."

Sean Pollock realised there was nothing he could say in response to this although he was experiencing a mixture of emotions. Dismay at being reminded of his previous mistakes; relief that the man he'd come to see was prepared, as much as he could, to forgive and forget; and a little bit of optimism that perhaps something good could come from this meeting which might enable him to arrest the right man. That being the case he nodded his agreement and settled himself into the chair indicated by Eugene McPhillips, looking around the room for the first time as he did so.

It was surprisingly spartan. There was, Pollock noted, no separate room for a secretary, nor even space in this room. Obviously the psychologist was entirely on his own – for the present anyway. There was only a minimum of furniture. A large, old-fashioned desk with drawers on either side of the knee space. Like the two chairs, the filing cabinet and the solitary bookcase it looked second hand. Despite his many qualifications Professor McPhillips had clearly decided to start on a very small scale.

"Right," said the Professor, "let's get down to business. Why don't you tell me about this new case of yours and how you think I might be able to help you?"

For the next ten minutes or so Pollock described the recent events, detailing the background of the three victims, outlining his own theory about the motive behind the killings, explaining the evidence of the crossword clues and, finally and briefly but without naming them, giving a short explanation about why the three men in particular had ended up as the main suspects.

There was a long pause when he finished. McPhillips sat back in the old leather chair, closed his eyes and began to weigh up all that he'd heard. The room was completely silent. Pollock waited, hoping against hope that his journey hadn't been completely in vain.

"I think," said the Professor, at last, "in fact I'm almost certain, that you're one hundred per cent correct about the motive. From what you're telling me – and I'd agree with Dr Mason, the killer has to be a man – it would appear that he is acting out a set of revenge killings for the many humiliations he's experienced during his life at the hands of the women he's been involved with. For whatever reason he cannot punish the actual women who made his life misery: they might be dead or out of the country or he is still too frightened of them. So instead he's seeking to do so, as it were, by proxy.

"I also agree that, given what you've told me, the three, if they witnessed a mother, a sister or a wife each as abusive as his own, must certainly be considered as prime suspects. However, that is only true if you can find out for definite that these men were themselves victims. I don't know how you're going to do that without arousing too much suspicion on their part but without that evidence your whole theory collapses. You say all three suspects have, or had, at least one sister but you can't be sure whether two of them were ever married. You definitely need to check that out. But you already know that, of course.

"And although you can probably assume that none of the women have any role in their present life you will obviously need to confirm that as well. I'm practically certain that, if any of the dominant women still has a part to play for one of these men, he will not be your murderer. He will be too weak to act."

All of this was reassuring for Sean Pollock. Although McPhillips was right and they had a lot more research yet to do into the backgrounds of the three suspected men, it was still a relief to hear an outsider – especially one with expertise in dealing with the way people's minds worked – agree with him.

"And that," continued the Professor, "is a very important fact, if not the most important. You see, your killer is basically a very weak man. That's clear from the way he accepted, or we must assume he accepted, the bullying throughout much of his life. Remember, I'm speaking very much from personal experience here. The fact that I was able to spend time at school away from my mother helped but I was only truly free from her when she died not long after my seventeenth birthday. Until then, much as I still hate to admit it, I could be reduced to a nobody by her. Her death freed me. It may be that the same has happened to your killer. But what you've yet to discover is the catalyst behind his current actions."

"The catalyst?" Pollock was puzzled.

"Something very dramatic must have happened which acted as a catalyst and sparked off this killing spree. If our theory is correct these men might have put up with various forms of verbal abuse from their women folk for years. You say there's no sign of any woman in their lives now so, in that case, they are now free from further abuse. In which case there would be no need for any them to take this dramatic action.

"So it's logical to assume that some major incident took place recently which pushed the killer over the edge and onto this dreadful road of vengeance. I would say without doubt that, whatever it was, it was caused by a woman. However, given that he has already dealt with – in his own mind at least –mother, sister and wife, this has to be a woman who's not necessarily related to him. She will probably, but not necessarily, be connected with him in some way – at work, perhaps, or in a club – or he will have had some unpleasant contact with her, perhaps in a supermarket or some other public place. Whatever it was she'll have behaved in a way that made him feel weak and foolish yet again. And probably in front of others. What you have to do is look into recent events in each man's life and see what you can find."

Sean Pollock had been listening intently to all this and was fascinated by the obvious logic of it all; a logic which he and his team had, as yet, failed to recognise. Once again he was glad of his decision to consult an expert.

"I take it you can't give me any idea what the catalyst could be," he now said, "but we have to look for some recent event in this man's life involving a woman."

"Exactly."

"Will he try to kill this woman?"

"Without a doubt, if he can. And soon. You only have to think how close together the three murders so far have been. As I say, he's basically a weak man and before long the weak side of his nature will take over once more. He's probably desperate to finish off the job he's set himself before his courage fails him. If he's already made up his own mind to get his own back for all the humiliation caused him in his life that only leaves this other woman and then he's free. He'll definitely want to deal with her as his final act of vengeance. So it is, of course, vital that you find her as quickly as possible."

Chief Superintendent Pollock sighed deeply.

"That's where it's beginning to get complicated," he confessed. "I want to investigate all three suspects without alerting them – or anyone else – to our suspicions or causing harm to an innocent man."

"Listen, Sean, you have the facilities and, to be quite honest, it's far more important to try and prevent another murder than worry about an innocent person's reputation. You know that's true. Reputations can be restored, lives can't."

He spoke without rancour and Pollock readily accepted the sense of what he was saying.

"Take it from me," the Psychologist continued, "it's possible to find out a lot through simple conversation with these men. And, since they are all witnesses to events you think are connected to the case you have every excuse to send your people off to interview them again. It will help if you an interview them at home where they'll be more relaxed. You'll be surprised what you can learn just by letting them talk. I know: it's what I've been doing with people for years," he added, smiling.

Eugene McPhillips was right: Pollock knew that. The visit had definitely been worthwhile.

"I'll not keep you much longer," he now said, "but there is one other thing. What about the crossword clues? Where do they fit in?"

"That's what makes all this so interesting," McPhillips replied. "This man is obviously quite clever and certainly has a devious mind. That shows in the clues he's devised and the way he's presented them to you. And, again, I think you're right. He's using them as a message to explain to you just why he's behaving the way he is. He's not only challenging you to find out his identity, he's challenging you to work out his motive. And he's chosen a method which particularly interests him.

"In fact," he went on, "I think that's very important to him. It's another way of showing that he's not a complete nonentity; that he is, in his own mind, very smart. I think he's trying to prove that he's not the fool that these women made him feel."

There seemed very little more to say and, after a moment or two pondering all that had been said, Pollock started to get to his feet. Eugene McPhillips' next words stopped him in his tracks.

"There's one other thing you should bear in mind, although I could be wrong."

"Go on," said Pollock.

"I think that when you do catch him you'll have no difficulty in getting a confession. I think he'll be more than willing to admit everything."

"Why on earth would you think that?"

"Those crossword clues have given you the story behind his actions. I feel he will want to take you to the end of the story. And that means admitting his guilt. He'll be hoping that you can figure it out from the clues he sends you – and it appears you have someone on your team who has a talent for these things – but, just in case you don't, he's quite possibly going to want to tell you the whole story."

"I'm not sure I understand your logic." Sean Pollock was confused. "Why should he want to confess?"

The Professor laughed.

"This man isn't your usual vicious killer doing it for kicks. He's not even like those who act out of a hatred for what they see as some form of betrayal by their victims. This is someone who's done what he's been told to do for most of his life, and not in a pleasant way. Now, for a short while, he's stepped out of line.

"But think of the child who disobeys his mother. For a while there is a bit of a stand-off, a minor mutiny if you like, when the child apparently enjoys showing the parent that he has a mind of his own. And yet, nine times out of ten, before long the child relents and admits he's done wrong. I think this man is like that. He's staged his rebellion but in the end he's going to need to confess. He's far too weak to do otherwise. Unfortunately," he concluded, "there's another life at stake and you can't afford to wait."

"Well," said Pollock, and this time he did stand up, "hopefully we'll get him before he gets to her – whoever she is. At least that way we will save one life."

"I hope you do," replied McPhillips, though Pollock thought he detected a certain element of doubt in the man's tone. He decided not to question him about it, suddenly very aware of the grave dangers; that his failure to do exactly what he'd said would place yet another death on his conscience. It was not a happy thought.

He reached the door before speaking. "Once again, Eugene, I'm sorry for my failure to help you when we first knew each other. Now, however, I am deeply grateful for your time and all your help. It really has been very useful. And I will bear in mind what you've said. You won't be hearing from me again."

Professor Eugene McPhillips nodded and this time he held out his hand.

"Chief Superintendent Pollock," he said, "I was able to make a fresh start many years ago and, slowly but surely, I've got my life back after some very unpleasant experiences. There really is no need for any further recriminations on your part."

They shook hands.

"Good luck. In everything," were Pollock's parting words.

IX

As arranged they were all waiting for the Chief Superintendent when he got back and if anyone on the team was surprised that Pollock had decided to consult a psychologist - and not even a local one - no comment was made.

Pollock was pleased – although not really surprised – to learn that, rather than using Saturday morning for their own affairs they'd each tried to find ways of furthering the investigation.

Geoff Hughes had, in fact, taken advantage of the situation and suggested to Mags Power that they might be able to combine business with pleasure.

"If I collect you at about ten o'clock we could maybe head back to Church Road and talk with some more of the people there. Most of them were out when Phil and I called yesterday: at work probably. There's a better chance of catching them at home on a Saturday. And afterwards," he added, with a smile, "we could get lunch somewhere. A nice, long, leisurely lunch before we have to meet Pollock again. If," he hastened to add, "you don't think that fiance of yours will object to you lunching with such a handsome man as me."

"O.K.," Mags had agreed, with a laugh, "but not quite so early, please. There are a few things I must get done at home first. How about eleven? Call for me then. It'll still give us plenty of time."

Lunch, as expected, had been very enjoyable; especially as Geoff had decided they would have enough time to drive out of the city, find a quiet place to eat, spend an hour or so over their meal and still be back in plenty of time for the meeting. Their lunch time had been very successful; their earlier police work had been far less so as Hughes explained to the Chief Superintendent.

"We did get to see a few more people," he said, "but they didn't really add anything to what we already know. A couple of them repeated Mr Moroney's story of the fight in Muldoon's garden a week or so back and they agreed that there was something a bit off-putting about the Muldoons as a couple that made people reluctant to try getting friendly with them."

"What about Henry Moroney?" Pollock demanded. "Were you able to find out anything more about him?"

"Not really. Of course, we had to be a bit more circumspect about him. We didn't want to arouse any suspicions and start a load of gossip. So we were left with very general remarks. You know the sort of thing. A nice man, quiet, friendly, keeps to himself pretty much."

Hughes looked questioningly at Mags to see if she had anything to add.

"To be quite honest, Sir," she said, "that was the general impression I got of the whole street. That, for the most part, they all keep pretty much to themselves. Certainly," she added with a smile, "not the same sort of neighbourhood as Maureen Connolly lived in. If Sammy Ferguson's to be believed."

"Did you get to see Mrs McLoughlin? Is that her name? The one who lives next door to the Muldoons? She seems to be the one who could tell us most. And she seems to be quite friendly with Moroney so she could really be of some help."

"She's still away by the seem of things," Geoff replied. "And, unfortunately, no-one could say where she was or when she'll be back."

"Pity," said Pollock. "Still, at least we have confirmation of the kind of woman Siobhan Muldoon was and that might prove useful if we ever get to the stage of having to prove motive."

"I have a bit more about Howard Morrissey," offered Phil Coady.

Like Geoff Hughes he had managed to combine business with pleasure and had, during his phone call to his friend the nurse, persuaded her to meet him for a drink when her shift ended. His

241

usual charm had been such that Carol had ended up spending the night with him and although he'd had no intention of spoiling the mood by talking about work – hers or his – he had managed to get a little more information about one of their suspects.

"Of course," he announced, with a wink and a broad grin, "I had better things to talk about but I did realise it was too good an opportunity to miss. Especially as it was Carol herself who brought the topic up in the first place. Annie Morrissey is a regular visitor to that ward and I got the impression they all have a bit of a soft spot for her."

"So what did you learn?"

Sean Pollock was in a good mood, not only because of his successful trip to Derry but also because of the obvious dedication of his team. Not that that surprised him. One of the reasons he'd kept this particular group of officers was because of the commitment and the initiative which they so often displayed. He was therefore prepared to be far more patient than usual.

"Apparently Annie always gets three regular visitors when she's in hospital. Her housekeeper, her next-door neighbour and her nephew."

"Howard."

"The very same. And Carol says the nurses are always amazed that he keeps showing up, especially since it seems the old woman can be quite unpleasant to him. She's a sweet old lady to everyone else, a perfect dear according to Carol, but has very little time for him. Even though," Phil went on "she gives out yards when he doesn't visit."

"It sounds as if our Mr Morrissey is a real victim when it comes to women," Inspector Murphy murmured.

"And that might give him an even stronger motive for attacking these so-called spiteful women," added Geoff Hughes.

"During all your noble exertions," said Murphy, very tongue-in-cheek, "did you find out any more about Morrissey's family?"

"Not directly," Phil replied "although I did learn that there was a cousin, Annie Morrissey's daughter, but she was killed in a car crash a good few years ago, while she was working in the States. And before you ask it appears Annie and her sister both lived in England for many years and, in their innocence, both were taken advantage of. Those were her words, according to Carol, so I take that to mean that neither woman was married."

"We can also add something can't we, Noel," announced Chris Murphy, when it became clear that Phil Coady had nothing further to offer.

Noel Lawson nodded and began shuffling up the sheaf of papers that was on the table in front of him. Unlike his colleagues, he'd had a far less successful time in his private life. His attempts at persuading his former girlfriend, Ruth, to renew their relationship appeared to be foundering.

They'd met the previous evening for what he had hoped would be a reconciliation but all his attempts at winning her back had been swiftly thwarted with the arrival of two of her friends. They were on their way to the grand opening of the city's newest and, it was claimed, trendiest nightclub and had soon talked her into joining them. Noel had gone with them but it hadn't taken long for him to realise that not only was it not his kind of place but the volume of noise made it impossible for him to have any kind of conversation with Ruth, let alone one on something as serious as their future together. Disappointed, he'd finally made what he knew was a feeble excuse , arranged to call Ruth sometime during the weekend and made his lonely way back to his flat.

Surprised – and more than a little dejected – at finding himself at an unexpected loose end on Saturday morning he'd eventually made up his mind to head back to the incident room and see if he could find out any more about their three suspects. It was there that Chris Murphy had found him engrossed in the computer and surrounded by various pieces of paper. Noel had welcomed help in his research and between them they had managed to fill in a bit more of the profiles of Mellor and Morrissey.

"So what have we got?" asked Pollock, his optimism increasing all the time.

"I'm afraid I didn't get as far as I'd hoped," Lawson apologised, "although thanks to Inspector Murphy I was able to access a couple more websites."

"I was able to call in a few favours," explained Murphy. "Although," he added with a grin, "I wasn't too popular. Not on a Saturday morning."

Sean Pollock smiled.

"I also had a brief word with Dr Mason.," the Inspector continued. "Nothing surprising in the pm. Exactly the same as the other two. Which we'd already assumed. However, there was one interesting find." He had their full attention now. "It seems the murder weapon in this case was quite old. Dr Mason described it as what her grandfather would have called a muffler, although that's neither here nor there. The thing is, it has what are possibly the owner's initials embroidered on it and guess what."

"H.M.," said Pollock, flatly.

He shrugged as Murphy confirmed that that was indeed the case.

"Well," he admitted, "at least that tells us we're definitely on the right lines. Trouble is, we still have no real clue as to which of the three is the killer. So, Noel," he turned to the younger man. "What did you discover?"

"We now know that both Hugh Mellor and Howard Morrissey were married but neither wife is on the scene now. From what we can find out Mellor is divorced and it looks as if his wife is completely out of the picture."

"And Mrs Morrissey?"

"Dead."

In the circumstances that single word, uttered with great solemnity by Lawson, was bound to rouse interest. Pollock raised his eyebrows questioningly.

"Heart disease," Lawson explained. "Which, I'm afraid, tells us nothing about her or about their relationship. However," he went on quickly, seeing the disappointment in the Chief Superintendent's face, "I do have one interesting piece of information regarding Hugh Mellor.

"I popped down to the canteen for a bite to eat earlier on and got talking to Peter Hynes. I said that we were interested in three people in particular and when I mentioned Mellor's name he said it sounded very familiar. In fact he's almost sure that was the name of a chap involved in a traffic incident a week or so back. He didn't have the details but he contacted the guard who dealt with it and it seems that some woman ran into the back of Mellor's car. She blamed him for all the damage done and, as it turned out, she was absolutely right although he wasn't too impressed."

"Did he remember this woman's name?" Pollock demanded.

Could this be the breakthrough at last? Could this be the catalyst Eugene McPhillips had spoken of? And, if so, was Hugh Mellor their man?

"Eileen Regan," Lawson informed him. "I have tried to get in touch with her but only got to talk to her partner. Apparently Ms Regan is away on business until Monday evening."

Superintendent Pollock decided that, in a way, this was good news. Not only was there a good chance that they might have found a possible reason for the killing spree – and therefore the killer – but, if McPhillips were to be believed, his next, and possibly final victim was, for the present, safely out of the city. Was the end now in sight?

****

"How did you get on?" Murphy asked Pollock, taking advantage of the lull in conversation that followed Noel's information.

Chris Murphy thought his friend and colleague seemed in a far better frame of mind than he had been for a long time. Certainly he was far more like his old self. It was as if he'd at last been able to clear his head and see a potential end to this particularly upsetting case.

"Well," replied the Chief Superintendent, "as the saying goes there's good news and there's bad news."

And with that he began to tell them exactly what Professor McPhillips had suggested.

"So unless we're able to stop him there could be at least one more victim," said Geoff Hughes, when he'd finished.

"It's looking that way and, naturally, it's up to us to try and prevent that happening at all costs. The trouble is we don't know who, we don't know when, we don't know where and we don't know who the killer is."

"But apart from that it's a doddle," Phil Coady couldn't resist commenting.

Pollock allowed himself a brief smile before continuing.

"We do, however, know something. According to the expert I spoke to, our three suspects could certainly fit into our particular profile although as he said – and as we already know – we need a lot more evidence that any one of them was victimised by women.

One of the best ways to do that, according to him, is actually to get them talking about themselves. Obviously it would all have to be approached very carefully and he did say it might be easier if it's done in the relaxed atmosphere of the man's home. Less likely to rouse suspicion than the formal set-up of an interview room.

"What I'm going to suggest, therefore, is that we do that tomorrow. I think it's probably a bit late to go calling on them now. It's already nearly five and I'm not sure we'd be welcome at this hour on a Saturday afternoon. And the one thing we don't want to do at this stage is cause them any annoyance. That'd shut them up faster than anything. But tomorrow afternoon – fairly early – might be far more acceptable. They might not expect a visit from the gardai on a Sunday but they might be far more willing to chat then than now. And I want us all involved: two of us for each of the three men."

"What happens if, in the meantime ...." began Margaret Power.

"In view of what Noel found out about Hugh Mellor's confrontation with Eileen Regan it's quite possible that she was the catalyst that we've been advised to look out for. And if that's the case she's probably safe enough as long as she's out of town," Pollock cut in. "On the other hand we do not know for sure either that she is the next victim or that he's the killer. I've already had a quick word with Sergeant Overton and we're going to set up surveillance of all three men. I think we'll go ahead with that idea, just to be on the safe side. Uniform will help but I'm afraid we're all in for some overtime over the next twenty-four hours. I'll leave you to decide how you're going to share the load but if any one of them makes a move tonight I want us to be on his tail."

"And tomorrow?" asked Murphy. "Before we get there?"

"I honestly don't see him trying anything during daylight hours," Pollock answered. "The risks of being seen are too great. He wants to punish this woman for what she's made him do so he'll do all in his power to avoid being caught before then. The chances are that tomorrow afternoon they'll all be at home so that's when we go and talk to them. And, if we're really lucky, by this time tomorrow we'll have a pretty good idea which one is the killer and we can then take him into custody.

"And remember, it's vital that we try, if possible, to find out if there's any woman in particular who might have caused one of them the kind of embarrassment or humiliation that started these murders. If we have a better idea of who the next likely victim is we can take measures to protect her."

He then began to get the team organised.

"Chris, take Mags with you. You deal with Mellor. His attitude to Mags last time was interesting. Let's work on that. Geoff, you and Phil go to Morrissey. He's seen you a couple of times, Geoff, so he may well relax in your company. It's the same with Henry Moroney, Noel. He's already met you. I know he's also met Geoff and Phil but you're the man who helped him with his crossword. And those crossword clues we've got are, according to the professor, an important part of this man's actions. You and he share a common interest which may well help us find out more about him. So you and I will interview him together. And if you'll do the early part of the surveillance I'll take over from you at midnight."

Lawson felt quite relieved. At first he thought he'd drawn the short straw, having to partner the Chief Superintendent. Now he realised that it wasn't going to be so bad after all.

"Now. Any questions?"

"Let me get this right," said Coady, a grin playing at the corners of his mouth. "We watch him all night. We talk to him tomorrow. And, if it all works out as you plan, by this time tomorrow we all go to the pub to celebrate."

They all laughed. Phil Coady could always be relied on to bring that much-needed flash of humour to the often grim reality of a murder investigation.

"Yes," replied Inspector Murphy. "And if you're really clever, really efficient I might even buy the first round."

The meeting broke up then. As they each began to prepare for the long night ahead Chris Murphy turned to Pollock.

"Your visit was a success then," he remarked.

Sean Power knew what he meant; knew that, although he didn't know all the details, his friend wasn't just talking about this particular case.

"Yes," he replied, "I think you can say that it was a very definite success.

X

After a long and uneventful night it was just after two o'clock on Sunday afternoon when Geoff Hughes brought his car to a halt outside the large terraced house where Howard Morrissey lived.

It was large, double-fronted Victorian building, three stories high. Geoff knew that these had been the homes of the city's wealthy industrialists before huge detached houses in their own grounds, like the ones on the outskirts of the city, had taken over as the way of demonstrating the extent of a man's success. There was no front garden, just black railings framing the steps which led down to the basement, while a second flight of steps led up to the front door. And beside this second flight of steps was a large For Sale sign.

"If he's our man," Coady commented, "you don't think he's going to do a runner after his killing spree ends?"

"You never know," replied Hughes. "We'll certainly have to ask him what his plans are. Mind you, this is one hell of a big house for one man, don't you think."

"Well, since we know he was once married maybe he chose a place like this in the hope of having a large family to fill it. Anyway, let's see what he has to say for himself."

Howard Morrissey was very prompt about answering the doorbell, almost as if he'd been expecting visitors and had been waiting just inside the door. It was clear from his look of surprise, however, that the two officers were not the expected callers.

"Detective!" he exclaimed. "I certainly didn't think I'd see you today."

"I'm sorry about this, sir," apologised Hughes. "I don't know if you're aware of it but there's been another murder and ...."

"I read about it in the local paper," the school master cut in, "but I don't see how I can help you. I didn't recognise the woman at all and I'm quite sure I didn't know her."

"Well," continued Hughes, "we're just checking a few things with one or two people like yourself who have already been so helpful to us. We're pretty sure now that these murders are all connected in some way so we have to look at all possible links. You knew or at least you had contact with the other two victims so we wondered if maybe you'd seen or met this woman at all."

Before answering Morrissey looked up and down the street as if he was expecting someone at any moment.

"Alright," he said, although somewhat reluctantly, "I suppose you may as well come in for a moment or two."

"Sorry," said Coady, alarmed that their interview might have to be cut short. "Are you expecting company by any chance? We don't want to interrupt anything. We can always come back later if that would suit you better."

Howard Morrissey looked annoyed, although Geoff Hughes had the distinct impression that his irritation was not directed at them. He was right.

"Not so much visitors. To be honest I'd far prefer to be talking to you than dealing with them."

"Who's that, sir?"

"You see that sign. It would appear that someone is supposed to be coming at some stage this afternoon to view the place. Didn't have the courtesy to give an exact time so, of course, when I heard the doorbell that's who I thought it was. Anyway, come on in."

He led them into the house, leaving Phil Coady to close the heavy wooden door behind them.

A tiled hallway led the whole length of the house towards a rear door. To the right a flight of stairs covered in worn brown carpet led to the upper floors while to the right of the staircase was a door, firmly closed. On their left was a half open door and it was into this room that Howard Morrissey now led them.

"I must say this is a fine big house" Hughes remarked, looking around him. "Plenty of room for a family to get lost in. Much better than these modern places where everyone gets under each other's feet."

"That was what I thought when I first came here," Morrissey agreed. "In fact that's why I took it. And the rent was quite low. And, of course it's very convenient to the school."

It struck Geoff as a typical schoolteacher's room. It appeared to be crammed full of books, the two bookcases and every available flat surface holding books of various kinds. On the small coffee table was a pile of school copies, the top one open with a red pen resting on top of it. But it was more than that: it was a male room with no sign at all of a woman's touch. Yet even in the apparent chaos there was definite order. Hughes would have bet anything that if he'd asked for a specific book Morrissey would have laid his hands on it almost immediately.

"What exactly is it I can do for you?" asked Morrissey, settling himself back into the armchair he'd obviously been using, leaving the other two to settle themselves on the rather worn settee opposite him.

"So you're moving then," said Hughes, choosing to avoid the question for a few moments and concentrate instead on a subject he found rather curious.

The answer surprised them.

"Not if I can help it," said Morrissey.

"I'm not sure I understand," returned Hughes. "I thought you said people were coming to view the house. And that sign outside."

"Oh no. It's not my house. My new landlady inherited it a few weeks back and has decided to sell. No warning. No consideration of my position. Just a brief solicitor's letter. Look, I'll show you."

Before they could stop him Howard Morrissey hurried out of the room, returning a few moments later with a plain white envelope in his hand.

"I must have destroyed the letter," he apologised, handing the envelope to Geoff Hughes, "but look at that. She couldn't even get my name right. All those years," – it struck both Hughes and Coady that it was almost as if he were speaking to himself at this point – "and still people can't use my right name."

Sure enough, there was the error. The letter had been addressed to Mr H Morrison, 73 Parnell Row.

"This is now a very desirable part of the city," Mr Morrissey continued, "and she's decided that, since she doesn't want the place, my whole life must therefore be completely disrupted. Talk about callous! It's all about money, of course."

"In the current climate you can't really blame her for that," Phil Coady pointed out.

"That's as maybe," replied Howard Morrissey grudgingly, "but I've lived here for nearly twenty years, almost as long as I've worked at St Saviour's. And it wouldn't have hurt her to give me a bit of warning, talked it over with me even. But no. The first I knew was when I came home and found that sign outside. Naturally I phoned her straightaway. Her reaction was most embarrassing. Talk about putting me in my place. I felt a complete nobody. And I'm sure she was at work so there were plenty of people around to hear her. It was awful. Anyway, as far as I know I've got rights and Ms Eileen Regan is going to have to accept that whether she likes it or not."

The two officers found it hard to hide their surprise at the name. This was certainly an unexpected development although one which they knew was hardly going to please Chief Superintendent Pollock. Just when they were beginning to believe they might finally have one clear suspect coincidence was playing with them yet again. It was that type of case.

"You wouldn't think of buying it yourself," suggested Hughes, anxious to divert Mr Morrissey's attention away from what he thought might be their very obvious dismay.

"On my salary? I doubt very much if I could afford it: not at today's prices. As I say, it seems that this is now one of the city's desirable districts. And," he added bitterly, "since I didn't get the promotion I'd hoped for," he shrugged, "I'm not sure I could afford to buy anything; not anywhere I want to live that's certain."

'So,' thought Hughes, 'Collins was right.'

For a moment he couldn't help feeling a certain sympathy for the man sitting opposite him. Then he remembered that he might be dealing with a killer. There were already one or two comments he'd made which had aroused the detective's suspicions. Especially if the landlady's decision to sell was the catalyst Sean Pollock had told them to look out for.

Well, sir," Hughes decided to change the subject and give an explanation for their visit, "we're trying, as you might imagine, to piece together the background to these murders and, since two of the victims had connections with St Saviour's – Mrs Corcoran's son, Miss Connolly's brother – and you probably knew both young men, we wondered if, perhaps, you could think of any link between our latest victim and the school."

"I told you, I didn't recognise the name," replied Morrissey, "but it could be that she had a son in the school. We've a couple of lads with that name but I can't think of anything in particular that might make them stand out. Not like poor old Richard Corcoran or Mickey Connolly. You couldn't forget the likes of Mrs Corcoran or Maureen Connolly."

He thought for a moment then continued: "Maybe her husband was a past pupil. What's his name?"

"Zechariah, Zac for short," answered Coady. "But we know he didn't go to school at St Saviour's. And they didn't have any children either."

"Perhaps," suggested Sergeant Hughes, "this might jog your memory."

He took a photograph of Siobhan Muldoon and passed it over.

"Good heavens!" exclaimed Mr Morrissey. "Oh yes, I've come across this woman. And a nasty piece of work she was too. I know I shouldn't speak ill of the dead but, in my opinion, she quite likely deserved everything she got."

Both officers were very definitely interested on hearing this, although they were pretty sure they already knew what he was about to tell them.

"What makes you say that?" asked Hughes.

"Oh the carry-on of this one was unbelievable," answered Morrissey. "Which is strange, now I come to think of it."

"Why do you say that?" Phil Coady wanted to know.

"The fact that, in some ways, she was very much like those other two women."

The two detectives studied him closely for a few moments. Was this a simple observation from an innocent man or was he playing with them in the same way that the murderer was taunting them with those crossword clues? It was impossible to tell.

"So," Hughes prompted him. "What happened exactly?"

"I was visiting my elderly aunt in hospital about, oh, several weeks ago," Howard Morrissey told them. "This woman" - he indicated the photograph- "was in the bed next to her. Well, the abuse she gave her husband when he arrived was nothing ordinary. I told you, Detective, about Maureen Connolly and how she treated poor Mickey. Well, that was nothing compared to this woman. And in a hospital ward as well. There are some women who simply have no idea how to behave in public."

It was certainly useful to have their suspicions that Morrissey had witnessed Siobhan Muldoon's outburst confirmed but Geoff Hughes had noticed something more. One more little clue. Howard Morrissey had spoken of women not knowing how to behave in public rather than using the word 'people' which, to Hughes' way of thinking, would have been the far more obvious term.

He left it to Phil Coady to lead the conversation on a new direction.

"Strange sort of case this," said Coady, keeping his manner casual. "It looks as if there might be a link with one of the city's hotels."

Howard Morrissey didn't seem particularly interested but Coady pressed on.

"It turns out that two of the women had what ended up being their last meal at the Carlsworth. Ever been there?" He sounded almost nonchalant.

"That's that big posh hotel in the city centre, isn't it." At last Mr Morrissey began to show an interest. "We had a staff Christmas do there a couple of years ago. Smart sort of place but I thought it quite expensive. I was there the other evening as a matter of fact."

"Can I ask what took you back there?" Geoff Hughes asked.

"One of my colleagues is retiring at the end of the year and it's been decided that we should hold his retirement dinner there. I got roped in to be one of the organisers – I suppose that's what you've got to expect when you've been in one place for a long time. Mind you," he added, "it wouldn't have been my choice but I suppose he won't complain."

Hughes decided a small lie wouldn't hurt – and could be useful.

"I was there myself on Thursday evening. That wasn't by any chance when you were there?"

Morrissey thought back. "It was as a matter of fact although I don't recall seeing you there. But then, we were in an office talking to some woman there about costs and menus. That sort of thing."

Geoff Hughes pressed on. "That would explain why we didn't bump into each other. I was in the bar."

"That's where my two colleagues ended up but I came on home. I don't like the bar there at all and in any case I'd had enough. I'm not much of a drinker anyway and I don't actually like being out during an evening. I always think that when I've done my day's work it's nice just to come home and rest."

"I suppose," said Coady, indicating the pile of copies on the table, "that there's plenty to keep you occupied. Correcting, lesson preparation, that sort of thing."

"Now you've said it. And, to be honest, I like being on my own. I can do what I like without any interference. It suits me that way."

"So," Hughes laughed, hoping that, by making it sound like a jest, his remark would be more likely to get an answer, "clubs and outside hobbies are not for you."

"As I say," Morrissey agreed, "home and hearth, peace and tranquillity. That's what I want. And after all I've had to contend with over the years that's what I deserve. Which is why," he stood, indicating that, as far as he was concerned, the conversation was at an end, "I'm definitely going to fight this house sale. She needn't think I'm going to take this lying down."

"Have you always lived in the city?" Coady asked as they made their way to the front door.

"Much of my life, although I was actually born in England. Mind you, I escaped from there as soon as I could. Which is why I was so pleased when young Mickey Connolly decided to make his own escape. That's why I'm helping him. Sometimes the only way to get a life of your own is to break away before it's too late," he added darkly.

"I wondered why you were encouraging young Connolly so much," Hughes acknowledged, "Although, from what you've said, his sister was in a league of her own. I doubt if there are many like her, thank goodness."

"Don't be so sure," said Howard Morrissey. "Believe it or not this world is full of women like her. I have to admit my sister wasn't much better and my mother ...." He stopped abruptly, as if suddenly aware he'd said too much. "You just have to be careful. Trust me. I know."

There seemed no possible comeback to that particular statement and Hughes decided that they'd probably got as much as they could from the interview. He stood up; Phil Coady followed suit and they began making their way towards the front door.

Half way along the hall Hughes noticed what appeared to be a small piece of yellowish card on the floor beside a small table on which were a pile of papers. It must have fallen when Howard Morrissey had been searching for the solicitor's letter. Hughes picked it up

254

and turned it over. It was a photograph, taken many years earlier, judging by its condition, and it showed two little boys.

"I think you must have dropped this," said Hughes, preparing to hand it over.

He couldn't resist looking more closely at the photograph and, in doing so, thought he detected a certain familiarity in the features of the taller boy. "Is this you by any chance?" he asked.

Mr Morrissey took the photograph and hurriedly pushed it into the pocket of his pale grey cardigan.

"Yes" there was a definite sadness in his voice. "Many years ago."

"And the other little boy?" Hughes persisted.

"My brother. He died."

There was a note of absolute finality in the statement and Geoff Hughes knew better than to pursue the subject. He thanked Mr Morrissey once again for his assistance and the two detectives made their way back to Hughes' car.

"Are we any further on?" asked Phil Coady, as Hughes slowly guided the vehicle back into the traffic.

"There were an awful lot of signs there," Hughes replied. "If you ask me he could well be our man. I think the chief ought to bring him in now before he does any more harm."

Phil grinned.

"So Spud Murphy could find himself buying me that pint after all."

XI

The first thing they noticed as they approached the semi-detached house in Carlton Park where Hugh Mellor had a flat was a rather large dent in the rear of the black Volkswagen Passat standing in the drive. The glass cover of the right hand cluster of lights had been broken and it was clear that the vehicle had been involved in some sort of collision. It looked as if Peter Hynes had been correct in thinking this was the same man as the one his colleague had dealt with following a traffic incident.

"I see someone's had a bit of a bump," Inspector Murphy remarked when Hugh Mellor opened the door of Flat 24A.

"Some bloody fool of a woman," the man growled. "Ran straight into the back of me and then persuaded your lot that it wasn't her fault and that I was to blame. Caused quite a scene, she did, and in front of a whole load of onlookers who were, naturally, thoroughly enjoying the free entertainment. Silly cow couldn't even get my name right. Kept calling me Mr Miller. Still, at least she actually used my name. I suppose that's something."

He was obviously thoroughly annoyed by the incident, a fact which was made even more apparent by his next words.

"So, of course, now it's either going to cost me a fortune or I lose my no-claims bonus. And she gets away scot free."

"When did this happen?" asked Murphy, mindful that the catalyst Pollock's psychologist friend had spoken of could be anything.

"A couple of weeks ago," Mellor replied. "And before you ask I haven't had time to get it fixed yet. Anyway," he went on, "what do you want?"

"We're very sorry to disturb you, especially on a Sunday afternoon," said Murphy, ignoring the man's rude manner, "but you may be aware that there's been another murder and, from what we've been told, you might be able to help us."

"I don't see how but I suppose you'd better come in before the neighbours start talking."

Hugh Mellor was obviously not in a particularly happy frame of mind.

He led them through to the rear of the ground floor flat into a large kitchen which also, it appeared, served him as a dining room. Judging by the dishes piled on the draining board and the lingering smell of cooking Hugh Mellor had not long ago prepared and eaten his lunch here.

'A lonely meal,' Chris Murphy thought, 'but I suppose it suits him.'

Apart from the fitted units and a cooker and fridge, a kitchen table and two chairs were the only pieces of furniture in the room. Without hesitation Mellor sat in one of the chairs. Margaret Power sensed that this was a deliberate move on his part and that he hoped that she, as a woman and a subordinate, would be bound to defer to the Inspector and thus forced to remain standing. It didn't bother her: she simply leaned against one of the worktops. She and Inspector Murphy had already agreed that she would play very little part in the questioning unless something important occurred to her. Instead she would act as an observer, watching Mellor's reactions as the conversation progressed and the Inspector gently prodded and probed.

"The latest victim's name was Siobhan Muldoon," Chris Murphy began. He took out a photograph of the dead woman and passed it over to Mellor. "I understand you knew her at one time."

"Can't say I did," he replied. "Mind you, I think I might have seen her somewhere recently, though I'm not too sure where."

"And yet," said Murphy, "I hear you were best man at her wedding."

Mellor looked a little taken aback at this piece of information and he studied the photograph again, more closely this time.

"Well, well," he murmured at last. "So that's who it was. Zac Muldoon. I haven't thought of that name for years." He laughed scornfully. "I think he bit off more than he could chew when he married her and that's the truth. But then," he added bitterly, "he wasn't the first and" – with a glare in Mags' direction – "I doubt if he'll be the last. Anyway, as I recall she was the boss from day one. I didn't actually know him very well but I got the impression that he had few if any friends. Which is why I agreed to be best man.

"Mind you," he went on, "I did try and warn him. It was clear to everyone. When she showed up in that trouser suit instead of a proper wedding dress it was obvious who was going to be calling the shots in that marriage. Still, some of us don't take telling when it comes to matters of the heart. More's the pity." Chris thought that sounded very much like the voice of experience but said nothing. "Mind you, I'm surprised he didn't get rid of her when he saw what she was like. It's the only thing to do, believe me."

He paused and Murphy took advantage of that pause to move the conversation on.

"It appears, Mr Mellor, that you might have been one of the last people to see Mrs Muldoon alive."

"Oh? How come?"

"Mr Muldoon has told us that you shared a ride in a lift with him and his wife last Thursday. In the Tower House Shopping Mall.

On the way down to the basement car park. And that was only a matter of hours before she was killed."

"That's who it was." It sounded as if Mellor had just solved a riddle which had been niggling him for some time. "I knew he looked vaguely familiar. Well, well." He smiled. "It must be at least fifteen years since I last saw him. More probably. Yes, I remember now. That was when? Last Thursday, you say." Murphy nodded. "Yes, I was in that lift with them. Couldn't avoid noticing them either."

"How come?"

"The way she was going on at him. Poor fellow. Never had a chance. Non-stop. Nag, nag, nag. Something to do with him being late and her going out. And in the cramped space of a lift you couldn't avoid hearing what was being said. It was embarrassing enough for us but it must have been awful for him."

"And how many of you were in the lift?"

"Four of us, I think. Me, the two of them and one other guy. I didn't know him. He looked as uncomfortable as I was and I also got the impression that he knew Muldoon. I seem to remember a look of horror on Muldoon's face when they were leaving and he actually looked at us. Fancy being humiliated so much in front of people, especially someone you know. It's not right."

"You didn't by any chance notice where the other man went did you?" Chris asked.

"Why? You don't think he followed them and did her in, do you?"

"No, nothing like that. But we do have to follow up every angle."

"Well, as it turns out you'd probably be wrong in this case. He and I had both parked our cars quite a distance from the lift. Muldoon was much nearer, quite close to the ramp. I should think he was glad of a quick getaway."

"And you didn't see Mr or Mrs Muldoon again?"

"I told you. Straight to my car and straight here."

Despite his initial grumpiness Hugh Mellor seemed surprisingly happy to sit and chat. Perhaps, Murphy mused, he's glad of the company on a dull Sunday afternoon. He decided to try a different tack.

"It's a very nice place you have here," he said. "Do you live alone?"

"Too right. It suits me. Once bitten, twice shy so they say – and it's absolutely true."

"How do you mean?"

Chris was genuinely curious. Despite what they already knew about Mellor it still seemed an odd statement.

"Got married. Didn't like it. Gave up," was Mellor's brief summary. "When you're on your own you can come and go as you please. Don't have to be at anyone's beck and call. Like I say, suits me. I get enough of running around after others at work. At least here I can be my own boss. I can watch whatever I want on T.V., eat what I want when I want with no-one to nag me. I tell you, Inspector, it's great."

Murphy smiled, thinking of his own situation: Fiona and the children and the warm, chaotic atmosphere which, for him, was what home should be. He declined to comment on Mellor's view of marriage choosing, instead, to move the conversation on to a different topic.

"You don't go out much then. You wouldn't go to the cinema or the theatre or anything like that."

"Not really," Mellor replied. "If something caught my attention I might but it's not something I'd do on a regular basis. You can get so much now on DVD or these Netflix type things it's just as easy to stay here. And far more comfortable.

"I'm very lucky, Inspector. I've learned to enjoy my own company. And when you get a bit of routine going it's fine. And I've got a few mates I usually meet up with once a week. There's a pool table in the pub down the road so we tend to go there for a couple of games and a couple of pints. It's walking distance so there's no problem about drinking and driving you'll be glad to hear."

"You wouldn't bother going into town for a drink then? Not to any of the fancy places? The Carlsworth, for example?"

"That's that big place in the city centre. I know where you mean. I've never been inside the hotel part so I haven't a clue what it's like; but I've been in the bar a couple of times. Was in there last Wednesday as a matter of fact. Me and my mates called for a pint after we'd been to a match the other side of town.

"Not my kind of place, mind. I don't know why these people think we need all these fancy bits and pieces in a pub. After all," he went on, warming to his subject, "a pub's a pub, a place where a fellow should be able to get a quiet pint in peace and quiet. Not some sort of fancy theme park. But of course, it's only since they allowed women in that they've felt the need for all this glamour."

"You sound," said Chris, deciding that in the circumstances a little lie wouldn't hurt, "like my father-in-law, God rest him. Only he blamed all the ills of the world on women being allowed out of the home."

"Too bloody true," Mellor agreed. "Look at them now. They think they can tell us what to do whenever they want. It's not right. Not right at all."

He really didn't like women, that much was blatantly obvious but he was so open about it that Margaret Power found herself wondering how much of this was simply based on his own experience and not really to be taken as proof that he was the killer. She couldn't help feeling that the murderer was far too devious to give himself away so easily. On the other hand, they were all fairly confident that the killer's actions were based on events which had happened to him so maybe.... It was, she knew, yet one more thing to be discussed when they got back to the incident room.

Meanwhile Inspector Murphy was leading the conversation in a new direction, taking advantage of the fact that Hugh Mellor was still so willing to talk.

"Do I take it then that you prefer to spend your evenings at home?" he asked.

"Like I told you, I am quite happy in my own company. I enjoy my evenings here alone. A bit of tele, a bit of reading. After a day's work that's grand."

"I know what you mean," Chris agreed. He'd sensed another opening and decided to try and follow it up. "Do you read much?"

"I enjoy a good thriller every now and then. And I'm quite partial to horror stories. Stephen King, James Herbert, that sort of thing. Don't go much on all these vampire things that seem to be so popular though. How about you? I doubt a man in your job gets much time for reading."

"Reading, no. The daily paper's about as much as I can manage. Although, to be honest, these days the news is usually so depressing that I tend to buy the paper for the sports pages and the puzzles more than anything else. I must admit I quite enjoy a good crossword. Keeps the brain active."

Margaret Power was impressed at the smooth way the Inspector was ferreting out information. They all understood that crosswords were an integral part of the case: it was important, therefore, to know whether their suspects had this particular interest. They already knew about Henry Moroney and Howard Morrissey's interest. She waited eagerly for Hugh Mellor's response. If he expressed no interest at all could they, she wondered, cross him off their list?

"As a matter of fact I don't mind them myself. As long as they're not too complicated. And you're absolutely right. It does no harm to keep an active brain though I'd have thought in your line of business you have enough puzzles to deal with."

"Ah, but they're of a different kind," Murphy explained. "It's a bit like the books you read. There's a big difference between the clues in a crossword and following up clues in a case like this."

"I guess you're right, though I must say I've not had much to do with your lot so I wouldn't know. That's until last week and that bloody stupid woman."

"As a matter of fact," again the smooth transition, "I was talking to a former colleague of mine the other day and your name came up in conversation. It must have been after we met the other day. Anyway, he seemed to think he knew you: or, at least, he thought your name was familiar."

For the first time Hugh Mellor looked decidedly uncomfortable.

"I can't think how," he said. "I've never been in any bother with the law."

"Oh no, don't get me wrong," Murphy hastened to reassure him. "No. It was your surname he remembered. It's not what you'd call a common Irish name. But, as he said, it might not have been you at all."

"Like I say, I doubt it. I've never had anything ...." He stopped abruptly. "Unless .... But that was a long time ago." His curiosity got the better of him. "So what did this chap say I'd done?"

"It was nothing like that," the Inspector pointed out. "Actually it was very sad and, as I told you, he wasn't even sure it was you." He paused. "It was something to do with a rather tragic accident."

261

"Ah." Mellor sighed. "That."

It was a single word but it seemed to both Chris and Mags that it spoke volumes, although that impression might have arisen simply because they already knew the story. They waited to see if Mellor would choose to enlighten them. They didn't have long to wait.

"It probably was me," he admitted, "but I'm amazed your mate remembered. It's got to be at least thirty years ago. He told you the details I presume."

Inspector Murphy nodded.

"Your brother," he said. "A terrible thing to happen. Your family must have been devastated Detective Power there would understand. A friend of hers was killed in a traffic accident when he was quite young."

Hugh Mellor looked at Mags for the first time but there was no sense of a shared tragedy in his look. She felt that it was, rather, a look of scorn. His words reinforced that impression.

"I bet it was a hell of a sight easier for you," he sneered. "After all, you were a girl and girls can lie their way through anything. Do you know something, Inspector?" He transferred his attention back to Murphy as if eager to exchange confidences, man to man. "My mother never forgave me for that accident. Made my life a misery she did. Not that it was complete accident.

"It was my sister," he continued. There was no stopping him now. "She was angry because Ian - that was his name – had taken her roller skates and wouldn't give them back. So she gave him a shove. Right in front of that car. The driver was right. He couldn't have avoided Ian no matter how hard he tried.

"But my mother was having none of that. She had to blame someone. It was the only way she could deal with the misery I suppose. And I became the whipping boy. And my sister" – they could sense real anger growing in him. It was as if he were speaking about this experience for the first time, having kept it bottled up inside him for so long – "sided with her completely. Even though she knew the truth. Not once did she try to explain. No wonder I left home as soon as I could. Between them they'd made my life hell."

He finally came to a halt, drained, or so it seemed, by his outburst. Inspector Murphy couldn't help but feel sympathy for him in spite of the fact that he might be the man who'd already murdered three women in cold blood.

"Didn't your father have anything to say about it?" he asked.

"Hah!" It was a scornful laugh. "Him? Inspector, my father left home when I was two. I have absolutely no idea what happened to him after that."

The room fell silent. There seemed very little else to be said after such an outpouring of misery and anger. The Inspector got to his feet.

"Well, Mr Mellor," he said, "once again, I'm sorry for disturbing your Sunday but thank you for your time. You've been most helpful."

Hugh Mellor made no attempt to move. It was as if his last emotional outburst had drained him of all feeling.

"We'll see ourselves out," Murphy went on.

"Right so," was Mellor's reply.

He sounded as if he'd drifted back into a past which, from all they'd heard, had been a time of great unhappiness.

"Not the most likeable man," Murphy declared after they'd closed the door behind them, "although it sounds as if he didn't get a fair deal when he was young."

"That's true," Mags agreed, "which certainly makes him fit the profile of our murderer. I'm not convinced he's our man, though. I think he's far too obvious."

"I was beginning to feel a bit that way myself," Chris admitted. "Still, it'll be interesting to see what the others think."

So saying he started the car and, with a final glance at Hugh Mellor's damaged vehicle, they made their way back to the incident room to make their report.

XII

Henry Moroney appeared delighted at the prospect of visitors. When Pollock and Lawson introduced themselves he welcomed them cheerfully, saw them settled in the same room where he'd previously met Hughes and Coady and then turned to Noel Lawson with an eager expression on his face.

"Just the man I wanted," he declared, much to Noel's surprise. "I have been battling with this final clue for the last twenty minutes and I still can't figure it out. So you have a go while I go and get some tea."

Without waiting for an answer he placed a newspaper, open at the crossword, in front of Lawson and bustled off into the kitchen. Noel looked questioningly at the senior officer.

"Go ahead," Pollock urged him. "We're probably not going to get any information from him until it's done and it's definitely a way of winning his favour. Just don't ask me to help. I'm hopeless at those things."

While Noel Lawson started working on the clue Sean Pollock took the opportunity to look round the room in the hope that it might tell them a little about the man they'd come to visit.

It was exactly as Geoff Hughes had described with few signs of comfort or homeliness apart from the solitary easy chair and the almost over-sized television. It was very apparent that, like Sean Pollock, Henry Moroney lived alone; but there the similarity ended. Although Pollock had been devastated by his wife's death and, he had admitted to himself at the time and on several occasions since, terrified of facing life without her, he had done everything he could to try and keep her memory alive within the house. As a result he'd managed to ensure that it was a home, a place of refuge full of memories of happier times. As far as he could tell there was none of that in Henry Moroney's house. Instead this struck Pollock somehow as a lonely room. Here there was no hint of a woman's touch. It was as if, for Henry Moroney, a wife had never existed.

'Still,' he thought, 'his marriage was perhaps so miserable that there was nothing he wanted to keep. Sad really.'

And perhaps a little curious but whether it pointed to Moroney as a murdering woman-hater remained to be seen.

It was at that point that Mr Moroney returned carrying two mugs of tea.

"Thank you, sir," said Pollock. "Are you not having one yourself?"

Moroney pointed to a half-empty mug in the fireplace.

"I've already got some," he explained, "although I've probably let it go cold by this time. So, Chief Superintendent is it?" - Sean Pollock nodded. - "What can I do for you today? I spoke to your

264

colleagues the day before yesterday about that poor woman from up the road so if it's about that I don't know that I can be any more help."

Although he was addressing himself to Pollock it was clear that his attention was still focussed on the crossword and he kept glancing towards Noel Lawson. At last his patience was rewarded as, just when Pollock was about to reply, the young man looked up with an expression of triumph on his face.

"You've got it?" Moroney asked hopefully.

"I think so but I'm not a hundred per cent sure," replied Lawson, while Pollock settled back and began sipping his tea, resigned to the fact that he'd get no more from this particular interview until Henry Moroney was satisfied that the crossword was completed.

He took the time to study their host who had now left his armchair and was leaning over Lawson's shoulder, eagerly studying the newspaper and nodding in agreement as the younger man began to explain his possible solution.

Nondescript was how he could best describe Henry Moroney. There appeared little real character to him although he seemed friendly enough. Was this the type of man who would suffer years of bullying from the women in his life only to snap at last when presented with some final and as yet unknown humiliation? Could this be the sort of person who could suddenly turn into a cold-blooded murderer? Pollock had not yet met the other two suspects. He had no way of knowing whether one of them might fit more easily into the role of a killer. But, at this point – and if appearances were anything to go by – he found it hard to picture the man in front of him undergoing such a dramatic transformation.

Henry Moroney returned to his armchair, satisfied that Lawson had successfully solved the final crossword clue. Hopefully Chief Superintendent Pollock could now enjoy his full attention.

"This seems a very nice part of the city," Pollock began casually. "It's not one I know too well. Have you lived here long?"

"About twenty years now," Moroney replied. "And you're right. It is a most pleasant place to live."

"You're here on your own I take it," the Chief Superintendent continued.

"I am now," answered Mr Moroney. "I was married for a short while but I'm afraid my wife grew tired of the game and went off to torment someone else."

He spoke cheerfully, jokingly, but his eyes told a different story. There was real hurt in them which Pollock considered might be due to the fact that Mrs Moroney had left or, just as easily, to the way she'd treated her husband while she was with him. Either way they now had an answer to one of their questions: added to which Moroney's choice of words left plenty of room for speculation on the nature of the marriage.

"And are you a native of the city?" Pollock continued his gentle probing.

"Born and bred here. Mind you, I was brought up on the other side of town. Out towards Stewarton Road. But, as I say, I've lived on this side of the city for nearly half my life now."

"So I daresay you've family living here."

Henry Moroney seemed a little perturbed by the question. If Pollock had been asked to describe his reaction he would have said that the man almost flinched at the word 'family'. He did, however, give an answer.

"Not that I know of," he said. "My mother's dead, so's my brother. My wife's gone. As for the rest, we didn't get on so I lost touch with them all a long time ago."

Another question answered – and more grounds for speculation.

Moroney seemed to shake himself at that point, perhaps sensing that he might have said too much.

"Anyway," he announced, "enough of me. What exactly can I do to help you? I think I told the other officers all I could."

"And we really are most grateful," said Pollock. "However there are one or two points we now have to follow up. If you don't mind us intruding on your Sunday afternoon. We won't take up too much of your time."

"So," Henry Moroney settled himself more comfortably into his chair, "what do you want to know?"

"First of all, as you know we're investigating the murder of Mrs Siobhan Muldoon among others. She lived just up the road from here so I was wondering, since you've lived here for so long, did you by any chance know the Muldoons?"

"No. I knew them to see but, like I told your colleague, they weren't the kind of people you got to know."

"Do I take it then that people round here don't mix very much?"

"Oh no, Chief Superintendent. Quite the reverse. Don't get me wrong. On the whole they're very friendly. Mrs McLoughlin, for example, she lives next door to the Muldoons, she's a very good friend of mine. I often go up to her house for dinner. No, it's not the neighbourhood. It's that particular pair. He was always like a scared rabbit and she always came across as a bit of a tyrant to say the least."

"But you say the rest of the neighbours are easy going enough."

"Oh yes. That's one of the reasons I've stayed here so long. They're such pleasant people. Don't interfere or want to know your life history but always there if you need a helping hand. You know the sort I mean."

This fitted in with what Margaret Power had told them, although Pollock suspected that there would possibly be fewer 'helping hands' than Moroney might have them believe. It had struck him as he'd driven along the road that this was a part of the city where people really did cherish their privacy. Still, he nodded in response to Mr Moroney's comment before continuing his questioning.

"And apart from dinner with Mrs McLoughlin do you go out with any of the others at all?"

"Not really. A couple of times over the years there's been an attempt at some kind of local get-together. Christmas party sort of thing, you know. But it never really worked. People round here can be very private and I suppose that's no bad thing."

Clearly Sean Pollock had been spot on with his assessment of the residents.

"Do you go out much at all?" He tried to make the question as casual as possible.

"Not really. An occasional trip to the theatre, maybe. If there's something really good on. Which isn't often these days. But I can't remember the last time I was in a cinema. It's not much fun on your own."

"You wouldn't think" - Pollock tried to put a smile in his voice to make the question appear light-hearted – "of using one of these new escort agencies we've got in the city?"

"Too right I wouldn't," came the reply. "I understand they're very pleasant young women, easy on the eye, but – call me old-fashioned – but it always strikes me that this is just a form of – how can I say? – high-class prostitution."

"I think there are quite a few who'd agree with you," Pollock said, "Although, from what little I've heard, they resent being seen in that way. As a matter of fact one of our victims worked for one of these agencies"

If the Chief Superintendent had been hoping for a reaction to that piece of information he was to be disappointed. Henry Moroney quite clearly had no interest at all in the matter.

Pollock glanced at Noel Lawson and gave an almost imperceptible nod. It was the younger man's cue to take up the questioning.

"I would imagine," Noel began, picking up the newspaper, "you must have spent years practising to get so good at these crosswords. That must have kept you busy."

"You're not so bad yourself," replied Moroney. "You've just got one that I couldn't work out."

"That was mostly pure chance," was the modest reply. "And it's always so much easier to come with a fresh mind, especially when someone's already worked out half the letters. As you'd done."

"You're right, of course, and it's very often a good thing to take a break when you're really stuck and come back to it fresh later. Although," he grinned sheepishly, "that's something I still haven't trained myself to do."

"So do you have any other hobbies like this?"

It sounded mere conversation but Pollock knew there would be a definite motive behind the question.

"My only other real passion," Henry Moroney spoke enthusiastically, "is chess. It's a game I really love. I suppose in a way it's like the crosswords because, unlike so many of these mindless computer games you see advertised, it really does force you to think. You don't play yourself, do you?"

"I'm afraid not," Lawson answered.

"How about you, Chief Superintendent?"

"Me? I haven't got the time for things like that."

"Come now. You should make the time. There should always be time for some relaxation. It shouldn't be all work and no play."

Sean Pollock laughed. "I'll try and remember that in future," he said. "You never know. I might take up the game. Do you play locally? Are you in a club or what?"

"Oh yes. We meet once a week, regular as clockwork. Spend about, oh, usually four hours challenging each other to full games or just working out new moves. And, of course, the beauty of it is that it's something you can practise at home on your own. That's how the experts get so good."

"So you go to each other's houses to play."

"Not at all. We meet in town. As a matter of fact that's where I hope to be this evening. Seven o'clock. Carlsworth Hotel."

Not surprisingly Sean Pollock's attention was immediately seized. Not only by the venue but also by the fact that it was exactly one week ago that Bridget Corcoran had been killed. To his way of thinking this was definitely proving to be a worthwhile exercise.

"So you were there last Sunday?"

"I was indeed. Started at seven and it must have been after eleven before the last of us left."

He paused, suddenly curious although not in a guilty way, or so it appeared to Pollock.

"You don't think I'm a suspect or anything?" he asked, almost amused at the notion. "Only I can assure you that if you'd like to go along to the Carlsworth this evening I know there will be several people there who can confirm that I was there last week."

"Don't worry about that, sir," said Pollock calmly, at the same time making a mental note that that was exactly what he'd get done. "No, it was when you mentioned the Carlsworth. Only, strangely enough, that's where two of the victims were last seen. They had dinner and drinks there."

"And you think that there could be a connection between the hotel and these deaths. That won't be very good for business." Moroney chuckled at the thought.

"It's hard to tell," admitted Pollock. "Unfortunately, from what we've learned so far, none of the three women was particularly likeable. You yourself told Lawson here about an incident you saw between Mrs Corcoran and her son."

"That's right," Moroney agreed. "Most unpleasant. She was vicious. But then" – again Sean Pollock noticed that strange, hurt expression in the man's eyes – "some women are."

"You didn't happen to know the second victim? Maureen Connolly?"

Pollock made it sound as if the thought had suddenly occurred to him.

"I don't think so. You come across so many names in my job, Chief Superintendent. It would be impossible to remember them all."

"I appreciate that," replied Pollock. "This was a young woman, in her late twenties and, it seems, a bit of a bully to her younger brother. Mickey his name is."

Moroney pondered for a moment.

"It's possible that she was the one I heard berating a younger man about something a few weeks back. I've no idea what it was all about but I remember now. I'd just been dealing with the lad. His name could have been Connolly, now I come to think of it."

Chief Superintendent Sean Pollock was somewhat perturbed. Henry Moroney seemed perfectly genuine in his replies and yet there was the feeling that each one was being carefully constructed. Almost as if the truth he claimed to be telling them was, in fact, only a half truth.

'Sins of omission, sins of commission' he thought with a slight shrug.

He got to his feet. They had probably got as much as they were going to get from Mr Henry Moroney. For the moment at least. He thanked the man for both his time and his hospitality and made his way back to the car.

****

"What's your impression?" he asked as he settled himself in the passenger seat beside Noel Lawson.

It suited him to let the younger man drive; it gave him chance to mull over what he'd just heard. He also knew the importance of first impressions when dealing with a possible suspect so he was more than a little curious to know what, if anything, Lawson had picked up from the interview.

"It's hard to say, Sir," replied Noel. "He definitely seems to fit the profile. I think that came through in some of his answers. But, by and large, he came across as quite open and innocent. And it appears he has an alibi for the first murder."

"That's easily checked. But remember, Bridget Corcoran wasn't killed till the early hours of Monday morning so his alibi doesn't actually cover the time of the murder."

"Still, it would be some trek from the Carlsworth out to where she was killed. There'd be no buses at the time. And don't forget Sir, he doesn't drive as far as we know."

"You could be right but I just get the feeling that he was playing with us. Telling us what he thought we wanted to hear rather than giving us the full story. I actually think Henry Moroney is a very clever man and that worries me."

XIII

"Damn! Damn! Damn! Damn! Damn!"

Pollock surprised the others by the mildness of his reaction. They all knew he didn't swear much at all. He had done in his youth but Claire hadn't liked it and so he'd got out of the habit. Still, in spite of his moderation, he felt that if ever an occasion called for some really strong expletives this was it.

It wasn't that the interviews had told them nothing. On the contrary: the trouble was they'd almost told them too much and although, in one way, they'd been helpful in providing extra information about their three suspects there was still one major problem. From everything they'd learned it was still impossible to say which of the three was actually the guilty one.

"And," remarked Phil Coady gloomily, "it might not be any of them. We could be barking up the wrong tree completely."

"Give over, Phil," said Hughes. "We don't need comments like that."

"But I'm right, aren't I," Coady snapped back. "We've got a lot of theories, many of them based on the ideas of a fellow who hasn't even met these men, but we don't actually know anything. And as for real evidence ...."

He left the sentence unfinished. They all knew he was right. It wasn't enough to believe a man was guilty based on such intangible notions as a problematic upbringing. They still needed hard evidence in order to prove their case. And, as far as they could see, there was none. No fingerprints, no DNA traces and the only motive was the very thing they simply couldn't prove.

"That's not completely true," Noel objected. "We've got that scarf with those initials on. And we must know from past experience that this isn't the work of some random killer."

"Why?" demanded Phil. "Why can't it be some nutcase who chose these women simply by chance?"

"For one thing," Chris Murphy reminded him, "the way that two of them were lured to their deaths. There was nothing random about that."

Being the only female on the team Margaret Power decided to keep quiet and simply waited, trying without success to stifle a yawn. Superintendent Pollock noticed and reached a decision. They were tired, all of them, and very frustrated. It had been a long night, it had been a long day, it had been a long week. And they all felt they were no closer to a solution.

Not only that, they also faced the distinct possibility of another murder taking place before they could find any way to stop it. According to the information they had, Eileen Regan was not due back until tomorrow so she was safe enough at present. If she actually was the killer's target. It seemed a strong possibility. They now knew that both Hugh Mellor and Howard Morrissey had reason to dislike her. But were either of those reasons strong enough to merit her death? And what if she wasn't the next target?

He remembered something Eugene McPhillips had said to him.

'*It's far more important to try and prevent another murder than worry about an innocent person's reputation. Reputations can be restored, lives can't.*'

"That's it," he said, bringing the team to order. "As far as I can see there's only one certain way of making sure no-one gets murdered tonight. We bring the three of them in."

They all looked somewhat surprised at this decision although there was a certain amount of sense in it. If nothing else they could get some much-needed sleep.

"It's far better," Pollock explained, "to save a life than to go pussy-footing around trying to spare someone's feelings. They'll get over it: they'll have to. So we stop playing nice guy. We bring them in and we now question them formally. If he knows how much we've already got to point to his guilt it could be the only way to get one of them to break and confess."

"They're not going to like it," suggested Murphy.

"To quote an old film," Pollock replied "frankly I don't give a damn."

"And they'll get their solicitors here in record time, I imagine," Hughes added. "That's bound to cause more objections. They'll all be questioning the legality of what we're doing."

"So be it," declared the Chief Superintendent. "We are investigating three murders here. We have strong enough reason to suspect any one of these men even if we don't have much in the way of concrete evidence. We are therefore perfectly entitled to bring them in for formal questioning. They can have their solicitors. It might even help us if they do. We'll ask our questions and then, if we're not satisfied, we'll just have to keep them in overnight. That's standard procedure.

"After all," he went on, "the psychologist said it's quite likely that, in the end, our killer will want to confess. So we're going to give him the chance. And if he's as weak as McPhillips led me to suppose then, with enough pressure, maybe he'll give in."

They were all agreed: it certainly seemed the most sensible move at this stage. The Chief Superintendent was right. They'd tried the softly, softly approach. That had got them nowhere. It was time to get firm.

There was, in Pollock's mind, a further important advantage. If no-one confessed during the forthcoming interviews – and he wasn't one hundred per cent confident any of the suspects would – he would definitely need his team at their best in the morning if they were going to make a renewed attempt at solving the crime. By keeping the suspects confined or just uneasy overnight the whole team could at least get a good night's rest.

"I'm sorry, Chris," he said. "I'm going to want you here for a while longer. You too, Geoff. The rest of you go home. Get some rest. If there are any developments we'll let you know. If there aren't be here prompt in the morning."

He turned to Inspector Murphy.

"Right. Let's get started."

XIV

Pollock was fascinated to notice how much the reactions of the three men varied as each was brought into the police barracks and led to three separate interview rooms.

Howard Morrissey appeared curiously resigned.

"I don't know why I'm here," he told Geoff Hughes, who was waiting to question him. "I've spoken to you several times now, answered all your questions, helped you all I can and yet you still don't seem satisfied."

"I'm sorry, sir, but we have reason to believe there are more questions you could answer."

"I think I'd better call my solicitor. And I don't think I should say anything more until he gets here."

This was only to be expected and Hughes was fully prepared to wait until Mr Morrissey's solicitor arrived. His offer of tea having been declined he left the suspect under the watchful eye of a uniformed officer and grabbed the opportunity provided by the delay to grab a cup of tea and a sandwich. He was quite sure it was going to be a long evening.

****

Henry Moroney was intrigued.

"They say you should have a new experience every day," he declared cheerfully, as he walked into interview room three where Chris Murphy was waiting to talk to him.

"I don't think we've met," he continued. "You know who I am, of course, but there you have the advantage."

"Inspector Murphy, Mr Moroney." Chris introduced himself.

"Well now, Inspector. I assume that this is a bit more serious than the quiet chat I had with Chief Superintendent Pollock earlier today so I think I'm going to wait until my solicitor arrives before we go any further."

"That's fine, sir. Would you care for a cup of tea while you're waiting?"

The Chief Superintendent had given instructions that, even though they were to be questioned as definite suspects, the three men were still to be treated courteously. Initially, at least.

"That, Inspector," Moroney said, looking around with interest at the stark bleakness of the interview room, "would be very nice. There's always comfort in a cup of tea."

****

Hugh Mellor was highly indignant.

"This is absolutely outrageous," he shouted at Sean Pollock. "I demand an explanation."

"I'm afraid, sir, that I'm not fully satisfied with some of the answers you've given my officers so I wish to question you myself," replied the Chief Superintendent. "You are welcome to call your solicitor if you wish and we can wait until he gets here. He will, of course, be able to advise you on the legalities of this interview."

"Too bloody right I'm getting a solicitor," he growled. "I told your inspector everything I know earlier today. I don't know what you're trying to do but I feel this is a set up and you're not going to get away with it."

****

Solicitors were summoned. Two of them were already known to Sean Pollock.

Angela Spenser seemed an odd choice of solicitor for Howard Morrissey. The fact that he should be represented by a woman – and a young one at that – was surprising if, as they all believed, each of the men had been the victim of abuse from more than one female during his life. The truth of the situation was soon made clear. She was the only person available from the legal firm Morrissey had always used. The fact that she was still fairly new to the job – although as far as Pollock understood this wasn't her first murder case – made no difference and she wasted no time in insisting that she talk to her client in private before any questioning could begin.

"I don't know why my client is here," she complained to Geoff Hughes, once she'd been briefed on the situation. "As far as he knows he's done nothing wrong and has, in fact, bent over backwards to be helpful to you and the other officers."

"There are still certain questions that need to be answered," Hughes pointed out, "in order that we can eliminate Mr Morrissey from our investigations. It's to his advantage, surely, that we get these things cleared up now."

Both solicitor and client had to be satisfied with that.

Barry Armitage, it turned out, had been Henry Moroney's solicitor for as long as he could remember.

"Not that he's needed me very often," Armitage confessed. "Conveyancing when he moved house, a couple of minor legal questions and, of course, that whole business when his marriage failed. I must admit that was pretty unpleasant. But there was never, ever anything like this. I think you've made a mistake, Inspector," he told Murphy. "I can't for a moment think why you should accuse him of these terrible crimes."

"We're not accusing, we're questioning," Chris Murphy corrected him. "There are certain questions we need Mr Moroney to answer, if only to eliminate him from our enquiries. He's not been charged with anything but we do have good reason to want him here."

Hugh Mellor refused to accept any solicitor suggested by the gardai. As he saw it, he'd had enough police pressure and wasted no time in telling them so.

"I've heard all about situations like this," he told Sean Pollock. "You can't do your job properly so you think you can pin everything on some poor idiot who has only the smallest link with your case. Well I'm certainly not letting any of you choose who represents me. And I'm not saying another word until I get legal advice. But I warn you; you're not going to get away with this. Not at all."

His final choice, made at random using the local telephone directory, did not please him. Andrew Kavanagh was quite elderly, certainly in his late sixties, and, it transpired, only worked for his firm on a part-time basis. He'd seldom been involved in such serious matters as murder but, like Angela Spenser, was the only representative of the legal firm Mellor finally chose available at such short notice. He tried to reassure his client.

"Don't worry, Mr Miller," he began.

"Mellor," his newest client snarled. "Hugh Mellor. That's my name."

He spoke slowly and distinctly as if to a child but in spite of his manner Mr Kavanagh remained unflustered and reassuring.

"Sorry, Mr Mellor. As I was about to say, I promise you I will do my best to guide you through whatever questions the Chief Superintendent may have to ask. I'm quite sure we can get this whole awkward business cleared up in no time. You just have to be a little patient, that's all."

This was Sean Pollock's first meeting with Hugh Mellor and, for reasons he couldn't explain, he found himself disliking the man from the outset. It wasn't just the aggressive attitude he'd shown ever since he'd been brought into the police barracks. There was something about his tone, his manner, even his appearance which left Pollock feeling decidedly cold. Nevertheless he was determined not to let anything colour his views and he proceeded with his questions in the same manner he trusted his colleagues were doing with the other two suspects.

****

They had already agreed a strategy. This time the three men would be facing a proper police interview, very unlike the almost casual conversations they'd experienced earlier in the day. And this time, Sean Pollock hoped, one of them would crack.

Over the next hour they were quizzed on anything that could have even the slightest connection with the case and, in particular, the three victims.

They were asked for far more detail about their family backgrounds, although the only new fact to emerge was that Howard Morrissey's wife had died just four years after they married. Judging by his body language and his expression, Geoff Hughes got the impression that it might not have been a particularly happy marriage. However, this, he realised, could simply be wishful thinking on his part.

They were questioned on their whereabouts on the nights when the murders were committed. The answers were far from satisfactory.

Howard Morrissey had already informed Sergeant Hughes of his visit to the Carlsworth on Thursday night, the night Siobhan

Muldoon was killed. Apart from that he'd been at home every evening, busy correcting school-work.

"I've been giving the boys a series of tests – we do that on a regular basis – and it's very important to get them corrected and returned as soon as possible," he informed Geoff Hughes. "Otherwise they tend to forget what they've done and the whole exercise loses its value. But apart from going into the school and asking the boys to show you their copies I don't know how I can convince you that that's what I was doing."

Hughes declined the offer.

According to Henry Moroney, his only night out was the previous Sunday when he'd been with his chess club; something which, he pointed out but without much rancour, he would, unfortunately, have to miss on this particular eveing. Apart from that he'd spent his evenings at home - alone.

"I can tell you what I watched on T.V. if that's any help," he offered. "I'm a man of regular habits so I tend to watch the same thing at the same time each week."

Inspector Murphy, going through the motions, took a note of the various programmes, knowing full well that there was no way of knowing whether the man opposite him had actually watched the programmes or simply got the names from the television guide.

On the night Maureen Connolly lost her life Hugh Mellor was at a match and then in the Carlsworth. He didn't even try to prove the truth of his answers.

"I told you I was at home," he told Sean Pollock. "That should be good enough for you. If you can't take my word for it that's your problem not mine. Honestly, you're worse than a nagging wife."

Each man could provide an alibi for at least one of the attacks but in each case the alibi only covered the early part of the night. All three claimed to be at home when the killings took place. There was no proof that they were: nor was there anything to prove that they weren't.

The detectives wanted to know whether they knew Eileen Regan, the woman they feared might be the killer's next target. Neither Sean Pollock nor Geoff Hughes was surprised at the responses they received. Hugh Mellor referred to her as 'a bloody, arrogant bitch, typical of most women these days.' Howard Morrissey was rather more restrained, choosing to refer to her simply as 'part of the

278

modern generation, more interested in making money than in the well-being of others.' As for Henry Moroney his reply, though perhaps expected, was disappointing. He had no hesitation in declaring that he certainly couldn't remember meeting anyone of that name.

Finally the three men were asked whether they'd recently suffered any particular setback in recent times; either at work or in their private lives. As expected Hugh Mellor's only complaint was the recent traffic accident and he was about to start another rant about women in general and Eileen Regan in particular until his solicitor advised him that such a reply was both unhelpful and unnecessary. Howard Morrissey's response was equally predictable: the prospect of losing his home and the thought of the struggle ahead if he wanted to keep it still very painful. And, once again, Henry Moroney could think of nothing particularly upsetting. Clearly, his was the kind of calm, quiet life most people desired.

At last the interviews came to an end. There were no more lines of enquiry to pursue, no more questions that might lead to an arrest. Despite Sean Pollock's initial optimism they had, in fact, learned very little new. After over an hour's serious questioning, broken occasionally for brief whispered consultations with solicitors or legal objections by those same solicitors, they were no closer to identifying the killer.

By ten-thirty everyone had had enough. Sean Pollock informed Andrew Kavanagh that he was taking a break and, getting up and stretching, he left interview room two and went in search of his colleagues.

"Anything?" he asked when Murphy and Hughes joined him in the corridor outside the interview rooms.

"Not a thing," the two men nodded in agreement.

"The trouble is," continued Hughes, "there is absolutely no evidence to support our suspicions and nothing to support their claims."

"Let's call it a day," suggested Chris Murphy. "We're getting nowhere fast. And who knows? Maybe we're barking up the wrong tree and none of them is involved."

Chief Superintendent Pollock was not convinced. He hated coincidences and in this particular case there were already far too many. And, yes, there might still be some surprising coincidences to come: what they'd discovered so far made that inevitable. However, he still believed that it was these very coincidences which lay behind the murders and, he was sure, one of these men was the guilty party.

He looked at his colleagues and sighed.

"O.K" he said, at last. "We'll tell them they're free to go. For the time being, at least. But let's remind them that we have to follow up some of the things we've been told and we won't be able to do that until the morning. Which means we might want to question them again.

"And, then," he went on, "get off home yourselves. You look done in."

So saying he returned to his office to consider once again what they knew so far. Somewhere, he knew, there was that tiny piece of information waiting to reveal the whole unpleasant story. He just needed to find the way to get that small clue.

XV

The following morning the team were all back in the incident room much earlier than usual but no-one was surprised to find that Chief Superintendent Pollock was way ahead of any of them. He'd set up three new boards and at the top of each he'd printed the name of one of the suspects: one board, one name. Beneath each name was a space and then a list of headings, repeated on each of the boards. Some had blank spaces beside them, others were already filled with the information they'd already learned.

"What we're going to do," he informed them, once everyone had arrived, "is treat this like a brain-teaser. A bit like those crossword clues I suppose. Noel gave me the idea with something he said to Henry Moroney yesterday."

"I did?" Noel Lawson couldn't for the life of him think of anything he might have said which could have inspired the Chief Superintendent's enthusiasm.

Pollock grinned. "You told Moroney that it was much easier to solve a difficult crossword clue when you came to it fresh and, more importantly for us, when someone had already filled in some of the letters." Noel nodded. He remembered the remark. "So we're going to try and do something similar with the information we have on the three suspects and, if we're lucky, it might lead us to a new clue and, better yet, a solution. And since we're all coming to it fresh this morning ...."

He left the sentence unfinished. It was time to put this new approach into effect.

"First things first. You've all had chance to meet and perhaps study these three men," he pointed to the boards. "So what do you think of them? In your opinion, what kind of men are they?"

For the next few minutes various words and phrases were added beneath each man's name as the detectives voiced their impressions of them.

Howard Morrissey, they all agreed seemed rather fussy, very much the old-fashioned, pedantic school master.

"He obviously cares for the kids he teaches," Geoff Hughes suggested, "but I don't think he's really in tune with them. I think he lacks imagination."

"Perhaps that's why he didn't get the promotion he hoped for," added Phil Coady.

"He seems almost colourless," said Chris Murphy.

"Hugh Mellor's the complete opposite," Mags Power declared. "He's definitely very anti-women. Certainly seems to have a temper."

"I agree." Inspector Murphy had seen for himself Mellor's apparent hostility towards his colleague. "He comes across as being both aggressive and resentful."

Once more Pollock scribbled these words below the man's name. Then he turned back to his colleagues.

"And what about Mr Moroney?" he asked. "What's our impression of him?"

"To tell you the truth, sir," replied Hughes, "he seems to be the most ordinary of them. A bit lonely, I imagine, but otherwise quite normal." He looked at Phil Coady for confirmation.

"He's not the kind of person who'd stand out in a crowd," the younger man agreed. "Not like Morrissey, though. As Geoff says, he's just normal."

"And, strangely enough, that's what worries me." Sean Pollock's words surprised them all. "I spent an hour interviewing him last night and the whole time I got the impression that he was thoroughly enjoying the novelty of the whole thing. But there was something..." he hesitated. "It was almost as if he was completely in control of the interview and all his answers were well thought-out in advance. As I say, that worries me."

"Are you saying you think he's our man?" asked Murphy.

"I'm not sure. It's just ....Anyway, let's see what else we've got before we rush to any rash conclusions."

So saying he drew their attention back to the three boards and, for the next twenty minutes, they concentrated on drawing together all the information they'd found out about Howard Morrissey, Henry Moroney and Hugh Mellor. Gradually a picture emerged. It wasn't a particularly encouraging one.

All three had admitted, directly or indirectly, to an uneasy relationship with their mother. They all had at least two siblings – there'd been no evidence of any others. All had sisters: Morrissey and Mellor had brothers who had died young.

"We assume Morrissey's brother died young?" Pollock asked Hughes.

"That was the impression I got," Geoff answered, looking at Coady for confirmation.

"That's what I thought," Phil agreed. "Something in the way he said that the boy was dead when he looked at the picture. It just made me think he'd died young."

"We got nothing more about Moroney's brother," admitted Pollock, "although he did say he'd lost touch with his family after his mother died. The trouble with Mr Moroney is that, as I keep saying, I got the distinct impression yesterday that he was in some way manipulating his answers so that he wasn't actually lying but was certainly using the truth to suit his own purposes."

Each man had experienced an unsuccessful marriage and everyone had got the impression when talking to them that there was a lot of bitterness towards their ex-wives.

"Morrissey didn't say so in so many words," Geoff pointed out, "but I think we can assume that, at the very least, it wasn't a happy marriage."

"They wouldn't have got divorced otherwise." It was Phil Coady who stated the obvious.

"But remember," Mags pointed out, "Howard Morrissey didn't get divorced. His wife died."

"He hinted last night that it wasn't a particularly happy marriage," Geoff told them . "Which perhaps explains why there were absolutely no signs in the house that there'd ever been a wife. No photos. Nothing."

Each of the three had witnessed an angry exchange between the victims and a male family member even though they hadn't actually known the victims.

"That's important," said Murphy. "It seems to me far too much of a coincidence that all three had unhappy lives and all three saw other men's unhappiness. Although we're talking about events that took place quite a few weeks ago – in Morrissey's case it must be years since he saw Mrs Corcoran with her son...."

"Do we know for certain that he did actually see them together at any time?" Noel Lawson interrupted. "I know we've assumed it because of his job but do we know for sure"

Geoff Hughes looked a little shame-faced.

"I didn't think to ask him last night," he admitted. "I was too busy concentrating on his movements last week."

"I think," put in Pollock, "that it's quite possible but we'll put a question mark beside it. It all adds to the overall picture."

They were almost at the bottom of the list of headings. There were only two left.

"We know all three of them are interested in crosswords so any one of them could be responsible for these clues."

"I'm not sure Mellor would be quite as smart at inventing them as the other two," Murphy argued. "It strikes me that they are both long-term enthusiasts but I got the impression that, for him, it's far less of a hobby."

He looked at Mags for confirmation.

"I agree," she said. "I also think he's just too obvious in his hostility towards women. He makes no bones about the fact that he doesn't like them whereas, from what you others say, Mr Morrissey and Mr Moroney are far more discreet."

"It's an interesting point," agreed Pollock "and we must certainly bear it in mind."

He stepped back to study the boards. They definitely had a great deal of circumstantial evidence – but none of it would stand up in a court of law. He refused to be dismayed.

"Let's take this a bit further," he suggested. "Let's get back to the victims for a while."

He moved over to the original board where the photographs and details of Bridget Corcoran and Maureen Connolly had already been joined by those of Siobhan Muldoon.

"As we can see," Pollock continued, pointing to the other three boards, "all three victims were known – and I use that term very loosely – by our suspects. But is there anything we can think of that might show a closer knowledge. For example, which of these three men would have known about Siobhan Muldoon's night out?"

"Or, come to that," added Chris Murphy, "what about the phone call to Maureen Connolly. Who was most likely to have her number?"

"It's certainly possible that Howard Morrissey would be able to get it," Lawson suggested, rather tentatively. "He was Mickey Connolly's class tutor and, in my day at least, the school always asked for a contact number for a family member. Just in case anything happened. It would make sense for them to have Maureen Connolly's number and very easy for Morrissey to think of an excuse to get it."

"Good point," agreed Pollock. He was now busily scribbling key words onto the boards; hints which, he hoped, would lead them to the bigger picture.

"I can also think," added Mags Power, "of a way in which Henry Moroney would get her number."

"Go on."

"Didn't Mickey Connolly say that she'd lost her job and was claiming the dole?" Pollock nodded. "Then, presumably, she'd have to put a contact number on her application form. And these days most people put a mobile number rather than a land-line."

It was a very valid point although it clearly meant that this particular line of argument was going to get them no closer to identifying a single individual.

"Can we at least exclude Mellor from this?" Hughes asked.

"Not totally," Murphy admitted. "Although he didn't take the bait when I asked if he'd ever thought of using an escort agency he was aware enough of them to have an opinion of the kind of girls he thinks they employ, albeit not necessarily the right one. It's possible that he may have approached the agency Connolly worked for and then changed his mind."

"It's equally possible," added Coady "that, since they both worked in the same place, he could have invented an excuse for asking someone for her number."

"Well in that case," Sean Pollock was determined not to be put off, "let's move on to Siobhan Muldoon."

"Can I just ask," said Lawson, "why you're ignoring Bridget Corcoran?"

"Mainly because she had a very definite routine. According to her work-mates she took the same route home every day when her shift was over. Any one of these three," he pointed towards the new boards, "could have found that out by following her. She would have been a very easy target. I also accept that it would have been possible – and in two cases highly probable – for them to get Maureen Connolly's number and lure her to her death. But surely there's no way all three of them could have known about Siobhan Muldoon's movements. So let's look at that logically."

"The obvious," said Chris Murphy "is Howard Morrissey. He was in the Carlsworth the same night she had dinner there. He says he left early once his colleagues went to the bar but do we actually know that's what he did? Is it possible that he was there when she arrived and then hung around long enough to check that she was going to be there for a while? He could then have written the note, arranged for it to be delivered and then waited out at the Business Park for her to show up."

"I only wish we could find the youngster who delivered that note for her but that's like the proverbial needle in a haystack. We have no idea where to begin and no description to work with. Still, you put forward a strong argument, Chris. What about the other two? Can we think of any way they could have discovered Mrs Muldoon's whereabouts?"

For the first time since the meeting began Sean Pollock felt they might actually be onto something. Murphy's' suggestion had a great deal of merit. It definitely put Howard Morrissey very much in the frame. And if there was no equally valid argument for the other two then maybe, at last, they'd found the crack they'd been looking for. Once more he was to be disappointed.

"I hate to put a damper on things," said Hughes, "but is it possible that she actually mentioned where she was going while she was in that lift with Hugh Mellor? As far as I remember he told Inspector Murphy that she'd said something about going out. Maybe she actually said where she was going."

Inspector Murphy looked troubled. "And unfortunately we can't ask him about it?"

"Why ever not?" Coady wanted to know.

"Because we, or rather I, told him that the Carslworth was the last place she was seen. How could we prove that that wasn't the first time he'd heard where she was going to be?"

"Can we at least exclude Henry Moroney from this?" asked Hughes. "He wasn't there the night Mrs Muldoon was – at least as far as we know – and he wasn't in a position to overhear her say where she was going to be."

"He's the least likely," Pollock agreed, the frustration beginning to show in his tone, "but I daresay someone's going to tell me that he could just have followed her there. After all, they live in the same road."

"Not really feasible though, Sir," said Hughes cheerfully, in an attempt to lift the Chief Superintendent's spirits a little. "After all, that would involve him being at the front of the house, just in case she happened to go out. That's unlikely in itself. And we don't even know if it's possible to see the Muldoon's house from Moroney's place. Those houses are supposed to be very private."

"And then," put in Lawson, "there's the question of how he would actually follow her. As far as we know he doesn't have a car and, since she drove to the Carlsworth, there's no way he could have followed her."

"So the only way Henry Moroney could have known where she was going to be was if anyone told him," Pollock conceded. "Was there anyone likely to do that?"

"The only candidates are the Muldoons themselves – and from what we've heard that's pretty unlikely," said Hughes. "Or that next-door neighbour of theirs. Mrs What's-her-name."

"McLoughlin," said Coady. "But she's been away for a few days hasn't she?"

"When we finish here check if she's back yet. And if she is go and talk to her. Find out if she knew anything and, more importantly, if she did know where Siobhan Muldoon was going to be, whether she told anyone else."

It seemed to Pollock that they were creeping closer to the answer. There was, as far as he could see, one more point to consider.

"What about this catalyst we're looking for?" he asked the others. "Are we happy enough that two of them had a recent experience which might have caused them to flip?"

They all nodded in agreement.

"Then if we take Eileen Regan as the catalyst can we ....."

It was at that moment that the phone rang.

XVI

For a brief instant everyone froze, apprehension on each face then Inspector Murphy who was nearest lifted the receiver.

"Murphy," he said abruptly.

In the silent room they could all hear the tinny sound of the voice at the other end although it was impossible to make out what was being said. Only Chris Murphy's changed expression told them that at least it wasn't really bad news, or rather, not the news they'd all been dreading in those few moments while they listened to the one-sided conversation.

"Well of course he's fully within his rights," Murphy said.

A pause followed while the speaker at the other end made some comment.

"Oh yes, but you and I both know that it'll go nowhere."

Another pause.

"But we were completely within our rights. We've done nothing that was in any way illegal."

More tinny sounds and then, finally:

"Yes, it does seem to me that that's the kind of man he is but thanks anyway for letting us know. Goodbye."

Slowly he replaced the receiver, a grim smile on his face.

"That," he told them, "was Andrew Kavanagh who, some of you might not know, acted as Hugh Mellor's solicitor when we interviewed him last night. It appears that Mr Mellor has taken exception to our actions and has decided to seek legal action against us."

"He's not likely to get far with that is he, Sir?" asked Lawson.

"Of course not," replied Murphy. "But I think it tells us something about the man."

"You don't think," Phil Coady suggested, "that this is some kind of ruse to try and put us off the scent."

"How do you mean?" Pollock wanted to know.

"Well there is a saying – Shakespeare or some such – that goes something like 'methinks he doth protest too much.' And possibly our Mr Mellor is actually guilty and afraid that we're now getting too close. So perhaps he's using this as a kind of diversionary tactic."

"It's a reasonable point," Sean Pollock agreed, "although it seems to go against what Professor McPhillips told me. His argument was that in the end the killer's going to need to confess. He will want to take us to the end of the story and that will mean admitting his guilt."

"But McPhillips could easily have got that wrong," Coady argued. "After all; think about it. These psychologists or profilers or whatever you like to call them are only putting forward theories. They've no way of guaranteeing that their ideas will prove correct every time."

Chief Superintendent Pollock nodded, although he was reluctant to abandon his former friend's theories completely. On the journey back from Derry he'd been so confident that McPhillips was on the right track but he also knew it would be a big mistake to rely solely on the opinion of someone who, as Coady had just pointed out, knew little or nothing about the three men concerned.

"You could be right," he said, "and we certainly need to keep an open mind on all this. And a close watch on Mr Mellor."

"Where is Mellor now?" asked Geoff Hughes.

"I would imagine," Pollock replied, "that he's back at work. I got the impression when I saw them off the premises that, as far as they were concerned, we'd finished with them and they could go back to their normal routine. And I suppose that means back to work.

"However," he went on, "even if this is all a ploy on Mellor's part I'm still pretty sure that, for the moment, there will be no further developments on his part or from the other two. At least not until tonight at the earliest. And hopefully by then we might have had more success in getting the proof we so desperately need. By then, I hope ,we'll have tracked down Mrs McLoughlin – is that her name? – Henry Moroney's neighbour."

"You think she might give us a bit more information about him then," ventured Murphy.

"I certainly hope so. More important, perhaps, we'll also have made contact with this Eileen Regan woman. We need to know just how serious this business was between her and both Mellor and Morrissey. That way we can decide whether or not she was indeed the cause of these killings."

"And if she wasn't?" asked Hughes, cautiously.

"Let's deal with that if and when we get to it," snapped Pollock.

It was a measure of how frustrating he was now finding this case that he would actually let his anxiety show, for he was usually the most patient of men.

He turned to Noel Lawson. "You say you spoke to her partner."

"That's right, Sir," Noel nodded. "Niall Brennan. And he said that she'd be back today."

"He didn't by any chance give a time?"

"Afraid not, although he thought he remembered her saying something about getting back before dark so I assume that means sometime this afternoon."

"Which means," announced Pollock, "we have to wait till then to talk to her."

289

"Yes, Sir. I did ask Mr Brennan to get her to ring us when she gets home. Said it was important. But as you say, until then...."

Sean Pollock turned to the others.

"I know it's going over old ground," he told them, "but there are several things we can now follow up on. And, of course, we're not leaving any loopholes. Who knows, we may find something we've overlooked. Or, for that matter, people we've already spoken to might now have remembered some vital fact that they forgot to mention earlier. It's worth a try."

He paused. They waited.

He'd been right about one thing. After the disruption of Saturday night and the disappointments following the previous afternoon's interviews his team had certainly needed the rest that Sunday night had given them. This morning they were well-prepared to try once more to follow whatever tasks he might give them in order to find the killer and bring the case to a close.

"Geoff," he said, "I'm going to get you to go back to that place where Siobhan Muldoon worked. I want you to talk to everyone there, not only those who were with her on Thursday night but all the staff. See if anyone might have let slip the fact that she'd be at the Carlsworth that night. And if so, who to. We also need to know if any of those with her at the hotel now remembers seeing anything unusual in her behaviour or if they noticed anyone paying particular attention to her.

"Talk to her boss," – he glanced at the open folder in front of him – "Paul Roche. We need to know if there was any way anyone outside the company could have known their plans for Thursday evening. I don't think it'll do any harm to have a look at her personnel file, either; just to see if she has or had any connection with our three candidates."

There was a pause while he considered his next instructions.

"Phil, Geoff, did you find out when this Mrs McLoughlin will be back or, for that matter, where she's gone?"

They shook their heads.

"In that case it's going to have to be a case of going back to Church Road to check. Still," he went on thoughtfully, "that's no problem since I don't think it'll do any harm to have another chat with Mr Muldoon. He's had a couple of days to start coming to terms with what's happened and it may be that he's had time to remember some odd fact that might be important.

"Noel, Mags, I'm going to leave you, if you can, to see to that. Have a chat with Muldoon. Nothing too heavy, mind. He's probably a bit shaky still. Mags, you seem to know how to deal with people in this situation. See what if you can get anything new from him.

"I also want you to try and track down this Mrs Mcloughlin. There must be someone who knows her well enough to tell us where she's gone and when she'll be back. If she's such a good friend of Henry Moroney's she could have some useful information for us."

"Don't you think," said Phil Coady, "it's a bit odd that a man who has been, as far as we can see, so mistreated by women all his life should refer to that particular neighbour as a good friend. I'd have thought if his past experience were anything to go by – at least from what we're assuming his past experiences might have been – he'd have avoided any unnecessary contact with women. Yet you say he goes there for dinner on occasions." He shrugged. "It seems a bit of a contradiction to me."

"That may be so," agreed Pollock. "Or it may be that we've misread him and she can tell us enough for us to cross him off our list. But," he added, looking at Mags once again, "we still need to find her and talk to her.

Satisfied that that particular link would be fully pursued the Pollock turned his attention back to Phil Coady.

"Phil, this job's just up your street." He smiled. "I want you to go back to Harmony Escorts and talk to the woman who runs it. You need to get information about anyone who might have gone out with Maureen Connolly. We have to be able to rule out any connection there with these three men. I know we've already been down this road once, after Maureen Connolly's death and it's highly unlikely there's anything to find. These men don't strike me as the type to use an escort agency although Inspector Murphy did say that Hugh Mellor had some idea about such agencies. So even as an outside possibility we need to check.

"Ms ..." again he paused to check in the folder, "McDonagh might not like it but I'm sure you can use your famous male charm."

Coady grinned, in no way put out by that remark.

"I'll do my best, Sir," he said.

"Meanwhile," Sean Pollock concluded, "Inspector Murphy and I will visit the other two victims' homes. Chris, you go and see Angela Molloy. See if you can find out anything that might link her mother with any of our three men. Even a link with one of them will do if it adds a bit more force to our views on the motive behind the murders. If," he added gloomily, "we ever get as far as finding out which of the three is guilty."

"And," he closed the folder abruptly: this was no time for brooding, "I'll go and track down Mickey Connolly again. I'd like to know a bit more about Howard Morrissey and he might be the best one to talk to, without giving rise to too much unnecessary speculation. I don't know about the rest of you but it strikes me there's something a bit odd about this extra interest he's showing in young Mickey and I want to know why he's doing it. The lad might be able to give us a bit more background and, as we all know, every little helps."

So saying he brought the meeting to a close and within a very short time the incident room had emptied. Each member of the team had left, determined, if possible, to bring the case to a successful conclusion by the end of the day.

XVII

Mid-afternoon. Monday. Exactly one week since the discovery of Bridget Corcoran's body and still her killer was at large. They were, Chief Superintendent Pollock believed, close – tantalisingly close – to the answer. Yet there was still no real proof.

At least there'd been no further killings. That, he supposed was something to be grateful for although the local press didn't seem to agree. According to Simon Moran, a reporter Sean Pollock considered decidedly unhelpful as far as the gardai were concerned, the gardai were doing little or nothing to catch the man (obviously he also assumed it was a man) who continued to be a threat to every female in the city. As far as Moran was concerned the official statement that they were following several leads was nothing more than the typical meaningless platitudes so common with the gardai while, he suggested, the city continued to live in a constant state of fear. It was, of course, the familiar media hype so often put out by that particular tabloid but sadly, Pollock reflected, there were plenty of people out there ready to believe it. And that didn't help their work at all.

****

As it was – and in spite of their best efforts – as the day began to draw to a close they didn't appear to have made much progress at all. Phil Coady had charmed Martina McDonagh from the escort agency sufficiently that she allowed him to see the relevant records regarding those clients who had been escorted by Maureen Connolly. She hadn't been with the company very long, however, and there were few names, none of them, it seemed, connected with their suspects. With a bit more persuasion Ms McDonagh had even gone as far as to let him see the list of clients on the agency's books. No-one was surprised to learn that there was no connection there either.

It had been a similar tale at Global Investment Company. Geoff Hughes had spoken at length to each member of the staff, many of whom were genuinely upset at their colleague's untimely death. She might have treated her husband badly but she'd certainly won friends at work. Hughes even had the impression that there might have been something more in Paul Roche's somewhat emotional response but this was not something he felt it necessary to pursue. Since they were unlikely to be looking for a jealous lover he didn't think any affair Siobhan Muldoon may or may not have had was particularly relevant to the case. The three murders were definitely linked and that, he was certain, ruled out either an ardent lover or a jealous husband.

At the end of his visit he had to accept that all his questions had produced no evidence that Siobhan Muldoon's presence at the Carlsworth Hotel for dinner on Thursday evening had been broadcast outside the office. There was, it seemed, no apparent way that Mellor, Morrissey or Moroney could have known she was going to be there. At least not through her colleagues.

Inspector Murphy had returned to talk to Angela Molloy, Bridget Corcoran's daughter, but since he had to cross the city he'd decided to call at the Carlsworth on his way, in case either the manager or the barman had remembered anything since their previous conversations. It was a vain hope although both Patrick Keane, the manager, and Anton the barman informed him that they had been searching their memories in the hope of finding some little clue which could help the gardai. Somehow the media had got hold of the fact that two of the victims had spent their last hours in the hotel and the manager, in particular, was quite troubled by this fact. However tenuous the link it was, he knew, not the sort of publicity any business would welcome.

"You can rest assured," Murphy had told him, "that we've said nothing but it's always amazing how these reporters manage to put two and two together to make a story. And I'm afraid there's little or nothing we can do to stop them."

Angela Molloy had not been pleased to see him. They had contacted her when they'd discovered her brother's whereabouts to tell her that, as far as they were concerned, Richard Corcoran was no longer a suspect and that as a result she was no longer in any obvious danger. They'd even phoned her again after Maureen Connolly's death to reaffirm this belief. Nonetheless it seemed to Inspector Murphy, as he followed her into the sitting room once more, that she and her husband had made an almost indecent haste to transform what had been Bridget Corcoran's home for many years into a place of their own.

Gone were both leather settees and the easy chair; they'd been replaced by two modern armchairs; the type, Murphy, noticed, which allowed the sitter to recline in comfort, since they even incorporated a foot-rest. The sideboard had disappeared although the bookcase and two small tables had survived the room's face-lift. Most dramatic of all, to Murphy's mind, was the absence of all the pictures which, he'd felt on his previous visit, had dominated the room. All that remained was a rather dramatic seascape and a photograph of the Molloy's wedding.

It seemed that Mrs Molloy was reluctant to spend any time talking to him and his visit had been a brief one. She told him she'd heard nothing from her brother, although she knew that he'd been informed of his mother's death. His lack of contact didn't appear to worry her in any way; as she calmly informed the Inspector she didn't expect to see him at the funeral and, if she were honest, she really didn't expect to see him ever again. They'd gone their separate ways and, while she agreed that her mother might have been a littler harsh on him occasionally, she didn't seem to think that any real harm had been done. On the positive side, as far as Murphy's investigation was concerned, although she confirmed that Richard had been a student at St Saviour's she couldn't remember whether her mother had ever attended any meetings there.

"What about the regular parent teacher meetings?" Murphy asked.

"Oh, she might have gone to one of those but I can assure you it would only have been once. She only came to my school once, so she'd hardly have bothered with Richard's. She told me she didn't see the point in those meetings and, to be honest with you, neither did any of us. As far as we students were concerned all it meant was that the following day the good ones would get a load of praise and the rest of us, most of us, would get long lectures on how we should improve our ways. And then everything went on as before."

When the Inspector asked whether her mother could have known any of the staff from the hospital canteen she told him she could see absolutely no reason why her mother would ever go there.

"Apart from the fact that it's closed during the night," she explained, "Mum and her friends made their own arrangements. I know that for a fact. They would get something delivered from one of the city's pizza places or from the local Chinese. She used to say they used to have great fun deciding what new thing they'd try each night."

Angela Molloy's eyes suddenly filled at the memory and she sniffed loudly. Such an unexpected surge of emotion seemed to contrast strongly with the speed with which she'd altered her mother's home although, Murphy realised, the dramatic changes might simply have been her way of coping with her grief.

"And," she continued after taking a moment or two to recover, "they had all they needed to make tea and coffee. So no, I don't think my mother ever set foot in the staff canteen. And it's very unlikely that she'd have known any of the people who worked there."

She also confirmed that Bridget Corcoran had always accompanied her son to the dole office.

"She just didn't trust him to get there," she explained. "She thought he was such a hopeless case that he'd probably forget to go unless she was there with him. But as far as I know she always waited at the door for him so I doubt if she'd have known anyone there."

In order to divert her suspicions in case she might begin to question why he was referring to those three places in particular Murphy then asked her a few questions about the neighbourhood: the local shop, the neighbours and any friends Mrs Corcoran might have had. When it came to male friends Chris Murphy knew he had to tread carefully but, to his surprise, Angela Molloy was quite open about it.

"Oh yes," she said, "my mum did have the occasional male companion although," she reflected, "not for quite a long time now.

In fact, not since I started going out with Colin and that's eight years ago or thereabouts. Still, I can assure you, I don't believe any of them had any reason to bear a grudge against her. But then," she looked at him sharply, "I still don't understand why anyone would want to do this to my mother. She was a good woman. She had her faults but then, don't we all. But she was a good person and she didn't deserve to die the way she did. So the sooner you lot find the bastard who did this to her the better."

She got to her feet, her sniffs much louder now, and Inspector Murphy suddenly realised that, beneath the facade she appeared to have built around herself, there was a very distressed young woman who was trying in every way she could think of to escape the reality of her grief and the pain that went with it.

Promising to let her know if there were any further developments he left Holly Avenue and made his way back to the station.

* * * * * * * * * * * *

When Noel Lawson and Margaret Power reached Church Road the sight of a car in Mrs McLoughlin's drive made them hopeful of finding her at home. It was not to be, although it was only as they walked back towards the road that Mags remembered Geoff Hughes telling her that, wherever Mrs McLoughlin had gone, she hadn't used her car.

"I suppose," she said to Noel, "One of us will have to come back later and check on her again. I must admit I don't mind doing that. I'd rather be out doing something than sitting in that incident room waiting for something to happen."

Noel agreed. It hadn't been so bad when he'd been able to research things through the computer or, for that matter, when he'd been working on those crossword clues. But now things seemed to be grinding to a halt and, like the others, he was feeling an increasing sense of frustration. There were, they both knew, other things and other cases they could be helping out with but none of them felt like abandoning what had become a very trying case. Still, there was nothing they could do about the absent Mrs McLoughlin at present so they made their way to the house next door to speak with Zac Muldoon.

Mr Muldoon's appearance when he answered the door shocked both officers. It looked as if he'd done nothing at all since seeing his wife's body on Friday afternoon. Three days of stubble darkened his chin, his hair was uncombed and it looked as if he'd slept in the

296

dull brown sweater and faded jeans that he was wearing. Clearly the grief and shock that he'd felt had totally overwhelmed him and robbed him of any will to go on living.

Naturally, Siobhan's death had come as major shock. Even more unbelievable was the sense of utter desolation he'd felt ever since he'd received the news. For fifteen years he'd endured his wife's bitter words, becoming, in effect, almost a slave to her endless demands. Throughout their marriage she'd told him what to do and he'd done it. Now, without her, he was totally at a loss. He couldn't even think straight any more.

Mags and Noel only stayed with him for a few minutes. It was blatantly obvious to them both that they would get few if any answers from him.

"He's completely traumatised," Noel informed the others when they met in the incident room once more. "I doubt if he's done anything since you saw him on Friday, Sir. He looks totally uncared for, almost lost. He's going to need help soon because otherwise he'll just fade away to nothing."

Sean Pollock nodded but said nothing. However, he made a mental note to contact a friend of his, a bereavement councillor, who had been a great help to Pollock himself when he'd gone through the same awful grief. He also decided it would do no harm to contact the local parish priest and get him to call on the poor man. Sean Pollock understood a lot of what Zac Muldoon was going through. The least he could do was send him some help; in the same way that, ten years ago, some thoughtful people had sensed a similar need in him and so had carried him through those dark days.

After listening to the others he told them of his own fruitless attempts to catch the one elusive clue which, they were all convinced, would lead them to the killer. The Chief Superintendent's day had been just as frustrating as the others.

He'd found Mickey Connolly back in Murdoch Street, busily sorting through a mountain of paperwork at the kitchen table. To Pollock's surprise he seemed genuinely pleased to see the Chief Superintendent and welcomed him with a cup of coffee and a definite willingness to talk.

"Unfortunately," Pollock informed his colleagues, "he had nothing of any great importance to tell us."

Since receiving the news of his sister's death Mickey had returned home and was trying hard to sort out his own legal position.

"I won't be eighteen until February," he told Pollock, "so I want to know whether I can stay here and if so what financial help I can get. I haven't finished going through all this yet," he indicated the pile of papers, "but I don't think Maureen had much in the way of savings. I think she spent money as she earned it."

"What about this house?" Pollock asked. "Is this yours?"

"Not as far as I know. Again I've yet to find the relevant documents but I'm pretty sure my parents rented it and Maureen just continued with the same arrangement. Trouble is she never thought to tell me anything about this sort of thing. Didn't think I was worth telling I daresay. But it hasn't made any of this easy, I can tell you."

"Have you got anyone to help or advise you?" Pollock wanted to know.

"Mr Morrissey has given me a few pointers. He's been a great help. It's a strange thing," he continued pensively. "When I was in first year I wasn't surprised to see many of the boys taking advantage him. And yet, poor old Mr Morrissey, I think he's only ever had the interest of his students at heart.

"Anyway, on his advice I went along to the Social Welfare people on Friday. They were a great help. So," he added, "was Mrs Fitzgerald from school. I've not had much to do with her in the past but Mr Morrissey told me she would be a good person to give me advice. And he was right. It's thanks to her that I've got an appointment with a solicitor for tomorrow. With any luck he can show me what to do."

"I suppose the neighbours have also been lending a hand," Pollock remarked. "With the basic day-to-day things, I mean."

"I can't complain" Mickey agreed. "Mrs Rafferty next door has kept me well fed. Too well fed if anything."

He glanced across to the worktop where Pollock saw a large casserole dish and a fruit cake.

"And what about Sammy Ferguson and his mother?" Pollock wanted to know.

He had taken a liking to this young man and didn't relish the thought of a scoundrel like Ferguson taking advantage of him at what was, understandably, a very vulnerable time.

Mickey Connolly smiled.

"Don't worry, Chief Superintendent," he said. "I know Sammy and his reputation well enough now not to get too involved with him. Besides, I've still got my Leaving Cert to think of and I need to do well in that if I'm to make something of myself."

Sean Pollock admired the lad's determination. He'd had, on his own admission, a very difficult upbringing – one which may well have defeated many others – and yet he seemed to have survived. Of course he wasn't totally unscathed; there was no way he could be. Yet Sean Pollock felt certain that Mickey Connolly was destined to make a good life for himself. Once again he found himself thinking of the other two men, the other victims as it were. Richard Corcoran had already escaped and was making a new life for himself. As he'd told the others those two were lucky. He doubted whether it would be the same story for Zac Muldoon.

They chatted for a bit longer while Pollock finished his coffee but it was clear that Mickey had nothing to add to the information they already had. He knew nothing about his sister's job at the escort agency so could shed no light on the people she might have met. It was a similar story with her previous job at the hospital.

"She never spoke of it," he told Pollock, "so I honestly don't know anything. Not what she did there or who she knew. As far as I know she may have gone to the canteen for lunch or she may have gone somewhere else. I don't think she ever took anything in with her from here. Certainly she never got to make sandwiches or anything like that for her lunch. And you can be assured, Chief Superintendent" he added ruefully, "that's definitely the kind of job she'd have expected me to do."

Similarly he could suggest nothing to link his sister either to Henry Moroney at the Social Welfare Office or Howard Morrissey at St Saviour's School.

"I've told you about the only time I saw her at the dole office" Mickey reminded Pollock. "although, of course, she'd have had to go there a couple of other times once she'd lost her job at the hospital. I'm pretty sure she would still be claiming the dole in spite of having that job with the escort agency. She probably didn't think that counted as proper work.

"And," he went on, reddening slightly at a memory which, it seemed, still haunted him, "you know about the one and only time she visited the school."

Pollock nodded. "And you say she knew nothing about the arrangement you have for extra lessons with Mr Morrissey."

"I'm positive she didn't," Mickey agreed.

"Tell me," Pollock said carefully, "why is it that Mr Morrissey is giving you these lessons? And free of charge, I understand."

Mickey grinned and yet again Pollock was struck by the basic charm of the young man – and by the fact, awful though it seemed, that his sister's death had, in many ways, freed him.

"To tell you the truth, Chief Superintendent, I think Mr Morrissey has some notion of me becoming another Colum McCann or someone like that and he's determined to do all he can to push me in the right direction. He means well and I do appreciate it. It's been a great help, that's for sure."

There seemed little more to say and Pollock drained his mug and got to his feet. Placing the empty mug on the draining board he turned to leave.

"So when's the next lesson?" he asked casually.

"I was supposed to go tonight but Mr Morrissey rang me earlier to say that there's a meeting at the school tonight so he won't be free. I suppose it'll be tomorrow or Wednesday before I go to his place again."

Alarm bells began ringing in Pollock's head. Was there really to be a meeting at the school or was the sudden cancellation evidence that Morrissey had something else, something murderous, planned? Pondering this new piece of information Chief Superintendent Sean Pollock made his way to the door. As it closed behind him he let out a sigh. Mickey Connolly might be making some progress in getting his life sorted out: Maybe, thanks to his last comment they'd soon be able to say the same for the investigation into his sister's murder.

300

XVIII

It was late. Five o'clock had come and gone. Still no progress. Still no answers. And still no word from Eileen Regan. Even their one possible lead - Howard Morrissey's apparent school meeting - hadn't really taken them much further; although the fact that, according to the school secretary, not all of the staff were involved gave some slight hope. However, since she couldn't say whether or not Mr Morrissey would be there was of little help. Otherwise: nothing.

The others had returned, exchanged information about their respective interviews and, having finished the written reports of these visits to add to the ever-increasing file which Pollock always insisted they keep up to date in any investigation, they now all felt very much at a loose end. There were, naturally, other jobs which they could be doing although, technically, their day's shift was almost at an end. Others would soon be taking their place although, in reality, there was nothing urgent, nothing very pressing, except this case. And this, they all agreed, was their case.

Three women had been murdered in the course of one week and the officers investigating these crimes could not help but share the public anger which was being so thoughtlessly whipped up by the tabloid press. Yet another long and apparently fruitless day had passed and they were no further forward.

At this point even Sean Pollock appeared to be at a loss over what to suggest next. He'd been involved in various murder enquiries during his career. Some had been very straightforward, a family affair they could almost be called. A jealous husband, an angry daughter, a violent brother. Others had been part of a new and increasingly troubling trend: the tit-for-tat gang killings which were so closely connected to the country's ever-growing drug problem. It was a sad fact that while the recession had brought hardship to many it had brought increased prosperity to the so-called drug lords as it seemed that more and more people –young people in particular – turned to drugs as a temporary relief from their daily problems.

But this case was different. In this case they were confident they knew everything: motive, method and even, if their theories were correct, the possible identity of the killer. Except that the killer was one of a possible three and that final, elusive link which would give them his name was still missing. It was small wonder that the atmosphere in the incident room was one of rapidly growing despair.

Strangely enough, and although their working day was almost over, none of them, it seemed, was in a rush to go home. Even Chris Murphy who, more than any of them, had something to go home to, seemed reluctant to leave until they had at least heard something positive to mark the end of their day. The case had really got under their skin and each of them wanted to be there when the breakthrough - which they all believed would happen - came. The trouble was, although no-one was prepared to say so openly, that breakthrough might not happen for another twenty-four hours or more.

By this stage in the day the only thing any of them could think of with any glimmer of hope, was the expected interview either with Mrs McLoughlin or Eileen Regan. . An hour or so earlier Margaret Power had returned to Church Road for a third time in yet another attempt at tracking down Mrs McLoughlin. Now it was a great relief when the door of the incident room opened and in came Mags with what could only be described as a satisfied expression on her face.

"Well?" It was, of course, Chief Superintendent Pollock who spoke first.

"The good news, Sir," repliedMags, "is that I've finally met Mrs Mcloughlin. And that's where I've just come from."

"And?"

"And she can only be described as a dear little old lady. She is, as she proudly informed me, eighty-five, still surprisingly sprightly and she was full of genuine shock at the news of her neighbour's death."

"Did she know the Muldoons? Especially Siobhan Muldoon?" Inspector Murphy demanded.

"That's probably the bad news," Mags replied. "In spite of the fact that she's lived in that house for over forty years and so had known Mr Muldoon's parents – and consequently known him from childhood – she didn't have much to say about them. According to her they were never friends in any real sense of the word. They might have exchanged a passing greeting if they met in the street but she could never remember being inside the Muldoon's house and she certainly knew nothing at all about Zac Muldoon or his wife. In fact I got the distinct impression that she was quite nervous of young Mrs Muldoon, seeing her as a rather unpleasant character."

302

"That goes very much against what was being said at her workplace," interrupted Geoff Hughes. "According to everyone there she was a lovely person and a real friend."

"Ah yes," suggested Inspector Murphy, "but that's probably because she was always on her own there. Probably, unlike her neighbours, they never saw her with her husband."

"You're right," agreed Mags. "Mrs McLoughlin repeated what we've heard from the other neighbours. Not the type of people you would stop and chat with nor the type who would encourage neighbourliness. In fact she was of the opinion that they were the type of neighbours you wouldn't really want anything to do with."

"More importantly, what about Henry Moroney?" Pollock demanded. "What could she tell us about him?"

"According to Mrs McLoughlin, Henry Moroney is a perfect gentleman. Unlike her other neighbours she's got to know him well. That started soon after her husband died. There was some trouble with her car. It broke down in the road and he was able to fix it for her. That would be about fifteen years ago; she couldn't remember quite when. Anyway they got talking and have become quite good friends.

"She confirmed that he comes to dinner at her house from time to time although he's never returned the invitation. I actually think," Mags concluded, "that she's been mothering him in a way. And it's certainly in a very caring way."

"Hang on a minute," Phil Coady objected. "What about all this business of him hating women? Where does that fit in?"

"I was thinking about that on the way back," answered Mags. "And I don't think he actually hates women in general. I think it's just a certain type of woman. The type that the three victims represented. Mrs McLoughlin, on the other hand, is very different. I know it's a bit of an old-fashioned notion these days but she struck me as a real lady. In the best possible sense. She's a bit like everyone's ideal grandmother. And I can't imagine her ever creating the kind of scene we've heard about with the three victims.

"Anyway," she went on, "according to her, Moroney is a very sad person who's had quite a difficult life. Obviously she doesn't know all the details but she does know that his wife left him after only eleven years of what she thinks must have been a very unhappy marriage. She did say, however, that he is a very private person and she actually knows very little about his background.

"The bottom line," she concluded "is that, as I say, she definitely treats him as a friend and quite possibly - and in the nicest possible way – as a son."

"So do you think we can rule him out?" Pollock demanded.

"I'd ..." She hesitated. "I'd say yes ....."

Again she paused.

"Come on. Out with it."

"Well, the only thing she told me which might have a bearing on this case – and perhaps fills another blank – is that in return for him acting as her driver when she wants one – and if he's free - she does let him use her car occasionally. Noel says he doesn't have a car – which is true – but we now know he can drive and he does have access to a car. He even has a spare set of keys. That's all, I'm afraid. Of course she has been away all week so has no idea whether he's used her car during that time or not."

"So," said Pollock, "just like the other two he had the means to get to the murder sites. It still doesn't help us ...."

He was interrupted by the phone. The shrill ringing caused less tension in the room this time. Everyone was hoping that this was the call they'd been waiting for, from Eileen Regan. More to the point they all hoped that she might be able to help them since, in spite of everything, they all felt that the interview with Mrs McLoughlin had proved rather disappointing and had really left them no further forward. If an interview with Eileen Regan produced the same result they really would be left completely in the dark as far as this case was concerned. It was a scenario that didn't bear thinking of.

XIX

The young woman who opened the door to Sean Pollock came as something of a surprise. Hardly more than five feet two, Eileen Regan was very slim with very short brown hair and what were probably, Pollock thought, very expensive designer glasses which looked almost too big for her small sharp features. Barefoot and dressed in what was clearly a well-worn tracksuit she looked so young that – had he not known better – Pollock may well have been tempted to ask this almost child-like figure if her mother was at home. Before he could speak, however, and saving him from further embarrassment she introduced herself.

"Hi. I'm Eileen Regan. And you must be ..."

"Chief Superintendent Sean Pollock." He finished the sentence for her.

"Do come in," she said, turning and leading him into her ground-floor apartment.

It was the most unusual apartment Pollock had ever seen. Very modern and not at all to his taste, although he had to admit that it was very eye-catching. Whether this was the original design or whether it had been done according to her specific request he didn't know but the whole apartment was, in effect, one large room cleverly divided into various highly functional areas. As he looked around him he realised that, surprisingly, it all worked very well. No single area dominated and the furnishings necessary for each section in no way intruded on the rest. He thought back to other, similar places – bedsits they used to be called when he was young – which he remembered from his past and knew that there was absolutely no comparison.

"Do sit down, Chief Superintendent," Ms Regan urged him. "I'd offer you something to drink but I get the feeling that this is an official visit and I doubt if alcohol is allowed. However, if you'd like some coffee...."

Leaving the sentence unfinished she pointed in the direction of the kitchen area where he noticed rich brown liquid filtering into the glass jug of a coffee-maker. That, he now knew, was the source of the tantalising aroma which had greeted him when he'd first entered the room.

"Coffee would be nice," he told her. "Black please, no sugar."

"Do sit down and I'll get it."

He settled himself where she'd indicated, on a small two-seater couch and discovered that, in spite of its modern metal frame, the thick rose-coloured velour cushions made it surprisingly comfortable, even for someone as tall as he was. He took a few moments to study Eileen Regan's surroundings. From what he could see it was remarkably tidy. It appeared that everything had its place, although he couldn't see beyond the corner of the L-shaped design where, he assumed, were the sleeping and washing areas.

"Here we go," said Ms Regan, returning with two mugs of coffee, one of which she placed on the glass-topped table in front of him. "I hope you're not one of these people who insist that all hot drinks should be served in a cup," she went on. "That's O.K. for afternoon tea, I suppose, but I always think coffee is best served in a mug. Unless it's one of those terrible espresso shots that the French drink. I don't think anyone could take a whole mug of that."

She stopped suddenly, aware, possibly, that she was talking too much.

"No this is fine," Pollock reassured her.

He took a sip. It certainly was excellent: not too strong, just the way he liked it. And just what he needed.

Eileen Regan took a sip from her own mug before speaking again.

"I'm not sure what this is all about, Chief Superintendent. I certainly don't understand what it is you need to talk to me about so urgently."

She settled herself into the big leather armchair opposite him, pulling her feet up under her.

"I really didn't think," she continued, "that a minor traffic accident would merit the attention of a senior officer but since that's the only contact I've had with the gardai I'm assuming that's why you're here. I can't think of any other reason."

Pollock took another sip of coffee, a gesture which allowed him a moment to decide exactly how best to approach this conversation. He knew he had to be very careful. He didn't want to frighten this young woman unnecessarily but at the same time he certainly needed to know whether she was in any danger from either of the two men she had so recently annoyed. Equally important, on the other hand, he didn't want to do too much damage to the reputations of either man if they were innocent. Especially not to Howard Morrissey who was, after all, her tenant. It was a delicate situation which was why he'd chosen to make this particular visit personally.

"That's part of the reason why I'm here," he began, slowly. "I understand from the officer who dealt with the incident that there was a bit of – how shall I put it? – unpleasantness from the other driver."

She grinned at him, and again he found himself thinking how childlike this young woman seemed – in appearance at least – and how unlikely a candidate she seemed as Professor McPhillips' 'catalyst'. But there again, maybe that was it. Perhaps, in the circumstances, it was her very youth which had been the cause of so much anger.

"I think," she said, "that unpleasantness is putting it quite mildly. He really did seem to lose the run of himself, absolutely convinced that I was in the wrong. He didn't take it too kindly when I tried to point out just how much he'd been at fault.

"The trouble is, Chief Superintendent," her expression turned serious, "people look at me and because I'm small they decide I must be a bit of a walkover and they can take complete advantage of me. They don't realise that over the years I've learned to stand up for myself. I learned that lesson very early. And, believe me, when I know I'm right I make sure I stay in the right. And that man was definitely at fault. I had right of way, the lights had changed in my favour and he certainly should never have pulled out in front of me the way he did. He was very lucky I only clipped the tail-lights of his car. It could have been a lot worse for both of us."

"But he didn't see it that way."

"Not at all. He was going to take further action; sue me if necessary. Told me I obviously didn't know how to drive. Of course I stood up for myself and gave pretty much as good as I got but I must admit I was quite relieved when those two gardaí arrived and calmed him down a little."

"Did he apologise once he accepted he was in the wrong?"

"Good heavens no! He didn't actually admit that he was in the wrong. To be honest, I got the impression that it wasn't just me he was angry with, it was women in general. And women drivers in particular. I do have a sneaking suspicion, though, that he knew straightaway that he was in the wrong but then, as so many people do, – and men in particular, I'm afraid – he tried to cover up his mistake by attacking me."

Sean Pollock smiled. His initial assessment of this young woman had been completely wrong. She was definitely no push-over and he could now well imagine how Hugh Mellor would have been more than a little irate to have been put in his place by this feisty young female.

He took another drink from the mug, looking around the room as he did so.

"I must say," he remarked, "it's a most unusual place you have here."

"Do you like it? Niall, my partner, is an architect and he designed it for us. I hate to feel closed in and this gives me the real sense of open-ness that I wanted." She laughed. "It also means, as Niall pointed out, that it stops me getting too much clutter or being too untidy. That's the trouble when there's too many cupboards and too many rooms with doors. You can hide a whole load of stuff away instead of dealing with it. With this," –she waved her arm to encompass the large open space – "I don't have that problem."

"You have another property, though, don't you," said Pollock casually. "A very different one, I understand. In Parnell Row."

"Why, yes." She looked surprised that he should know about this. "My godmother's old house. She died a couple of months ago and left it to me in her will. She had no children of her own," she explained, "and she and I were always very close. Especially after my parents died. But, Chief Superintendent," a puzzled expression clouded her face, "I don't understand how you know this or why it's of any interest or importance to the gardai. For that matter, I still don't understand all this interest in me. As far as I know I've done nothing wrong."

She was beginning to look a little anxious in spite of the tone of indignation that had crept into her voice. Pollock decided that, at this stage, she deserved to know some of the truth, although not necessarily the whole truth.

"It's like this, Ms Regan," he began cautiously. "We're investigating a series of murders which have taken place in the city over the past week and it so happens that both Mr Mellor – the man in that traffic incident – and Howard Morrissey, the man living in your house in Parnell Row, have been able to give us a great deal of useful assistance in our enquiries. And in both cases your name cropped up. Naturally, we need to follow up every link no matter how unlikely it might be."

"But I still don't understand. I've read about these murders, obviously, but I didn't know any of the victims that's for sure. Neither do I know either of those two men."

"But surely," Pollock interrupted "you must know something of Mr Morrissey. I believe you've had contact with him very recently about selling his home."

It seemed to Pollock that she blushed at this remark making her embarrassment quite apparent.

"Oh Chief Superintendent," she murmured, "I wish you hadn't mentioned that. I feel so awful about it.

"You see," she went on to explain, "Niall and I had talked about what I should do with Aunt Noelleen's place and he said that one of the first things I should do – especially as I was almost certain I'd sell the place - was look at what was involved in putting it on the market. After all, it's in a very good area and, since it's far too big for me, I might as well sell it. The money would be far more use. Anyway," she seemed to realise that she's strayed from the point a little, "Niall said that, if I was thinking of selling, one of the first things I should do would be to get a solicitor to contact the tenant to advise him of my plans."

"Which is what you did."

"No. That's the point. I know we'd had a few drinks – a bit of a celebration – and I know I agreed that it was a good idea. But I didn't expect Niall to go ahead and act on it. I was horrified when I heard what had been done. I didn't realise, until after, that the house has been Mr Morrissey's home for so many years. Certainly I've no intention whatsoever of causing him any upset. That's why I was so glad to get his message."

Pollock seized on this immediately.

"What message," he demanded.

"He left a message on my voice mail suggesting that we meet up this evening to discuss everything and, hopefully, we can come up with an arrangement that suits us all." She looked earnestly at Pollock. "I know that Mr Morrissey was so upset that he was talking about taking legal action but I do hope it won't come to that. That's why I'm meeting him," she repeated. "To sort this out."

Sean Pollock was now in a bit of a dilemma. Howard Morrissey was one of their suspects. The letter from Eileen Regan's solicitor had, they knew, upset him greatly. It could even have been the catalyst to these murders. And, as far as he understood the situation, if that were so then, by going to meet him, this young woman could in fact be walking into a trap. And a fatal one at that.

He didn't want to alarm her, especially if he were wrong. Yet again there was that uncertainty which seemed to have dogged this whole case. He decided to try and find out a little more before he faced the question of whether or not to warn her against meeting her irate tenant.

"Mr Morrissey," he told her, "appears to be a reasonable man so I'm sure that, between you, you can come to some arrangement. You're meeting him this evening you say?"

"Yes," she replied, glancing automatically at the large slate clock on the wall to her right. "In about half an hour. He said he should hopefully be free by then although it might be a little late. I'm hoping Niall will be back in time as I want him to come with me." She grinned. "He can help me out if I put my foot in it again. Especially since this whole misunderstanding is as much his fault."

Chief Superintendent Pollock felt a wave of relief. If she had someone with her at this meeting then there was little likelihood of any danger. Not yet anyway. He got to his feet. There was, he thought, little more he could ask her.

"Well," he said, as he began to make his way to the door, "I'm sorry to have troubled you; especially when, I understand, you're only just back from a weekend break."

She gave a laugh as she followed him to the door and her face took on a rueful expression.

"Oh believe me, Chief Superintendent, it was no break," she said. "I've recently had a very important promotion at work and though, of course, I'm delighted, it can be quite difficult for someone quite young and" – she looked down at herself and smiled – "tiny like me to create the right sense of authority. Especially over older staff members who may feel put out by having me as their new boss. And more especially if they'd tried for the same post themselves. So," she opened the door for him, "I've spent the weekend on a course learning just how to deal with any tricky situations which could arise in my new role."

As he stepped outside Sean Pollock looked at her appraisingly.

"Well, Ms Regan," he declared, "I'm quite sure that you can bring the right measure of authority to any job. And I wish you well on your promotion. Where is it you work?" he added, almost as an afterthought.

At that moment they heard the musical sound of a mobile phone from inside the apartment. The insistent tone demanded an answer. Glancing back to where her mobile lay Eileen Regan hurriedly answered his question before, with a swift goodbye and an apologetic smile, she turned back to the phone, closing the door behind her.

Sean Pollock was already hurrying to his car. He was now absolutely certain he knew who the killer was. He didn't hear Eileen Regan answer her phone. So he didn't hear Niall Brennan telling her he was going to be delayed for a couple of hours and that she would have to go to Parnell Row alone.

****

3 DOWN, 20 DOWN, 23 ACROSS

I

The evening traffic was as busy as always. It was home-time and, with a fog already drifting over the city, everyone was in a rush to get to the warmth and safety of their homes. Sean Pollock cursed the restriction caused by the build up of traffic but, driving as fast as he was able and negotiating short cuts wherever he could, he made his way back to the garda barracks.

"O.K." he shouted, as he hurried into the incident room. "There's no time to explain. Geoff, I want you to come with me. Chris, get back to Eileen Regan's place. 15 Gilmore Place. Don't go in; just wait in your car until you see her leave. And then I want you to follow her. Take Mags with you. We might need a female officer.

"Phil, Noel, wait here. I'll call you when I need you. Come on, Geoff. Quick. And here," he handed over his keys, "you drive."

****

They hadn't gone very far before Pollock's mobile phone rang. It was Noel Lawson.

"Someone's just delivered another large envelope, Sir. It's exactly like the others."

"Open it."

There was a pause while Noel did as instructed.

"More clues Sir. Shall I read them out to you?"

"No. Just get on with them straightaway," Pollock snapped impatiently. "And let me know when you've solved them. Now, let me speak to Phil."

There was another pause and the muffled sounds of the phone changing hands.

"Sir?"

"Phil, I need you to check out a couple of things for me. And let me know as soon as you've found the answers." He stopped speaking for a moment, obviously trying to consider every possibility. "And if you can't reach me or if I don't answer then speak to Geoff."

Moments later he ended the call and turned his attention to the road ahead.

It didn't take long to reach their destination.

"Now, Geoff," Pollock ordered, "I want you to back up a bit, pull in and then we wait. And, if I'm right, I don't think we're going to have to wait for too long."

"Can I ask, Sir, exactly what we're waiting for?"

"I think that, before too long, that car," he pointed towards a small Seat Ibiza parked in a drive not far from where they were waiting, "is going to move. And when it does we follow it. And whatever you do, don't lose it."

Sean Pollock had thought more than once in his long career that, in their job, it was often the waiting that was the hardest to put up with. He was now quite sure in his own mind who the killer was and, since they all knew how devious the man had shown himself to be, he was equally sure that he knew what was being planned. However, the only way to prove it was to do precisely what they were now doing and trust that, as events unfolded, they wouldn't lose their prey. To do so might literally be fatal.

He was right about one thing. They didn't have long to wait. After about twenty-five minutes they heard the sound of a car door slamming and saw the lights of the car they'd been watching come on.

"Don't get too close," Pollock instructed Hughes, as they pulled into the road behind the small vehicle. "We don't want him to know we're here. On the other hand, whatever happens, I repeat, don't lose him."

Pollock soon realised that this was perhaps the best time of day to follow another vehicle. The evening rush-hour had eased off but there was still enough traffic around to make it difficult for their target to spot them. At the same time, there wasn't too much traffic so there was less chance of losing him.

The Chief Superintendent's mobile phone rang. It was Phil Coady.

"I've checked Mickey Connolly's story again, Sir. It's definitely this evening but there's no time limit so no-one could say when it would end. And I spoke to Sergeant O'Dwyer. Apparently they were taken to the canteen and he says there appeared to be quite a lot of chat between them. I suppose their mutual troubles and certainly their annoyance with us gave them plenty to discuss."

"Thanks, Phil. How's Noel getting on?"

313

"Nothing so far but we'll keep you posted."

No sooner had the call ended than the shrill tone of the mobile began again. This time the caller was Inspector Murphy.

"She's just leaving now," he reported.

"Has she anyone with her?" demanded Pollock.

"Can't see anyone. No. No, she's just heading off and she's on her own."

"Bugger it," snapped Pollock although he'd already begun to fear that this might happen. The killer was definitely both clever and devious. "Stick to her, Chris. And, for God's sake, don't lose her. She may well need your help when she reaches her destination."

"What do we do when we get there?" Murphy wanted to know.

"Wait in the car until you hear from me. But, Chris, this is important. Make sure no-one is aware that you've followed her. Especially not Ms Regan herself."

He ended the call. Inspector Murphy had known better than to ask any questions. He'd worked with Sean Pollock on several cases and understood him well enough to know that the Chief Superintendent now had the scent of victory and was following it through with all his usual enthusiasm.

****

Neither Pollock nor Hughes spoke as they continued to follow the small Seat through the city streets until the driver finally indicated that he was pulling into the kerb. His destination was exactly what Pollock had expected. Hughes pulled in a little way behind and, as he turned off the engine, they saw their target climb out of his car and then, turning back, reach in and pull something towards him. It looked like a long piece of fabric – a scarf probably – which he quickly rolled up and tucked inside his jacket.

"A murder weapon," breathed Hughes.

"Exactly," Pollock agreed.

"Do we make our move now?"

"Not yet. At the moment he could just give a load of excuses. Visiting a friend, a cold evening, anything like that. We have to let him go a bit further."

314

Their target looked round once more but, apparently reassured that he wasn't attracting any unnecessary attention, then moved towards the house. Geoff Hughes was surprised that he didn't immediately walk up the few steps to the front door. Instead, however, he gave another quick glance round and then disappeared in the direction of the basement. One look at Pollock's face told the younger detective that this was pretty much what his boss had expected.

In the wing mirror on his side of the car Sean Pollock saw two people approaching, heads bent as they hurried to get out of the cold, damp evening. They were almost at the spot where the two officers were parked.

"As soon as these two pass," he told Hughes, "I'm going to get out behind them. I want you to wait here but whatever you do keep your eyes on that house."

Using the two unsuspecting pedestrians as cover Pollock stepped out onto the pavement, pushing the car door gently shut behind him. With any luck their target wouldn't have seen him either leaving the car or approaching the house. Now all he had to do was get as close as possible without being spotted. Not for the first time in his career he was grateful for a dark night and a rapidly descending autumn fog.

Sheltered by the large hedge of the adjoining house Pollock thought he was probably as close to the target as he could risk getting at this stage. His one hope now was that, when the time came, he'd be able to move quickly enough to prevent a tragedy.

He felt a small vibration in his coat pocket. His mobile phone. He knew better than to risk trying to answer it and, in any case, was confident that it was another member of the team and, if they couldn't contact him, they would immediately try to speak to Geoff Hughes.

Hopefully it was Noel and by now the young detective had cracked the last few clues although if the Chief Superintendent's theory was right – and everything now pointed that way – those clues would now be almost irrelevant.

He glanced back to his car where he thought he saw, for the briefest of moments, a flicker of light and a slight movement. Hughes' phone he guessed, as he turned his attention back to the dark house and the even darker basement area.

II

Back in the incident room Noel and Phil had been working on the crossword clues. There were three of them.

16 Across: A lot without the indefinite.

19 Down: As the old writer said this, when good, is an immediate jewel.

21 Across: Eight with six, Tom Jones, Tin Lizzie – they all had the same first.

Phil was honest enough to admit that he still couldn't follow the complex deductive reasoning that had enabled Noel to solve two of the clues. Noel hadn't bothered to explain.

"Just take my word for it, Phil. The first one's 'my' and the second is ...." He paused, a look of intense concentration on his face.

"Well," said Phil, "if it's any help Tom Jones is a pop singer and Tin Lizzie was a pop group so maybe that's the link."

Noel Lawson shook his head.

"It was Thin Lizzy not Tin Lizzy" he said, absentmindedly and then, to Phil's astonishment, slammed his hand down on the desk.

"Of course," he cried. "How stupid."

Phil Coady stared at his colleague, wondering what had caused this particular outburst.

"If we work backwards," muttered Noel, his eyes fixed on the white-board at the front of the room "then the answer is blatantly obvious."

Coady was completely at a loss as he watched Lawson reach for the phone, hurriedly dial a number, wait for a moment and then hang up and redial. This time he got an answer. It was Geoff Hughes, still watching and waiting in the car.

"He's not here," said Hughes in answer to Noel's question. "What's wrong?"

"Tell him I've solved those clues," Noel told him. "Tell him I've got the answer."

Geoff Hughes smiled ruefully as he ended the call. It looked as if the Chief Superintendent was right and, although that didn't surprise him, he couldn't help feeling slightly disappointed at his own inability to figure out just who the killer was.

'Perhaps,' he said to himself, 'that explains why he's in charge and I'm not. Still, you never know. One day.'

And with that he resumed his study of the dark and almost silent street.

****

A car came slowly down the road, tentatively, as if the driver were looking for somewhere to park. As it turned out there was a space just a short distance away on the opposite side of the road from where Hughes sat. He watched as the small Fiat was skilfully manoeuvred into the space and the driver – short and probably female although the heavy padded jacket she wore made it hard to tell for sure – climbed out.

Sean Pollock was watching as well and he'd also seen a second car pull over, just four vehicles away from the Fiat. The parking, he observed cynically, was slightly less efficient. It didn't matter as long as the occupants – Murphy and Power he assumed – would be poised ready to move as soon as the need arose.

Eileen Regan walked slowly away from her car, remaining on the far side of the road until she was directly opposite the address she was seeking. Then, with a quick glance in either direction and finding the road empty, she hurried across to the foot of the steps which led to the front door.

A figure emerged from the basement steps, startling her.

"I'm sorry, Miss Regan." The voice was very quiet. "I didn't mean to startle you."

It sounded very familiar. The one she'd heard on her voicemail. She relaxed.

"I hope I'm not late," she said, as she began to turn round.

The man's next words stopped her.

"I think," he said "that you've left your car lights on."

She turned away from him so that she could check her car and in that brief moment he moved towards her. The next thing she knew there was something soft around her neck, something which was being pulled ever tighter, something which was dragging her

317

backwards towards the basement She started to struggle and then, thankfully, the scarf began to loosen as she heard a loud voice.

"I wouldn't do that if I were you, Henry."

III

By common consent they'd all adjourned to the Seanachai. With the adrenalin rush still high and the sense of satisfaction at a difficult case solved strong, none of them was in a hurry to go home. Even Inspector Murphy was with them. Having phoned Fiona to tell her the news he was pleased but not surprised at her reply.

"Go ahead, Chris," she'd told him. "This has been a hard week for all of you and I understand completely that you now need time to celebrate. I'll see you when you get back."

As so often in the past, Chris Murphy thanked his lucky stars to have found such a wonderful and understanding companion. He knew that many men in his job were not so lucky.

"What I want to know, Sir," Phil Coady was saying when Murphy rejoined the group, "is what led you to be so sure it was Moroney."

"To be perfectly honest, Phil, I wasn't when I first went to talk to Eileen Regan although, having said that, I'd pretty much decided that it wasn't Mellor."

"Why not?" Noel Lawson wanted to know.

"For pretty much the same reasons that Mags gave."

All eyes turned to their attractive companion whose charming smile and sparkling eyes had them completely hooked as usual. She shrugged modestly.

"It just struck me," she told them "that he was far too open in his dislike of women, which was not the impression I was getting when we began to investigate the victim's relatives or for that matter when we started to build up a profile of the killer. It just struck me that Mickey Connolly and Zac Muldoon disliked the way particular women treated them but it didn't seem that they had any axe to grind against women in general. Mellor, on the other hand, when we" – she nodded in the direction of Inspector Murphy – "interviewed him was very blatant in his mistrust of and even dislike of my being there."

318

As Pollock nodded in agreement Murphy added a further point, repeating something that had been suggested earlier in the day.

"I was beginning to have my own doubts about him," he confessed, "after that phone call from his solicitor. Mellor came across as an unpleasant individual but, despite what Phil suggested, I didn't think he'd have the intelligence, if that's the right word, to play such a devious game of bluff. Crossword solving is one thing, bluff and double bluff take a certain amount of extra mental agility and, to be honest, I didn't think he had that. If he was planning to sue us for wrongful detention then it struck me that he probably felt he had a genuine grievance and so was an innocent man."

"Fair enough," Phil acknowledged, "but that still doesn't explain, Sir," – he turned back to Pollock – "what made you finally choose Henry Moroney as the killer. Why not Morrissey?"

"Morrissey was a very strong candidate in some ways," said Pollock, "although Geoff had a point the other day after he'd visited him at the school."

Hughes looked slightly bemused.

"I did?" he said, not at all sure what point the Chief Superintendent was referring to.

Pollock helped him out.

"When you and I were chatting after that visit," he said, "you passed a remark about wondering how someone like Mr Morrissey managed in the classroom, controlling a bunch of disinterested teenage boys. And then Mickey Connolly when, I spoke to him earlier, also referred to the fact that at one stage, when he was younger, he'd not been surprised to see many of the boys taking advantage of the man. Poor old Mr Morrissey he called him.

"And, of course, there was the fact that the school principal had told Geoff that it was unlikely that Morrissey would get the promotion he'd hoped for. Although we have no idea what that promotion was it was obvious Howard Morrissey wasn't considered the kind of person to win the school's confidence. I did think that, if that was the case, he might not be a strong enough personality to convincingly lure these women to their deaths.

"On the other hand," he went on, "I knew my reasoning had no real backing. And there was the fact that he had one very good reason for being angry with Eileen Regan."

"The house sale," said Hughes.

"Exactly. He'd lived in that house, as he told you, for years. It must have been a huge blow to have this jumped-up young woman suddenly announcing that she was going to sell his home. As we all agreed, that could easily have been seen as yet another example of him being abused by a woman.

"Anyway, when Eileen Regan told me he'd left a phone message for her, arranging to meet him that evening I still had my doubts. In fact," he continued, "I was about to warn her and try and find a reason for suggesting why she should postpone that meeting when she told me that her partner was going with her."

"But she ended up going on her own," Chris pointed out.

"Ah," said Pollock, "but that's just another example of how devious our Mr Moroney really is. What I didn't know then was that the phone call she took as I left – the one in which her partner told her he was going to be late – was actually part of a put-up job engineered by Moroney."

"Engineered how?" Noel Lawson wanted to know.

"I now know that Mr Moroney has spent part of his time this past week or so researching his target; so he not only knew that Ms Regan had a partner, he also knew what the man's job was and where he worked. So all he had to do was phone him and invent a situation that would prevent him being with Ms Regan this evening.

"Of course by the time she got that call I'd assumed she was safe from Morrissey but I also knew that Moroney was the real threat. And that," he turned to Geoff Hughes, "is why you and I had to tail him."

"You still haven't said what finally convinced you that Moroney was our man." Coady was nothing if not persistent.

Pollock smiled.

"It was when she told me where she worked. She'd just been promoted, she'd already told me that, and when she said she worked in the same place as Moroney I was certain it had to be him. I now know that it was a promotion he had hoped for; I'd suspected that when she spoke of it. It seemed obvious. A broken rear light or a change in landlord was nothing in comparison. Here was a man in his mid-forties who was going to be told yet again what to do and how to do it by a very efficient woman – and a much younger one at that. And I think – and he has admitted – that's when he snapped."

"But what about Howard Morrissey's phone message to Eileen Regan?" prompted Chris.

"That wasn't Morrissey at all," Pollock explained. "It was Moroney. He only had to change his voice slightly to fool her. Remember, she's never met Morrissey so she wouldn't know his voice. I'd figured that out by the time I got back here which is why I needed her to be followed as well. It struck me that someone who'd been clever enough to fool both Maureen Connolly and Siobhan Muldoon into going to meet him so late at night could certainly trick Eileen Regan into a much earlier meeting."

"So how did he know about Morrissey and Eileen Regan in the first place?" asked Lawson.

"As I said, he'd already done some research on her and I got Phil to check whether the three men had had any contact while they were here. It transpires that they had coffee together last night before they left. Sergeant O'Dwyer saw no harm in that. So it would have been very easy for Moroney to control the conversation so that he could find out exactly what he wanted to know. Of course, when we began following him I wasn't sure just what he'd got planned but I know that area and I reasoned that the layout of those houses where Morrissey lives might lend itself to some kind of dark deed. Especially on a night like tonight although," he laughed "I don't think even our clever Mr Moroney could have actually engineered that."

"There's one other thing," said Mags, as the laughter died down. "We know he fooled Maureen Connolly with a phone call and Siobhan with a note but how did he fool Bridget Corcoran?"

"He didn't have to. All he had to do was find out her routine. And we've been told it was the same every night. Which meant he just had to follow her until she reached a spot where he knew he was unlikely to be seen."

"So he's confessed to it all?" asked Murphy.

"His confession is signed, sealed and locked away. Like him. There's also a rather pathetic document which he had with him; his justification he called it."

"And?" Murphy clearly expected his colleague to say more.

"And we were absolutely right. This is a man who was abused throughout most of his life and when he feared it was about to start again he simply snapped. But no matter how sad his life we can't ignore the fact that he murdered three innocent women. And no matter how bad they were in his eyes they didn't deserve that. "He sighed. "A new twist I suppose on the idea of the sins of the fathers."

"And the crosswords?" Noel Lawson couldn't resist asking.

"Just his idea of a challenge apparently. Despite everything the women in his life have told him he still believes he's quite a clever man. This was simply one way of proving it. And, believe it or not, he was quite pleased to have met his match in you. He made up all the clues and eventually you were able to solve them all. That appears to have given him a great sense of satisfaction"

So saying Sean Pollock drained his glass and placed it carefully on the table in front of him. In the ensuing silence he studied it for a moment or two then spoke once more.

"I seem to remember Inspector Murphy saying at some stage that he was going to buy us all a pint."

Chris Murphy looked blank and shook his head.

"Well, I'm quite sure that even if he didn't, he meant to. And I don't know about the rest of you but, I'm more than ready for mine."

****

322

12 ACROSS, 18 REASON, 21 DOWN

Because

It's true. It is the last straw that breaks the camel's back. I'd never believed that: experience taught me better. My mother, I feel sure, had never really wanted me: her obvious preference for my sister - shown in the many ways she used and abused me - was ample proof of that. My wife eventually tired of making my life miserable. I think that, for her, marriage to me was a bit of a game, an experiment to see just how much power she had over me. But even games become boring if they are played for too long. She taunted, I endured: but, after eleven miserable years – well, miserable for me – she grew weary.

She'd done well out of the game. Not only had she had her fun she also got a very good divorce settlement. I didn't mind. At least I was free. I could become my own man. For the first time in my life I had no woman ordering me around and making my life an almost unbearable hell in the process.

At last I was content. I had my home – not a palace but a comfortable place where I could live my life the way I wanted – and I had my job. I'd finally discovered what it was like to be happy.

It couldn't last. I should have known that. But happiness can sometimes make you very blind.

She really shouldn't have treated me the way she did. Such a public humiliation. To address me in front of all the staff.

"So sorry, Mr Malone. I know you were hoping for the job"

And as the rest of them patted me on the shoulder – "Sorry about that." – before gathering around the successful candidate, anxious to win her favour straightaway, I realised that, like the others, she couldn't even call me by my proper name. That was when I knew that everything I'd finally achieved – my home, my job, my life – all was being destroyed. I was back where I'd started all those years ago as an unloved child who didn't even deserve to be called by his real name. Nothing had changed.

I finally cracked. I admit it. I had to do something. I had to prove to myself, and to everyone else, that I was a man, that I wasn't a nobody.

It was then I understood what I should do. I'd suffered in silence and, as a result most of my life had been misery. It was up to me to try and save others from the same fate.

I remembered instances when I'd witnessed others suffering the same awful humiliation. Three stood out. And in two of those cases the victims were still young men, hardly more than boys. Surely there was some way I could rescue them so that they could enjoy a proper life.

The die was cast. The decision was made. The rest was easy. And, of course, she who had brought me to this terrible course of action, she was to be the final sacrifice.

****

And the crossword clues?

They were my bit of fun. My challenge. My proof to myself that I was no fool.

It's a great pity they never realised that. I never was.

Was I?

****